Valerie Thornhill studied at Cambridge before living through student protests while at the Sorbonne in Paris and during the Red Brigade era in Rome where, inadvertently, she became entangled in the underworld. She has written since childhood, followed in the footsteps of five generations of her family in India to travel widely, and has taught in America and Asia as well as Europe. Her publications include *The Children of Kumbhalgarh and Other Stories,* a collection of short stories set in India, the USA, Russia, Japan, Italy and England; a novella *The Tycoon's Tale* and *Cynthia Loves her Fiat 500*, a story of 'swinging' Rome in the Sixties. She gardens speculatively, creaties outside sculpture from random natural objects and divides her time between Yorkshire and Italy.

www.valeriethornhill.org.uk

IN RESTORATION

This book is a fascinating read for several reasons. There is a strong story line... the characters are memorable and credible while the descriptions and details paint a full, visual picture. One is transported to specific English and Italian landscapes and their buildings, characters and views.

Rosalind Smallwood, Artist

In Restoration is a moving and subtle novel in which the central voice explores both historical and personal losses which bind her British family to Italy, and reaches out to find inspiration in the Etruscan past, in the partisan experience of the farming people of the valley, and in the house she undertakes against the odds to restore to a family home. The opening is quite brilliant in its brief conjuring of a whole historical period.

Elinor Shaffer, literary historian and critic

I began reading *In Restoration* on the return flight to the U.S. after my first visit to Italy and did not put it down during the entire trip until I'd completed it. I found it very evocative ... while the complex relationships and revelations at times brought tears to my eyes.

Susan Quick, American Museum Curator

This is a book about love – for Olivia's absent and unknown father; for her mother 'wise through lost hope'; and heartbreaking, aching love for her dead son Tim, intermingled with the extreme joy of Dan, witnessing his 'journey out of childhood'... It is also about betrayal, understanding, acceptance and the healing power of landscape and a house... above all it is about human emotions, intensely experienced and sensitively and truthfully revealed.

Silvia Gavuzzo-Stewart, Italian Art Historian

Against the contrasting settings of England's quiet colours and Tuscany's vivid sunburst yellows and radiant skies, this tangled web of family loyalties, feuds, tragedy, loss, loves and passion is played out with consummate skill. This finely wrought novel is a compelling read.

Kathleen Tarrant, Teacher

In Restoration is not only entertaining, but also full of emotions and ideas ... To me the very best part is Olivia's journal... and I especially loved Mia Pia's description of life in the mountains, some beautiful writing there. Gianni is a wonderful character. He really steps off the page.

Lynn Ftzwater, American Connoisseur and Explorer

Nature plays the leading roll in Valerie Thornhill's book. Passages as fresh as plein-air sketches evocatively capture the changing landscape, in turn informing and revealing the complex personalities that populate the densely woven fabric of her story... Our involvement in the experience of loss and recovery the permeates the novel is such that on closing the book we feel as though we are parting with friends.
Francesco Nevola, Italian Art Historian

Valerie Thornhill looks with both a poet's and a novelist's eye at people and places – at the landscapes of central Italy, and the reality of life and work amongst them through a period of economic and cultural change, conditioned by the heroine's experiences of loss and transformation.
Robert Cockcroft, Poet and Scholar

I absolutely loved it! Reading it has brought back so many enjoyable memories of Tuscany... I found the characters enthralling, loved the story of the search for the house, and felt that the way the Italian and English stories were interwoven was clever and engaging.
Margaret McIntyre, Australian Physiotherapist

In Restoration was a wonderful companion during my two weeks by the sea. I lived, literally, a Tuscan life through the various characters and their interactions and was completely caught up with the plot.... A true tour de force!
Cordelia Richards, American Traveller

Valerie Thornhill's work comes from the heart; it is expressed in an intense vocabulary of emotions, events and images which glow like richly woven tapestries. Her narrative threads, compulsive in their own right, are enriched by the tints and dyes of her phraseology and acutely observed minutia, woven with apposite precision and understanding.
Robin Horspool, Artist and Writer

I found *In Restoration* absorbing and was pulled into a specific atmosphere that felt like a real reflection of a certain life which I lived in part, alongside the narrator. It's like when one remembers a dream, and isn't sure whether it did in fact occur as one slept or was something that had actually occurred in real life... a strongly communicated and atmospheric unfolding of events.
Samantha Beste, American Artist

Valerie Thornhill

IN RESTORATION

AUSTIN MACAULEY

Copyright © Valerie Thornhill

The right of Valerie Thornhill to be identified as author of this work has been asserted by her in accordance with section 77 and 78 of the Copyright, Designs and Patents Act 1988.

All rights reserved. No part of this publication may be reproduced, stored in a retrieval system, or transmitted in any form or by any means, electronic, mechanical, photocopying, recording, or otherwise, without the prior permission of the publishers.

Any person who commits any unauthorized act in relation to this publication may be liable to criminal prosecution and civil claims for damages.

This novel is a work of fiction. The names, characters and incidents portrayed herein are the work of the author's imagination. Any resemblance to actual persons living or dead is purely coincidental. The thoughts and opinions of any of the characters are not necessarily those of the author

A CIP catalogue record for this title is available from the British Library.

ISBN 978 1 905609 321

www.austinmacauley.com

First Published (2009)
Austin & Macauley Publishers Ltd.
25 Canada Square
Canary Wharf
London
E14 5LB

Printed & Bound in Great Britain

Dedication

To John
Susan and Robert
Erica and Kate
for their infinite help and encouragement

Acknowledgements

In addition to those mentioned in the dedication, many have helped in the creation of this book.

Sylvia Ashwell, Azadeh Bagherzadeh, Susan Bates, Ruth and Sam Bergman, Annunziata and Maria Cosimi, Pietro Afan de Rivera Costaguti, Nigel and Martine de Lee, Elisabetta Ferrero, Orietta Floridi, Alec French, Robbie Griffiths, Peter Hunt, Annalisa Izzo, Jill Jones, Robert Maccubbin, Nicola MacGregor, Enzo Magini, Sarah Morgan, Mario Pedicelli, Ada Persia, Martha Hamilton Phillips, Alexander Stewart, S.E. il Cardinale Roberto Tucci, S.I., Emanuela Vesci, Neville Ward, Stephen and James Wilton-Ely, Bernardo and Cristiana Zanchini.

In particular, I would like to thank Annette Longman, Frances Moldaschl and the production team at Austin & Macauley for their advice and encouragement.

IN RESTORATION
Truth

'Love, Olivia,' said my mother, more to herself than me, 'is the most overused word in the English language.'

At five, all I wanted to know was what 'love me, love me not' meant as I watched the last dandelion seed blowing away on 'love me not'.

'Do you love me now?'

'Of course,' she said absent-mindedly.

'Did you always love me?'

'Always.' She was gathering her skirt to get up from the grass.

'When I was little? When I began?'

'Passionately!'

Seeds in time
1983

In the stillness after my grandmother's funeral, I lie on her bed still smelling of lavender, a child again, feeling miserable but cosseted. My earliest memory is of curly patterns of colour, looking like chunky marmalade, on an Indian counterpane that had travelled halfway round Gran's globe to delight me. She held my finger and we would trace her father's adventures on faraway plantations, before he returned to found Palmer's Tea Merchants in Guildford, Surrey.

Everyone who has lived in this house crowds into my mind. My great grandfather, Eric Palmer, bought the property when his son, Frank, was two. Three years later Alice, my grandmother, was born in this bed. The mantelpiece opposite still holds treats for a good child being quietly restored to health: the sweet tin with women in skirts like bells and men in jackets with swallow tails; a yellow and blue jack-in-the-box given to great-uncle Frank and passed on to Gran, who occasionally let me wind it up. Gran's globe is still there, the one I spun round to swirl all the countries into a rainbow quilt when she was out of the room.

No combs and grips for her unruly hair now; no pile of old envelopes kept for messages in large faltering script; no books on her bedside table. Only the photographs remain. The nurse has tidied her away. To Joan, her only child and my mother, she has left this house. To me, her only grandchild, this room, its contents and the photos in her corner shrine.

Next to Eric Palmer's sepia wedding photograph is five-year-old Alice, in fur-trimmed coat with muffler and bonnet to match, looking up at brother Frank in a sailor suit. He reappears in an officer's uniform. Gran didn't know I once saw her slip a letter behind this photo. She told me that, when Frank was fighting in the trenches to protect her and everyone at home, he remembered in his letters how they used to play ducks and drakes on West Poynton village pond and that he taught her to tell the time by the church clock. Or he recalled the thatched cottage next to the vicarage, with the hedge cut into funny birds and pyramids, and imagined himself back there with her. Not even the trench warfare could take these memories away from him. It was their shared childhood landscape.

Gran would move her bedside gallery around, choosing each night's closest companion before going to sleep. Most often she would place Frank in uniform next to her wedding photograph – she married his best friend George Taylor, my grandfather. Frank did not come back from the War; George did. Sometimes Gran would pick out children's photos to show me, jumbled images from the family past. My mother Joan is the little girl wearing a dress so beautiful that I imagined she'd escaped from a children's book. Or Gran would settle on her photo with Frank. There was a snap of me as a child just after the Second World War, but the one she preferred was the last image of Tim with Paul and me, sitting outside a café in Italy.

In the garden the afternoon is daubing the forsythia too sharp a yellow. Framed by the window, I imagine their spirits animating the garden. Alice, an Edwardian child in coat, hat, muffler and gloves bobbing in through the back gate, a hop in front of sailor Frank. They were the first to play, before my mother and later me, on this lawn edged by forsythia and cherry blossom, sprinkled with daffodils and yellow and purple crocuses. They disappear into the living room below, sighing with the last of the mourners. In my reverie again, the gate opens to spill out my mother and her pert friends with ringlets, all skipping towards the house. Then there's me in a check dress cut from old kitchen curtains after the War, running across the lawn to play with our cat. A generation later, my son Tim is sitting under the chestnut tree sketching the house or gathering conkers with his school friends in autumn, alert, then full of life.

The front door is closing on the last of the mourners and the spirits have slipped back into their frames. I stand by the window to look at the photo I took of Gran tucking a bunch of poppies behind carved laurel leaves. All her life she had yearned to cross France and find her brother's name. Her posy lies under Frank Palmer, inscribed on the monument to all who died in the Battle of the Somme and have no grave.

Mother is distanced by melancholy.

'Your father,' when I asked, 'was wounded in 1941 in Libya. He came to England on a troop ship with other injured soldiers.' Later I found out that he was a prisoner of war. The handsome young Italian from a village south of Florence met my mother when she was a landgirl working on a Surrey farm. But he disappeared before I was born, parachuted back into Italy to help the anti-Fascist partisans. Or so she told me.

CHAPTER 1
April 1974

Across France, rain slashed the train window into grey green trapezoids, slurring trees into meadows and roofs into splodges of red and yellow. Why hadn't Paul come to Tim's funeral? Bumpity-bump. Why hadn't he phoned me? Bumpity-bump. Didn't he care? Bumpity-boom into alpine tunnels, hollow rings of emptiness. Other people were slumped asleep, smelling of damp wool and leather. After hours of darkness, I traced 'Why?' in the beads of morning condensation, then angrily rubbed it out on the descent from the Alps to Milan. In the valleys, clouds foamed round pines and larches. Raindrops, like tadpoles, swam across the windows as the train sped south over the Po valley.

Hours later, in Florence, fear disguised as fury propelled me from the station past Santa Maria Novella to Paul's flat in Via della Scala 9, interno 5. Watery sunlight played over the heavy door and sounds seeped through shuttered windows: a child crying, a radio spluttering, a patter of words over the phone. Stealthy movement down steps to an alley – tawny cat or sewer rat? No lines of washing, no rush-bottomed chairs on each side of street doors, just scurrying figures too cold to loiter, and a crimson-mouthed, fur-wrapped woman balancing a tapering heel against the corner wall. No answer to the grubby bell push under number 5 – he hadn't even bothered to stick his name over the previous tenant's. Scant care, little consideration, less tenderness and no love, whatever that word meant. High on rage, I hammered at the door. Hurt, I paused, looked up, saw a window opening and a woman peering down from the third floor. The last breath of morning coffee escaped from the houses along the street to taunt me. No breakfast, no consolation over coffee, nobody, nothing but a drumming headache.

Even more than the screech of brakes, the skidding van scattering children and shrieking mothers, then the sudden hush at the school gates, I can still feel the clamour inside – Tim spread-eagled on the pavement and the sheer senselessness of it all.

I leant against the wall to ease my back, head against the tidemark left by the Arno flood which had drawn Paul here in 1966 to clean sodden manuscripts. Because I was teaching in Guildford, I had to stay behind with two-and-a-half year-old Tim. But I missed Paul. His life, his work, his skills were his to do what he liked with; and so, in theory, were mine. Our relationship was to be based on trust, not conventional vows.

'It suits us both,' he'd say. At first I agreed.

Paul had left us in February 1974 for another assignment in Florence; he telephoned on the last day of March, Tim's tenth birthday.

'Dad's got a very special present for me,' he announced, handing me the receiver. 'It's too heavy and complicated to send, so he'll give it to me at Easter.' Paul explained that he had enjoyed making an unusual gift as a surprise for Tim, 'and for you too, Olivia.' It was clear from his tone that he was looking forward to seeing us. He hadn't rung since.

I lurched backwards as the door opened, letting out a surprised housewife.

'*Permesso?*' I slipped inside. Before the stair light clicked off leaving a glow by the switch, I had glimpsed what I half suspected: the middle letterbox with Paul's name under it was stuffed full. On with the grim light, yank out the futile publicity; the real mail remained locked inside. I hooked my fingers down and felt one, no two, letters, and rattled the silly little door, tugging and pushing against the side until a buff corner appeared over the slit. My telegram.

It was to recall Paul to share the funeral rites; to face the condolence of flowers, the solace of strangers, the silent touches of kindness; to shoulder fate as it cast a shudder over the mourners, sparing them this time round.

When you fret whether you've thought of everything, something unforeseen always happens. Better to address another telegram to his flat, I had thought, even though I'd already sent one to the studio. He said he sometimes worked elsewhere, went to a client's home, or visited some remote museum to compare other works by the artist he was restoring. Surely he would have returned to sleep?

Clearly not. Someone else had signed for that telegram. Stuffing the envelope into my handbag, I rushed along side streets and across the Ponte Vecchio to his studio.

'Paul, Pa-o-lo, Pa-o-lo!' burst out of my mouth and ricocheted round the vast studio; spotlit heads lifted from recumbent Madonnas, flurries of angels, a saint in ecstasy, a dolphin fountain... as my voice receded in echoing space. A woman looked up in irritation from her archangel.

'Why do you want Paolo? He's not here.'

A man in a stained overall took his eyes off a saint covered by a cobweb of cracks. He pointed with his brush.

'That's his place.'

Another uplifted face, 'Who are you, anyway?'

Hesitatingly I said, 'I sent a telegram here. And a letter, days ago. What's happened to them?' Eyes turned on me, uncertain. Silence. I moved to his worktable. On his easel beside it stood part of a triptych, the panel with a child falling from a window and being saved by an airborne saint. No saint had snatched Tim to safety. Paul's worktable seemed strangely tidy. My other telegram and letter were propped unopened against the lamp stand.

'Why didn't he get this telegram?' Still staring silence. 'Who signed it for him?'

Waving the buff envelope, shrill, accusing, my face scored by tears, 'Our son has been killed in an accident!'

The woman with the archangel turned away, shutting her eyes with a muffled 'Oh, no!' The man at the easel next to her blurted out, 'He has a child?' Everyone stirred; a cup of coffee appeared in front of me. In the office, fingers scurried through papers.

'He's on a job in Naples. We're looking for an address... He's been away for nearly two weeks. He should be back by now...' – by the weekend, by next week, month, year... century?

No one had a key to Paul's flat or knew exactly when to expect him. Someone remembered a man from the British Consulate talking to the head of their studio, who was away this week. Another, perhaps the woman restorer, asked me to stay, but I had to leave and disentangle grief from panic-driven fear. I stumbled out through the courtyard. Drizzle blurred the buildings on the far side of the Arno as I careered towards the station crying,

'I forgive you, Paul, as long as you're safe!' I had somehow to find him in Naples.

Curled up again in the corner of a railway carriage, wet-eyed, withdrawn, I ignored wires and poles racing past grey Florentine suburbs. Grief is unpredictable; you don't know how you are going to react from one second to the next. Minutes, an hour later, my eyes widened, entranced by terraced hillsides dotted with olive trees, warm-tiled hamlets with dovecotes and towers and cypresses piercing the skyline. Framed in the train window, a hilltop town in the Tuscan landscape reflected my childhood dream. It was my father's homeland, as my mother had imagined it. It was a world I yearned for. Irresistible, it beguiled me.

A spasm of panic. How could I find Paul in the tumult of a million Neapolitans? He wasn't expected to be away for long, and had left no telephone number or address. The British Consul in Florence had contacted the local police, scoured every hotel and boarding house, gallery and restoration studio, hospital ward and prison cell in Naples – without success.

What could I do? Sit somewhere by a phone with my suitcase and survive for an indefinite agony of time until he returned to Florence or finally called me in Guildford? Me, a mere speck on the crust of the earth, only existing to wait, with nothing to do but grieve.

I had to act. Do something. Find somewhere with a telephone number to give to Paul's colleagues and my mother at home. Anxiety corrodes and resolves nothing. I could imagine my way out of this predicament, create a fantasy, make something – anything – happen to while time away and dispel the torment of not knowing.

Desperate for something to shorten the agonising wait and stifle the unrelenting wordless howl inside me, I got off at the next station, the stop for the hilltop town I had seen from the train.

From my Italian journal:
Arriving at Montesasso – April 1974

Open space outside the ticket office, solitary bar and a couple of shops – hardly inviting. A bus with a Montesasso sign stood deserted in the early afternoon. Not a soul in the square.

'Cappuccino?' Just the barman. An imaginary interview flickered through my head.

'Signorina, what are you doing here in Montesasso Scalo?'

'Waiting for the bus to go to Montesasso.' (A silly, obvious answer.)

'Why is a foreigner stopping in the middle of nowhere?' (Seeking an avventura with a mythical Latin lover, I thought, distractedly.)

'To see Montesasso.' (Lame answer.)

'There's nothing to see. Move on along the plain; go to Perugia, see Assisi, Saint Francis.' (Or did he mean, 'leave us alone'?)

A door banged, jerking me out of my daydream. The youthful driver heaved my luggage on to the bus before the other passengers climbed inside.

Avventura?

Hairpin bends, olive groves, small Fiats speeding, fields of winter wheat, and higher up neatly tended vineyards on terraced hillsides – the world I had dreamed about.

From the plain, Montesasso looked like Bethlehem in the huge 'presepio' I had admired with my mother on an earlier visit to Italy, an elaborate Nativity with scenes around the stable and outside the town walls, set in a countryside with ploughs, oxen, and sowers scattering seed, eternally caught in the everyday rhythm of life. On the surrounding hills, the shepherds were gaping at the heavens as their flocks grazed unaware.

Montesasso had perched for centuries inside walls enclosing the higher land for olives, kitchen gardens, chickens and pigs – a larder in times of siege. Cyclopean fortifications hung over the bus as it wheezed up the steep curves. My eyes ran across the terraces, tilled and sown under the shimmer of olives into green and brown ribbons, and down slopes with vineyards to the fresh furrows on the plain below.

A jolt. Should I get off? 'Si scende qui per Montesasso?'

The driver winked at me and shook his head. The bus growled on towards the mountains, stopping perilously close to a precipice. A domed church on an outcrop stood out against the pale green sweep of a mountain valley. Above, cypresses stitched their ridge to a misty blue sky. Opposite the steep incline a gate opened in the city walls.

'Si scende qui per Montesasso, signorina.'

I was the last to get off. Gallantly the driver hoisted my suitcase across the road. A firm handshake, slight smile and another athletic leap back into the driver's seat.

Wood smoke was seasoning the city gates. A milky-white ox plodded through them, pulling a painted cart laden with olive branches. The scene could have come straight out of the frescoes in Siena's Town Hall.

Just inside the gates elderly men sat by what seemed like a door to a private house, puffing or rolling their cigarettes between stained fingers and exchanging grunts on life as it passed. At that moment for them I was 'life'! Above the door an olive branch poked out from a hand-painted sign: 'Taverna Etrusca'. I felt a strange tug, an urge to look inside. Impulsively, I put my fantasy into words, linking Paul's longing to paint throughout summers of cypresses, olive groves and vineyards under cloudless blue skies to my yearning for a place to be together with him, and asked.

'C'è qualcuno che ha un rudere da vendere?' Anyone here with a ruin to sell?

Silence. Five pairs of eyes focused on me. Casually one pair looked down to flick cigarette ash, adding texture to the earthen floor. Rising slowly, leaning to one side and eyeing me all the time, he replied.

'Sì. Sono Panichini Gianni.'

'And I'm Olivia.' We shook hands. Taking my elbow and suitcase, he steered me away from his companions into the street. I dithered, uncertain of his intentions, but I was propelled on. The street was steep and, as the pace slowed, I noted Gianni was

taller than he appeared, his weathered frame lost inside a tweed jacket and trousers too wide for his legs. A sudden gust blew dust and empty cigarette packets past the Franciscan church; a notice on the door announced it was sinking into its crypt.

'If they don't do something quickly,' he glanced up at the church, 'it'll keel over into the Saint's hospital below. They've both been around since the twelve hundreds, so I suppose their time has come!'

Crossing the road he rang a doorbell in a street of houses that curved up the hill. I was curious to go on and up to see what lay beyond the arum lilies and herbs in pots marking the bend.

'Chi è?' A head poked out of the first floor window and the door clicked open. The ground floor seemed to be for storage, filled with chairs, an old single bed and various cast-off stoves. I followed him up the narrow staircase to the first floor.

'This is Ada, my wife.' He introduced me as 'Signora Olivia'.

Gianni's wife eyed me warily from the kitchen doorway and moved to the living room threshold after Gianni had 'Venga-d' me inside, still staring as her husband settled me on the minute sofa. Squeezed behind the sitting area, a beech table partly blocked the stairs up to the second floor.

'La signora dorme qui.' Gianni had caught me off guard and I couldn't think of a polite way to refuse and look for a cheap hotel with a telephone. My invitation was to stay, he informed me, in a medieval house, built on top of Roman stones laid in turn on the original Etruscan foundations!

He commanded Ada, 'Caffè!' I warmed my hands round the cup; the rusting gas heater had already been turned off for fear of singeing the furniture. Swallowing his coffee in one gulp, Gianni rose.

'Andiamo!' Time to move outside. It was warmer there.

Gianni's tiny car was parked by his front door. He drove about two miles outside Montesasso, stopping at a cluster of mottled yellow houses leaning over a general food store, a petrol pump and a bar with bedraggled hydrangeas in pots and a stray dog.

'Silvano is a friend,' Gianni explained. *'I'll phone him from here. He's the agent for a British property dealer and lives locally.'*

Silvano eventually arrived in his Land Rover, stepped out and shook hands enthusiastically.

'There's a real bargain available. An Englishman who lives in Rome owns it. Two cottages, one inhabited, but the family is moving out.'

Silvano could evidently command a quiverful of builders, electricians and plumbers all ready to *'fix it'* in our absence. We could easily move in by the summer. He walked Gianni and me along a path past empty pigsties to a long-abandoned stone house, one room deep. Though it didn't command a straight, conventional view, there was a sense of space. It felt good. No brooding hills nearby. Paul would like the subtle mix of shapes and colours: near purple evergreens on the distant mountains, the contrast of grey-green olives on narrow terraces and the arthritic shapes of vines not yet in leaf. Blessed by the labour of centuries, this biblical landscape matched my dreams. This was it!

'There's another cottage,' Gianni reminded me. It was squat, square and splashed over with cement-like rendering. Smoking outside, a man watched us suspiciously. Silvano's price was a special one for me, but only if I decided there and then.

'We would have to sell the smaller cottage pretty quickly. We'd need the money to start restoring the main house.'

'Of course,' Silvano said obligingly. *'No problem. Vacant possession.'* A woman and small child joined the man at the door. Eyes first scrutinised us, then Silvano, roaming defiantly over his corpulent contours and halting on his dough-like face. He regarded them like shrubs that could be uprooted from the doorway. I should contact the owner or risk losing this advantageous property.

Fatal indeed to show one is smitten. I really believed that the stated amount was just for me, and that others were keen to pay a far higher one. A few days to think it over were conceded grudgingly, with the warning that prices were rising dramatically. Italians, as well as foreigners, were interested. Restored *farmhouses in the country were now more fashionable than villas at the seaside – too expensive, crowded and polluted. This deserted building had most interesting views and was easily within walking distance of Montesasso.*

'Hurry,' Gianni whispered, driving me back and parking outside Porta Etrusca. On our way to his house, I vainly looked along the street and up alleys for a hotel to slip into before he could prevent me. But as far as I could see, there were none in Montesasso.

Ada was busy in the kitchen preparing the meal; another figure stood in the doorway. Alberto, a sturdy eleven-year-old, was waiting hungrily for his supper. Gianni introduced him and we sat opposite each other at the table. Ada piled pasta on to plates and a local version of Chianti flowed. Before I'd even finished, my plate was refilled without asking. Gianni pushed his away and lit a cigarette. My blunted appetite struggled with the next dish – chicken stewed in tomato sauce and a salad doused in oil and vinegar. Finally liqueurs arrived with a dry sponge cake followed by coffee, 'corrected' with grappa.

As I jotted down my first impressions of Montesasso in Alberto's bedroom, I felt uneasy; I had displaced him to sleep in the living room on a spare bed that sprang unexpectedly out of a cupboard. Whoever descended to the ground floor would fall over him. This was uncomfortably generous hospitality.

I can still feel my desperation all those years ago and my anxiety to conceal, as well as I could, the deep scar of despair. That impulsive move to get off the train must have been fuelled by my futile situation, or was it also the call of the land and the hilltop town? After all, I'm half-Italian. With unknown time on my hands, I could at last spend it in a place I had imagined for so long and keep my mind occupied writing about it until Paul returned to Florence. He was expecting to see Tim and me at Easter.

I recall too how it struck me, as I stepped off the bus, that my father could have looked like this driver.

I hadn't asked my mother much about him until I went to school and my friends were curious. I began to picture him just like this young man with dark curly hair, bright smile and firm handshake. Convinced that my father had been made a prisoner of war and then released to become a famous partisan, I fondly imagined he had grown up near an ancient town like Montesasso. He was my childhood hero.

It didn't occur to me at the time that Gianni might not have a telephone. That first evening I went out to call Paul from a bar. No answer. He hadn't contacted either the studio in Florence or Gran and Mother back home. Parcelling my hopes and fears into manageable space and time, I frenziedly conjured up a ruin to be lovingly restored in the Arcadian countryside around Montesasso.

CHAPTER 2

'Why doesn't my father come back and love me?'

'He would if he could, Olivia.'

'Why can't he? All my friends' daddies have come back from the War.'

Nearly six and starting school.

But some fathers did not return. Would not. Post-war confusion. 'Tragic losses.' Accidents.

'Where did my father come from?'

'San Giuliano. A place in Tuscany.'

I grew up thinking all Italians must be dark and good-looking and passionate. I did hear that some were small and smelled of garlic. But my father didn't, because he wouldn't have found much garlic in Surrey when he loved my mother. In my make-believe he would kiss her endlessly, and never a whiff of garlic. There in a meadow I'd sit blowing dandelion seeds with, 'He loves me, he loves me not,' or 'he will come, he won't come,' puffing extra hard on 'loves me' and 'will come' so the last seeds would fly into my fabulous future.

Later still, as an inquisitive ten-year old, I asked, 'If Italians are dark, and you are too, then why am I fair?' Mother sighed.

'Don't you ever listen, Olivia? Gran's always telling you that you're a Palmer like her.'

Gran explained, 'You have fair wavy hair, just like Frank'. Her own hair was greying, but it had been fair and wavy too.

'Like your brother, like me, Palmers three,' I chanted to make Gran smile.

My adolescent curiosity nibbled unsatisfied at Mother's assurances, 'Your father'll come back if he can,' repeated over and again, until she added, 'if he's alive.' Time stopped like hay-dust drawn into the throat when you can't cough or breathe or speak.

'Why don't you **do** something? Find out?' I snarled at her as only a teenager can.

Turning away, she murmured, 'What do you imagine I've been doing all these years?'

I often think back to my sad angry mother working all hours as a librarian. Of her coping with whispers about her 'wartime encounter'; of time spent researching what happened to Italian prisoners in England, helped by a man in charge of the archives; of her journeys to Italy to learn the language, leaving me behind with Gran.

One year – I must have been about fourteen – she took me to different parts of Tuscany, talking to the priests at every San Giuliano church she could find. I relished the anticipation, like a detective never sure what might happen. Once she stopped by a fresco of the Last Judgement whispering, *'nessun maggior dolore...'* – no greater grief than to recall happy times in present misery. They were Dante's words, I learnt later, about passionate, illicit love. Mother's Michelin guidebook curtly dismissed Montesasso as a grim little hill town, lost and forgotten in the mountains without great saints, famous buildings or notable museums. We had passed it by.

A fledgling teenager, I would pause under the clock jutting out over the cobbles in Guildford High Street, before practising my hip-manoeuvring walk down the steep hill to the bridge. I chose my strip carefully: not a place to provoke catcalls, just to set men's eyes on stalks. On other days I'd become the leggy athlete, cycling to the top of the bumpy incline, more to amaze than attract. By my late teens I promoted my own style: a blithe self-awareness, creating space for admiration without seeming skittish or shrill. It served me well at university in London. Swooping in and out of themes and theories (a pattern I knew intrigued men) and vivaciously juggling ideas when I felt like it, I reigned over a group of mostly male friends. We sat in earnest discussion, peppered with pinches of wit, and created blueprints to reform the world. I soon learned how to charge the atmosphere around me with intellectual and physical promise. Using fresh ingredients in right proportions, the spell never failed.

One day, breathless and late as usual for the lecture, I slipped into a seat next to a pleasant looking first-year girl. Over lunch I learnt that we had both been incarcerated in single sex schools, and agreed there was no time to lose. Sarah was serene, with mouse brown hair, small and settled in her rounded breasts and pear-shaped hips like a fertility figurine. You might forget her appearance, but not her presence; there was a liveliness and brightness about her. We lived in the same hall of residence and she was studying history like me.

We trotted after other first-years to wine and cheese parties, a recipe for mixing undergraduates from all disciplines. Sarah quietly smiled at no one in particular while I perfected a come-hither stance, though avoiding all direct eye contact. Women were not supposed to reveal desire in 1960; it was called 'brazen' behaviour. I couldn't help noticing one interesting man always surrounded by minimally clad females. Steering Sarah closer, I glanced sideways at this sinewy, animated elf with white-lashed eyes, a pointed nose and chin – perhaps ears too, but they were hidden under his startling blond mane. Busy gesticulating to emphasise the points he made, his smiles revealed unexpected creases like half-moons in a lean face. He tilted his head back and stood so upright that he seemed taller than he really was. He was the first I knew to use aftershave. Meticulously casual or smart as occasion required, he had an apologetic penchant for the blazer, a silk handkerchief peeping from crested pocket.

'It makes me look like an art dealer,' he said. Mike was cultivating an eye for stylish bargains. He gave me an Art Deco toast rack picked up in a junk shop. Prowling around Portobello Road, he found me a cut-down oil painting of a saint at prayer, eyes rolling heavenwards, in a chipped rococo frame. Later I gave it to Paul.

Sarah preferred Mike's friend. I had hardly noticed Joe, dark-haired and overshadowed by Mike at the wine and cheese party. A few days later Mike and Joe remembered us when we went to a wine tasting at the Italian Society. We didn't know anyone and gravitated towards them. Joe's father, a wine importer expanding beyond the usual Chianti and Valpolicella, had supplied Sicilian wine. Joe filled everyone's glasses while Mike entertained with a witty barrage of anecdotes fired with prancing energy.

'What are you studying here?' I asked him.

'Nothing,' with a wicked smile. 'I'm at the Courtauld Institute, doing History of Art. Joe's reading Law at University College. We were at school together in Nottingham.'

Mike never mentioned his family, except once to say that the house where he was born was now part of a slum clearance scheme. Shrugging his shoulders, he remarked casually, 'As we talk, my youth is being demolished,' and never referred to it again. He'd won a scholarship to the local direct grant school where he met Joe. When Sarah knew Joe better, he confided to her that Mike had stopped other boys bullying him. It was by chance they both ended up studying in London. Sarah liked quiet people. Taller, endearingly vulnerable and less obviously exciting than his conspicuous friend, Joe was shy and out of tune with the sixties.

Our first university year passed in a blur of new experiences, sporadic studying and a general revolt against war-torn parents. We shocked them with our way-out clothes and behaviour. At the start of the second year, Sarah and I moved out of university accommodation to create a homespun sense of natural living with huge wooden salad bowls, endless scarves and bean cushions in the five-bedroom house that Mike found in Islington.

I saw Paul for the first time as a prospective tenant when Mike showed him the fifth room. Tall and strongly built, he moved with energy rippling from his feet through his legs, hips, arms and slightly rounded shoulders. I remember feeling tempted to run my fingers round the dark brown curls just touching his collar. A day later Sarah brought William to inspect the room. She'd met him through a cousin who was doing research in the English department. I was impressed that she actually knew a post-graduate student.

'He's awkward looking, long and leggy, but friendly,' Sarah said over mugs of coffee in the kitchen after he'd been unofficially interviewed. 'Do you think he'll take the room?'

'I don't know,' I said, hoping Paul would want it. 'It's men who are supposed to look at women and undress them! Now what are you doing, Sarah? Poor William!' Sarah laughed.

'I'm only pointing out that I prefer slim men, even skinny, if it means they don't go to fat. Why can't I state my preferences?'

'Of course you can. So can I. William's red hair, white skin and freckles put me off. The class bully at my school had the same colouring.'

'Not fair, Olivia. You're linking an unpleasant character to physical appearance. Tough on everyone with red hair. It's really because you like the look of Paul.'

'Oh well, it doesn't matter.' I shrugged it off. 'Paul probably won't take the room.'

I was right. I can still see Paul walking out of the front door and along the street and feel the emotional thud when William took the room instead. I tried to contrive another meeting with Paul through Mike, but nothing came of it. Convincing myself that Paul was probably less interesting than he looked, I learnt it took more time to get a man out of one's mind than to pick one up.

Frankly I wasn't surprised when Sarah fell in love with our new flatmate, who was finishing his Ph.D. thesis on eighteenth-century travellers in Italy.

'Find the vulnerable child in any man,' she told me, 'and you'll know what he's really like.' William was teased at school when he was ten. They chased him chanting 'Ginger mop, carrot top, lollipop!' Sarah liked the idea of protecting him.

It was 1963, the summer of my finals. I had finished the exams and, at a loose end, happened to see Paul again in a Bond Street gallery. He stood out in the way he contemplated paintings from about two yards, then close-up, nose almost touching the surface. It was much more interesting to size him up than examine the works of art. I'd nothing better to do, so I shadowed him, angling to talk. When he glanced in my direction, I was struck by his eyes: deep brown with specks of green at the edges and framed by eyelashes almost too long for a man. I hung around until he turned and couldn't avoid bumping into me. He was training to be a picture restorer, was three years older, and taller than me by a hand's width, intelligent and unpredictable. I found him alluring and feared others might too. For three weeks we drifted together, walking, snacking at his studio, visiting galleries and fooling around before collapsing at his digs. We were both working out how best to earn a living, he as a restorer and me as a teacher, while still finding the time to paint and write as we really wanted to do. And to love, passionately. In September he would start his apprenticeship in a leading London restoration studio, and I had a place at a teachers' training college for, as my mother would have it, 'safe' future employment. That summer would be our last chance of freedom together.

Paul came to meet my family in Guildford. Gran and Grandpa approved of him, as did Mother, who lent us her Austin Mini to drive all over Surrey. I remember sitting beside him on a bench by a village green, both holding ice cream cones and contemplating the scene in general and the parish church in particular.

'I've always thought it funny how that spire looks as if it's about to fall on us,' I said, 'but we know it won't.' Paul listened, licking his ice cream.

'When I first went to Florence,' he laughed, slightly embarrassed, 'it was to follow in the footsteps of artists I'd read about. In his first church, San Lorenzo, I remembered that Brunelleschi had explained its proportions to Donatello by showing how the floor pattern – and the church's proportions – were worked out in circles and spheres, squares and cubes, all perfect forms.' He stopped, glanced at me, and continued. 'Imagine how I felt standing just inside the church, feeling the light from the high windows touch the stone floor and glide along parallel lines of dark grey slabs to the altar. Your eyes say, "There they meet" but your brain says, "No they don't!" Brilliant!' I understood exactly what Paul meant by that special thrill when your senses argue with your mind – and both are right!

I'd never felt such companionship with any of the other men I'd met. We both enjoyed going to the theatre and cinema, expeditions to the countryside or just looking at pictures. However, he didn't read as much as I did, probably because he was usually holding pen or charcoal in one hand and sketchpad in the other. He teased me with fun in his eyes and, unusually for a reserved man, he was sometimes disturbingly direct. He could only tell the truth. That was his way, his guiding principle. I realise, looking back, that I should have done so too.

There was a lot of friendly banter about Sarah and William in the Islington house. Paul joked about 'the long and the short of it!' referring to the way Sarah had to lift her hand up to hold his and William needed almost to bend double to kiss her. We didn't tease them any more after they married, though Paul was tempted to in his best man's speech.

Paul had promised his parents that he would go home in July before starting the apprenticeship. The day after Sarah and William's wedding I bought a student's train ticket for Greece, convinced I could gather ideas there for a novel inspired by a book Gran had read to me. I remember her gentle voice conjuring a magical light that glowed stronger and stronger when I shut my eyes and pictured the sun radiating from a turquoise sky on to sugar-fine sand by a sapphire sea. Gran laughed when I told her I was leaving for Greece, saying the book she had read to me was about Pharaohs and pyramids; I should have gone to Egypt!

Greece turned out to be both a dream come true and a savage nightmare that I couldn't speak or write about. If Paul had come with me, our lives might have turned out differently.

When I came back in August, he had already found a small flat for us in Camberwell. He was brimming with excitement and energy. Days at home, in spite of his mother fussing over him and his father's cursory comments, left him time to think and space to feel how much he missed me.

'I managed to finish these while you were away.' He held out two pocket-sized sketchpads. Parallel sloping lines, dark wriggles and light flicks of ink evoked hillsides, leaves fluttering and birds planing over clouds – all on blank pages of cartridge paper. In the second drawing book one wash of colour flowed over another, bonding into gradations of blue skies and green and brown countryside with touches of white walls, thatch and red bricks. The watercolours seemed quieter than the line drawings, more reflective. True to his home landscape or true to his feelings, or both? I wondered. Interleaved here and there, rarely inside the landscapes, were deft sketches of people – a middle-aged man with a nose that didn't quite fit either cheeks or chin, children skipping, suspended in space, and one of me – or his memory of me.

'Do you like it?' He was anxious, looking at me, not the sketch. 'The watercolours I did of you weren't good enough. I tore them up. It's much harder to recall the tones. Lines are easier; they catch movement.' His smile was so direct that it thrilled through me. 'Your face is never still – eyebrows, eyelashes, nostrils, lips, always about to see, smell, say... It's exciting, even disconcerting.'

I had never seen or heard myself analysed like this before. He didn't show me as I saw myself in mirrors, but his perception was closer to the way I felt.

Not long after returning from Greece I realised I was pregnant. Paul assumed I had been taking the new 'pill', but I worried about meddling with my body chemistry and used other methods. We had hardly spent any time with each other, scarcely enough to learn how to love and live together and make our careers. Neither of us had even thought, let alone talked, about having a family. Paul was stunned by the news, though it helped a little that there were months for him to adapt to it. Above all, he understood when I told him I couldn't think of adoption or abortion. The unborn child was an inextricable part of me. After all, Mother had kept me.

Ten years later that young life came to an end when the skidding van hit Tim, numbing me with horror. Compassionate leave followed, but the void only grew blacker inside me. Tim looking out from the photo on Gran's bedside table nourished my despair. He sits there, stripped to the waist on a hot summer day, gazing out with his long-lashed dark eyes, mouth half open, tousled hair curling brown over his forehead. Paul is half smiling at him. I'm opposite Paul on the other side of the table, glancing thanks to the waiter taking the photo for us. Now I needed to cut Tim's image out of my mind, though it left a dark negative form within.

Turning my back on senseless grief, I remember how I woke up in Gianni's house in Montesasso, contemplated the endless repetition of tomorrow and tomorrow and tomorrow without Tim, and reached for pen and paper.

Of houses and hens – April 1974

Italians rise early. I dressed, feeling slightly queasy. Already 7.30 and someone knocked on my bedroom door. It was Gianni. He sat me down at the kitchen table with dry biscuits and the sharp mental jolt of coffee, concentrated into barely two mouthfuls and bitterly strong. It evidently revs Italians up for the day ahead.

'*Would you like to see some other farmhouses for sale? Nobody is living in them.*' He understood my reservations about the property Silvano had shown us.

'*Yes, I would.*' I was keen to see more of the countryside.

'*This afternoon. We'll meet here at two.*'

I phoned Paul's studio in Florence from a bar, but he hadn't returned. With Gianni at work, I had the morning to explore Montesasso. The tourist office was hidden in the depths of a run-down palazzo just off the main square. I picked up the town guide, pausing to look at some blue smudges and dribbles of ink on a large map by the door.

'*It's by Leonardo da Vinci.*' The middle-aged man behind a desk was watching the only movement in the room. '*He did it for Cesare Borgia – some military whim.*'

Coming over to stand by me, he pointed out Montesasso. Wriggling lines fed the amorphous blue area spreading over the plain below us. Strange, I hadn't noticed any vast expanse of water.

'*You're from England?*' I nodded, embarrassed by my slow Italian sentences steering their cautious way along familiar structures. '*The original is in your Queen's collection at Windsor.*' I smiled and left. The map in the guidebook showed Gianni's house on a parallel street higher up the hill. Turning under an arch I drifted over uneven paving slabs towards it, finding a bar and a slice of cold pizza for lunch on the way.

Gianni was waiting in his minute Fiat 500. He jarred the engine into first gear, grinding along tiny alleys to the Porta Etrusca where roads fan out into the plain to the west and the supposed site of the Etruscan necropolis. Few tombs had been discovered, Gianni remarked, though farmers lived in hope of finding valuable objects like the famous vase in the Montesasso museum. Pausing to glance sideways, he added that it was decorated with erotic scenes and intrigued scholars and tourists alike!

'*They come to the local museum just to see it. Now it's rumoured to be a forgery,*' he chuckled, '*but what an entertaining one!*'

We passed the Cinquevie where five roads meet halfway down the hill. Gianni explained there had been a fierce battle here between the Allies and the Germans. I imagined weathered men leaning on their long-handled spades as they had done for centuries, wearily contemplating their damaged crops as age-old hostility repeated itself.

'I was a partisan,' Gianni said casually as he hurtled past the main Etruscan tomb. We bumped over large, flat stones back towards the mountains.

'Etruscan road,' he said laconically. 'Here long before the Romans.' Braking under the outside staircase of a farmhouse, he hooted. Two faces peered over the top of the stairs.

'Venite! Venite!' Up the steps, past the pots of basil and parsley and the winter-worn geraniums to a landing that opened into a huge kitchen. In the dim, smoky room Gianni was kissing everyone in sight before commandeering a chair and waving me to sit down as if it were his home. Perhaps he did own it. Could this man be in fact a 'closet' property owner?

'Da bere!' he ordered. Wine was placed in front of us; Gianni drained his glass before pushing it away with the other hand over it to avoid a top-up. I tried to do the same, to no avail. I endured a second glass of sharp and healthy 'vino genuino' produced from their own grapes.

After pleasantries, keys were jangled and Gianni, accompanied by a gaunt and silent man, led me away from the kitchen hearth, down the outside stairs past skinny chickens that ran half-heartedly after us and a chained dog, bored and mangy. Two pole haystacks stood like natural sculpture, jauntily lopsided with gaps where hay had been sliced off during the winter leaving enough on the other side to last until springtime. A stone's throw from the haystacks stood an uninhabited house.

'Eccola!' Gianni took us upstairs first. It was like the one we had just come from, except the doors were drunkenly askew, the windows swinging off hinges and roof tiles missing.

'Sound timbers,' Gianni stated, watching me closely.

No view. Too low down; too close to the other house and the farmyard chickens. Smell and flies, recited a voice at the back of my mind. I attempted to translate my thoughts tactfully.

Gianni and the gaunt man led the way to the stables below. Some broken mangers remained, evoking contented munching and warm animal smells rising to heat the rooms above. Outside, open fields ended in olive groves and vineyards where the first leaves were pushing out from savagely pruned and bound vines.

'Saint Francis lived a while up there,' Gianni was pointing up a ravine. 'The Franciscans often settled near waterfalls.' Ten strides above the abandoned farmhouse the waterfall cascaded into a pool. It was a remote spot but, as Gianni pointed out, cool in summer. The land in front rose blocking any view of the plain. The masonry was as impressive as the price. We left passing two Franciscan monks and an old man on a donkey carrying bundles of twigs returning up the valley. Smoky twilight engulfed us. Church bells startled me; almost time for vespers. I hadn't realised that Montesasso was murmuring above us unseen. House too hidden, even if shady in summer, I thought. And oppressive to have those rocks almost hanging over you with the feeling of being spied on by the town, peering down from the hilltop like an over-anxious matron. Far out beyond the ravine the sun, behind clouds all day, was sinking blood red into mist.

The prospect of another huge meal and having to converse in my tired Italian did not appeal. I escaped Gianni and Ada as politely as I could to write with the day fresh in my mind. Before supper I had telephoned Paul; after it I packed, ready to leave for Florence early the next morning.

After so many years I still see myself dodging into a café to telephone Paul, Gianni kicking his heels outside. The dialling tone again and again and again. The same resounding absence. The receiver was halfway back when,

'*Pronto.*' It was his voice. I paused, eyes closed, sighing in slowly diffused delight. He was safely back in Florence! I breathed in deeply before.

'Paul. It's me.'

'Where are you?' He could hear the café clatter. He sounded excited, in boyish mode. That woman restorer hadn't told him about Tim.

'I'm in Montesasso.' He'd be frowning in concentration, hair curling over brow.

'Where?'

'Montesasso. South of Florence. About one and a half hours' away. I'll be with you tomorrow...' He interrupted me.

'They told me you took a letter and telegram from my worktable. Why?' Too cruel to tell him when alone.

'I can't hear you properly. It's too noisy here. I'll explain it tomorrow. See you at the studio.' Better not to allow him to ask about Tim. Better to tell him when we're together, better... 'Bye, darling. A big hug.' I replaced the phone.

Your mind jabbers on in futile argument with fate, haunted by a shape lying still, skidmarks and scattering children – a cacophony of fear. I cluttered it with plans and projects, listing the two houses in an exercise book followed by a description, the asking price and my comments. Closing it, I stared at the back cover with its useful information: inches into centimetres, miles into kilometres, pints into litres, highest mountains, the speed of light in both measures, capital cities – but all I could see was Tim's absence.

CHAPTER 3

Settling into the corner of the carriage the next morning, I waved *ciao* to Gianni and to the emotional shield provided by Alberto's bedroom, Montesasso's alleys and squares and the flights of house fantasies. Dew had scattered beads over the olive groves; leaden clouds weighed on the plain glimpsed in patches of ploughed and fallow fields.

A mere month before Tim was born, Paul had declared (my fist hit the small table under the window as the train sped towards Florence and my memory hurtled back ten years) that there was not enough space in our London flat for a baby. People in the carriage were chatting, smoking, moisture drying off them in stagnant smells; I was too distressed to care. Fields freshly furrowed, five-branched olives clutching out of stumps, slender cypresses greentipping the mist were fleeing faster away. Paul had sketched our baby 'looking like you', with the blond curls that everyone found so fetching. Gran pronounced crisply, 'Tim's like himself!' and defied anyone to challenge her. Paul assumed the women would take over the unplanned addition to the life he and I had barely started together. Tim would have his surname and any money left over from his work as an apprentice restorer until he became independent. Then he hoped to earn enough for a larger flat with space for Tim.

The train's repetitive clinkety-clank, clinkety-clank, clinkety-clank, made me think of just what we had sworn to eliminate from our lives: routine. We'd do what we wanted, keep our freedom, all we needed was love – no ties, no succession, no stake in the future. That was before Tim was born.

'*Caffè, signora?*' Yes. No. Perhaps. No, leave me alone.

I was desperate for Paul's wide embrace smelling of white spirit and latent energy, his enthusiasm for paintings, for trees in wide-open spaces, for tales of great-uncle Bob and the 'House Beautiful' in his childhood landscape. Carriage doors slamming. Figline Valdarno. Last stop before Florence; more inquisitive eyes watching me. Clinkety-clank, closer to telling; clinkety-clank, closer to consolation; clinkety-clank, closer to shared misery.

Paul and I lived a semi-detached life after Tim was born, my work an hour out of London in Guildford, his in the capital.

'But that's the way you wanted it,' Sarah warned. 'An open relationship. Excitement and insecurity.' Paul and I chose to cultivate our individual lives and careers with loving flexibility; Sarah and William were emotionally shackled. The morning cup of tea William took Sarah and the way they dovetailed around their three children was predictably familiar.

When Paul left every Sunday, I would tidy up and sit on our bed to plan the week as I wanted. Mondays and Tuesdays were spent calmly preparing for lessons and catching up at an agreeable pace. Wednesdays hurried by. I worked late, relishing the prospect of Friday, and savoured moments of yearning in the silent house with Tim asleep, Gran and Grandpa in bed and Mother out late at book club or film. Thursdays passed in tingling anticipation and Fridays throbbed by in feverish efforts to clear work before the weekend started at four o'clock. Paul might surprise me at my school gate, or meet Tim leaving his school with Sarah and her son Andrew. (She began teaching there after William had started lecturing at the University of Surrey.) Then I would find Tim and Paul engrossed at home, small and large heads poring over the ingenious games Paul concocted out of bits of sandpapered wood, cereal boxes and the insides of toilet rolls. Other times there was a message through Gran asking me to meet his train, or inviting me to a surprise assignation in London. He would sometimes go away without warning, creating the thrill in anticipation of an unexpected return like the Prodigal Son.

In November 1966, more than two-and-a-half years after Tim was born, the Arno flooded Florence and Paul left to help. Ink sketches framed a brief message in capitals: 'TERRIBLE DAMAGE IN FLORENCE. AM DOING WHAT I CAN. SPECIALS. PAUL.' 'Specials' was our word for all conventional affection: love, hugs, kisses, words worn threadbare by others. Days later he called from a noisy bar.

'I'm working in the Uffizi, cleaning and drying manuscripts.' Framed by Christmas lights round his bedroom window, the child waited for his father to come back from cleaning nasty mud off books in faraway Florence. Paul returned, bursting with excitement at meeting the great Ridolfi, who had offered him a chance he could only have dreamed of: an apprenticeship in the most prestigious Florentine studio! Just right for his career. Of course he would return often to see us, and I could travel to Florence with Tim whenever I was free. I agreed reluctantly, relying as always on Gran's help.

Following my mother's pattern, I juggled work with caring for a young child. From Tim's 'special' father flowed messages and drawings on gold-edged paper with red and blue petals and green leaves intertwined, from the city of flowers that floods itself. A little face expecting the postman kept vigil at an upstairs window.

Despair sidled up when I left the train from Montessasso, slipped inside me as I bridged the Arno with a scurry of chattering schoolchildren, dragged my feet alongside Brunelleshi's church of the Holy Spirit and caught my breath as I arrived outside Paul's studio near Palazzo Pitti.

I saw him the moment I stepped inside. In the ten years we had been together he had filled out a little; his brown hair curled shorter over his forehead and longer at the back. He looked up, worn and worried. They must have told him everything after my phone call. His arms tightened round me as he nuzzled my hair and laid his cheek on the crown of my head. The others in the studio were looking and trying not to, though it was after one, and they should have left for lunch. The woman working on the archangel actually turned round and stared.

'Tim is dead. An accident outside his school.'

'They've told me,' was all he said; then, 'I wish you had called me home.' He made me feel I had pushed him to the periphery. I held him at arms' length, voice trembling.

'I did! Telegrams here and to your flat. Letters too. Why didn't **you** call **me** more often?' He looked stranded, silent in his stained white overall with its warm smell of paint and white spirit. He reached out to me, but all I could see over his shoulder was the dark shape on the road, our child's future ripped from us by the van skidding. Then he stepped back, leaving stillness between us.

'If only I'd known. At least in time for the funeral.' The others had quietly left for lunch before he took off his overall.

'Why didn't you say you were going to Naples when you phoned for his birthday? That was two days before the accident.'

'I didn't think it important. It was for such a short time and I would've been back in Florence before Easter to meet your train.'

There was a chill in the drizzle over the demands, questions and reproaches that skimmed the vast piazza sloping down from Palazzo Pitti. We didn't even have an umbrella to huddle under as he took a side street away from the bars and the people he knew. He found a bustling tavern, the better to muffle our misery. Two crumpled figures, we sat by a window blurred with drops of condensation, the interior redolent of wine and smouldering logs. The landlord cut us hunks of unsalted Tuscan bread and, unasked, sliced salty *pecorino* cheese and ham unhooked from the rafters. Two plates, two glasses and a carafe of wine. So our grieving journeyed into the leftover day. It was agreed...right from the start... Tim was unplanned... how can a child run around a studio with bottles and jars and strange concoctions like an alchemist's den? Who looks after a child? Who should have done this or that or the other? Searching for pointless exculpation from past guilt; agreeing, dissenting and groping forward. Pauses. I spread his hands on the rough table and traced the stains, brown with a touch of green, a fleck of red. Scraps from a shared past, fragments of memory: Tim chuckling as Paul played with his toes and fingers; his first tentative steps from me to Paul and back; a sandcastle competition on a short seaside break; Paul pushing him on a swing or turning up unexpectedly to collect a surprised, over-excited child at the school gates. That was where it all had ended. An absence settled between us.

'How can I tell you what's happened if I don't know where you are?'

Under wide lampshades casting smoke-filled cones of light into the dark interior men looked up from their cards, silenced by my shrill voice.

Paul paid and followed me out, almost running.

'Be fair. I didn't stop you keeping Tim...'
'Didn't **you** want the child?'
'I did.' He hesitated. 'A lot.' I wasn't sure if his face was streaked with raindrops or tears.

We sat in Brunelleschi's Santo Spirito looking across candles at Michelangelo's carved wood crucifix. Together on a bench we contemplated it, hand beside hand.

'If only you'd been in Florence I could have contacted you...'
'You knew I'd return –'
'Not when I needed you.' So much. So very much. 'Tragedies never happen when expected.'

We spent the evening adrift from the world; no telephone, no radio, no newspaper, sinking together into a vortex of grief, hopelessly recalling a child clutching Paul's teddy, a fair-haired boy feeding ducks; a slender, brown-haired one climbing an oak tree so high that he panicked and Paul followed to coax him down. A taller boy with darker, curly hair winning the hundred-yard sprint at school as I had years earlier. Paul scrutinised him as he often did, remarking that **he** had never excelled at sport. Like Olivia, like Tim. And he kept on looking at Tim, making little portraits which he gave me, and a watercolour inspired by the photo of us three round the table on our last holiday. We spiralled down into the void, in shades of irrevocable loss.

The following days I drifted along streets, in and out of shops and into any museum that would not remind me of Tim. The child's face peeped out from intricate flower patterns on cabinets and table tops, from behind vases or statues in the Archaeological Museum and came reflected in the glass cases of the Science Museum. He should have been with us in the crowd outside the Cathedral when the Easter dove whooshed along the wire from its high altar through wide-open doors and ignited the pyramid of fireworks on a cart by the Baptistery's 'Gates of Paradise'. I felt him but I couldn't find him.

Montesasso – Easter 1974

Not long after I left Montesasso to join Paul in Florence, Silvano phoned the studio and left a message that the Englishman's property was ready for us to purchase. I was relieved that Paul was eager to see it with me. We found the tenants still in the smaller house; they knew they could legally stay as long as they liked. I wondered how many times the owner had done this to unsuspecting compatriots. He probably made a good living out of forfeited deposits!

From spring to summer the weeks were punctuated by sporadic calls from Silvano or the Englishman's lawyer in Rome promising that the family was about to move out. Gianni wrote once, then twice a week. Why didn't we return to Montesasso in the summer as we had promised? We could stay in his house. The weather was perfect. He would happily take us to look at houses. The prices were not too high if we avoided agents like Silvano and took our time – wise words in the circumstances.

Gradually the fantasies returned. Why not try again? Paul was as keen as I was. We decided to jettison Silvano and the Englishman for Gianni.

I recall feeling sick and listless after Easter when we returned from Florence, my body still in shock after Tim's death. Though I looked at schoolchildren as if from the wrong end of binoculars, I decided to return to teaching in the summer term. I lacked the will to change my career as both friends and colleagues advised. Thinking back, I must have been too distraught to realise I was pregnant. Paul knew I would keep the baby and accepted the general consensus that we would welcome a child to love again.

After Florence he spent most of his time in London catching up with work. There was a *capriccio* from a country house in such bad condition that it required more time than he anticipated. Paul found this genre of painting strangely fascinating. I remember being with him in London when he showed me an eighteenth-century traveller's souvenir of a once-in-a-lifetime journey to Italy. The Colosseum, Apollo Belvedere and Laocoon in the Vatican Museum and tombs on the Appia Antica were all reassembled in the imaginary space of an artist's fantasy. Paul fretted about finishing it. I was advised not to travel abroad that summer; the baby was due in September.

At weekends in Guildford the older members of the matriarchy fussed over Paul. He lay in bed all morning, curled over three-quarters of it. Once I panicked and shook his shoulder.

'Are you all right?'

'Exhausted... too much work...' he murmured and curled his fists tighter under his chin, drawing knees up to elbows. When he came down to lunch he looked worn, eyes shrunk into his head.

Gran saw me worried.

'It's hard for him to lose one child and know another is coming but not feel it. He hasn't got the baby inside him.' She fussed over him even more.

'I don't think he takes much to babies,' she observed one lunch when we had started to eat without him. 'Tim was older and his companion as well as his son.' She would be thinking of her brother Frank in his sailor suit, playing with her at about the same age.

Both Paul and Grandpa had stopped going to the workshop on the top floor as they used to before the accident. The stairs were perhaps too much for Grandpa, but it was really because the room was next to Tim's. I, too, avoided my son's bedroom after he died. On the day William came to discuss a short story that I had written for the journal he edited, Andrew was with him. He must have slipped away while his father and I were talking and didn't answer when we called. I left William with my grandparents and mother in the living room and climbed slowly up the stairs to Tim's bedroom. Andrew was sitting on the floor strewn with everything he and Tim had last played with, eyes wide and filled with tears. I can see him there now, mouth moving silently as if talking to Tim about the Hornby train at the station they had made together, the model ship, Paul's old teddy with boxing gloves falling off its paws, and of future adventures when they would always be best friends.

'Take anything, Andrew. Anything you'd like to keep of Tim's.' I wanted him to take everything.

'I don't know where to begin,' he said looking up at me, hazel eyes under ginger hair. 'It's like there's a terrible empty space and I don't know how to fill it.'

'Just take whatever you want.' We were both crying. 'They still have a feeling of him about them. Carry that with you.'

Looking back, I don't know if he understood. He had to move on, leaving part of his childhood behind.

Mother started to clear away Tim's possessions before Dan was born in September. I remember that on one of Paul's visits in August she asked us to take whatever we wanted to keep, but by then Tim's spirit had evaporated. I removed one or two things blindly from the top of the boxes, and went to see if Paul was still lying in our bedroom.

He had left for London.

Tim's clothes and toys, once humming with his presence, were bundled off to orphans in India. His bedroom door closed on a room emptied of all but the furniture.

CHAPTER 4

The first time I watched Paul carrying out restoration was before Tim was born. He was working on a wooden statue of Saint Dominic riddled with wormholes. I watched him hold surgical pincers lightly in his wide fingers, dipping swabs in white spirit and stroking them over the black surface to reveal traces of brown – a Saint Francis?

'How do you know what to clean and where to stop? Why don't you just wipe the candle smoke off Saint Dominic and leave it at that?'

'It's the starting point that counts. People want to see the original; to be singed by the fire of creation, I suppose, and then follow the work's miraculous survival through time.'

'Where do you start? On the surface, with Dominic? Is there a lot of grime?'

'You mean discoloured varnish? Yes,' Paul explained, 'and that's why it's taking me such a time!'

Sitting beside him as he wiped away the black friar, I had fun inventing a story.

'In a church somewhere in Italy, the brown robes of Saint Francis were painted black. Why?'

'The parishioners decided to change their patron saint, and the church's name, to Saint Dominic,' Paul continued.

'Why not another Dominican saint? What about Thomas Aquinas, the Theologian, or Peter Martyr?' That was all I could manage on Dominican saints. My favourite, Peter Martyr, was always pursued through a dark forest, black cape flapping over white robe, by red-tongued dogs baying him into sainthood. Paul's statue was too static to tell that tale.

'More likely a local donor gave money on condition his patron saint Dominic was portrayed,' Paul suggested.

'Of course! So they had to do it quickly...'

'To satisfy the impatient donor...'

'Weren't given enough money...'

'Took some of it to repair the crumbling church tower…'

'Or support the parish priest's illegitimate child…'

'Who turned out to be a famous painter like Filippo Lippi!' As we improvised Paul finished cleaning the folds over Dominic's right thigh, handing the body back to Saint Francis. He saw himself excavating the past, restoring the artist, known or unknown, to his creation. As more conservation work came in, we merrily speculated over tempera and oil paintings, angels and saints.

But after Tim was born everything changed. I brought him to the studio in a carrycot. The baby liked watching Paul's face as he concentrated under the lamps and his hands delicately lifted the veil of time off a painting and stabilised what remained. Eventually he'd start whimpering, making Paul edgy.

Ten years after he was born in March 1964 memories flooded my mind. The accident happened two days after his tenth birthday and Dan was expected in September of the same year. The birth of the second child would inevitably recall that of the first, when I needed to forget completely or have Tim restored to life. If there were a benign fate, it might this time favour the child to be born in September.

After so much apprehension, Dan was launched easily into our lives. He ate, slept and put on weight to everyone's approval. There were no complications at all. I sailed a choppy course around child, chores and work Monday to Wednesday, navigating to calmer waters by Thursday and into a haven on Friday with everything shipshape for the weekend and Paul. Waiting for him gave a thrill that heightened as Friday approached. But before going to sleep, when autumn winds blew branches across the street lamp and skeletal patterns convulsed over the curtains, I thought I heard Tim humming in his room and his laughter when playing 'snap' with us; felt his loveliness of being, saw his smile – then his shape on the ground. I'd click on the light and work over what I'd written; fall asleep and try to dream of going away to restore a ruin near Montesasso.

Like Tim, Dan was cared for by three generations of women; their love beamed forcefully on to him. Around Christmas 1974 Paul began to show more interest in the child, now not only smiling but also sitting up. It was Paul's idea first, but Mother also was keen for me to return to Montesasso at Easter and find, with Gianni's help, a place to restore. She would take care of Dan after work. Gran could look after him in daytime and Paul offered to help, though he had so much work to do, so many fraught deadlines. He even spent an evening in March planning weekend shifts with Mother and Gran. I accepted Gianni's invitation to stay that Easter and bought a new exercise book to write our dream place into existence.

A plot for paradise? – March 1975

Gianni met my train at Montesasso Scalo. In the widened square a petrol station and two houses under construction now stood near the bar and general food store. New blocks of flats were enticing families down from Montesasso's ancient, unheated palazzi, and hillside farmers impatient to flee leaking roofs and crumbling houses. So many were up for sale, and Gianni knew it.

He drove slowly up the panoramic route for the landscape to work its spell on me. I absorbed the olive groves and vineyards on terraced hillsides and the farmhouses with wisps of smoke, enthralled. In the distance, an avenue of cypresses wound up a ridge to a fairy-tale castle. Gianni parked outside Porta Etrusca, walked me briskly to his house and rang the bell – he never used a key. Ada buzzed the door open from the kitchen on the first floor. A tall girl with long brown hair was looking over her shoulder.

'Giuliana!' The normally serious Gianni smiled at his daughter.

A stocky forty-something man looking oddly familiar was sitting at the kitchen table. Gianni shook hands and introduced me perfunctorily: 'Olivia, my boss. My daughter.' Giuliana began to tell me about her work in Turin. She likes it there. Montesasso is small and provincial with everyone minding their neighbours' business. She's lively and nervous, always smoking and moving about, hands gesticulating, legs crossing and uncrossing, getting up to sit in another chair, then returning to the first one. Restless. Like father, like daughter.

'There's a lot to show you.' After lunch Gianni hurried down the stairs into the narrow street spiced with wood smoke, across the main square with scarcely a nod to friends on the Town Hall steps and into an alley below a statue of the local saint.

'The dark Madonna or "Saracena",' he explained, before stopping at a house with its first floor jutting out and beams so weathered I was afraid to enter.

'Ecco!' Gianni pointed to the outside water tap, *'acqua'*. Two rooms up, two down. No water or WC inside. No WC anywhere. Had they been hopping over the wall into the fields for centuries? There was a small abandoned herb garden at the back and a spectacular view down vineyards and olive groves and over fields crosscut with drainage canals to ridges etched against distant mountains. Gianni watched me intently.

'The house is from the time of Dante.' I turned, startled to hear him speak English. *'Only little words,'* after a pause, *'learned in war.'*

A chicken clucked, ending in a squawk. Two children were quarrelling. Just sounds of life. Then a cackle of laughter from a television programme cut a swathe through the afternoon siesta.

'No, Gianni. Too noisy. We need quiet, and the countryside.'

He nodded and returned the key to the neighbour with the raucous television. Out through Porta Contadina, down the hill and along the Roman Via Cassia to a bar and general food store; further up a few houses and farm buildings lay scattered round a medieval church.

'Don Luigi!' Gianni commented without actually greeting the priest as he shot past him and accelerated the blue Fiat up a rutted track, risking its underside. I remonstrated.

'Non importa! It doesn't matter,' he replied driving with erratic bravado. We went still higher above the last olive groves. On the far side of the valley Montesasso straddled the hill, leaning out from the mountains behind to peer over the plain below, hardly on nodding acquaintance with the distant range that separated it from the coast. Here was the ideal view, I was almost sure. We passed a house on an isolated outcrop being busily restored.

'A local builder has bought it.' I had been warned. When Italians became interested, prices would soar.

'For resale?'

'Beh!' Gianni's favourite answer meaning he doesn't know, usually accompanied by a shrug. We bumped along to a more modest dwelling; a ramp led up to an outside passage with decrepit doors dangling into long deserted space.

'Guarda!' Gianni was inside pointing through a paneless window, *'Look, beautiful view!'* He had grasped my priorities. Spring scents wafted in. The buzz of the first lazy fly, harbinger of a hot summer. Below, chickens fussed and chortled.

'Safe from wolves; that's why the stalls below are used as chicken pens,' Gianni explained. The owner came once a day to feed the hens and collect the eggs. He would be glad to sell.

Wolves? I could hardly believe my ears. Would they find my baby Dan a tasty morsel? Ideas flickered through my excited mind and I began making wild plans, like a frustrated architect. Where was the water? A disused well. Vines projected from a ramshackle trellis in front of an arched area, originally for carts. It would make an ideal open loggia or summer dining room. Alone and responsible, I was uncertain I knew what Paul wanted. I glanced down the slope estimating the distance to the food store and bus. A car would be necessary. I had hoped while on holiday to avoid vehicle dictatorship.

The sun was moving behind the mountain ridge another hundred feet above us, unrolling shade along the narrow terrace. It was only mid-afternoon.

As we walked back to his car, Gianni looked up at the house in restoration. Ever practical, he said, *'You can take electricity from there. The builder will pay to get it up the hillside. It would hardly cost you anything.'* If they agreed to it.

'I was born in that house. I had to walk four kilometres to school – two there, two back. Then I usually looked after the sheep so mamma could bake bread and cook and care for the hens and rabbits. The landowner allowed mamma and my sisters to keep silkworms in the attic and sell the cocoons to the agent for

the silk factory. Our mulberry trees are still there. My sisters went to school for about two years, on and off.'

It was a largish, sturdy house; four families had shared it in Gianni's time, all working for the same padrone, all warmed by the animals in the ground floor stables. A single hearth in the kitchen; his draughty, cold, candle-lit youth.

'It took two hours on foot to get to the nearest shop and back. There wasn't much time for anything else because we got so tired. Up at six for school. Papà left even earlier to try and get work as a casual labourer. We needed money. Sunday was the highlight of the week. You put on clean clothes to go to church and ogle the local girls. Down there at Don Luigi's church, I met Ada.'

He described himself returning from the War, twenty-five, unmarried and, in the parish community, highly eligible. He was a stonemason. Most of the others had returned unskilled, all avowed partisans, to unprofitable hillside farming for absentee landowners.

Progress was slow as we bumped down the track. Though his brother worked in Milan and his sisters were married and lived in Florence, everyone in the vicinity was Gianni's relative and had to be greeted. That meant driving into muddy yards, scattering chickens and stopping right by steps up to the smoky kitchens and a glass of their 'vino genuino'.

Looking back, I saw that the narrow house below Gianni's birthplace lay totally in shadow. The sun was setting behind it in full glory and twilight spread over olive groves and cube shaped houses. In Montesasso there was a chill in the smoky air. Placing a Campari in front of me, Gianni casually mentioned a figure.

'We don't have much money, Gianni. If we spend a lot to buy a place, then there won't be enough for even basic repairs.'

This is not the most favoured area between Florence and Siena, so I had expected the prices to be lower. Camping in a ruin with a young child was unthinkable without water, and that would mean sinking a well.

'I can't help if you go further away,' Gianni warned me with a touch of severity. 'Petrol's expensive,' adding, 'I'm a stonemason,' almost as an admonition.

More ruined houses, more thoughts, more uncertainties. Wrong price, wrong place, no view, no water...
I lay in bed that evening dreaming of a farmhouse with the view down the valley below Gianni's birthplace, tentatively imagining Paul and me settling into the landscape, putting down roots.

Flowing out of my dreams early the following morning I found Gianni waiting for me in his kitchen. March had been unusually wet, he said, even for this rainy time of year. It had started with sleet, but was now warming up. The fields were still sodden. The terraces too, yet the first Florentine lilies were flecking the banks purple. Sowing had started late. The narrow terraces of the hillside farmers were better drained than the huge farming estates on the plain where the cereal crops were in a bad way. His tone suggested, 'Serve 'em right, they've already profited too much!'

He headed south towards the plain, stopping in his usual abrupt way by a group of houses.

'Ossegno. Where the Romans were slaughtered by Hannibal.' Gianni's direct way of presenting history turned Hannibal, the Carthaginian general, into a superhuman figure.

'They say some Romans fled and married Etruscan women in Montesasso.' A conveniently arranged affair, a sort of peaceful rape of the Sabines. This makes historical sense and explains why Gianni resembles figures on the Etruscan vase in the town guide: strong nose, dark, lank hair, almond-shaped eyes with slightly drooping eyelids and a lithely expressive body. Feeling unexpectedly merry, I began humming something about the 'Vecchio Etrusco Giannino'.

He walked up a track to a low building and disappeared. I peeped after him to catch sight of a wide hearth, a small girl in a smock and a huge double bed capable of welcoming a tribe of children with the *genitori*. The female 'generator' eyed me with wary curiosity as three members of the tribe returned from school. The grandmother was cooking over an open fire. I had no idea where she slept; hardly in the tribal bed too?

Gianni interrupted my thoughts, took my arm and pointed the way with a key he had been given. A stone's throw higher up stood a handsome dwelling more befitting an estate manager than farmers.

'*Costa poco.*' My ears pricked up. Only '*nove milioni di lire*'. Rapid calculation: £6000. More than I wanted to shell out at this stage, but as we moved from the fine entrance hall with a huge fireplace and solid beams into the kitchen and adjacent rooms, my spirits soared. Found at last! My gut feelings rarely betrayed me. It boasted an inside stone staircase, already a sign of status, and four habitable rooms on the upper floor, one leading off the other. The roof looked sound. The price was suspiciously low. Perhaps more repairs were needed than I realised. Electricity? A pole fifty metres away; just a small job to connect it. Water? A well with a convenient tap by the kitchen door.

Great, I thought. But where's the snag?

Gianni narrowed his eyes as he looked into the sunset behind the hills; a handsome young man trapped in an ageing body. Some agent who managed the detested *mezzadria* or sharecropping system for an absentee landowner would, he was sure, have lived in this house. A few *padroni* kept their side of the contract: repaired farmhouses, outbuildings and carts, and replaced trees, plants and breeding animals for their *contadini* in exchange for half of the farm produce. His father's employer had not been a good *padrone*, and came only to collect his portion at the appropriate season, neglecting everything else.

'I learnt to dress stone and build walls before the War and this got me a job afterwards on an estate.' He pointed to an imposing villa halfway up the mountain to Montesasso with ochre walls enclosed by deep green cypresses. 'We had a *cita.*' His use of the dialect word to refer to his daughter made me feel fully accepted.

'Every summer we had two weeks off to help with the harvest.' He only had a few valleys to cross to return to a rustic culture from a world of privilege. He had learnt to love plants and care for the garden. The villa owner's wife was English and seemed to enjoy teaching him words and phrases. However, I remembered him telling me that he'd picked up some English earlier when he was a partisan. He used to return every summer to his people in the valley. Girls flirted with him even when he came back not only married, but a proud father. He couldn't help it! They just threw themselves at him – or so he said. He recalled Ada looking out of the house we saw being restored as he made love in the long grass, but not out of her sight. This was recounted without remorse, even with a pinch of pride. Regret only came some years later when he had to leave the cottage in the grounds of the ochre villa. They were allowed one child, but Ada could hardly cook and serve at table with two hanging around her. Gianni professed amazement that she was pregnant with Alberto as he had only planned for one. Beh! That happens.

I stood up. Copper clouds were sagging over us, pushing the deep red sunset beyond the horizon, and the first drops were falling. Why hadn't I noticed before? On the other side of the road was a high wall, but the gates were open. Right in front of us small lights were blinking in the cemetery set on a west-facing slope, like the Etruscan cities of the dead. Places have affinities, threads of usage linking them across centuries and cultures. I felt the spirit of the estate manager nodding at my side, at one with my thoughts.

But I had also found the snag.

We returned to Montesasso Scalo for an aperitif. Unaware of my ambivalent reactions to the house, Gianni was certain he had made a deal and keen to celebrate.

'Un caffè? Una birra, un campari?'

I was the only woman in the smoke-filled bar. At six, on the edge of evening, supper would be on the hob and all females dutifully employed, daughters with mothers, age-old patterns of rural harmony within the extended family, or so it might seem to outsiders. I was allowed my eccentricities. Gianni was obviously known to the groups of card players. They looked at him, then me and back again.

'Un campari per la signora,' ordered with a swagger in his voice.

A sudden yell at one of the tables made him scurry over.

'Il sette di cuori!' exclaimed Gianni, 'porta fortuna.'

Seven of hearts – the harbinger of fortune.

CHAPTER 5

Bereft in the present, I wanted to write about realising a dream. A mind in shock seeks refuge in memories of intense happiness, like Paul and me before Tim was born. Paul, the 'black sheep' of his family, had turned his back on generations of upright suburban bank managers for the exciting but unprofitable realms of art. In the liberated sixties he was an irresistible amalgam of sensuous allure and courteous reserve, his body more sportsman's than artist's. Intrigued, I remember on our first visit to the National Gallery observing him in thrall to portraits and absorbed by the misty landscape with poplar leaves flickering behind the Perugino Madonna and Child. I arranged for us to do everything together, leaving no space for anyone else to inch in between him and me. He had to be my partner at the university ball – though he didn't dance nearly as well as Mike. Paul would have preferred to stand on the sidelines laughing and teasing me; but I refused to dance with anyone else except Mike, because he and Paul were friends and Paul didn't mind. Sarah was amazed to see me, as she put it, gallivanting after a man, when I was always complaining about males pestering me.

Preoccupied as she was with William and her wedding plans, my obsession with Paul appeared to her comic, even frivolous. But too much had happened since then.

Gianni's patch – March 1975

Though we talked late by the living room fire, Gianni was up early the next day. Seven is late by the countryman's clock, and if he's on the stretch of road he maintains before eight, he can justify returning for lunch by one instead of two when his stint officially ends.

From the years working at the villa, Gianni told me he had saved enough to buy a narrow section of an ancient building backing on to Montesasso's thirteenth-century hospital. The widow of a wealthy lawyer who owned the palazzo across the alley, seeing him busily pointing his own place, asked him to do some building work for her. One job led to another till he was regularly employed in the building boom of the sixties. They were, he thought, the golden years, though he worked too hard to see much of Ada. Then came the accident. Slipping on the scaffolding, he shattered his left hip on the paving below. That's why he limps slightly and leans to the left when standing. After many months and endless form filling, Gianni found a coveted half-day government job. Secure, with low pay but a reasonable pension, it left time for tacitly acknowledged moonlighting. Because of his accident, he had been accepted before others higher on the waiting list, but his skills as a stonemason counted too.

He loved his strip of road in the mountains behind Montesasso, the companionship of the scattered and hospitable mountain people and the way he was often summoned to rebuild a crumbling parapet or create a new retaining wall. Crucially, the foreman in his area was a close friend. He certainly seemed at home when we met in Gianni's house, a genial, heavily boned, bespectacled individual about eight years younger than his host.

Gianni backed his vehicle with brio, squeezed my knee as if to say, 'Now for the adventure!' and hurtled down the hill, past a superb Renaissance church. We were careering away from Montesasso to where Life, as Gianni would have it, really goes on – Montesasso Scalo. Life was in the bustle of the bar on the corner of the station square. All male, they were talking of weather, pigs, the moon waxing or waning, the sowing to be done, the lightning tax on something or other and whether one could escape paying it. Andrea the barman pushed across Gianni's usual espresso. I was given what's rapidly becoming my unchosen usual; grappa splashed the back of my hand as I clumsily attempted to stop Gianni 'correcting' my coffee. At this rate I'd be uncontrollably merry by ten in the morning! It had not yet struck eight. Gianni nodded towards a posse of gnarled faces grouped round a table, placed the small cup with finality on to the saucer and turned on his heels, to leave Andrea and his weathered clients looking at me with naked interest as I followed Gianni out. Not a twinkle of recognition from the barman, though he had served me when I first arrived in Montesasso.

Inexplicably we retraced our steps. The western flank of Montesasso was still in shadow. Alternating cypresses and umbrella pines beat out our slow climb as we hugged the perimeter walls. Surging past at eye level were the massive cyclopean blocks that must have been hauled up the steep mountainside by oxen. I imagined them straining, nostrils distended, with Etruscan drivers, lean and bronzed like Gianni, goading them on in a ruthless rhythm. We left the town to wind over a sequence of hills to an upland valley, oaks and beeches supplanting cypresses and umbrella pines.

'My brother-in-law, Carlo, gets his timber here. He's a builder's merchant.' Still further up, a dark green reservoir drained all sound, even birdsong, into the depth of the waters. The air shivered for an instant, dimpling the surface.

'Montesasso's water supply. Plenty of it.'

Then back to the narrowing mountain road. 'E la mia strada.' His stretch of asphalt, his pride. Perched on the watershed was a hut painted the muddy purple of Italian road maintenance buildings. Unlocked, the dark interior welcomed with enclosed memories of wood smoke and snatches of conversation over cigarettes and coffee. Gianni busily lit a wood fire after settling me on a hollowed tree trunk with spindly branches as legs. He sat beside me and smoked while the percolator, poised on a spirit burner, popped and hissed coffee into the top section. He poured it into two cracked mugs and spooned sugar into both.

Ten o'clock already. The weather wasn't bad enough to spend the morning brewing coffee or occupying the best kitchen chair in a farmhouse while the signora prepared lunch – always generously offered to him and always refused, Gianni assured me. (What was Ada doing, after all, down in Montesasso?) He pulled out a scythe, a long-handled shovel and a broom, before handing me a wrinkled three-day-old newspaper and disappearing down the road on an unexplained mission.

With nothing else to do I set off to climb Monte San Leo and survey the land beneath. I tackled a rocky path formed by flash floods and woodcutters. Stacked pine logs displaying the weave of the wood grain tingled my nostrils. Higher up strands of smoke escaped from a carefully layered woodpile packed with earth. On the other side of the clearing a log hut, built as meticulously as the charcoal pile, was locked, but in use.

It's so rare to be unbothered, to drift out of time, place and expectations, just conscious of the birdsong, of the damp interlacing scents of the mountain ruffled by the faintest of breezes.

A dark shape leaped up the woodpile from the far side. A wolf? Backing away in fright, I slipped and fell, aware of a hairy creature with tusks and snout cantering up the path in the direction I was going. I had overheard men in the bars talk about the cinghiali – wild boars – both a delicacy and a proof of virility among hunters. Though it had only looked at me and lolloped off, I decided to take another path to the summit.

A speck in the light clouds moved like an eagle. Sky-filled space rose above me, and beyond lay range upon range of conifers. I sat on an outcrop and wanted to sing. Not a habitation in sight. Moss and heather were glistening into life after their winter hibernation. It was peaceful beyond belief.

One o'clock. I reluctantly began retracing my steps towards the hut in the distance and Gianni's figure in the shape of a question mark.

'Cosa facciamo?' I felt I had to put some shape into the rest of the day.

'A mangiare.' Well, I had to admit I was hungry. When had I got up? It seemed almost a day ago; six hours to be exact with two black coffees and a shot of grappa to survive on.

Eating red meat, Gianni explained over a mound of tagliatelle, is a sign you are no longer poor. Red meat was only served on feast days if you were lucky, as chickens, rabbits and guinea fowl came, like lettuce and common vegetables, from your own back yard – as long as the landowner didn't seize them as his share.

'Caffè?' Ada obliged, slightly grudgingly.

'A dopo.' See you later. Gianni was up from the table and down the stairs without any explanation. Their son Alberto had long since left.

The day before we had seen a house that gave me all the right vibes, except for its position facing the cemetery. I had tried to phone Paul in London, spending a lot of money, only to find that he was out. He always reassures me that he trusts my judgement, little suspecting what a fraught situation I would be in.

'Pazienza!' I muttered to no one.

After lunch I drifted into the local museum with row upon row of Madonnas, interrupted only by the local saint. Nothing was happening. I was going to return home, mission incomplete. The last room displayed the famous Montesasso vase decorated with the erotic scenes Gianni had mentioned. It certainly held pride of place. Yes, what was discernible would intrigue Paul.

Walking slowly away from the museum, I ignored a voice calling from the steps of the Town Hall. Then a hand grabbed my shoulder. Couldn't I see him? Was I deaf? I half turned to look at Gianni, who was very excited.

'Una casetta. E di un mio parente.'

Gianni, too, had been rather dejected that morning. Convinced I was keen on the house at Ossegno, he hadn't planned to show me others. After lunch he had decided to try one last time. Some distant relatives had a ruin but he never thought they would agree to sell. I followed Gianni back to his house and into the Fiat 500 tucked snugly below the balcony. A hazardous four-point turn nosing or bumping the buildings on both sides of the alley, and away we went. Through the Porta Etrusca where we first met, then down to the Via Cassia, turning at the small store and bar towards his valley. We took a different route across a farmyard where children chasing skeletal hens stopped to watch us. Up a steep incline in first gear and, instead of turning sharp right, Gianni jolted to a halt mid track. Nose snubbed on windscreen, I was looking up a wide valley to the chestnut clad ridge and could just make out the house where Gianni was born.

'Una valle ridente. La mia.' Then he paused and, turning to look intensely at me, said in hesitating English, *'it is my smiling valley'*. He got out and pointed.

'Eccola!' Straight ahead, at eye level across fields of buttercups under olive trees and terraces of vines bursting into leaf, lay a small stone house with one window on the first floor and two doorways below, all topped by a caved-in roof.

'It is of distant cousins,' he repeated. *'Massimo, the cousin who's a builder, says they sell it for little. We look?'*

CHAPTER 6

'Any luck?' Gran picked up the excitement in my voice when I called from Montesasso.

'Yes. Yes and no. I don't know where to start. Tell me about Dan first.'

'Sitting up and smiling more everyday. He'll start crawling any time now…'

Gran's grit and sparkle through war and post-war hardship sprang from unfathomable energy. Action, that was how one had to overcome mourning. Her mother died first, then her brother at the Battle of the Somme, followed years later by her father. Now Tim. I spent a lot of time with her and she would tell stories of when she was a suffragette, with exciting allusions to being in prison with famous people. Tales to unfold when I was older and she had more time. Though I asked, they never were. Her past was her property, and she travelled back to it when and how she wished. Mother inherited the same reserved nature and defended her vulnerability with romance. By the time I was old enough to pelt her with questions, she had already honed her fantasy about my father. By the time I was a teenager I had mine. My mother's youth was an alien territory. First she was a landgirl, then met my father, studied to become a librarian, went to Italy to look for my father, and always left Gran to care for me. I too enlisted Gran, older and now frail, to help with the next generation. Her skin had been quilted by time, with tight stitching round her eyes and light brown dots on the back of her hands.

Without Gran all would have unravelled. She knitted together our patterns, mended the holes, darned over stresses and tension. 'Women shouldn't have children too early,' she laughed complicitly with me. When my mother was born in 1920 Gran was eighteen; my mother, in turn, was twenty-two when I arrived. I continued the family with a child at the same age as her, compromising my name, career and life choices. She patched together a loose routine with Dan as she had with Tim, interweaving strands of time and care.

Gran had never been to Italy, but loved to travel there in her imagination, first with my mother, then through Paul and me. I told her about the book I wanted to write and she could hardly wait to read it.

Alchemy – March 1975

The small house on the other side of the buttercup fields was gradually crumbling into the slope. It looked unexciting and rather low set, but had an air of friendly unpretentiousness. A spasm of panic. Would Paul take to such a ruin?

'Andiamo!' Gianni returned to the car and switched on the ignition. We continued through another farmyard (strange the way public roads were routed through others' poultry runs!) where a sullen faced boy ran after the car gesticulating.

'Perchè?' Gianni shrugged his shoulders when I asked why the child was doing it. Behind the run down farmhouse we turned into another track snaking along the edge of an olive grove. To our left green shoots were already visible in the narrow strips between the rows of vines. Instead of pollarded field maples and stone posts to support the vines, cast-off railway sleepers were being reused. A pale yellow farmhouse, its outside stairs rising to a long balcony, overlooked the way down to the ruin. Gianni waved to a younger man harnessing oxen by a neighbouring stone farmhouse, before tackling the overgrown path. The tumbledown house he led me to was perched on a spur of land, like the prow of a ship about to surge between terraced hillsides, across fields and over the plain towards Monte Amiata.

Gianni took my arm, steadying me up a ramp to the gable end. Abundant ivy covered it right up to the amputated stump where the chimney had been. He pushed ahead through a door askew on rusty hinges. I hesitated. For someone who had suffered a serious fall from scaffolding, Gianni was bold. What sort of weight could the floor bear? I peered inside to find him standing in the middle of a large room looking up at the sky through the half open roof and scanning the remaining beams. To the right, the single window we'd seen from the track; another gaped on the far wall above a stone ledge. Following my eyes, Gianni moved towards it, tested the floor tiles and pointed at a hole in the wall. The lead waterspout from the shallow basin had been wrenched out.

I stayed cautiously in the doorway. On the windowless north wall to my left was a diagonal spy hole like a leper's squint, directed towards the track. Who would they be looking for? I felt drawn towards the contadini families who had subsisted in this long-abandoned room.

Under the hole in the roof there would once have been the capacious matrimonial bed, proudly bought by a young couple after years of saving. Their clothes would be kept in the wall recess, and there was just enough space left at the foot of the bed to wash themselves and the plates in the bowl on the window ledge. Only chimney brackets remained of the hearth where food was cooked and hams hung to cure. I imagined it radiating a dusty smell of warmth and endurance on to the smoky walls. Around a scrubbed beech table, strong and reassuring like Gianni's, the ever-increasing family would have congregated. The parents aimed to stop at three offspring, Gianni explained, not to run out of space: one child between them and one on each side, heads down towards the bottom of the vast bed.

He squeezed past me to stand by the ivy-covered wall and look down the ramp.

'Strange there's no bread oven,' he said. 'It must have collapsed into the rubble beneath this ramp.'

Already recreating this former home from what Gianni had told me of his childhood, I found him below tapping beams with the heel of a shoe. I followed suit. They were sound. The stables glowed in the silvery light shining through the openings behind us on to pruned olive branches. Someone was storing fuel. They were dry to crackling point. Gianni looked at me; our excitement was kindled, imagination fired.

'Sound beams. A good start.'

Outside again, we moved to the prow of land and turned to look back at the ruin.

'Could we perhaps add a kitchen with an open eating space in front?' Gianni surveyed the ramp, then nodded. It was wide enough for both.

Water! Why hadn't I thought of that before? But Gianni, a child of the valley, was already on his way past the yellow stuccoed house and the rough stone one with oxen next door. Down a path between fruit trees and allotments crowding the edge of the stream we came to the ford.

'It never dries up,' Gianni told me with assurance. This was a good valley for water. I recalled Leonardo's map in Montesasso's tourist office; we were standing on the same veins of water nearly five hundred years later! Romantic notions of walking in the footsteps of a great artist as topographer slipped into a dream of summers simply spent in a sunlit paradise.

Voices below the ford. Two women were washing clothes in a series of natural basins; garments cleansed in pure mountain water, dried in clear unpolluted breezes. One was soaping and pummelling white sheets in the hollowed stone bed of the stream. Above her, another rinsed in fresh water dammed to bypass the washing area.

Gianni clambered down the bank to talk to the women, who glanced up at me; the older one waved. I smiled back in pleasure at their rural companionship as they washed clothes together in dappled shade by the stream and hung them out in the sun.

Gianni and I looked upstream. I breathed in delight from the profusion of overhanging plants, the mottled – pearl, dun, grey – tang of water in skittish sunlight, and heard the rustling of early leaves with the first birdsong.

'See the watercress? And the toad over there?' There were freshwater crabs too, which Gianni had caught barehanded as a child and even tiny fish, all small fry and tasty in the thoughts of a boy returning uphill from school, tired and ravenous.

Returning along the track Gianni broke off branches, looking at them critically before stripping the twigs with a penknife. He discarded all except a forked one grasped firmly, palms upward. For the next ten minutes he walked around the ruin, water divining. I picked up one of the discarded branches and copied him. There did seem to be a strange pull towards the earth, or was I willing it?

'The well.' Gianni pulled a stake from a sad-looking vine and struck it into the ground, like Moses.

It was then I noticed the rickety pole supporting a single wire. Some electricity, not much, but at least it would mean no oil lamps and candles; they seemed less authentic than washing garments in the stream. Brambles filled the channel between the ruin and the electricity pole and invaded the yard where visitors would have trodden warily, avoiding the competing cacophony of hens, dogs on chains and children. The far side of the outcrop above the stream had been sliced away to form a retaining wall. For what?

'Il vecchio mulino.' Gianni had come up behind me, unnoticed. He knew of at least five such mills up the valley, all on the same stream. Three millstones were lying where once they had ground wheat so that, Gianni knew, the contadini could conceal some of the flour from the landowner. The spy hole inside would pinpoint him or his agent approaching to claim his contractual share of the crop down the only path to the house.

'Allora?' What about it? I looked up the valley, over the terraces of olives, the rows of knobbly vines just in leaf, the trimly planted crops of broad beans and beet between small buttercup meadows, then turned towards the plain and the distant hills defined in the play of sunlight and shadow. To the left Montesasso, and on the horizon Monte Amiata, poised in the centre. But was the spur high enough? Would we catch the hill breezes? I knew Paul disliked intense heat. Others would object to the uphill walk. Could we reach a general store on foot?

'Come!' Gianni was at the top of the ramp, a buttercup between his lips and mischief in his eyes. He seemed decades younger, the Etruscan spirit of the place, arms opened wide to embrace the ruin, the mill remains below, the whole plain in front and the valley on either side. A few battered cars bumped along the track, returning sons working elsewhere to mother's steaming plates of pasta.

'Un gioiello!'

Gianni, the alchemist mason, would transmute a wreck into his masterpiece, a jewel of a house.

* * * * *

Ada refused to let Gianni light a wood fire on our return that evening. He went to bed early, leaving me to write by the light of a candle-strength bulb and breathe in the ancient history of the stone walls around me. Only a few days left before I had to return, but Gianni unsettled me. In his nonchalant way, he now appeared less loyal, hinting at other 'clients'. Worst of all, I had to make a binding decision for Paul too. However encouraging he had been at the far end of an indistinct line, this ruin might not match the picture in his mind.

* * * * *

I was woken at seven the following morning by the sound of Gianni making coffee in the kitchen below. Dressed and shivering, I descended to meet his disapproving glance. He rises with the sun, his best time of day, and he'll enthuse about the freshness of the dew and the dawn chorus with the innate jauntiness of early risers. Childhood memories of early risers being closer to godliness came to my mind as I sipped the bitter but mercifully uncorrected espresso he handed me after announcing that he was taking two mornings off work.

I needed to talk to Paul. It was difficult to hear him in the din of the bar, but I did snatch a quieter moment to tell him what was happening.

'Go ahead. It sounds perfect.' He didn't say much about our baby, just 'Dan is fine, don't worry'.

Gianni's relation, bearing the same name and from the same valley, was to inspect me in Montesasso Scalo. Half an hour later Claudio Panichini was surveying me from behind brooms and basins, coils of hosepipe, garden chairs and humdrum household goods. He was affable and composed, evidently considering himself a cut above his labourer kinsman. Just a stonemason, that Gianni, his gestures were saying. With fine features framed by greying hair, Claudio looked a lean and fit fifty-three year-old, though Gianni told me he enjoyed a handy war pension for unspecified injuries.

Claudio was non-committal. Italian law decreed that he should consult the family, even though the ruin was in his portion of the property. His parents bought the house they had lived in all their lives, as well as the land with the ruin, when new legislation offered *contadini* favourable terms. I gathered that they now lodge with Claudio's younger brother in Montesasso Scalo. Their sister has married a *carabiniere* officer who works in Pisa. All three had to agree.

'I must leave tomorrow afternoon,' I ventured in a thin voice. Long faces, chins drawn in under pursed lips, shoulders shrugged and hands upturned. A worm of unease was squirming into the pit of my stomach.

Then sudden action. Papà Panichini was with the tenant farmer now working his land and living in Claudio's childhood home. Gianni followed his large Fiat saloon along damp streets and out into the countryside towards the Panichini's tribal valley. Up the sodden rutted track, prelude to the discovery of the ruin on the far side of buttercup meadows – so clearly etched on my distant memory of yesterday. At the top, an old man stood talking to a younger one in front of a farmhouse.

'*Papà! Eccoci qua!*' Claudio braked his car noisily, the commotion bringing two women and a small child to the landing at the top of the outside stairs. Gianni parked discreetly to one side so the father and son could talk to their tenant, lit a cigarette and stared meaningfully at trees in the middle distance like a true countryman.

'*Signora!*' Claudio introduced his father, ignoring the tenant farmer who withdrew, staying within earshot. Yes, there might be the possibility of a sale, but only at the right price. They would have to go and inspect it. The property lay five hundred yards up the valley, but walking was out of the question. Ingrained in ancestral memories are centuries of trudging mile upon mile to remote fields. So we bumped up the road to the bend where I first saw the ruin, through the farmyard, but no child this time to chase us, along the ridge and down the slope to brake on the prow of land.

'*Terreno davanti e dietro soltanto. Uso del viale con voi...*' Gianni was talking to the others, leaving me well out of it. I grasped they were discussing conditions, amounts of land, rights of access; I left him to it and tried instead to look meaningfully at trees in the middle distance. It augured well that Monte Amiata was clearly visible across the plain.

Silence. Where had they gone? I found them round the back talking to Giulio, the neighbouring farmer, across brambles in the channel. We were introduced. The father of that strange child who chased our car seemed agreeable enough. Lots of nods and '*ci vediamo*'.

Papà Panichini and Claudio turned to shake my hand.

'*A domani, signora!*'' Tomorrow? Gianni helped his kinsfolk back their car up the slippery path. No price had been mentioned. They assumed my consent.

'*Va bene,*' Gianni reassured me. 'Not much land, but you said you only wanted a place to sit out and a small kitchen garden.' The price I should trust him with. The important thing was speed. Speed to find a solicitor to draw up the *compromesso*, or provisional agreement and deposit; the rest of the money to be paid in the summer. This could only be done after all the adjacent landowners renounced their right to buy first. Twixt cup and lip, I thought...

Back in Montesasso it seemed to me time for a good meal and a break to take stock and update Paul. But for Gianni there wasn't a second to spare. He turned into an alley off the main square and pushed at a mighty door with wrought lion-head handles and deeply recessed panels. A brass plate with '*Cecilia Ferrarini, notaia*' had been screwed on to wood worn by centuries of hands pushing the door open. A dark hall, lights in a room at the end and a bustle inside. Gianni walked purposefully towards the sounds of activity, greeting the receptionist behind a huge desk before stationing himself by the office entrance. Around him, leaning against faded frescoes, people sat or stood waiting *patiently. I spied space on a bench and, thinking we'd have to wait, moved towards it.*

'No. Dobbiamo entrare subito.' Puzzling. How could we get in ahead of the others? Gianni seemed to know as, nodding to one, a few words to another, without any resentment we were the next to enter the inner sanctum. (He must be the boss of an unofficial Montesasso Ways and Means Committee!)

From behind a sturdy walnut desk with a slimline lamp illuminating scattered files came a 'Ciao, Gianni' and a bright smile. Dottoressa Ferrarini was alert, striking in an unconventional way, and very business-like.

'Compromesso? Domani? La signora deve partire...' Gianni was persuading her to draw up the initial contract, as I had to leave. Still no price had been mentioned. I couldn't bear the suspense any longer.

'Stop, per favore!' I stood up. 'Quanto chiedono?' What's the asking price? Gianni and the lawyer looked surprised, probably for different reasons. I explained I must talk to Paul before signing an agreement.

'Sei milioni,' Gianni said, observing me. I felt sick. It was too much for a ruin. Even allowing for the way all those thousands of lire had of striking fear into a head unused to zeros, I'd already told him that price was too high for other properties. Why was Gianni raising my hopes? Huge amounts would have to be spent on restoration. Just think of the roof! No mention, typically, of what his cut would be – from Claudio Panichini or me or both?

Through the open window wafted tantalising foretastes of lunch. The lawyer started to gather papers together, looked up, smiled and held out her hand.

'A domani.'

It's sewn up, I thought, as I followed Gianni past all those querying eyes. I quickened my pace and touched his arm. Already pulling out a cigarette and mumbling we would be late for lunch, he blithely added that his kinsman would cut the stated price, he himself would do masonry for us out of friendship, and he didn't want anything for finding us the ruin. I was stunned silent.

'Mangiamo.'

I called Paul after lunch but he had just gone out of the studio. My soul yearned for an undefined tranquillity. I decided to explore the church of San Domenico, and there calm my thoughts.
 No such luck.
 'Ormai abbiamo il tempo di provare quella macchina.' I had completely forgotten that, at some point, I must have told Gianni we needed a small car to cope with a baby and building materials. What was Gianni up to now?

The best time to find Paul was in his studio late morning, inconvenient for Gianni and me. I tried later at his flat in London, where we had briefly lived together before Tim was born. It was difficult to return by train over Easter, but Monday would have been Tim's birthday. He was born prematurely on 31 March. That was just two days before the accident. I needed to be closer to some sort of remembrance of him.

'Olivia,' the pulse startled inside me, 'any luck?' His voice was deeper than it had been since that Easter in Florence.

'Yes. A ruin.' I paused, then, 'in an idyllic setting.' I heard him breathe in sharply.

'Olive trees?'

'Yes. A lot.'

'Any umbrella pines? Cypresses?'

'No. I can't remember. But we can plant them along the drive, the ones with long trunks that Fra Angelico painted.'

'Any poplars?'

'Lots. By the stream.' I didn't tell him that it wasn't on the land we were buying. 'And plenty of wild flowers.'

'I can't wait.' He sounded more cheerful.

'Too much has been happening to tell you now. I'm writing it all down so I don't forget anything.'

'Good. I'm glad you have time to do your writing.' Yes, in the cold and under the weak bulb Gianni used to save electricity.

'It's a place to create together what we want. Gianni will help and – I'll tell you everything when I get back.' Paul was a good listener, but I didn't know where to begin over the telephone. I wanted to tell him my writing would bring a ruin back to life, reaching beyond into remote times. It had to be true to the spirits of the *contadini* who were whispering to me as words glided over my exercise book, victims of the *mezzadria* with nothing in their pockets and only half of what they produced from the land the worked on.

'Are you writing a diary?' he asked,

'No, not exactly.' It wouldn't be a diary. I had no mind to record the daily hum of life.

'A journal?' No, it would be something different, not just selected highlights.

'It will be a book about our adventure, Paul. About us restoring a ruin together.' I chose the word deliberately, 'an elixir to share.' I waited for a lull in the bar's conviviality, 'and it will all come true.'

'Oh, Olivia,' emphatically, 'I hope so.'

CHAPTER 7

My account of Montesasso had an immediacy I couldn't express to Paul in a hurry or try to tell Gran and Mother between Dan's demands and meals, or even explain to Sarah and William. When it was ready for them to read, they could savour the people and events in their own time. I might discourage Paul with all that was already happening and remained still to be done. Better to tread carefully when initiating anything. Better to write than recount.

Paul was as particular about people as he was about restoring paintings. Our first meeting at an exhibition had reassured him that at least I'd be interested in his work. He sent me only a few brief notes, but I shall never forget the first.

18 JUNE 1964 OLIVIA, 'VARIUM ET MUTABILIS SEMPER FEMINA' VIRGIL WROTE AND DRYDEN TRANSLATED 'WOMAN'S A VARIOUS AND CHANGEABLE THING' LEAVING OUT 'SEMPER'. ALWAYS YOU ARE UNPREDICTABLE. I LOVE IT. PAUL. His messages bore his grammar school armature of quotations. Another brief note mentioned my 'infinite variety'. So I was his Cleopatra, sailing on a barge into his mind and heart.

He worried about the presents he gave me, almost as if I'd laugh at them. He once handed me a slender box, too long to be the perfume he liked me to use. He watched my hands unwrapping it; inside an orchid, pale yellow with speckles. I felt I couldn't make the right comment, so I smiled and exclaimed, 'How lovely!' thinking he was implying, 'You have a sallow complexion and spots, or freckles,' and maybe the protruding stamen meant I wag my tongue too much? If I'd asked him, he'd have laughed it off. But Sarah suggested he might be indirectly referring to himself, adding that men don't usually share their emotions and I shouldn't fret.

Compromising Olivia – March 1975

Anxiety swung into elation. I was about to buy a ruin and a car! Gianni's Fiat 500 buzzed down the hill to Montesasso Scalo, accelerated through amber lights into the station square and veered left down a mud track parallel to the railway, squealing to a stop by a shack-like house.

'Ecco la macchina!' Chickens were pecking dispiritedly around a mustard-coloured three-doored, snub-nosed Fiat 500. Dismayed, I stuttered.

'Funziona?'

'Of course it goes!' he snorted and yelled 'Pina!' An anxious face appeared at the open door. Her husband was out. Only Carlo could decide about the car.

Pina has the worn physique of someone inured to tiresome tasks and marital servitude. Wisps of hair frame a face creased by memories of pain with a smile revealing absent teeth, drawn to relieve when too late to save. Her voice has the tone of a shepherd's pipe from the alpine valley where she was born. We sat drinking coffee by the hearth that spread a glow over the stark interior. When Carlo is angry, she told me, he reminds her of the Tuscan proverb, 'moglie e buoi dei paesi tuoi', meaning it's better to find both oxen and wife in your own home town! I was loath to leave Pina, the warm room and her reminiscences but Gianni called peremptorily for the keys, impatient to try the car out.

In his hands the Fiat 500 lurched into action with a throaty growl of protest, nearly ramming the yard wall to the consternation of both hens and neighbours. All went well for twenty minutes or so. Then the car spluttered to a stop by the Bar dello Sport on the Cassia. The creature refused to budge. Gianni turned and re-turned the key in the ignition, each time rewarded by a fainter gasp. I diagnosed the inherent weakness of the Fiat beast.

'The engine's flooded.'

'Ingolfato,' Gianni agreed glumly. 'Ingolfatissimo!'

To escape the stench of petrol we took refuge in the bar for an espresso and, for him, a consoling cigarette. The regulars stared at this unknown foreign woman with Gianni, the local 'lad'. I asked him for the keys. Gingerly easing the choke halfway out, I tried starting the engine. A gurgle, then silence. Then more guttural throat-clearing from the jaded engine until all mechanical activity again foundered. Gianni, ensconced in the passenger's seat, encouraged me with a friendly squeeze of my thigh. Was it because of that encouragement I was third time lucky?

'*Gira, gira,*' he insisted as the engine shuddered into life. Cautiously I turned into the road towards the ruin. He distracted me as I was struggling to engage the second gear by pointing to a builder's yard in front of a half-finished house.

'*Ciao, Carlo!*' he shouted to a puppet-like figure with a loosely moulded face and jerky limbs unloading breeze blocks from a truck. Carlo turned, his hand rising in a jaunty wave. Half ignoring Gianni he strutted, hands in pockets and abdomen thrust forward, to the car.

'*Buona sera, signora.*' This was Pina's husband, Ada's brother, and by a strange coincidence his land was about half a mile down the valley below ours. In these few hours I had already begun to think of the ivy-strangled, roofless ruin as ours!

'*Difficoltà con la guida?*' I nodded. It was a difficult car to drive. Carlo was looking me up and down, as far as that is possible in a tiny Fiat 500. He lost no time in prising Gianni out of the passenger seat to shift me into his place. Gianni pushed his lips out in a masculine pout as he tilted the seat up to bend into the cramped space at the back, his cigarette almost singeing my neck.

Carlo proved to be a good teacher. As he demonstrated the mechanical intricacies, he casually touched my left knee. It was a small car, such limited space, Italians so friendly and physical, unlike the cold sons and daughters of Albion. (Mussolini, so I'd been told, referred to the English by this ancient Roman nickname.) How kind of Carlo to take such trouble.

After the lesson Carlo announced he would '*give*' me the car for 400,000 lire, roughly £180, a fair amount for a hard-worked out-of-date model. The fatal way to buy, as we all know, is in a hurry.

'Ciao. Il compromesso domani mattina presto!' All 'compromises' or preliminary agreements were to be made on the day I had to leave. I was anxious and Gianni was glum driving the vehicle back.

'Tutto bene.' Nothing was the matter, he insisted unconvincingly, and looked straight ahead. Pina came to the threshold followed by fourteen-year-old Vincenzo.

'Volete mangiare?' Gianni handed her the car keys, declining for both of us her invitation to supper.

Back in Montesasso, Gianni smoked his way moodily through the meal in spite of being offered his favourite broth veined with egg yolk, and went out immediately afterwards. I tried to keep Ada company, chatted about her younger brother Carlo and the car and gave her parting gifts of chocolates and flowers, before retiring upstairs to worry about advance payments and slump asleep over the calculations.

The day of my departure dawned chilly, with a bell-like clarity. Rising at seven, I worried about getting to the bank, giving Gianni some money, signing 'compromessi' for both ruin and car, all in one morning.

After the bank, straight to our lawyer Cecilia Ferrarini. Claudio and his father signed the provisional agreement with the air of a reluctant favour. Papà Panichini pocketed the cash deposit. Carlo was waiting for us by a truck in front of his unfinished house. He greeted me rather formally, I thought, considering his behaviour the day before. At the Italian Automobile Association's office we were kept waiting while the two officials behind the desk busily ignored us. It was, after all, the last working day before Easter. Eventually, with a scarcely stifled yawn, one held out his hand for the documents.

'Non ha la residenza la signora?' What was this? Residence? Without it, I could buy property, but not a car. Gianni and Carlo looked at each other.

'Ci penso io,' said Gianni, deciding the car should be bought in his name but with my money. Time dictated my decisions. The paperwork was completed and paid for in a matter of minutes, the first instalment passed to Carlo and the keys given to me to hand on to Gianni. Back we went to Carlo's yard where the vehicle could remain until our return.

'A Massimo,' stated Gianni as he nodded me towards his car. Massimo? A cousin, of course.

Massimo lived halfway up the valley below Gianni's childhood home, now under restoration. An aproned woman with a child hanging on to her skirt appeared at the top of the outside stairs.

'Massimo non c'è!' she called, beckoning us up for coffee. Gianni was in a hurry. 'Grazie.' He walked to a slope in front of the low-lying mill house and cupped his hands to his mouth.

'Massimoooooooooooo!' echoed into the mountains. A balding man in his early forties stepped out of a half-roofed house above his yard.

'Eccomi! Gianni!' No telephones in the valley, yet he seemed to know why Gianni had come:

'The signora has to leave in five hours' time. The ruin she's bought needs work on it before she returns in July.'

Massimo followed us to the tumbledown house half a mile away in his Ape three-wheel open truck, an Italian scooter concoction with a practical loading area behind. By midday all three of us were edging inside the top storey. The men spoke rapidly of re-roofing the whole lot, and reconstituting the fireplace using the two surviving supports. What about a bathroom? A well would have to be sunk. It was becoming too complicated for the time remaining. Twelve thirty already with my train leaving just after four.

'Pazienza!' counselled Gianni.

He and Massimo peered into the stables below. Still dry, still filled with the dusty fragrance of olive branches. The floor could be cemented immediately, a window reused. I was relieved, apprehensive of still more expense.

'Quanto costerà? I asked nervously. Gianni and Massimo looked at each other. They made a few mental calculations. Many million lire. Dazed, I feared I was spending a fortune.

We shook hands with Massimo, unruffled and promising everything would be done by July. Into Gianni's car and a rapid ride past the church, Carlo's yard and along the Cassia, up the steep hill to Montesasso, round the Etruscan walls to park and walk to his house. A bowl of pasta, an omelette, an apple, and off to Montesasso Scalo.

Gianni clasped me for what seemed an epoch, then planted large kisses on each cheek as the train arrived.

'Ciao! A presto!'

I waved until he was a speck on the platform. He had welcomed me into his home, fed and accompanied me everywhere, found the ruin, arranged its purchase and initial renovation, not to mention the car – all for no charge?

The train began to speed as it passed below the valley, now 'our' valley, the next small town along the line and others. No stop until Florence. The die was cast. In the space of a few days I had agreed to spend a hefty sum of money buying a house of sorts and an ancient car. Repent at leisure? What would Paul say?

Mixed reactions came from friends who were the sort of people I'd want to read my book, all curious to know what had happened.

'That's not a house – it's a challenge!' exclaimed an architect friend looking at my photos. He knew. He was right!

Others were serious and cautioned us.

'Beware of being taken over by it.'

'You'll never spend enough time there to make it financially worthwhile.'

'You'll feel trapped. Instead of the freedom to go where you please, you'll be ensnared in one place.'

'You'll get bored with it.'

'How could you face going to an empty place, having to set it up each time... even if you find people to help, they're never around when you need them!'

All was capped by one semi-jocular accusation:

'You masochists! How can you enjoy a holiday restoring a ruin and washing sheets in a stream!'

Mother was supportive, in a detached sort of way. Sarah and William were more encouraging, offering to help with the pioneering stage. Paul turned out to be the keenest of them all.

CHAPTER 8

Our excitement mounted in anticipation of Gianni's weekly letters. I had left Montesasso at the end of March. By May Massimo had begun the most costly operation of all: roofing with hand-baked tiles.

As the evenings grew longer, Paul would leave London on an earlier Friday afternoon train and meet me at school. He'd stand, tall and intent, away from the gates and watch the children as they hopped or huddled past. I remember him giving me a necklace about that time with stones that scattered pink, blue, clear watery green like minute mirrors returning light to anyone looking.

'Multi-faceted, like you, Liv,' he teased. I twisted them round, so hard and bright, and fingered them tentatively. 'They couldn't be diamonds?'

'Don't know. My mother said I could take them, so they probably aren't.' Perhaps he'd bought me the necklace and didn't want to admit how much he'd paid? In the evening we went out to dinner and I wore it with a dress I'd chosen that summer.

'Keep the necklace on,' he said, 'it suits you,' and it stayed on all night like the one he admired in Cranach's painting of Venus, though wanting her wide-brimmed hat with smoky, ticking feathers curling over its brim.

Gran re-established the daily routine at the house in Guildford as it had been when Tim was tiny. Mother was in charge of breakfast while I got Dan up and checked everything for my day's teaching. I dropped Mother at the library on the way to work. In the daytime Gran would dust as the mood moved her, reading to Dan or to herself when he slept. The moment I returned from work she went off duty and sat with Grandpa. Mother walked home from the library; she said it aired her mind. I prepared Dan's tea, but Mother cooked the evening meal. First call on the car went to whoever was in charge of Dan, though mother used it most evenings during the week. I claimed it to fetch Paul when he came by a late train, often taking Dan with me. Gran enjoyed working on her routine like a patchwork quilt, sorting our age, skills and availability into different pieces of time. Shirking would unstitch it all.

By June there was consternation in Guildford when Gianni wrote that he was building a garage. I had visions of a makeshift eyesore plonked on the tiny bit of land behind the house, or even worse, on the terrace that jutted out into the valley! We curbed our curiosity, impatient for the end of term. On long June evenings after dinner, when Dan was in bed, Paul and I would wander along sunken lanes with roots twisting through fern and moss on the banks, or meandered in woodlands with the last of spring cowslips, primroses and bluebells. Then we'd leave the trees for the Downs where heather was losing the battle with bracken and larks sang into scumbled clouds over wild and open land. Paul grew up in an arable countryside, a pattern of fields and copses alive with birdsong. He would often talk of his home landscape, of the wind passing over the fields leaving a light shimmer on the underside of grass, oats and wheat, and how in July and August the greens deepen and dry back into darker shades. He recalled his childhood hero, great-uncle Bob, and the 'House Beautiful' they painted together. Then he would have been the same age as Tim, but we avoided any mention of him. At that time Paul never took me to see the house and I even wondered whether it existed. In late July I left for Italy.

Gianni starts his reign – July 1975

Gianni was waiting for me at Montesasso Scalo, punctual and brisk as ever. His natural reserve gives him a dignity suiting his unpretentious clothes and deeply scored mahogany face. I'd been sent ahead to prepare the house, but he was clearly in command.

His letters had warned me. It was already one of the hottest summers in living memory, and at three in the afternoon the air was snapping. He forecasted wells drying up and crops ravaged by beetles. I worried about the stream flowing below terraces bequeathed by a widow, he said, to the local church in the hope of a little place in heaven.

The dark green of the cypresses each side of the Via Cassia absorbed the glare from the sun, leaving a pallid glaze over the burnt-out fields. The sunflowers were already drooping in bronze ungainliness. Gianni's little Fiat buzzed onwards like the persistent flies that gathered whenever we stopped. Off the Cassia, up the hill past tumbledown houses, over the stream already reduced to a trickle, across the church square with two old women in black but no Don Luigi, along the rutted path too fast for me to glimpse the house where I'd first seen it, through Giulio's farmyard to turn along the ridge and stop at the top of the drive. I got out and walked slowly down to the house in excitement, and apprehension.

Massimo came to meet us, bare to the waist with trouser belt holding up his paunch. All smiles, he had clearly been rehearsed by Gianni to show me the restoration and especially Gianni's masonry skills. The chimney had been completely reconstructed. It topped the roof, now mottled in hand-made tiles, gentle and welcoming, unlike the strident cement ones alien to the spirit of the place. Paul would approve. The grass ramp that straggled up to the gaping doorway in April had disappeared. Steps now led to a platform giddily open on all sides.

Gianni parked his car and joined me. He was immensely proud of the frost-resistant tiles he had laid on the platform floor where we would eat, gazing over the plain to Monte Amiata.

'Venga, signora!' (Odd the way Gianni was calling me 'signora', while at Easter I was 'Olivia'.) He pointed at the chestnut door marking the entrance to the upper storey. I pushed it open with a thrill, recalling the worm-eaten one hanging on rusty hinges only three months earlier. Inside, the rays that had poured in through gaps in the old roof now slanted through new windows. One lit the first bathroom the building had ever known, clad in mossy green tiles to reflect the peaceful countryside. The open peephole was now glazed, all ten square inches of it. One third of the room had been walled off into a bedroom with the recess now for our clothes.

Beds, mattresses – I was beginning to feel weary at the thought. Odd bits of used furniture were being sent out from England, but there was so much to do before Paul and Dan arrived. As if to seek inspiration, I stared at the floor. Gianni promptly explained that the traditional earthenware tiles he had chosen to line it would polish up well. This expectation made me even more tired. Was he casting me in the role of the Italian 'mamma-moglie', a perfectly imagined amalgam of motherly and wifely virtues?

He turned me round to admire the wide chimney-hood built up from the two stone brackets, certain it would draw well. I was of no mind to try it out on such a scorching day, though he was searching for a bit of paper to light brushwood in the hearth.

We went back across the new platform, down the steps and turned to the stables. I gasped, recalling weeks of anxiety about the garage. Here it was! Where else could it be? A shadow above my shoulder fell on to a massive half-open door of pristine chestnut; Gianni was expecting my reaction. I let him wait, judging it imprudent for him to note my delight at the way he had neatly tucked the garage under the future kitchen and veranda.

The old window from the large room above had been reused for the bigger of the two stables. Little otherwise had changed. The olive branches had been removed, revealing an earth floor.

'Bisogna abbassare il livello.' Gianni was right. The floor had to be lowered.

'L'orto. Venga!' Still stiffly formal, Gianni invited me to survey the kitchen garden at the back. Shaded by our few olives were rows of beans drying out for minestrone; ripening tomatoes round or pear-shaped, staked or tumbling all over the ground; celery, parsley, basil, potatoes in the process of being dug out – abundance in the space of three months!

'Vado via! A domani!' Massimo was going home for supper. The shadows under the olives were deepening and the earth sighing with relief. We trespassed above the old mill and looked down at the poplars marking the stream's progress below. Silence. A dog barked. A child called from the farmhouses above. No sound of water. It could be heard from here in April. We scrambled down the church's three terraces and along the bank to where there was usually a cascade. Water was still flowing over it. Two black irrigation tubes snaked up the far bank to drain from

the pool where the women washed clothes. Could be worse. How did Gianni water his flourishing vegetables, I wondered?

'Il pozzo.' Funny, after all the thought I had given to a well while looking for a suitable ruin, I hadn't even asked him where it was!

The well stood behind the back wall of the house just where Gianni divined it should be, twenty metres deep, and all the better for constant use. He had surrounded the top of the cement tube with rough stone masonry and padlocked the lid. Well contamination, he warned, was the age-old way of settling grievances in the valley, and while we had no reason to fear, people can turn strange.

'Is the stream running dry, Gianni?'

'We see,' he said in English, 'no rain this year'. We could judge how it was flowing higher up. On the way to the ford I noticed a bunch of flowers wedged behind a stone with 'Marco Dio ti benedica' scratched on it and picked out in red paint.

'Gianni. Who's Marco?'

'A child who was hit by an ox-cart. Giulio swerved because of the spirits by the stream, and he didn't see the child. It happens...' His voice trailed into silence.

'Who's Giulio?'

'Your neighbour. I introduced you to him at Easter. The one with the vineyard below your bedroom window.'

Gianni was satisfied there was enough water in the stream, though if the heat continued then wells might dry up.

'Speriamo bene!' He hoped not. We returned past Marco's shrine to the house and Gianni's vegetable garden. He told me which to pick – tomatoes, celery, parsley, beet or onions – and what they were for, in this case a tomato salad and ingredients for pasta sauce. I was following his orders, and he was obeying Ada's.

He looked at his watch, bent down to gather his tools and headed for the garage. Time for dinner. Back in Montesasso I longed for a bath or shower, but while Gianni's bathroom had every fitting from bidet to hipbath, the lock didn't work. With the light on as a warning, I decided to risk washing bits of myself in the basin and bidet. Trickles of grubby water squiggled out from under the bidet pedestal to superimpose a rakish design on the blue and white tiles. Searching in vain for a floor cloth, I used my towel and opened the tiny window, to be promptly rewarded with pinlike mosquito bites.

The itching kept me awake. Though restless to move into the half-converted ruin, I overslept; Gianni had long since left for work. When I asked for the keys to my car, Ada shrugged her shoulders. Nothing could be done until Gianni returned. A morning for thoughtful inaction. The flavour of croissants, cakes and loaves floated up from the corner bakery, leavened with chatter and an occasional song to enliven the house martins' squabbling under the eaves. The best way to think what to do was to find a bar with tables outside in the shade.

Sitting down at a café in the Piazza della Repubblica, I leant back, and a generous cappuccino appeared. *Tutto bene.* I closed my eyes in a moment of relaxation. On reopening them, to my astonishment, I met Mike's jubilant grin. He bent down to give me a kiss.

'I've come to lend you a hand.' I had forgotten that, without a telephone, one had to frequent Montesasso's main square to find out what was happening.

'I felt like a bit of fresh air. It's impossibly hot in Naples,' Mike continued, settling at my table and ordering a Martini. 'Paul's given me names of people there wanting to thin out their collections – unsavoury ancestors are stealthily leaving the walls!' He laughed almost too loudly, pushing his hair back from his forehead.

Mike was blithely unaware of the complications stemming from his unexpected appearance. I wondered whether Ada might let him use the makeshift bed on the ground floor; Gianni would be less keen.

'Paul won't be here for another two days,' I said.

'I know. I wanted to help you get things ready for him.' He scanned the square and the steps of the town hall shimmering deserted in the midday sun. Gianni would return in under an hour, if we were lucky.

'Mike, I'm desperate to get hold of the car I bought at Easter. It seems to have been spirited away. There aren't any mattresses. The bed linen should arrive on the same train as Paul.'

We made our leisurely way to Gianni's house, Mike hovering at shop windows or disappearing inside to inspect the local ceramics. (He's always holding up his hands in an exasperating gesture of saintly wonder, noting profound artistic content in the simplest pottery!) We sauntered along a narrow alley imbibing the savour of Tuscan lunches piquant with green gold olive oil. If only we could produce our own!

Ada peered out from the first floor balcony, disappearing to press the button. She looked coy as we climbed the stairs, and giggled irritatingly when I introduced Mike.

'Mike's a friend,' I explained. 'He's arrived unexpectedly from Naples. We need the car to get the house ready and move in.' She tittered, waving us to the settee by the balcony. After serving an aperitif, she stood in the doorway to stare at the very blonde, blue-eyed man. Unconcerned, he observed the odd interior, starting with their sepia wedding photographs under a crucifix with a sprig of olive: Gianni, smooth-faced with an oiled moustache long since shaved off, and Ada, fresh and hesitant. Both had startled eyes and hung side by side in drab wooden frames.

The doorbell rang imperiously. Ada pushed the button and Gianni clomped up the stairs, narrowing his eyes at Mike before I introduced him, an instant later embracing the newcomer into his home. Hungry after his usual dawn start, Gianni went straight to the head of the table and placed us on either side. Ada put Alberto next to me and made sure she sat by Mike. In fact she hardly sat, being constantly ordered around by her husband.

'Vino! Più pane! Ancora per la signora. Per il giovane…' the ancient rite of offering bread and wine to guests while waiting for the meal to be served. He ate rapidly, anxious to be back outside.

I asked Gianni if I could have the keys for our car. Of course. Where could I buy mattresses? Montesasso Scalo. They'd have to lie on top of his roof rack. My car had one too. The rag-and-bone man sold bedsteads for a song opposite the Bar Etrusco where I met my 'Mr. Fixit', Gianni: unworried, capable, firmly in command. At that particular moment his role both suited and amused me.

We left in his car. Mike squeezed into the back seat. I sat uneasily as Gianni's eyes followed his friendly hand lingering on my knee whilst we all hurtled down to the plain. Luckily most of Italy, Gianni excepted, was enjoying a siesta on this sultry afternoon. The mustard-coloured Fiat with a large roof rack was parked in the merciful shade of Carlo's house, which had risen to the first floor since Easter. Apparently Gianni had been moonlighting in the afternoon for his brother-in-law as well as for us. I let Mike go on ahead with Gianni to the former ruin so he could deposit his bags while I drove cautiously after them. His knapsack was the only object inside the building not shrouded in dust. No broom; no brush and pan; no dusters – nothing. Where does one start?

'Reti, bedsteads,' said Gianni sensing my dilemma. His car buzzed back to Montesasso. It was no easy job following him uphill with unsynchronised gears. As my car grated and shuddered I muttered, 'Silly old thing' or as Gianni said (since Italians view cars as female), 'Mammalucca!' So Mammalucca she became. Inside the Etruscan Gate to the rag-and-bone man. Four worn bedsteads were hoisted up, two on each roof rack, secured by elastic rubber 'spiders' stored under the bonnet of Gianni's car. Down the hill again, fearful that the iron protruding over bonnet and boot would either condemn us to take flight or pay a fine. The bumps along the track swung my bedsteads sideways. If I stopped, there was no one to help me as Mike was ahead in Gianni's car. I jolted on, and just made it, the bedsteads festooned with shreds of vine, oak leaves and olive sprigs. Mike and Gianni unloaded speedily, placing two bedsteads in each of the upstairs rooms.

We proceeded in convoy along the plain to buy new mattresses in Montesasso Scalo where there are shops with bargains, according to Gianni. From the 1960s all who could afford it, usually two former contadino families together, had saved up to build their two-storey houses near the station.

Etruscan Montesasso, perched on the mountain spur, watched with elderly disapproval the new buildings engulfing a large villa down on the Cassia.

The four purple and white striped mattresses were cheap and light and served our purpose. All the to-and-fro with bedsteads and mattresses had taken less than two hours. It was still stifling. I took a mini breather to stock up with bread, butter, cheese, ham and fruit – we had no stove – as well as a brush, pail, soap and floor cloth with all the housecleaning products imaginable.

A cool corner was found inside for the food. No table and chairs.

'Ti do la mia.' Gianni was offering me, in familiar terms, his own table, the one he had eaten off as a child! I felt honoured; it suited our rural surroundings and would, in effect, return to its native valley. Giving Gianni a grateful hug, I told him I wanted anyway to find a present for him and Ada, perhaps a new dining-room table and chairs? When could we do it? Gianni, unstoppable, turned towards his car expecting me to follow. Mike willingly stayed behind. It was only six and shops closed at eight. The afternoon was yet young.

Ada was opening the door to go out when we arrived.

'Vieni!' Gianni was to be obeyed. I sensed her surprise, even displeasure. Whatever she planned to do had to be jettisoned, or postponed. She started to get into the back of the car, but I protested, pulling the passenger seat forward and cramming myself behind. Down the hill, as I expected, to Montesasso Scalo, then out along the Cassia. Driving the car at top speed into the forecourt of a furniture emporium, Gianni skidded it to stop in a burst of gravel dust. Inside smelt of wood shavings. Ada seemed pleased enough with what she chose: a shiny mahogany-coloured table that looked moulded rather than cut into shape, and six chairs with imitation leather seats.

Ada was released outside her house to go on her undefined errand. Gianni busied himself, loading his roof rack with a gas cooker from the ground floor storeroom. A bottle of wine and two glasses followed it. I reminded him we were three, and asked if I could borrow a knife. I had forgotten to buy any cutlery.

Mike had been creatively scavenging during our absence. On the platform above the garage discarded shutters were now balanced on stones from the mill to make a table of sorts with benches. The sun was setting as we perched on top of the garage laughing round Gianni's three glasses and bottle of wine, merrily rolling from side to side as the boulders shifted under us.

'Alla casa dell'avventura!' Gianni said. To the house of adventure – or good luck! And so it was named. The stream below helped cool the evening air. Across the valley the shadows lengthened and the tip of Monte Amiata appeared, blushing above the heat haze. Our view faced south; we were in the middle of the valley on our own spur, poised between sunrise and sunset. The plain now seemed like a huge misty lake below a sky fading blue into green. The setting sun cast rose dust over olives, a tower, umbrella pines, cypresses, knuckled fruit trees and twilight submerging the lower terraces and fields. A dog barked. I imagined a wolf's howl; Gianni said it could be one. A thrill of fear rippled into evening calm after daytime frenzy. Since our last meal we had equipped the house with its basic necessities. I tore open a packet of cheese biscuits and refilled the glasses.

'Auguri! Alla Casa dell'Avventura!'

Precisely at the moment the red ball of sun disappeared to our right, I heard the first whine. Then it struck. Another two followed. Ahhhh, the night attack had started. Gianni stood up. Did he feel them? What? The mosquitoes. No. Nothing

'A domani! See you tomorrow!' He unloaded the cooker and surged off in first gear in search of his supper. Mike and I were left alone, the mosquito attack intensifying.

'Any candles?' he asked helpfully. No. My sense of achievement evaporated when I thought of all the things still needed, from crockery and cutlery to candles. I needed a generous helping of time before Paul and Dan arrived. Mike glanced at his watch.

'I've got some money. Have you any left?'

'Not much. About 8000 lire.'

'Enough. Quick. It's nearly eight and we could just make it before the general store closes.'

Mammalucca jolted down to the local Generi Alimentari next to the Bar dello Sport on the Cassia. It was brightly lit, with a plastic ribbon curtain in the doorway to keep sun and flies out, and cigarette smoke in. Perched on a raised platform behind the counter, an attractive woman with a seductive smile was dispensing jollity with the stores to more male than female customers.

'Eh, Sibilla! Dammi la pasta come sempre...' She pouted and shook back her thick black tresses while packing groceries into a plastic bag. Next to her a quiet bespectacled man was doling out food and goodwill. He welcomed us patiently as we tried to guess what we needed. Candles. Plenty of the rough and ready household ones. He laughingly warned us there could be electricity cuts. I told him we hadn't any electricity. Not yet. Silence. All eyes on a thirty something foreign woman with a very blonde man. Under the pressure of so many concentrated looks, I began diffidently to explain: my family is coming in two days' time and Mike's our friend, here to help me get the house ready. I could almost cut the air of disbelief. Do you have any disposable plates? Plastic knives and forks? No. People around here don't buy them.

Sibilla was silently laughing at all this, sizing us up and amused by the male reactions around me. She disappeared and returned with four plates, two knives, forks and spoons.

'Ecco!' Return them when you've bought your kitchen stuff.' I smiled thanks, paid for the candles and extricated myself from those looks.

'Did you notice?'

'What?' Mike's mind was elsewhere.

'Oh, nothing.' My imaginings?

The candles perched on stones did help. So did the moon. As we ate our picnic supper of bread, local salted ham, goat's cheese and Gianni's wine, ending with peaches and apricots, we contemplated the last of the glow-worms in the rough grass along the drive. Then we walked up and down the track, tracing the Milky Way and the Plough, plotting the points of the compass by the North Star. It was elemental and comfortable, soothed by the crickets in full orchestra.

'We must be up early. I don't know if Gianni's working or coming here. He seems to be able to do just as he wishes. If he does come, he'll be around before seven.' Mike agreed. He helped me wash the plates and cutlery using water from the plastic containers Gianni had thoughtfully lent us to fill in Montesasso. Then, after throwing the dishwater over the solitary geranium Mike had found, I tipped the plates up inside the washing-up bowl to drain. It gave me a primitive satisfaction.

We took candles inside. Mike had already arranged his bed in the main room, and done mine as far as he could in the small one, so he wouldn't have to disturb me if he rose earlier.

'What about the mosquitoes?'

'I can wear pyjamas.' Finding myself the favourite target for the local predators, I wore a blouse over my night-dress and shoved feet and legs into the skirt of a dress that needed washing. It seemed early still, so we left the door open and commented on the day's events. Mike thought everything had gone amazingly smoothly. He had reconnoitred and talked to neighbours in the two farms above us. They'd given him the geranium and let him take some old planks and cast-off bricks that he had used to prop up shelves for plates and pans. I rapidly sketched out the next day's plans.

'Leave time for the unexpected...' Mike's voice trailed away. I sat on my mattress to jot down the day's events by the light of a candle, but the crickets soon lulled me to sleep.

I often woke up in the quiet of the night, my heart thudding when I thought about our neighbour, Giulio. They said he had been frightened by the spirits down at the ford when the oxen panicked and the cart overturned, crushing Marco. It was an accidental death, I repeated out loud. This mild, balding fifty-something in an earth-stained shirt and frayed trousers caused a child to die. And we had to live with him as our neighbour.

CHAPTER 9

Mike liked to wave his wand over events and make them happen to his own and everyone else's delight. His magic didn't always work, but he never gave up trying, and was usually around when needed. I shall never forget how, after Tim's accident, he turned up purely by chance. I was sitting by the window of my bedroom in an unquiet house empty of youthful patter and chatter, aching for Paul to call me and return in time for the funeral. Mike arrived and stayed.

The local paper carried the inevitable headline: 'Teacher's son killed in tragic accident' followed by an account of a van skidding on to the pavement outside the school. The report added that the driver had never had an accident before. Mike dealt with reporters before and immediately after the funeral. I can hardly bear to think of it, yet I was consoled to see all Tim's class there, many in tears, and each carrying a flower to place on his grave. The report gave my name as Olivia Taylor-Wyatt, Wyatt being Mike's tactful addition. It added:

'Michael Smithson, a family friend, expressed appreciation on behalf of Mrs Taylor-Wyatt for all the messages of condolence received. She will be replying to everyone individually.' In fact it was Mike who composed the short note of appreciation, had it printed, went through my address book and posted the letters.

It might have been any child outside any school gate – why Tim? I could have left my job, house, everything, to flee the cacophony of woe and disappear. Action or inaction, both were choices, but I couldn't choose to have Tim back.

I didn't then know I was expecting Dan.

Mike answered a knock at our front door the day after the funeral, calling me to speak to a man I didn't recognise. He stood apologetically, anxious to say something, but hesitating and clenching his hands.

'I'm very sorry. There was oil on the road outside the school. I wasn't speeding.'

That was the pity of it. The inquest found it was 'accidental death' and the van driver didn't contact us again. Mother took legal advice, but there was no one to blame.

Facing Neighbours – July 1975

'Giulioooooooo!' The call was followed by a long conversation with someone in the house above us. Sunlight was spreading over the fields Giulio farmed and into my bedroom window. I groped for my watch. Seven o'clock. Was Gianni already around, waiting? I put on my old housecoat and crept through the large room where Mike was still sleeping on to the veranda. No sign of the little blue car. No way to heat a cup of coffee either, though the gas stove stood tantalisingly where the kitchen should be.

I felt eyes travelling over me. I looked round as far as I could see in front and on both sides. No one. I walked under my bedroom window and peered across the dried-out channel. The younger woman I'd seen washing clothes was standing, arms akimbo, in the vineyard, staring at me. I waved. She continued staring. Giulio's wife, I surmised, and backed out of sight. Someone else was looking at me. My eyes searched under the olives sheltering Gianni's kitchen garden and glanced up our drive to the two farms. On the balcony of the faded yellow house a corpulent man sat in the green shade of a corrugated plastic roof, contemplating the land like a Buddha. He must have been shouting across to Giulio, who now stood with his wife in full view of our house. Probably they judged it improper for me to drift around in a dowdy housecoat, even if it covered every inch of my uncomfortably hot flesh. I escaped inside to wash. The prospect of pouring cold water over myself did not appeal. No pump in the well, no electricity, no water. A cat's lick would have to suffice. Mike was stirring.

'I've bought coffee, Mike, but I can't heat the water. We must find some butane gas.' He moaned. His toes, ankles and instep had been bitten all night and walking was painful. I dressed and left for Sibilla's shop to buy fresh rolls and to fill my thermos flask

with two cappuccinos from the bar next door, congratulating myself on being resourceful. The day was shaping well.

Sibilla had glanced at me, murmured *'lo spirale,'* and reached for a pack of coiled green spirals. My neck was bitten red; a few unkind mosquitoes had even sampled my cheeks. The fresh pasta Sibilla was arranging in the display case tempted me, before I realised I couldn't cook it.

'Butane gas?' She put my thoughts into words.

'Orazio!' Horace, the defender of the Roman bridge, married to Sibyl, the oracle of the valley! I felt like giggling but restrained myself.

'La signora needs a gas cylinder.' He would deliver it to the *'Panichini ruin'* later in the morning.

I returned with rolls to find the butter almost liquid and Mike trying to eat dry bread, fresh only the previous afternoon. My dream of rural life at a restored ruin with family and friends, of candlelit evenings in pastoral tranquillity light years from any modern workplace, seemed likely to be marred by daily shopping.

There wasn't much laundry, only one bulging plastic bag. Following the sound of distant voices, I set off up the drive, turning left on the track below unpruned plum trees purple with fruit and passing the small house where Ada'a grandmother once lived, which seemed deserted, and Marco's shrine. Below the ford by the natural stone basins two women were perched on a rock soaping and pummelling sheets, just as I had seen them before. They were hot and scarcely communicating. I had fondly imagined washing sessions would be times of gossipy fun and social integration. Now it seemed sheer slog. I hovered on the edge of the track, looking down. The younger woman raised her head and I recognised the sullen face that had eyed me critically earlier that morning. She scowled, saying nothing. The older one smiled. She had tightly-curled black hair flecked with grey and a bright look about her rather squat body broadened by years of toil on the land, much washing and many children.

'Venga, signora!' Maria Pia introduced herself, making space for me and, seeing my hesitation, opened my bag of washing with her reddened hands.

'Poco,' she observed encouragingly. *She took out a blouse, cheerfully dipped it into the upper pool, slapped it dripping on to the slanting rock where I was standing and attacked it with her green soap. I rummaged around for mine and took over. Dipping, soaping, scrubbing, then dipping again, I realised these country women were accustomed to far more grime than city people imagine, smears of machine grease being more stubborn than ordinary grubbiness.*

Maria Pia marvelled at the electricity recently brought to the valley.

'E un miracolo!' she beamed. *'Light at the flick of a finger!' She didn't care if the current wouldn't be strong enough for the washing machine she couldn't afford. She was content with a pump in the well, a sprinkler in the kitchen garden and a hot bath.*

'We have television!' she concluded with satisfaction.

Maria Pia invited me back to her stone farmhouse next to the pale yellow one. The other woman went off without a word. I paused by Marco's shrine before leaving my wet clothes at the top of our drive to help Maria Pia take her far heavier load across the farmyard. Pigs snorted, identified by a dry, bristly smell, which lodged in the nostrils, but not unpleasantly. She stopped at the ground floor stables to show me two creamy-brown oxen.

I murmured, 'Moglie e buoi dei paesi tuoi,' the old saying I'd learnt from Pina: wife and oxen are better chosen from your home area, and Maria Pia laughed.

'That's Giulio's problem! He did his military service up north and married Roberta, a woman he met there.' She was 'strana.' So I wasn't the only one to find Giulio's wife odd. Maria Pia showed me her goats, guinea fowl, hens and a mangy cock scratching the farmyard dust in desultory fashion before inviting me to follow her up the steep stairs to the smoky-walled kitchen. Chairs waited at angles to the scrubbed table, with sooty pots and pans crowding the fireplace. The lid of a wooden cupboard tilted back to reveal well-kneaded loaves rising inside. No shade over the low-amp bulb; no softness of weave except in Maria Pia's clothes; no armrests, not one ornament to introduce blue, yellow or red into this grey and brown hearth and home.

It was long after eleven. Renzo had been working since dawn and was looking out of the only window, hungry for his midday meal. He had an unhurried look, a generous, gap-toothed smile and high-pitched staccato delivery, liberally peppering standard Italian with dialect. I was encouraged to sit down, offered a glass of their wine and assumed to be hungry. Maria Pia hooked a shoulder of ham off a rafter to cut slices from it and hunks of bread from the largest loaf an oven can hold. While Maria Pia was busy round the stove, Renzo asked me about my family. I confided that I didn't have furniture in the house for when they arrived. It wouldn't be easy to buy things with a small child in tow. Then Maria Pia said something in dialect and Renzo smiled, asking,

'Chi e quel giovanotto?' Everyone wanted to know who Mike was. He must have been the main subject of morning conversation across the terraces. I told them briefly that he was just a friend on business in Italy and shrugged it out of my mind. Paul and Dan would give our neighbours more food for gossip.

I stood up to go, thanking them for their hospitality. Maria Pia dried her hands on her apron and grasped mine, pressing me to return soon. Renzo accompanied me down the stairs and across the yard to a shed.

'Lo vuole?' He pointed to a chest of drawers without its marble top and with chickens roosting in it, and to another worm-eaten one with a hinged lid. How much did he want for the two pieces? He shrugged his shoulders, as if wanting nothing, and picked three eggs out of the open chest.

'Tornerò. I'll return with Paolo,' I assured him. Paul would want to give a second opinion and help me find a tactful way of overcoming their dignified indifference to money.

Mike, having brushed out the top floor, was upset when I hardly ate anything of the scratch lunch he had prepared. Though mad dogs and Englishmen are said to enjoy the midday sun, it defeated us and we sat inside with the shutters closed, picnicking in semi-darkness.

I could scarcely believe it when Gianni disturbed my siesta. Every surface outside was burnished by heat and it was not yet three.

'Faccia pure, carry on!' he said with studied consideration when I explained we had adopted the fine Italian siesta habit. He walked over to a bay tree and lit a cigarette.

I tried to shut out his sullen disapproval. Thirty minutes passed. Outside I could hear him clear his throat, kick at the gravel he had spread in front of the house, and wander around crunching it as much as possible. The sound of a vehicle and Gianni's call of 'signora!' ended my siesta. A small trailer hitched to an Ape scooter was bumping down the track piled high with Gianni's beech table and assorted chairs, followed by Orazio with a butane gas cylinder in his scooter-powered miniature lorry.

'C'è da pagare Domenico.' The benign Ape owner sat smoking in silent company with Gianni. I emptied my purse and feared he would snort at the contents. It was foolish of me to take the morning off to wash clothes and talk to neighbours, rather than go to the bank. However, Domenico seemed satisfied enough.

That evening the first cooked meal was prepared at sunset. Maria Pia strolled down to see how we were getting on – was it to look at the signora inglese and the man with her? Supper was nothing exciting: tortellini from a package with a makeshift sauce of Gianni's tomatoes and basil, tossed in olive oil with all the panache I could muster. Simple fare, which became a candlelit feast for two hungry people.

* * * * *

I awoke from dreams of lire floating around the frescoed Venus as she ogled the reclining Mars, worrying about money. Both deities were painted on the wall of the old palazzo used by our Montesasso bank. It was later than I thought; the sun seemed high and critical. Mammalucca protested loudly up the track as we ground along the ridge down to the Cassia and up the steep hill to Montesasso. We parked outside Porta Etrusca and I rushed ahead to the most ancient bank in the world still in business. It was crowded with people silently jostling for position. As Venus contemplated the hum of activity she seemed more placid than in my dream. Firm of step, gaze fixed on a particular clerk, an elderly man moved purposefully in front of me to make some perfunctory transaction. I defended my turn. The clerk, tired and hot at the nagging end of a long morning fuelled by two espressos and a pastry, blinked slowly as he counted out wads of lira notes. It was after midday when I escaped into the narrow street. Mike was still waiting.

'Let's eat!' Not much choice. A couple of restaurants, a trattoria, and bars with leftover sandwiches.

'I'll treat you to lunch.' Mike chose a trattoria in a tiny square tucked down an alley. Children were playing in and out of tables spread across cobblestones and congregating around the central well. We collapsed in relief at the only free table, ordered wine, mineral water and the speciality of the day. I leant back to observe the people around us, and conjured up other families in the square from the garments dripping in refreshed intimacy outside upper storey windows. Mike enthusiastically described his success at the market; for supper he had found roast pork with rosemary embedded in the crackling, and had bought golden yellow and green beakers from the local pottery as a cheerful gift to the house. Meanwhile we ate lunch while the hot and humid air lay heavily on the little piazza. The garments stopped dripping and the children stopped playing, slumped over half-eaten desserts, heads sinking, feet dangling. Mike couldn't tease me into having tiramisu – an aphrodisiac by hearsay. At the end of lunch I felt more inclined to snore through the siesta than meet Paul and Dan. Black coffee came at last!

Mammalucca was too small to fit in Mike as well as Paul, Dan, and the luggage, so he chose to spend the afternoon in Montesasso. At Montesasso Scalo the station square drowsed in a white daze. No parking places in the shade, but plenty in direct sunlight at the station entrance. It was nearly three, and the train was due in ten minutes. Half an hour on, and still no sign. An elderly man protested to me: 'They always arrived on time with

Mussolini... but of course, I didn't support him!' Most people expected the train to be late, and adjusted their actions accordingly. Sounds of clinking and casual conversation drifted out from the bar opposite the station.

The clock ticked up a forty-minute delay. No station staff – all probably snoozing in the airless main office strictly out of bounds to the public. At last, exhausted by its long haul from Calais, the train pulled into the half-deserted station. Passengers peered out, surprised to see their international train (complete with wagons-lits, couchettes and a dining car) stop at such a one-horse set-up. At the far end the familiar figure of Paul stepped down, turning back to lift out a squirming Dan and pushchair, followed by case after case handed down by some helpful person inside. A small crowd of bystanders gathered proffering advice, intrigued to see a foreign male coping with a blond bambino.

'Have you forgotten anything?' It was an unkind way to greet Paul, in spite of my hug. I took charge of Dan, cuddling him close. They had arrived safely and this was all that mattered.

'Phew, it's hot! Wait – I may have left some luggage in the guard's van!' Paul bolted towards it just in time. The train started to pull out while he frantically checked the cardboard boxes and yet more cases. Everything was there.

'Signora!' I'd forgotten I'd told Gianni the time of the train. It was kind of him to come. He ambled towards Paul slowly, with his slight limp, and embraced him solemnly in the local manner, with kisses on both cheeks, followed by 'Pleased to meet you,' in English. Paul looked slightly annoyed. Later he protested he had managed to shave in a dribble of water on the train, yet Gianni's stubble was at least two days' old. He was glad, however, of someone to help him move the luggage while I was happy to deal with Dan.

Huge notices warned that only railway personnel could walk over the tracks, but Gianni, with confidence in his network of connections, ignored them. Paul nervously carried the other end of a long package over the rails to hoist it on top of our vehicle. Gianni settled on his roof rack two bundles of bulky sheets, blankets and cushions interspersed with odd plates, pans and cutlery. His small car was rapidly filled, including the passenger seat. There certainly would have been no space for Mike! We shoved suitcases inside ours, cramming assorted plastic bags round hot and tired bodies and slowly shuddered along the Cassia. It was after four; Italians were beginning to stir on to the tarmac. The sun was still high, the heat oppressive.

It had been a dry journey for the travellers. Their store of tepid lemonade had soon run out. The drinks sold on the train to captive passengers were as costly as champagne in a theatre, and too sweet to be thirst quenching. Whispers of 'povero vedovo' had run around the compartment. Wine was offered to the presumed widower and biscuits for the child. Assailed by offers of help, Paul felt the urge to shout out that he could manage on his own, but it would have seemed churlish. He kept himself going, he confided, imagining us all relaxing under olives, with him sketching the view from our small piece of paradise.

Paul got out to stop our overloaded Mammalucca scraping its exhaust along the rough track above our house. A lazy fly settled on the sweat dripping down my forehead. Oh for a seat under a tree, a cool breeze and a drink!

Paul followed the car with adrenalin-fuelled curiosity.

'Show me everything!' He had only seen the photos of the ruin I had taken in the spring. Walking slowly down the drive he paused to look around him, then came up the steps to the platform to contemplate the view. Halfway over the plain the heat haze intensified to obscure the three mountain ranges. The valley was wide; the terraces around us mostly cultivated, though olives on the higher slopes showed signs of neglect. Inside, Paul seemed content with the chestnut doors and shutters, the division into two rooms, the bathroom, and the large fireplace. All was well on the ground floor, except that his head hit the beams.

'Ci penso io!' Paul offered to lower the earth floor; Gianni left his pickaxe in the room as a pointed reminder.

The journey was beginning to tell on the travellers. Gianni helped us unpack a trestle table and put it under an olive tree, the only shade. All I could offer was warm mineral water with a few dry biscuits.

'L'acqua è bell'e fresca.' Drawn in a small plastic jug on a cord from the depths of the well, the water was cool and told of rocks and minerals in the deep veins of the earth. We could use it to cool food in the large blue enamel pan I had bought for pasta.

As I caressed a half-asleep Dan, Paul and I began to unwind together, relishing the sweep of olive groves and vineyards and the harvest quilt on the plain to the ranges emerging from the haze to shape the horizon. Shadows reached out. With a jolt I remembered that I had promised to collect Mike at six, and it must be after that now. Disturbing Dan, who began whimpering, I leapt to my feet explaining I would have to buy more food for supper and fetch Mike.

'Mike?' Paul was surprised.

'Didn't you know? He came because you told him I was here.' Paul mumbled something and turned back to his drink. Dan, who didn't want to return to his pushchair, burst into tears.

'Please cope!' I fled to our car, but before I could reach it, Gianni appeared from his kitchen garden, took hold of my arm and steered me towards Bluebottle.

'*Ti aiuto.*' His offer of help was now firmly familiar. Almost humming with relief from its burdens Bluebottle, as I called Gianni's car, bounced over the ruts. I explained that I had promised to fetch Mike. He stiffened at the name but drove me silently back to Montesasso.

The local band had mustered below the town hall, its wide run of steps a grandstand for teenagers and knots of older men. Musicians were massed on one side, shirts open to the waist displaying hairy chests and gold chains; their identical hats were tipped back, lending an air of tipsy jollity. A rotund balding figure raised his hand and shouted. Pom pom di pom, pom pom di pom... and the band started, eyes swivelling to pick out pretty girls on the steps and ignoring baldy who got hotter and angrier.

'*Per Ferragosto,*' Gianni explained. They were getting into practice for 15th August and the Assumption of the Madonna. A hand waved from the steps. It was Mike, enjoying himself. I would willingly have lingered with him to savour the local colour. Instead I shouted, 'Back in a quarter of an hour. We've got more *shopping to do for dinner. Sorry, but Gianni insisted on driving me here, so we'll have to go back with him!'* Mike nodded, relieved not to be asked to help.

Could I shop for two days without a refrigerator? It was difficult to think with Gianni hovering around me. Milk wouldn't keep. Not easy with a small child. Nor would butter. Gianni was amazed, even offended, when I asked for fruit and vegetables reminding me there were plums, tomatoes, onions, garlic, celery, parsley, and all the vegetables and herbs for pasta sauce in his kitchen garden. I grabbed six eggs for an omelette, spaghetti and tins of plum tomatoes in case there weren't enough in his vegetable patch, and a hunk of the well-matured local pecorino cheese that shouldn't suffer too much in the heat. Olive oil. Was that everything? I bought the largest loaf I could see. What about breakfast? Coffee we had. A little milk for the first day. I bought some honey to put on the bread and hoped that would do.

Gianni carried the bags. Back in the main square we found Mike contemplating the dispersal of evening strollers. Up twanged the bonnet of the car for Gianni to fit the shopping into the minute luggage space. I quickly pulled the passenger seat forward and squeezed sideways. Mike climbed in beside a tense Gianni.

'Mille grazie, Gianni*!'* he enunciated in textbook Italian, to bristling disapproval.

When we got back Dan was burbling in his pushchair on the veranda and Gianni's table was set with the newly arrived plates and cutlery. The mosquito spiral was already alight at the ceremonial centre of the layout. Chairs were awaiting us. The two-litre bottle of red wine Gianni had given me stood surrounded by a circle of glasses. Water was simmering for the pasta. Everyone was famished except for Dan, quietly bloated on biscuits. When Mike spread out his offering of Montesasso rosemary pork, Gianni dumped his emptied wine glass loudly on the table, glanced at the sunset murmuring something about hot days to come, and solemnly kissed us all. On both cheeks, so it took ceremonial time.

'Tomorrow morning,' he stated in English.

It was Saturday. The weekend so no electrician.

'You ought to ask him to find an electrician for Monday.' Unwilling to go back to 'olden days' and work in harmony with nature, Mike disliked liquid butter, curdled milk and dried up bread and cheese. 'Without electricity, no refrigerator. Without a pump for the well, no shower.'

That evening, over our first family meal at the ruin under restoration, we crazily imagined improvements: a sun-heated shower behind the house; an outside oven for pizzas; a millstone table beneath a bower; two fridges, one for drinks only and even a washing machine. What about a swimming pool using the water from the stream? Impossible without electricity. Rustic life without at least a modicum of modern comfort seemed less appealing. Part of our rural idyll was tacitly jettisoned that evening.

CHAPTER 10

Connections – August 1975

Drifting dreamlike over stone walls and around pines, cypresses and oaks daubed green and shaded bronze, I felt rays stroke my eyelids open. Shafts of light through chinks in the shutters bore specks and tingles of scythed grass. A bird see-sawing on two notes; chip, chopping of tool on earth; a fly buzzing into a spiderless web, a membrane suspended between shade and sunlight. I awoke under the shelter of russet tiles, thinking about the generations that had lived here. The aroma of coffee. I jerked up on my elbows, swung my legs over, toes on cool slabs searching for the carpet, the transition between sleep and school. The other half of the bed was companionably rumpled, not the smooth surface with Paul away in London on a working weekday. I leant back, eyes closed; warmer and warmer motes began dusting my bare legs, a gentle tickling along my arm, a mug on the bedside table, a closeness, lips and tongue waking me. This bliss, this paradise.

When I opened the shutters, the sun had risen enough to irradiate the valley. Chip, chop. No one on the prow of our land. No one in sight from the platform. Then I saw Gianni chopping and hoeing his vegetable patch. I went over to be rasped ceremoniously on each cheek.

'Caffè?' He nodded. The sun was already beaming me into the shadow of the eaves. Midday, and the kitchen area over the garage would bear the full glare of the sun. Drinking coffee under light olive shade at the back, I asked Gianni about electricity.

'He's taking me to find a plumber and electrician,' I informed the others over our frugal breakfast. This suited Paul and Mike. Dan could not yet express his views, but was happy for the moment playing with the pebbles and small stones his father had washed clean for him. Paul preferred to stay in the countryside

pottering and looking after Dan. It was too hot to concentrate on anything else.

'I'll start lowering the floor downstairs.' Paul had not forgotten the pick. 'Mike said he'll help too.'

Gianni's electrician lives at Sant'Anselmo, a hamlet by holm oaks shading a pool. The church serving this small community is covered in flaking honey-brown plaster. Even in summer it feels dank, smelling of stale incense and candlewax. It was deserted except for a tiny woman dressed in black from headscarf to tightly laced shoes, watching us from behind the altar. Gianni hailed her:

'Angelo, l'elettricista?' She shuffled towards him and glanced at me with a toothless smile of welcome. Escorting us to the church door, she spoke rapidly in slurred dialect, stabbing the air with an arthritic finger to punctuate her phrases. Gianni nodded, then strode off without even a glance, descending the slight incline as she shouted more unintelligible instructions after us. He occasionally raised an arm in acknowledgement without turning round until the gravel road veered to the left behind a bank, silencing her visual control. We stopped in the stable yard of a picturesque house with a tower and pigeoncote.

'Angelo?'

A woman peered out of a small, single-storey dwelling..

'Al lavoro.'

'Dove?'

'Da Carlo.'

Gianni turned on his heel to head back to his car. I smiled at the woman who ducked back into the room at the sound of an infant crying. She returned with a small bare-bottomed two-year-old, plonking him down in the yard. The little boy stared at me as he relieved himself. I recalled Paul taking me to the Brancacci chapel where Masaccio had painted such a mother, a similar bare-bottomed child in her arms, witnessing one of Saint Peter's miracles set in fifteenth-century Florence.

Carlo and a tall, well-built man in his early sixties were installing electricity in the half-built house. Affable, but busy, Carlo bobbed over to grasp my hand. I wondered if he was expecting the balance for Mammalucca, but that seemed far from his mind. He had just bought an electric saw on credit, finding, like me, that in building one expense inevitably leads to two more.

'La signora needs electricity in her house.'

Angelo reassured Gianni he would go to the 'Panichini ruin' when he had finished at Carlo's.

Gianni moved to sit on some logs in the shade. A good moment, I thought, to tell him I had a cheque account and could settle bills, by cash if preferred. Nothing could be better, Gianni indicated, smiling. His is a gentle smile, rarely seen. I was beginning to realise that all jobs had to be mulled over and duly digested by the specialist in question.

Gianni's plumber is one of the few who still live up in Montesasso, shunning the commercial zone down by the Scalo. The heat hung over row above row of buildings, each set a street-width further back. Deep shadows of still air absorbed dust and warmth from the burning stones rising four storeys above us.

Sergio Palombini wore a lugubrious look, enhanced by a long, curved nose and nostrils lost in a straggling moustache. A pretty young woman eyed us from the kitchen door, and a teenage boy stood silently watching. We were delaying their meal, I presumed, though no one seemed to be doing any cooking. Sergio agreed to see us that afternoon.

The half-restored house was deserted and unlocked. How trustingly careless! Fretting for lunch, Gianni left. All I wanted to do was to find Paul, Mike and Dan, and forget about electricians or plumbers. They were playing by the ford trying to catch crabs and dipping Dan's toes in the water, to loud gurgles of delight.

After lunch Paul, dreaming of a hammock, was braving the dragonflies to sit on the rocks by the stream, dabbling his feet in the water. I was sunbathing in front of the house with Dan dozing, like Mike, in the shadow of an olive tree, when a car stirred the silence of the siesta. Gianni's Bluebottle stopped tactfully halfway down our rough drive, snuggling into the bank to find shade and leave space for other vehicles to pass. I raised my head. There he was under the olive tree by Dan, observing. He thought I didn't know he'd arrived and I maintained his illusion. Returning to my book, I found the print impossible to read in the sunlight and snoozed off. Snorting myself awake, slightly embarrassed, I found him squatting in the shade two yards away. I jumped up, fully alert. Is this how a person feels when caught unaware in a photograph, visually violated and irrationally angry?

'Buona sera, signora.' Gianni was either unaware of my discomfort or ignoring it.

'Arriveranno?' I wondered whether the plumber and electrician were equally active in the hottest hours. 'Ma!'' He didn't know. I escaped inside to pour a few jugs of water over myself in the unfinished shower, wondering what I could do to entertain Gianni until someone came. These were precious hours, with Dan soundly asleep.

Gianni took me to his kitchen garden, picked me the ingredients needed for minestrone and helped in the tedious preparation of that wholesome country dish. The only advantage is that it costs virtually nothing when all the ingredients are there ready to be thrown willy nilly into the tallest pan. It's a vegetable patchwork, created with whatever's available and invented by someone like Gianni, with a flourishing kitchen garden, no freezer, time on his hands and infinite patience.

Nearly five and still no sign of electrician or plumber. Gianni strolled over to see how Paul and Mike were progressing in the ground floor rooms. Mike had wandered off, giving the excuse that there was only one pick. To Paul's annoyance, not only had Gianni insisted that morning on giving him a lesson in the use of the tool ('it's only common sense,' he growled), but now came back to assess his progress. Condescendingly, or so it seemed to him, Gianni observed the floor hadn't been lowered much. Paul bashed the pick into the ground and it rebounded as fast, hardly leaving a mark .

'Rocca viva,' Gianni muttered.

'Live rock!' Paul repeated, 'and how!' holding out his blistered palms. Gianni suggested gloves; I, tea. By now the day was cooling off.

Angelo would come, but Gianni was not so sure about Sergio who had family problems. Over a mug of tea and with time to spare he was unusually talkative, for he disapproved of gossip.

'Everyone in Montesasso knew his wife. She was so pretty. It took the town by surprise when they married and had two children, less so when she ran off with a younger man. The thirteen-year-old daughter was taken out of school to run the house. The son often works with his father when he should be at school.' Sergio had installed Gianni's unused central heating and leaking bidet at a huge discount, just between friends. It was the same Sergio who had fitted the lavatory and hand basin in our waterless, candlelit bathroom.

At last, a dusty green Renault drew up in front of the house. Sergio and son charged past us to inspect the bathroom. The shower would be installed on Monday as well as the water heater. Paul suggested connecting the electricity first; Gianni agreed, without really listening, and led Sergio round the house talking of gutters. Out came a ladder, the son steadying it while his father measured the eaves. They had just about finished when Angelo turned up. After a quick glance at the electricity pole in Giulio's vineyard, he bustled about measuring distances and asking us to mark where we needed switches and sockets, certain he could get the electricity company to link us up. He, too, would start on Monday.

Paul offered wine; a few crisps rescued from Dan were refused. Angelo sat on the platform and surveyed the valley. We gave him our binoculars, and then handed them round. You could just make out the occasional vehicle on the Cassia, and almost recreate the advance of General Alexander's army while Angelo recounted his war experiences. Like every man of his vintage, he claimed to have been a partisan, and by 1944 he had returned for safety to his own valley.

They all left together. The cicadas tuned up, sporadically. Paul and Mike laid the table and cut the bread ready for Gianni's minestrone. I watched them as worries chattered away in my head: Angelo and Sergio would return and hang around for instructions just when Gianni wanted to shuttle me to and fro to settle the bills. And that meant leaving the valley for a very early visit to the bank. Sarah and William would also be arriving with three children. Paul said I was crazy to invite friends even though they did offer to help. It was hot so I'd imagined we'd require less of everything. No blankets certainly, but everyone needed food and a bed!

So I continued, writing about the house and the people in the valley all summer in spite of being teased for my efforts.

'Who would ever want to read about us?' Paul said, forgetting that when we'd met he was training to become a restorer, though he really wanted to be a painter, and I had planned to write in the time left over from teaching. William laughingly agreed with Paul. Friends might find tales of curious habits and rustic folk amusing, but not the reading public. He knew, because he was setting up a creative writing course at his university. Sarah whispered that I shouldn't listen to them. Better to write and hone my tale of a dream coming true, hoping some time, some day, somebody might be interested. Even if no one was, writing, as far as I was concerned, would have served some purpose.

CHAPTER 11

Paul's Italian was better than mine then. He had lived in Italy for months at a stretch and should have been dealing with the plumbers and electricians, not me. Still, it was important for him to stay with his son; I liked seeing our child in his arms, waving goodbye with Dan's little hand in his. Rushing around with Gianni and making payments and arrangements kept my mind and feelings off children. When I was with Dan I inevitably leap-frogged ten years back to Tim as a baby, to new-born apprehensions. Blue for a baby boy: blue wards off the evil eye. Dan always had blue on him. Tim growing older had obliterated his younger self; now Dan was bringing it back to me. I feared that he was usurping my memories of Tim at the same age. It seemed to be a sacrilege against Tim's childhood – his lost stepping-stones into the future. Paul and I were complicit and silent. All associations with the house we were restoring in Italy would be Dan's alone.

Paying the Way – August 1975

The Tuscans (maybe it is an Italian characteristic?) never name a price, however hard they are pressed to do so. No one seemed in a hurry to be paid for the house and car.

'It's our holiday,' Paul kept reminding me. 'Time to relax and not think about money.' I argued that we were surrounded by people who needed it and had, after all, done the work. There might be bad feelings if we took our time.

'Olivia, you haven't a clue about what makes Italians tick,' he muttered, looking at Dan's prehensile toes before sketching them. There must be millions of paintings depicting the Virgin and Child, I thought as I watched him, but none of Joseph and Child, no veneration of paternal love. Joseph is always in the background.

Paul was rather proud of the way he had fitted nappies around pencils, charcoal and watercolours, rusks, baby wipes and toys in his knapsack and strapped a rolled-up rug on top. One day, before leaving with easel slung over his shoulder and sketching pads tucked into Dan's pushchair, he told me he had found a perfect place to paint near a church and a farmhouse with a tower. They could see the buildings while in the shade of holm oaks surrounding a pool. But that day he had to stay near the house to deal with the electrician and plumber while I was out paying bills.

Gianni hustled me to Montesasso on Monday, my self-appointed guide through the purgatory of payments. He was unruffled. After the bank, Gianni moved on to the lawyer's office. Dottoressa Ferrarini was in the waiting room coping with people milling around, more spectators than clients, I suspected. In Montesasso, Gianni says, they are unaccustomed to a woman dealing with legal matters. She was relieved to see us. The contract was ready and she would arrange a meeting. Gianni could speed up matters by calling on his cousin Claudio.

The bank notes weighed me down physically and psychologically. Gianni led me into a bar, though I wanted to get on with the payments. I suspected there was a hidden agenda behind this leisured manner, but one could never prise out of Gianni what he did not want to say. Suddenly he leapt into action. We sped down the hill to Montesasso Scalo braking in front of a half-stuccoed house.

'Carla!' yelled Gianni. A woman appeared on the balcony in the usual company of geraniums, basil and parsley. She looked familiar.

'Venite.' We climbed the stairs to a narrow hall with a scrupulously polished terrazzo floor. Gianni introduced me to Ada's, and therefore Carlo's, sister.

'Enzo?' Her husband, who had sunk our well, was expected at any moment. Gianni sat down in the kitchen and lit a cigarette. Footsteps on the stairs awakened expectations. It was now well after midday. Two boys, aged about eleven and fourteen, dumped their school bags in the hall, waved to us and disappeared.

Carla's sons are a strange pair. They could not look more unlike each other or their mother. Carla is small and slight, her hair mousy brown with blond streaks. The elder son is dark and heavily built; the younger lean with very fair hair and pinkish complexion.

Carla returned to the balcony. She seemed restless. Her sons reappeared to forage in the fridge and kitchen cupboards, opening the plastic doors of the much-vaunted cucina americana. Renzo and Maria Pia are saving up for a similar American-style Formica kitchen whilst Paul says he'll restore the old farm furniture they sold to us for a song.

'Carla!' A swarthy man with muscled, half-bowed legs was standing in the hall, expecting us to follow him into a room with a deeply polished table and ten chairs crowding the space. Carla raised the Venetian blinds and turned off the light. The atmosphere of gloomy coolness, even in summer, was slightly dispelled.

Enzo invited us to sit down, calling Carla for the ceremonial drink; strong liqueur accompanied crumbly sweet biscuits on a silver-plated dish. Hunger was in the air, betrayed by the restless to-ing and fro-ing of the sons outside the open door.

'A pagare!' To business. Enzo held out a scruffy piece of lined paper with figures scrawled over it. I asked for a proper account.

'Allora, signora, you'll have to pay more!' This was a very special bill for me alone as I was Gianni's friend. If I wanted the official bill, then there would be taxes to pay on top, and much else of unimaginable horror! Or so it seemed. I felt out of my depth and looked to Gianni for help. Pay up, he intimated. I began to burrow into my bag, then paused. Enzo cut thirty thousand lire off the bill for the well, exclaiming, 'In omaggio!' More drinks were poured while the money was counted. I stepped, lighter, into the scorching sun.

Mike was standing outside Orazio's bar with Sarah, William, their children and a taxi. The driver had stopped to find the way to our house and Mike was helping. With the three children there was no room for him, so he got into Gianni's car which led the way. Conveniently, Mike asked Gianni to drop him at the station on his way back to Montesasso. He gathered his bags, explaining that he'd been making phone calls from Orazio's bar and needed to meet clients in Milan, though he was sad to leave.

We settled into a leisurely, relaxing meal at the trestle table in the scant shade of an olive tree, discussing plans. The fun was that everyone proved so resourceful. The two mattresses padding the trestle table sent from England were for the older children, Andrew and Penny. All had to follow the ad hoc rules of the house: comfort starts with the oldest, and is shared downwards, with Kate and Dan sleeping on makeshift cushion mattresses until we could afford more.

Sarah and William rose to the challenge and offered to stock up at Sibilla's shop. The children were lured there by promises of ice cream, rationed to one a day. There was a serious discussion over whether the treat should be in the morning or afternoon, and Elevenses won. The reward would be fresh rolls for lunch, and Sibilla's selection of cheese and ham, limited, but preferable to the longer haul into Montesasso Scalo.

Dan had given no trouble, Paul reported, happy in his carrycot watching Sergio and his son as they fussed in and out of the bathroom and hitched up gutters. Angelo had come and installed the electricity with the help of a friend employed by the State electricity company. He had connected the pump in the well and the shower, and fixed the electricity points where we had agreed. We would soon have light 'at the flick of a finger'.

After lunch Paul moved the two deckchairs under an ageing plum tree in Gianni's kitchen garden, away from our guests.

'The plumber and electrician arrived one after the other.' He was worried. 'It was impossible to deal with two lots of work going on simultaneously. Sergio turned up with his son who did nothing but hold the ladder. They worked with much shouting and swearing, madonna-ing this and madonna-ing that.' Paul looked around to make sure Gianni hadn't slipped in unnoticed. 'The gutter attachments don't look strong or at all secure, and,' he put his hand to his head, 'the water heater in the bathroom is so bulky you can't help knocking into it! Sergio didn't ask me about size. He just installed it. By then it was too late to say or do anything.'

We went to inspect, and the first pear-shaped raindrops fell. I thought I heard distant thunder. The bathroom door opened outwards, but I too had to bend over the basin to squeeze through to the shower and WC.

'I tried to protest, but he kept on repeating that a smaller cylinder would cost more and not provide enough water for everyone. I tested the shower right in front of him, and it only dribbled out. There isn't enough pressure.' This crucial point seemed to be lost on Sergio, who looked at Paul and listened intently, only to repeat exactly the same explanation.

By now the raindrops had turned into hail and driven the children inside, leaving the adults to gather up books and discarded clothes. Unprotected on the kitchen platform and trestle table lay all our remaining food. As we rushed everything under cover hailstones, big as marbles, hurt as they hit. From the sitting-room grandstand, the window wide open, we watched forked lightning etching patterns on the copper-grey clouds louring over the mountains. Hail rapped olives off branches, pock-marked bunches of ripening grapes, and knocked neat holes in fig leaves. No chance to try out the electricity; it had gone off of its own accord! There was a surge of rushing water. The gutters couldn't cope. Instead of tipping into Sergio's rainwater drain and discharging into the channel beside our house, they sloped in precisely the opposite direction, spilling water into the garage! Paul glanced at me, before laughing at the children who were dashing in and out of the hail to test the lash of nature's fury.

As suddenly as it had started, blue skies nudged the storm westwards. Birdsong. Sunlight dancing on the leaves and caught in jewelled raindrops. Monte Amiata appeared on the other side of the plain as if by courtesy of nature's orchestration. Hills were rippling under the patchwork of fields that, in the hot stupor of a summer day, had previously seemed so flat. The lilies Gianni had planted in the front garden were prostrate and geraniums lay shattered; but the fury past, the air was breathing again, the skies freshened and the heat quenched.

Sound of voices. Up from the fields on the left and across the channel came Giulio with Gino, Maria Pia's son from the farm above. They nodded at us and walked in front of our house to the land opposite, which was not theirs either. As far as we knew, it was still owned by the Panichini who sold us the ruin with a meagre bit of land fore and aft. Paul and I waved, feeling affinity as owners of a tiny plot (even cultivators, with Gianni's help!) who nourished great intentions to grow vegetables and even plant an orchard.

We, too, wanted to inspect the land, ours or not. The children ran ahead of us across Don Luigi's terraces down to the stream. It was pouring into the pool that Paul and William had just hollowed out with the children, the waterfalls cascading down in liquid sculpture. We splashed around, to dry out in the mid-afternoon sun. Up the rough drive and along the track we hurried for no reason but excitement, past the one-storey house where Ada's grandmother was born and under the plum trees, their fruit, battered off the branches, all over the ground. Could we gather it? Sarah dashed back to the house for plastic bags.

The others hurried on to see what had happened to the ford. The natural basins used to wash clothes were swirling with muddy water. The older children splashed through the ford while Dan clung to me, crying to follow them. Paul carried him as we waded across, and up we went to the outcrop, our Montesasso viewing point.

Sarah called us back. Rural economy and our own finances dictated that nothing was to be wasted. We found her kneeling below the largest of the plum trees to gather the fruit less hammered by the hail.

'Gianni's come for you, Liv,' Paul warned me, hearing the Bluebottle turn into our drive. His car was there all right, but no sign of Gianni. I found him staring at his storm-battered kitchen garden.

'Tutto rovinato!' Gloomily he added, 'destroyed,' in English.

'Carlo wants to see you.' His excuse to leave the scene of disaster?

Every time Gianni and I passed Carlo's yard, the house was a few breeze-blocks higher. He was aiming to roof it before the summer was out, and needed the money for Mammalucca. When

Gianni arrived at the wheel of the car to be paid for by me and registered in his name, Carlo motioned him into the back seat and insisted on driving us all to the Italian Automobile Association.

To back out of the forecourt Carlo put his right arm round the passenger seat, and kept it there. It slipped slightly, touching my shoulders. There it paused. Then slid lower. I pretended not to notice. Shoulder or knee, these Italians were certainly fond of friendly physical contact. Rightly or wrongly, I didn't tell Paul about this. Out of sight, it should be out of mind.

Documents and payment completed in the office, Carlo drove the car back to his yard; I got out to thank him and he kissed me farewell for the first time. His brother-in-law remained in Mammalucca, puffing with indignation. He didn't really look it, but Gianni was quite a bit older than Carlo. We drove off.

'Prendiamo un'altra strada.' Gianni chose another route back, stopping at a rough farmhouse smothered in flame-coloured flowers that stood below a handsome villa.

'Villa Fontanina,' Gianni remarked before a woman greeted us, bringing a homemade cake and fresh lemonade out to a table shaded by a walnut tree. In her mid-thirties, small and rounded and full of welcoming smiles, Marisa made good, if undemanding, company. When she went to fetch glasses, I asked Gianni who she was.

'L'amante di Carlo.' So Carlo consoled himself with Marisa after a hard day's work in his yard, before returning to his wife and son in the shack by the railway line. Cannily, he used to drop in as we were doing, before Marisa's husband returned home at sunset.

The children had eaten when Gianni dropped me at the top of our drive.

'Scorpions!' Andrew came running up the drive. 'Scorpions! They'll poison us!'

Hysterical shrieks interrupted Sarah reading to the younger ones at bedtime. I pushed past Penny and Kate into the larger room below. A pale glow from the single electric bulb threw shadows where Sarah, William and Paul were searching under beds and cushions and in corners.

'Scorpions!' shouted the two at the door, 'big, black, shiny and waving their tails!'

Gianni had warned us about vipers but not a word on these alarming creatures.

'Scorpions thrive on fresh cement,' he informed us the next day. Harmless, unless they sting a newborn child, they usually appear at dusk and are easily mesmerised by torchlight, so a quick flip with a shoe sees them off.

Cement. Scorpions. The exciting prospect of buying a much-desired fridge. The daunting ones of paying Enzo for the well and Carlo for the car now accomplished, there might just be enough money, after settling with Massimo the builder and the final payment for the ruin, to build a kitchen above the garage.

It was an exciting time at the Casa dell'Avventura with Paul, Dan and our friends. I enjoyed making plans with them, but how could one's memory be wiped clear when Giulio was hoeing his vines below my bedroom window and Marco's shrine stood on our way to the ford?

After Tim's accident, I stood transfixed at the school gate, choking, hand over mouth – I didn't break down, sob, or yell. Not at first. It was Gran who wept and moved her photo of Tim, Paul and me to the front of the bedside shrine beside her brother Frank.

'At least you know where you are and what to cope with,' Mother said, silently sorrowing. 'It's easier to come to terms with certainty,' adding wryly, 'it knocks your dreams back under control.' She forgot I'd lived almost as many years as she had with a missing person: her great love, my father. She referred to her way of coping as her emotional 'loss adjustment'. At St. Mary's she prayed for my father's safe return, her longing offered with a candle lit in quiet hope. I simply despaired, forever wanting.

I shall never forget Sarah's help with Dan and Mike's with the paperwork and funeral arrangements. William came with Andrew to see me and ask what they could do, grieving reminders both of my father and my son, but their kindness lingered.

Andrew was found weeping in Tim's room. Comments were made about him growing 'too old for his years'. He sat where they had been playing with Tim's train set the Sunday before he was killed. He had lost his best friend and his childhood.

CHAPTER 12

Paul treasured his reproductions of sketches from Leonardo's notebooks – ideal churches based on perfect forms: squares, equilateral triangles and pyramids; cubes and circles that have no beginning or end – spheres of the mind. He kept these luminous shapes, bought on a visit to the Carrara quarries, on a shelf in his studio to take down and feel the cool texture of marble. He often pored over his copy of a painting he had seen in the Ducal Palace at Urbino. It's like the computer-generated image of an ideal square: no building more than four storeys high; paving in perfect patterns and perspective. A birdcage, plants hanging out of windows with half-open shutters; no people, no movement, no sound – a still silent scene waiting. It depicts an ideal city, Paul thought; he had read about somebody who planned and built one five hundred years ago.

A Pope's Paradise – August 1975

'You were snoring,' Paul teased me as he sat on the bed, coffee in hand. Plans. No meeting yet to sign the contract. All members of the family inherit equally, so all have to be present. The Panichini daughter lives in Pisa. She'd be coming soon. Pazienza!

Before I was awake, Gianni had changed the configuration of the land. Sand was heaped beside four large bags of cement behind the well. The other side of the drive, on Panichini territory still cultivated by their farmer, a neatly assembled pile of stones. They recalled dry-stone walling on Paul's childhood holidays in Cornwall but, although he was itching to get his hands on them, Gianni's presence inhibited him.

'Ci vuole la cucina.' Gianni looked up and smiled, leaning on his long-handled spade. 'A kitchen,' he stressed in English. I managed to extract from him a crumpled piece of paper with spidery figures written on it.

'Quanto ti devo? 280,000 lire?' He nodded. Here was Gianni waving his magic wand, without even knowing whether we had the money to pay for a transformation.

We had agreed that all family excursions would be on weekdays. Mammalucca was temperamentally unsuited to Sunday traffic and we were reluctant to deal with weekend crowds and drivers. Paul and I had already planned to go to Pienza, the others to Lake Trasimeno – one car, two excursions. Paul dropped Sarah, William and their children off first to swim in the lake, returning to take Dan and me on our expedition across the plain to Pienza.

The plain in itself was a discovery. From our spur of land it normally looked flat, criss-crossed by drainage canals and dotted with farmhouses, but after the hailstorm we had glimpsed hilltop towns beyond, tipping the heat haze like fairytale castles. Mountains edged the horizon; beyond them, the invisible sea. Driving across the plain we found ourselves circling hills or winding up steep roads to small run down market towns topped by a ruined castle or forlorn monastery. The patchwork plain had seduced us from our vantage point into its intricacies of character. Fields were cultivated around deserted farmhouses with dovecotes like stunted towers. Grey, then sandier stone gave way to pinkish bricks as we passed south of Siena. The battle between wheat and the sunflower crop had started on the lower land, while the higher slopes, a tender green in springtime, now lay shorn and bronzed. Cattle were hidden inside barns, with only a few sheep let out to graze on the stonier hilltops. Some slopes shouldered vines festooned to field maples and stone posts. Others, deserted olive groves. The isolated farmhouses were built after the low land was reclaimed two hundred years ago, but the hilltop towns told of ancient settlements and centuries of rural husbandry. The footprints and ruts of the more frequented tracks were now smothered in tarmac.

Pope Pius's spirit was expecting us at Pienza. Paul was intrigued by his Commentaries, written as if the pope were Julius Caesar surveying the dry land of moonscape ridges while *recording the creation of an ideal city in his native village of Corsignano.*

'Aenea Silvius Piccolomini,' Paul informed me, 'started by supporting the Holy Roman Emperor. Sent as his envoy to Scotland, he fathered a daughter, one of the many children lost to history. What would she have thought of her forgetful father who, turning forty and fearing damnation, entered holy orders? He rapidly became Bishop of Siena, then Cardinal and Pope in less than ten years!'

Thank you, Pius, for the travertine seat round the square in Pienza. A solitary figure was crouching in the shade on the far end of the stone ledge, arms around knees, apparently snoozing. We sat and watched, devouring a late lunch in the half-deserted square. The façade appeared more temple than church. Inside we expected cool darkness, but instead it was airy with the aisles reaching as high as the nave. Creamy travertine columns with whorls of darker brown linked the church interior to its façade and the square. This miniature cathedral calmed the light and life of the piazza into its serene interior of pale yellow walls and cool-to-touch carved water stoops. Pius's original delight radiated through his creation out to us.

'It remains as he dreamed it should be.' Paul was ecstatic. 'Pius saw it like this in 1464, before he died. It's perfect, exactly as he decreed!'

Walking towards the altar we pitched slightly forward, to halt by a fissure. The altar end was keeling over into the valley.

'Pius wrote about sulphurous flames when digging the foundations.' Paul had prepared notes. 'His architect, Rossellino, a Florentine, was disliked locally. He had also lied about the cost. When Pius found out he declared, "we are glad Rossellino did not tell us the truth, otherwise such a superb building would never have been built!"' Paul smiled. 'And all this from the pen of a Renaissance Pope!' But a sad story is embedded in the outside wall of the apse, pitted by gunshot when, in 1944, the Allies' armies passed though the Val d'Orcia.

We bought Dan an ice cream in the piazza and sat on the seat round the papal palace. Shadows had lengthened. The siesta ended, the original lone inhabitant of the ledge moved, talking and gesticulating, to a strip of shade under the town hall. A couple of men strolled over from the café to sit by the village idiot, victim of centuries of inbreeding in once remote market towns like Pienza.

The massive doors to the papal palace opened and a figure in a striped white and wine-coloured jacket looked out furtively. He was about to close them again when we rushed over to ask, 'Si può visitare?' Inside the empty courtyard we missed the warmth of the evening activities in the square. There was a shivery atmosphere; few echoes of the pleasure-loving Pope. The gate into the hanging garden was open. Ignoring the shouts of the man in the butler's jacket, I left Paul to deal with him and Dan, and escaped into the deserted garden.

'Hurry!' Paul called, Dan in his arms, from the stairs where the butler stood by an open door looking at his watch.

'Il giardino no, signora!'' The garden isn't open, reproaching me as if I was a child. Inside we joined four others on the first floor, all Americans. Our guide breathed in to expand his torso and look fiercely at the group. Dan made disturbing noises and the Americans stirred uneasily. They were glad of my sporadic whispered translation and anxious not to disobey orders. The rooms on the main floor remained, we were informed, exactly as the last descendant of the papal family had left them. In a fading yellow photo taken in the 1930s, the Count and Countess Piccolomini looked out of a palace window making a slight gesture to acknowledge whoever was watching below, exactly where Pius had witnessed festivities five centuries earlier.

Their only son, the last of the direct Piccolomini line, had died in an air crash. The widowed Count lived on alone in this vast ancestral pile, watching winter freeze the harsh clay ridges succeeded by the blossom, the birdsong and polka-dot poppies in the spring wheat, and then the parched summer fields shading into autumn.

All was strangely still. We were intruders, stirring the dust of memory. Paul was disappointed that few objects remained from Pius's time. He whispered that the Pope used to sit in the window alcove conversing with a companion, reading or gazing over the valley at the pageant of the seasons. He was the first since Antiquity to build with a view in mind and hold a dialogue with the moods of nature in the valley of his childhood. His books were written by the light of the adjustable candlestick still in the room – a constant fire risk. Immediately outside the corner bedchamber was the second of the three loggias and a vast hall.

The custodian began to hurry. We were too interested; he was impatient (his guiding time doubled by my translating for the Americans), and apprehensive about the child in his pushchair touching the furniture. We lingered on the loggia where Dan began innocently babbling to an Etruscan couple lying at his eye level on their urn, part of the antique bric-a-brac pushed back against the wall of the papal palace. Right hand poised on the brass handle of the door opening on to the stairs, his left palm opened towards us, the butler craved his tip and his supper.

We took a wrong turning on the way back from Pienza and found ourselves in a land of dry clay ridges, clawed by ploughs into strips of grey curls touched pink by the sunset. Across the valley a road zig-zagged up and round a stark hillside, its path marked by the darkening green of cypresses. Paul stopped. Dan was asleep on the back seat. We both got out to look at it in silence. Then, 'It's like a painting,' he stated. We watched the deep blue above us pale into pearlescent mist behind the cypresses tipping the road up and over to the other side of the hill. Making our slow way homeward behind vehicles and carts as they trundled from fields to hilltop town, we witnessed the ancestral call to seek shelter inside high walls, known rivalries preferable to unfathomable fears of isolation amid woods and spirits in the dark.

'What about Gianni? We should have returned earlier.' Paul was annoyed by my concern. It was the first day we had done something for our own pleasure. However, he understood. Gianni needed to be cherished, and we hadn't meant to be away for so long.

Paul dropped Dan and me off near Sibilla's store to return to the Casa dell'Avventura on foot and in pushchair, while he pressed Mammalucca as fast as she could go to collect the swimmers at the lake.

Gianni had left. The front parapet to the veranda and half a column to support the roof were there to admire, with no one to thank.

Paul found the lake party in the local café consuming ice creams to placate tired and fractious children. One car of limited capacity had to cope with six individuals and different priorities. We had rapidly acquired the Italian habit of being ignorant of the law! In addition we were ready, if challenged by the traffic police, to lose our collective knowledge of the language! Think of a minute three-wheeled car, then add a wheel, whip the engine round to the boot, and cram it illegally with three adults and three variously-sized children – Mammalucca that evening!

As the adults prepared a hasty meal lit by an almost full moon, they felt reassured by the parapet. Gianni had used channelled paving stones for the top, 'liberated' from a pile left one evening on his stretch of road. The cement had hardly dried but the wall served as a handy buffet and protected the younger children from a nasty fall past the garage doors.

We toasted the prospect of a kitchen under a starlit sky, cheered on by the chorus of crickets. Dan fell asleep but the older children played 'catch the sparks' as the last stragglers from the June festival of fireflies danced up the drive in front of them.

CHAPTER 13

These could have been the happiest of times. Paul was drawing and painting; he filled two large sketchpads with farmhouses and haystacks, cypresses, umbrella pines and poplars down by the stream. I, too, was writing and reshaping my narrative at odd moments during the day. He and William played with Dan and the other children, relaxed as rarely before.

I did try to tell Paul about Giulio being frightened by the spirits at the ford and Marco's shrine, but he didn't respond, turning away to get on with his sketch or to take a solitary walk searching for trees, rocks and water to draw or paint. You didn't talk about people being 'in denial' then, but he was. That's why I still couldn't confide in him, apprehensive of how he might cope with my shame and deep self-disgust, of his reaction to what happened while I was in Greece before there was much talk of women's rights. Paul looked after Dan, drawing him and helping generally – in his own way. It was far easier to talk to Mike, and I missed him.

'What on earth is Mike doing in Milan?'

Paul was surprised at my question. 'Don't be nosy,' he said. 'Mike might want to meet someone. A business contact, or another dealer. I suspect Angélique is there waiting for him.'

Mixed Emotions – August 1975

A paragon of propriety, Gianni didn't wake us up next morning, though he clearly wanted to make plans. The cement had to be mixed. He needed bucketfuls of sand. He needed a hosepipe. He needed a workmate. Paul was keen to build a wall but, Gianni warned, it meant getting up earlier. There was no cover and by ten-thirty it was already hot.

Pressures on time and car use were causing friction. The rural idyll was fraying under conflicting needs: to have plenty of food and also a respite from shopping. No fridge meant visiting Sibilla daily, fascinating though it was.

I asked Gianni where to buy a fridge, preferably a second-hand one.

'*Ci penso io!*'' Just leave it to him!

Meanwhile he and Paul laboured until sweat was running in rivulets. Gianni enjoyed having someone to command. His workmate was resentful because Gianni assumed he was a complete novice. Though he might have become an expert in drystone walling on his Cornish holidays, this was serious masonry with cement, and Paul's task was to mix it to match Gianni's recipe. Gianni was forever testing the grey consistency and finding it wanting. Tensions grew when Paul was regularly turned back with the wrong stone. He decided to transfer a pile close to the first courses of the kitchen wall, but Gianni still returned to his original ones across the other side of the drive, lit a cigarette and drew deeply on it, silently contemplating the stones. Five minutes were spent sizing them up while Paul hung around. Then he had to shift them rapidly to the wall being built in the order Gianni prescribed. A shame Gianni didn't scratch Roman numerals on them, as medieval masons did, to make Paul's task easier.

Gianni returned after lunch, his Bluebottle leading three cars: an Ape-powered mini truck, a clapped-out Citroën Deux Chevaux and the plumber's now familiar green Renault. Gianni's magic wand again. The Ape parked in front of the veranda-to-be and kitchen wall gaping for a window. Someone had discarded a fridge, and for a mere 20,000 lire (almost as much again for the mini-truck driver, Domenico), we had a functioning unfashionable machine. Whoops of joy greeted its arrival and installation in the roofless kitchen; the tinkle of the electric current generated sighs of relief at the prospect of cool drinks. The Deux Chevaux meanwhile disgorged smiling Massimo of the drooping belt with more bags of sand to unload on to the sandpit and Penny and Kate's sandcastles, condemning them to tearful oblivion. And still more bags of cement. Handshakes all round. Behind him emerged Sergio, summoned to tip his gutters towards the downpipes draining into the channel and stop them spilling over Gianni's garage. He galumphed off to sort it out with his son and a ladder.

Gianni announced that we had to select beams for the kitchen roof from Massimo's yard. He chose that moment to ask me about something inconsequential in the garage while Massimo drove off with Paul. Waiting until their dust cloud disappeared, he took my arm and walked me to his car. Lurching into second gear to hell-for-leather up the drive and along the track to the ford, and splashing muddy water over the windscreen, he laughed at me in a crazy recreation of youthful exploits. As the tiny car turned up the hill, Gianni's body swayed naturally with it, following the swing to the right into a kiss. I flinched and hit my head on the window. Far from being concerned, he was piqued. Watch it, I thought, he's easily offended.

He drove the car under a walnut tree, jettisoning it and me to join Paul and Massimo in the yard. An audience of eight hens, two guinea fowl and one disdainful deplumed cock surveyed the three men.

'Devono essere di castagno. Stagionate.' Wherever Gianni had learnt his English, it wasn't on a building site. He didn't try to say 'seasoned chestnut' as he moved with Massimo to a pile of tree trunks, both now lighting up thought-inducing cigarettes. Air lay heavily on us; waves of doziness called for a horizontal position on a Roman couch and sorbets with cool fruit cordials. Just as Gianni made up his mind and pointed to that and that chestnut trunk, Massimo's wife, Bianca, and their daughter, Rosella, came out carrying trays with glasses, bottles of white wine and spuma, a sweet and fizzy lemonade. She mixed them half-and-half, Rosella handing us each a glass before Massimo revved up the mechanical saw, took the measurements from Gianni, and cut the trunks he indicated. Paul stayed apart, drawing and watching the scene unfold.

Bianca took me to sit with an old man in the shade of a walnut tree.

'Olivia, I'd like you to meet Oreste.'(I felt I was entering an epic drama: 'Orestes will recount...') She was calling upon the seer of the valley to unfold the story of our house.

'I remember the last family abandoning it before the First World War. They still used it for storage. Hunters sheltered there.

When I was young' – a good-looking youth glimpsed in his smile – 'it was used for trysts, even after the roof caved in!' He was pleased to have me share his reminiscences.

'The stream in this valley flows from a spring above my house, pure and ice-cold. I remember, as a young man, the thrill of drinking it, bathing in it. Often there were snakes there, the harmless water kind, but they excited us young men. We made silly jokes before romping down to Sunday mass to look over the girls!'

Here he was, Oreste, over ninety and the oldest man in the valley, long a widower, living in his farmhouse with two of his five children, three grandchildren and four surviving great grandchildren – one had been killed in a farming accident.

'It was near your house,' Bianca said as we joined the others. 'By the ford.'

Ten-year-old Marco was hit by a cart about to cross the valley's artery flowing from the spring on his great grandfather's land. Oreste seemed resigned to the fellowship of memory. Children, like his great grandchild, were often tragically injured or killed in farming accidents.

'Not uncommon enough,' was Gianni's comment on Marco, che Dio ti benedica.

The tree trunks had been hoisted on to Massimo's truck and so the return journey started, at a decorous pace. No leaning over at sharp turns, no surreptitious kisses. I wiped them out of my mind as Gianni's temporary aberration (in spite of the painful bump on my head), fretting instead about how to keep him sweet, but physically distant.

Paul and Gianni unloaded the tree trunks with Massimo's help. He then drove off, busily ignoring Gianni's call for more manpower to raise the beams on to his pillar.

To his relief, William and Sarah emerged from Gianni's vegetable patch, followed by the clan carrying their booty of bugs while clamouring in a dissonant chorus for payment and ice creams. They had been doing profitable chores, like debugging aubergines of what looked suspiciously like Colorado beetles. Andrew threatened strike action if not paid more than ten lire a *bug, as they couldn't find enough to earn an ice cream each! The adults proved sympathetic. Other pests would be included in the count, and even dead scorpions for fifty lire each. But only two were found, hotly disputed by Andrew and Penny.*

That evening after supper, with Dan sleeping safely in my arms, we sat contemplating the view now framed by Gianni's beam, parapet and pillar. The white wine was cool. The children's Coca-Cola was just fresh to their liking, and three times as expensive as our wine. (They were blissfully unaware that a coke ration was to follow the ice cream one!) All was still, except for the occasional thread of lights as a train crossed the plain. The full moon rose to the accompaniment of the growing chorus of crickets; this was our dream come true.

More glasses, plates and chairs were desperately needed. Montesasso was too small for a medium-priced store with household goods and clothes. Our chronic inability to leave before eleven meant, once we'd parked outside the walls of a Tuscan hill town and meandered up the hill, there was barely half an hour before midday, when shops start closing for lunch and the afternoon siesta. That morning we were exceptionally early. By ten everyone had congregated on the roofless veranda. It was to be a shopping expedition to Arezzo with an adventure or two thrown in!

Feeling the heat, William chose to remain behind. Paul said he would stay too, as there wasn't much room in the car. It was my turn to drive Mammalucca along the edge of the plain already enveloped in haze. Six bodies again were packed into the vehicle. Dazed by the glare of sunflowers at their maximum spread and colour, I tilted my head to focus on the foothills. 'Look ahead! A mirage, or is that really a fairytale castle?' I stopped. Five bodies, Sarah with Dan in her arms, extricated themselves to gaze from the roadside. There on the nearest range stood the same castle that is painted behind Guidoriccio da in the Siena Town Hall fresco. A low, crenellated stone tower, curtain walls, and then a tall, slender tower crumbling at its crest.

'Let's go there!' Sarah suggested. To explore. To meet and enjoy the unexpected. Isn't that what holidays should be about?

Not buying glasses, building walls, and queuing up for a dribbling shower in one malfunctioning bathroom. I was tempted, but sterner duty dictated. After all, had I promised them it would be an uncluttered holiday? No. Shopping came first.

Leaving the plain behind us, we followed the road aligned on the distant cathedral spire. Like a beacon shining across an undulating desert of heat punctuated only by the odd umbrella pine or cypress sentinel, the Etruscan city beckoned. The superstore was on the left of the road just where we lost sight of the spire. Trolleys piled high with more than we had intended, we loaded Mammalucca and followed the city walls to park behind the cathedral.

The first plea for gelati came soon after finding the Pieve, a church with a vast, cool interior. The older children were asking me about Arezzo's history while Dan, in the pushchair, was pacified by a sponge finger every time he opened his mouth to protest. Rapidly skating over the Etruscans followed by the Romans to arrive at Frederick Redbeard and Saracen pirates, I ended with the Romeo and Juliet type feuds that flourished in thirteenth-century Arezzo, as well as Verona. Arezzo preferred Siena to Florence, and was rewarded with a superb polyptych for the high altar by the Sienese Pietro Lorenzetti.

We found the Pieve high altar bare, save for a cross. A notice: 'In restauro'. No Pietro Lorenzetti. Stymied yet again. The pitch and volume of their clamour rose. Gelati?

We licked ice creams in the sloping main square boasting one of the best medieval loos we had yet found. Stench medium to high. Paper and seat facilities non-existent. Flush weak but not splashy. Notices announced the jousting of the Saracens in early September and the clan demanded to go.

Peace was regained after purchasing exorbitant Coca-Colas as well as the ice creams, and cheaper cappucinos for Sarah and me. We ambled down the main street imagining the kitchen gardens, orchards and poultry yards in the late 1200s, turned sharp right and stopped in front of the Franciscan church.

'What a scruffy church!' Andrew observed. 'It's all rutted in front.' Ledges had waited centuries for a marble coat to dress the *bare façade. The sacristan peered out of the left-hand door with a key in his hand. I hustled our group into the one on the right, heading towards Piero della Francesca's frescoes behind the high altar and steering Dan away from the mesmerising flicker of devotional candles by side altars. A protest; another biscuit. He reminded me of a young cuckoo in the nest, mouth gaping. Behind the high altar, while the obliging five-year-old Kate clunked hundred lire coins into the light machine, I whispered the Story of the Finding of the True Cross from tales of popular piety. Amazing coincidences and improbable events were revealed as part of the eternal drama of life, elaborated and passed on by faithful congregations for centuries before they were even written down.*

'Let's start at the top right.' So far so good. 'Adam is the old man on the right, and he is dying. Weighed down by nine hundred years.' (Gasps of wonder.) 'Eve supports his head while his son, Seth, asks archangel Michael in the Garden of Eden for the oil of forgiveness.'

'Why are the angel and the man so teeny?' Penny piped up. I explained about the divisions into picture pages to tell the story because paintings don't move in space and time like words and music.

'How many pages are there up there?' The historian in me took over.

'The big pages are divided into three smaller paragraphs in this one: Adam's request to Seth on the right, the archangel giving Seth the oil of mercy, and finally on the left, Adam's death. There, right in the middle, is the tree for Christ's cross.'

'The tree of knowledge, especially of good and evil,' Andrew said knowingly.

'Now look at the next section, which would have been painted later to avoid being splashed from above.' Paul should have been telling them this. 'Where do you think the two pages are divided here?'

'At the column.' No stopping Andrew.

'I love the head things of the women near the pillar.' Kate looked up from feeding coins into the meter.

'While the Queen of Sheba kneels by the bridge, she realises it's made out of wood from the sacred tree.'

'Why? Who cut it down?' All three whispered, looking at the lusty tree above the queen, while I popped another biscuit into Dan's mouth.

'The man in the rich garments, Solomon...'

'Wasn't he supposed to be wise?'

'Yes, Andrew, but uninspired. The Queen of Sheba refuses to cross the stream on that piece of wood; she senses it's very special, that it'll be used for Jesus's crucifixion.' Dan seemed to be agreeing with a funny sucking noise.

'They have such wonderful clothes!' Penny was wide-eyed. 'Look at that man with a fancy hat matching his cloak. I like that.' Penny, following Piero, hankered after elegance.

Everyone except Dan was staring up at the frescoes, silently deciphering. He opened his mouth for the last biscuit.

'We have jumped ahead. Look at the man digging enthusiastically at the spot where the three crosses are buried...'

Penny interrupting, said, 'See, there's Gianni's spade; there, in the middle. The man with bare legs is leaning on it.'

'Exactly. Quite right.' The sacristan began jangling keys as he stood in the opening opposite us. Dan started to cough.

'Jerusalem is shown as Arezzo up on the left.' Sarah was busy deciphering the almost Cubist arrangement of churches and houses terraced up the hill above the man digging – with Gianni's spade – in search of the crosses.

'Look quickly at the battle scene at the bottom of the other side. After Empress Helena's son, Constantine...

'Ugggggghhhhhhh!' Dan began spewing biscuits in the direction of a white charger. The lights went out. A muffled cry from two women intent on studying the battle scene. Another group backed rapidly out, bumping into the sacristan who tripped on the step to the chancel, dropping his keys. The clang echoed ominously over the sickly smell of chewed biscuits beneath the kicking horse. Dan was chuckling at the epicentre of the pandemonium he'd caused.

'Out!' Sarah grabbed the two younger children and nodded me in the direction of Dan and his pushchair, expecting Andrew to fall in behind. As she and the two girls fled through the arch under the battle fresco, the sacristan, his retrieved keys raised in frustration, came through the opposite one to discover the cause of their rapid departure. He paused, framed for an instant in the archway; horror and disgust crossed his face, then resignation. He looked despairingly at the fair-haired Dan, smiling and gurgling angelically, his blue eyes opened wide.

'Mi dispiace tanto, tantissimo!' I held out all the change in my pocket, mortified that I had no means of clearing the mess up myself. *'Chiedo scusa.'* I bowed my head. Equally nonplussed, he stared, ignoring the money, and then turned on his heels muttering that the church was closing for lunch. Andrew lingered to watch the drama unfold, hiding behind the arch his mother had escaped through.

'Quick!' I give him a hundred lire for a candle. He sped sideways to a stack of them, slipped money into a box and returned. We were nearly halfway to the door. I handed Dan the candle, feeling it wasn't really his fault, and steered him towards a slightly neglected Madonna on the other side of the nave. The sacristan re-emerged from behind the blue-robed statue just when I was helping Dan light the candle from one already there. I started back, dropping the candle that went out in a flurry of sparks. He was carrying a pan and brush, both suspended on long handles, and a pail of water, steaming slightly, with a carefully wrung out cloth over the side. He didn't seem unfriendly; much of his face had sunk into chinfolds of flesh, making it difficult to read any reaction. A silhouette appeared at the church door.

'Are you coming?' The loud whisper shushshushed around the nave, up to the altar and into the chancel beyond. My rapid steps turned into a push chair race with invisible contenders to reach sunlight and welcome anonymity.

'What about some lunch?' Andrew prompted the adults. It was nearly one o'clock and the streets were deserted. Our choice was either to trundle back across the plain with a hot and hungry band, or hurriedly provide sandwiches and stop en-route. We left

Arezzo with fresh rolls, sliced in half and filled with contradictory orders from undecided children, to the shopkeeper's bewilderment. During the heat of the day I imagined Italian families consuming quantities of pasta washed down by the local wine and, after two further courses, wisely tottering off to darkened bedrooms. Not one impatient car was nipping the tail of overladen Mammalucca.

Thus my thoughts as we drove towards the phantom castle along deserted roads. Round a bend and it brooded over us. The children gasped. It appeared so fairy-like when we had gazed at it beyond the plain in the morning. Now it was close and threatening. We parked the car by the church and one-storey cottages clustered below. Carrying the picnic and two moth-eaten rugs, we skirted the walls under olive trees and through nettles, climbing further than we expected to reach the fortifications. There we sat and surveyed the plain, munching. Noises seemed oddly magnified: the call of a child, a shout, the revving of a motorcycle and the grumble of the first traffic stirring from afternoon lethargy. Perhaps this was another reason to build a castle on this site, not just the control of the route and the plain, but also the sound trap, like a giant's ear? We were innocently inside it.

Upon our return, Gianni was waiting anxiously for us on the roofless veranda.

It helped that our valley had never been Tim's territory. Sometimes, though, when I looked at Andrew, he faded into another child, his best friend still on the pavement outside their school. In the Arezzo church he asked and answered questions as Tim would have done, making it harder for me to forget.

CHAPTER 14

Two men alone in a landscape: one in a deck chair under a fig tree reading, thinking and writing; the other walking around the valley, easel and knapsack slung over shoulders, looking, reflecting and drawing. Paul didn't have to show us what he had done because we were clamouring to see. All the Thompson children wanted to be painted, so William half-asked Paul for a family group – his first commission. He had a way of imagining possible critical remarks: a withering 'too derivative', a kinder 'it's not surprising that old masters overawe his style – he's a restorer'.

'My way of painting is different,' Paul once explained when he was downhearted and haunted by such hypothetical comments. 'Artists are always being criticised as "unoriginal", as if novelty is all that matters. Well, my paintings may not be good enough, but they show how I feel about people and places.' I enjoyed his art, especially because it made him happier. It struck me at the time that on this particular day Gianni hadn't been around to blot his landscape.

Contracted into the Valley – August 1975

Visibly concerned, Gianni waved an envelope at me when we returned from Arezzo. He had bumped into Cecilia Ferrarini in the main square of Montesasso and she told him that the signing of the contract would be at seven that evening. There had been no advance warning.

Gianni couldn't allow us to sign it on our own. Authoritatively he made for Mammalucca, waved me into the driving seat and pulled up the one beside it to relegate Paul to the back.

Wearing an off-white trouser suit, her black hair tied back with a crimson ribbon, Cecilia Ferrarini looked less harassed than the first time we met. She was now ready to read us every monotonous detail of the legal agreement. Pasquale Panichini, the paterfamilias, sat crammed into the one armchair drawn up just that telling inch in front of the others. On his left sat his rotund and silent wife; could she speak only dialect, or could she speak at all? Their weather-chafed complexions were framed by thinning, softer grey hair worn longer now they were distancing themselves from their hard-earned, ox-tilled fields. Claudio, the elder son who had inherited his father's pomposity, was whispering to his sister. She had come especially from Pisa, smart in her Sunday best. The vast girth of her carabiniere husband underlined his professional presence but was unable to draw attention away from the most prepossessing of the lot, Pasquale's younger son. Franco was slipping humorous comments in between Cecilia Ferrarini's legal explanations. She laughed at the younger man, strands of hair curling out of the ribbon's grasp, lashes shading the corners of her eyes. She could be younger than forty, our previous estimate.

The contract specified the total price at just over half the amount agreed verbally. When I pointed this out, smiles shimmered round the legal studio affirming the collusion, and murmured grievances followed about taxes being so high that no one ever declared the price that was actually paid.

'What if one had to sell?' I worried.

'Similar arrangements. You'd still make the same profit.' We were trapped into their spiralling deceptions. No agreement on these terms, no sale, even though I had been rash enough to pay for the rebuilding and well! That was that. A painful burying of principles. Paul seemed oblivious, staying like Gianni on the periphery of the whole affair.

The documents were passed round for scrutiny. An air of smug contentment spread over the vendors contemplating the credulous foreigners foolish enough to pay a huge sum for a pile of rubble and a bit of land front and back, all comically unaware of the ruin's rapid transformation. Paul and I signed and escaped outside to buy food for the flock inhabiting the former ruin, now completely ours.

Over supper we discussed the party we were planning for our new friends in the valley to mark our first summer in residence.

Few had replied, perhaps because we didn't have a phone. Gianni had been non-committal; Ada might not be able to come, but he would ask her.

Though it had rained during the night, he arrived early as usual to poke around in his kitchen garden. He took his morning coffee with an air of urgency. It was barely seven, but late for the mushrooms. Hadn't I heard the rainfall? The first mushrooms of the season are always the tenderest. He strode up the drive, a plastic bag in each hand, with me trotting behind.

Wisps of mist were stranded on our side of the mountain while the sun was stroking away the last of the rain clouds. As we climbed to the ridge of the valley along bramble-lined tracks, I asked Gianni if we should stop to pick the berries. No. His mother had taught him to go for transient growths first: Wild asparagus in spring and mushrooms in summer, the most sought-after delicacies in nature's free feast. Blackberries can wait because they're plentiful and usually gathered by the older members of the family, being found lower in the valley and without bending. This last intrigued me, as Quinto's elderly wife is regularly propelled along the track above our house by an equally aged goat, its owner bent double under a bundle of hay which she must have scythed bending too. She also bends down to gather pinecones, shaking out the kernels that are scattered over the 'mantovana' sponge cakes – only for special occasions like Easter. Pleasure and necessity mingle in the hard struggle for survival. This, I feel, is Gianni's real education. It matters more than his basic reading and writing skills wasted through lack of use, except in letters to me.

We plunged over the ridge to the cooler north-facing side, and Gianni cried out in despair. A trampled mushroom. Others had got here first. He headed deeper into the woods, peering under the twigs and moving through undergrowth, plucking the few unnoticed by the dawn gatherers. On the way back he was more relaxed. We'd at least managed to fill one bag. After the next rainfall we had to leave at dawn. He promised he would wake me; it's clear he doesn't want Paul to come as well. Though Paul speaks more fluent Italian, Gianni likes the way I'm already picking up a few words of dialect.

Our rapid descent to the house allowed little time to discuss the evening ahead. Gianni's mood had altered. He sullenly enquired whether Carlo was coming to the party. When I told him both Carlo and Pina had been invited, he mumbled something about not being able to make it, and plodded off to his vegetable patch dragging a spade like the one in the Arezzo fresco. He had left by the time I was ready to go to the bank. The burden of providing a meal for an unpredictable number of people was weighing heavier by the minute.

I found a squeeze-in parking slot, a spare trolley, and mercifully few women to bump into at the food store in Montesasso Scalo. It was past midday and they were dutifully toiling over the main meal. I had lost my shopping list in all the haste. Ours was to be a simple, hearty, student-type party with plenty of pasta, cheese, and salad – no time to get to the open market for that – and a giant watermelon, always popular on a hot evening. Another rush to the co-operative wine cellar with the ten-litre plastic container Gianni had lent me for wine, poured reluctantly by a bored old man from a petrol-type nozzle to the amusement of any foreigner who happened to be there. A slow laden return along deserted roads to hungry family and friends. Paul had been looking after Dan while Sarah and William laid the table and put out what remained of the previous day's provisions, but I brought fresh Tuscan bread.

Sibilla and Orazio said they were coming when I dropped in at the bar. Carlo waved to me as I passed his yard on the way back from shopping. He planned to be there – presumably with his wife. Maria Pia and Renzo were engaged with relatives, but Gianni returned after lunch to announce he would accompany Ada. I was beginning to panic. What would they think of the simple fare? Paul took the car to get the largest tub of ice cream he could find.

I tried to involve Gianni in the preparations, asking if we could use some herbs from the kitchen garden he plainly regarded as his to flavour the salsa. He was reluctant to show me drying out vegetables and overgrown marrows in yellow disintegration beneath pock marked leaves.

'Needed for seeds,' he replied to my questioning glance. *There would be enough seeds in all those supine marrows for an acre-wide courgette field, but I was sad to see them dying. No more tasty courgettes, stuffed marrows, or 'flower power' as we called the flowers dipped in batter and fried. It was the children's favourite dish, which Gianni had explained how to prepare and cook, having watched Ada do it so often.*

Gianni paused before, I thought, picking the herbs for me; out of the corner of my eye, I saw his mouth protrude into a sort of snout. Turning towards him, I met his rounded lips planting a full kiss on mine.

Flabbergasted, I rejoined the others. Some nerve! He was old enough to be my father! Then I felt apprehensive, knowing how he could sulk. He was permaloso, Carlo had warned me when attempting a furtive squeeze. Prickly. We could hardly manage at the house without Gianni, but I had to cool his ardour – tactfully.

Sarah and William disappeared in Mammalucca to find more attractive additions to my menu. Andrew and Penny helped me count out plates, glasses and cutlery while I carried Dan around with me. Paul strengthened two wobbly chairs he'd bought from the rag-and-bone man and Gianni watched us moodily until he left to fetch Ada for the evening entertainment.

We were ready at half-past seven. No sign of any guests. Half an hour passed. Still no one. What was happening? Gianni and Ada arrived first with a large cake wrapped in shiny puce and silver patterned paper. Then Carlo with Pina carrying a flask of wine and a tub of ice cream, which caused a crisis in freezer space. Finally Sibilla and Orazio drove in with a huge bottle of bright green liqueur and lots of flinty, hard-boiled sweets. They eyed one another oddly, even though they had grown up together in the valley, except for Pina, the outsider from a village in the Alps. Paul poured wine and the rest of us passed round stuffed olives and crisps to accompany snippets on the weather, the grape and olive prospects and weddings coming or gone, culminating in a crescendo of scandals to a fully modulated chorus of 'ums' and 'aahs' as tongues were loosened.

Sarah piled pasta on to plates despite protestations. Italians seem to expect others to eat a quantity while they watch and wait, so it was their turn now! Sibilla looked up the valley, chuckling as she recalled the *partigiani* near her house. We leaned towards her, all ears.

'My parents lived higher up this valley. There weren't many of us around. My father began taking pans of minestrone or pasta into strange places, like the barns or stables. When I asked if I could help, I was allowed to carry the oil lamp and a loaf of bread across the muddy yard, steadying the flame to climb into the hayloft. Inside I saw two young men in tattered uniforms. They spoke strangely in undertones and jumped up when I appeared.' She opened her eyes wide to imitate them. 'They were escaped English prisoners trying to find their army. Some Italians had surprised them wandering in the mountains above us and asked my parents to help.' Sibilla knew how to hold her audience with suitable expressions and gestures.

'*Avanti!*' Go on! Hurry up! Her audience was impatient.

'My parents found old mattresses for the English soldiers. Two Italian partisans hiding from the Germans joined them. No room for four on two mattresses. My father laughed when he described how the Italians pulled the two mattresses together and lay in the centre, beckoning the English soldiers to lie on the outside of each. The wriggling started. A spasm, then a little snore from the partisans. Another wriggle. More squirming from the Italians in the centre finally edged the foreigners on to the floor on either side!' The guests roared with laughter at the Battle of the Mattresses. It seems the fugitive soldiers lay on draughty planks for the rest of that night. The Italians, refreshed and in good form the next day, confessed ignorance. Unable to argue a share of the mattresses, the English made themselves hay bunks, choosing not to fight for rights. Sibilla was clearly intrigued by these strange men, especially as her parents didn't allow her to see them, except when she was taking them food.

History had passed confusingly over their territory; partisans and escaped soldiers in the hills, armies advancing or retreating along the Cassia.

After everyone had consumed generous slices of watermelon, cigarettes were lit, coffee brewed and crickets chirped away in the moonlit night. Pina fetched a rudimentary tape-recorder from Carlo's car, and settled it on the kitchen table to blare out a selection of popular hits. Gianni's former table was lowered from the veranda to the drive; the chairs followed, then dancing. Sibilla and Orazio sat on the parapet while Paul swept Ada into a quickstep. Gianni grabbed me just before Carlo, who turned away to light up another cigarette and attempt a halting conversation with Sarah until William whisked her off. A tango came next, with three couples vying for space. This time Carlo grasped me round the waist and elbowed Gianni out. He sulked for a while, found Pina in the kitchen and whirled her on to the veranda.

The children were draped over chairs in the drive, when not in the roofless kitchen scavenging for leftovers. Dan, exhausted, lay asleep in our bedroom. Like two night owls, Sibilla and Orazio just sat and watched. The pace grew more frenzied. Carlo was pulling my hand on one side, Gianni's arm round my neck pressed down from the other. My command of Italian was severely tested in attempting to keep them both happy, and their hands decorously engaged. All this merely entertained the others. Paul was certain he had no serious rivals and that it was polite for him to dance with our female guests, if they wished. Gianni said little, but his actions spoke volumes. Carlo, instead, was the master of the provocative phrase, delivered in the most mischievous of whispers and only heard by me, but intuited by all. The rasping of the crickets, the thump of the music and the free-flowing wine followed by Sibilla's impish green liquid, soothed away tensions into the early hours of the morning. We had paid for the house and entertained our friends in the valley: the die was cast. It was our initiation, we thought, into the rites of the valley culture. We had 'made it'!

CHAPTER 15

'San Giuliano' had reverberated through my childhood. I imagined my father passionately embracing my mother in a dark wood or under a cobweb moon and whispering where he was born: San Giuliano in Tuscany. This mysterious place in Italy magnified into my favourite dreamland. I drew plans of the village, sketches of thatched houses and wells and stick versions of people or animals. I once showed them to Mother but sensed at the time that she wasn't pleased – perhaps she thought I was invading her memories of Gio (easier to say than Giovanni) and the odd way they talked in a mishmash of Italian and English, teaching each other. She laughed at my efforts and said that I had no idea of what the buildings were like in Tuscany. How could I, since I had never been there?

After she started taking me to Tuscany my dream world changed. I stopped drawing, at least on paper, but stored even more twilit scenes in my insatiable imagination. I sneaked an occasional look at my juvenile fantasies, but more often, I admit, I'd relive the story of Joan and Gio, their intimate meshing of English and Italian, their impassioned, uncompromising, war-framed love – and me, the olive branch. Mother thought his family name was Paese, until a priest told her it meant 'home town' in Italian and was rarely a surname. She couldn't find anyone who had heard of a Giovanni Paese in all the San Giulianos she visited. I never showed Paul any of my pictures, but Gran saw them. Now I had found a San Giuliano in Tuscany, I could place my father, even suppose he might have been baptised in the ancient stone font from the early Christian church, and had his first communion here, a slim, dark handsome ten-year-old – like Marco. Or Tim. It was strangely soothing to imagine them together.

from pre-war to the present, before following Don Luigi and the spaniel, Gianni and me outside. He had asked the priest to show us the church.

'Look at these doors!' Don Luigi's voice rippled in delight. 'Chestnut, cut on the slopes of Monte Amiata in the eleventh-century from descendants of trees used for Roman galleys. I love continuity; it's nature's apostolic succession.'

'Carved by local craftsmen?' Paul enquired.

'Of course! Here are the four Evangelists: lion, Saint Mark; bull, Saint Luke; the angel, Saint Matthew and, my favourite, the eagle of Saint John. Above and below them the usual Old Testament prophets: Abraham sacrificing Isaac, David dancing with his harp, and so on. The school children from across the stream love it.' He chuckled, picturing little souls gazing up at the figures as he recounted.

'I keep the doors ajar and the hinges well oiled so, just like this,' we were following him inside, 'the parishioners can bring light in their wake. It's evening now, but up here, high above the nave, creamy rays still shine through the alabaster windows to brighten our spirits. Look at our rose window above the high altar. A simple rose for the Virgin, the Queen of Heaven; beautiful tracery, with God's grace radiating through the dove.' He smiled and turned to Paul.

'You ask who painted the frescoes behind the altar. Signorelli, or school of. Our patron in those days, Cardinal Prudomini, paid for the Annunciation and a Count Prudomini commissioned the altarpiece you are admiring, signor Paolo. It's earlier, from some obscure Montesasso workshop in the late 1300s. Our other patron, San Giuliano, is there with more saints, so it must have been painted for this church, not salvaged from another on the Prudomini estate.'

Now I could ask about San Giuliano.

'So you want to hear about our saint? For centuries people here thought their San Giuliano was the one with 12 February as his feast day. Our saint's is on 12 April. The story my parishioners still prefer comes from the popular legend of the saint who killed his parents by mistake and, in expiation, helped

Folklore and Festivity – late August 1975

Don Luigi's church seemed as old and musty as the priest i[n] his long black cassock buttoned up to a dog collar. He was sittin[g] on the bench between two widows, just like the first time Giann[i] whizzed me bumpily past into his valley.

All tracks, from the chestnut woods above the olive line an[d] from the scrubland and peaks of the Apennines behind, reac[h] down into the valley to hold on to their church. All veins of th[e] valley flow into our stream, its main artery. All inhabitants cross over a rusty bridge into their earth-beaten church square. Don Luigi's habitual accompaniment of elderly ladies in black 'buona sera'-ed themselves away as Gianni bore down on their priest with us in tow. His face had rounded out, time mischievously contouring jaw and mouth; bushy ridges hid the colour and shape of his eyes, but not their sparkle.

'Saluti!' His handshake had none of the expected clerical clamminess. Gianni, Paul and I followed the diminutive priest along the side of his church and through double doors flaking green paint, to disturb a somnolent brown and white spaniel. The dog followed us up stairs into its master's study. Don Luig[i] avoided a pile of books with a landscape on the cover, handin[g] Paul one while skirting an acid pink exercise bicycle with blu[e] and russet rosaries over one handle, pausing under a bleache[d] portrait of Pope John XXIII with prayer cards and invitatio[ns] tucked randomly into the frame, before subsiding behind [a] paper strewn desk. Pushing an open bible and stray jawbone [to] one side, he excavated a large leather diary with a sigh of relie[f].

Gianni had brought us to talk about land, and he was vis[ibly] impatient throughout the desktop hunt. Don Luigi checked tha[t the] local administrator for church properties was to visit Montes[i?] the next day. He had told Don Basilio that Gianni (or Pau[l and] me) would like to buy the terraces above the stream.

'Va bene? Tomorrow afternoon?' He tipped his head to [one] side, clapped the diary shut and shot up before we eve[r sat] down, had there been empty surfaces to perch on. Paul lin[gered] over posters of religious, harvest and folklore festivals [

travellers ford a river and built a hospice for poor people – the first of many given his name.' I sensed he had to continue the story of this San Giuliano, treating us as new parishioners.

'One day Giuliano and his wife found a man almost dead with cold. They took him into their simple home, sat him down by their fireside and gave him stew from the pot hanging over the hearth. Giuliano and his wife passed that night on hard chairs by the embers while the stranger slept in their bed. The next morning their guest was up early, refreshed, glowing. Thanking them, he paused at the threshold, with the dawn coming in like a halo, and said, 'Christ has accepted your penance,' before he turned to glide through the ford without ruffling the water and disappeared round the bend'.

Don Luigi spoke with a smile, his eyes dreamily hidden as he told the tale, perhaps seeing our ford in his picture of San Giuliano and Christ in our valley.

'My imagination runs away with me! Our San Giuliano isn't nearly so exciting, just a fourth-century pope who fought the Arian heresy. He happened to be the family saint of a wealthy woman who married into the Prudomini family. But I must show you more of my church.

'Are you wondering why we have to climb steps to the altar, enough to suggest a crypt? I began poking around forty years ago. Some of my parishioners helped wielding pickaxes. I struck the first blow. It rang hollow as I suspected it would. We shone torches through the hole and squeezed down these steps to discover water in what, I found out later, was originally a small wayside church. Serpents were rippling the surface, the only sounds eerie echoes of lapping as water plopped against the walls. The capitals, each different, seemed to float with faces peering out of fronds above the sinuous shapes in the water, eyes squinting in the flash of the torches.' Even Gianni was agog. Don Luigi paused for us to sit beside him on a bench below the former water level.

'Well, the older volunteers wielding picks were soon joined by others with spades; they dug a ditch round the outside walls of the upper church apse that followed the foundations of the lower one.

The deeper we dug, the more people came to stare, especially when we reached the arches of the five slit windows and black trickles of water seeped out to wriggle like worms over the trench. Word spread. Truckloads of people with spades – and curiosity – jostled for space in the ditch; I had to organise them into gangs. Crowds gathered in anticipation of snakes leaping through the slit windows to slither up the bank and under the women's skirts – I shouldn't say this, should I? Anyway, the men were just as excited. We became briefly the main attraction in the area. It was so quiet before and, indeed, after the half-dead snakes slithered out with the last of the water.

'Here we sheltered during the air raids as the Allies bombed and marched northwards along the Cassia. We prayed on the original altar from the time the Roman Empire was crumbling and Christianity spreading outwards from early communities like this one. This is a column of Egyptian porphyry from an ancient temple on the site. Everything that could be reused, was. Not a bad rule, eh?' he said, hurrying us outside where his parishioners were gathering for evening prayers.

'This passage about Don Luigi is too long,' Paul said. What else should I cut out? I've omitted the longest feather duster in the world, six metres of gnarled bamboo canes bound together and tipped with feathers to waft across the rafters of the nave, unsettling motes into the alabaster sunbeams. Imagine the tiny Don Luigi running one way as the canes sway gracefully on a contrary path – I know, because I secretly tried it out! I've deleted the only museum in the world in a stable. Don Luigi, I reminded Paul, had opened up outbuildings on the other side of the church and shown us an amazing array of objects. It included a mammoth jaw and thigh bones, petrified jackal droppings, a votive offering in the 1940s of swaddling clothes from a young woman who had lost a baby, a wartime shell turned into a holy water stoop and the skeleton of a Roman matron with bad arthritis. I remember noting that Paul paused to look at bits of rusty metal with a lock.

'Don't let your wife see it!' warned Don Luigi, as he shook the dust off a hand-written card identifying the object as a chastity belt. The old ladies were waiting for him to say the rosary and he was fumbling for the keys to close the stable doors so his *omnium gatherum* wouldn't escape.

'I wish he'd given me a copy of that book with our landscape on the cover,' I lamented as we walked back.

'Take mine,' Paul said, handing it to me. 'It's only the work of some hack artist based on a fifteenth-century painting.'

On its bright cover are wheat fields with cypresses marking a road winding up the hillside. Inside, past figures fade indistinctly into rural scenes accompanied by poems in dialect and Don Luigi's essays in earnestly rotund Italian. Ada and Gianni, Don Luigi and the names inscribed on the war memorial outside his church: here is their youth, their history.

I shall never forget this day. The image of Don Luigi, a Saint Jerome of our times, in the company of trophies of passion, sources for meditation: skulls, primeval bones, an astrolabe, leather-bound books piled on ledges, quills, a peacock feather, curling posters, a crucifix, a learned volume packed with print open on a carved bookrest, sheets of paper with pen resting on a half-finished word in his cell, his upper room, with his emblematic spaniel at his feet.

* * * * *

There weren't many days to go before school started in September. Gianni made sure we didn't miss the appointment with Don Basilio, the ecclesiastical administrator in Montesasso. Beside him stood Dottor Riccioni, a care-worn solicitor and, Gianni whispered, the local secretary of the Christian Democrats. No chance of pulling in Cecilia, our elegant female lawyer, who is a Communist local councillor and in charge of cultural affairs. The cleric briskly signed away the little portion of land which, thirty years earlier, was a widow's mite to the local church. No discussion. Dottor Riccioni had already drafted an outline agreement. It was a small and honest sum; Don Luigi's tenant farmer had informed Don Basilio that most of the land was in the shade and the field at the top of our drive had only a few olives, some old plum trees and a solitary mulberry for silkworms. To us it was worth a few hundred pounds to keep Gianni happy. Done. Paul and I signed rapidly and put down about the same amount we had saved over the holiday, thanks to Gianni's vegetables. The rest was to be settled at Easter.

As he was gathering up the documents, Don Basilio leant over confidentially. Had we read the Gazetta? Which? I didn't realise that Montesasso has its own scholarly journal. In the most recent issue there was an article by Don Basilio. He gave us a copy (I noted it retained a quaint nineteenth-century layout), and asked for our comments. We murmured that it would be difficult, imagining the article to be ecclesiastical and out of our orbit. Not so, as we were to find out.

* * * * *

Summer was falling, days shortening and time trimmed down to essentials. We were closing up house for winter.

No invitation came to us without Gianni also turning up. On the evening before our departure he joined us outside Sergio the plumber's Montesasso palazzo. Who had told him we were invited? Perhaps Sergio himself. No sign of Ada. We entered a spacious, though cat-frequented entrance hall and dimly lit stone staircase. Smells alerted our ready appetites. Olive oil... ummm. Dan hates it. Garlic... aaah. Sarah can't digest it and few of the youngsters care for it. Sergio's son opened the door to the flat.

We were ushered into the largest room in the house, our children scrubbed silent before we left. There were traces of country scenes in a faded fresco inspired by Ovid or Virgil's Eclogues, Paul whispered, and probably by the same artist who decorated the bank. Sergio's plumbing business is prospering, and he, too, has indulged in the latest fashionable furniture. He rose proudly from the far end of a substantial black marble table, with a sideboard in the same moulded wood Ada had chosen for her dining-room suite. On it stood a large vase of artificial flowers.

We filled the table; Sarah by Sergio, Gianni next to me. No places were set for Sergio's children who titillated our palates by offering us liver paté, a mushroom concoction, caviar and spicy tomatoes all perched on mouthfuls of lightly toasted bread, before we tackled a mound of pasta served by Sergio's silent daughter. Stately, with clear-cut Giottesque features, she is best seen in profile as if serving in a fresco of the Feast at Cana.

'I don't like garlic,' Penny whispered pushing her plate away to her mother's fury.

'Nor do I,' copied Kate. I negotiated small helpings. We adults had to eat it all, or our host would consider himself dishonoured. Just fruit now, I silently begged. It was not to be.

Sergio is jovial, a man of few thoughts and even fewer words to express them, but of infinite capacity for laughter. He kept touching Sarah's knee or shoulder to make a point. Gianni beside me, visibly irritated, abandoned his knife and fork on bits of meat swimming in oil to put his arm round my shoulders – just a friendly gesture.

'I can't eat this meat. It's too oily.' Andrew looked at Gianni opposite him, not sure whether he would understand. Long past any comfortable stomach capacity, I struggled on. Sarah fiddled with her meat, trying not to imbibe all the wine poured by the attentive Sergio. A huge slice of creamy sponge cake soused in liqueur and half-chilled appeared in front of me. 'End, please end,' I pleaded silently with no one in particular. 'I Can't Eat Any More!' I gazed into the depths of the black table. Everyone else seemed to be giggling, almost gibbering, except for the son and daughter solemnly serving us. I felt queasier and queasier; the lights were fading into a murky yellow, the dim walls throbbing, and the flowers on the sideboard looming closer and closer. I was keeling over. Paul called out from the other side of the black marble. I veered back upright, drew in a deep breath, and swayed out of the room in the direction of what I hoped was the WC. Without the Giottesque daughter, I might never have found it.

It is a marvel of nature how a total vomit, disagreeable at the time, quickly restores the sufferer into circulation again. I was soon cautiously back at the table. Voices seemed muffled. Dan had nodded off on a leather armchair. The other children's heads were lolling. Sergio rose to push a tape into a worn machine, jerking everyone out of inertia with sounds of amorous gurgling.

'Lisa dagli occhi bluuuuuu... Lisa dagli occhi bluoouoou...' Blue eyed Lisa never appeared to get anywhere in words, though the tune babbled on with Sergio and Sarah moving heavily and vaguely to its beat. Would the evening ever end? William, normally one for a polite turn to music, was slumped as far as he could in his straight-backed chair and smiling benignly in an alcoholic haze. I wanted out! Gianni was determined to follow Sergio's example with a floor shuffle, though I was far too wobbly to match his movements. My delicate stomach came in as a saving excuse. I just had to rest.

'Mille grazie, Sergio, ciao, ciao, ciao... mille, mille, grazie di nuovo,' and many, many thanks to your children. They stood in the background, staring at us, the daughter upright in front of the dishes and scraps strewn over the table, her dark-lined eyes prematurely sombre. She seemed too young to have managed such a hefty feast. I stumbled back to thank her and noticed a tear on one cheek... for her mother who had abandoned them all?

Paul came to look over my shoulder while I was writing about Don Luigi and his unique medley of random objects, like mental attributes spilled over his desk and spreading up the walls of his study. When I complained, he justly reminded me, 'Well, you watch me sketching,' so I had to get used to it. He didn't want me to hold out too much hope for 'my sort of book' and be bitterly disappointed, still convinced that no one would want to read about Don Luigi or Sergio's party. I carried on despite him.

CHAPTER 16

All summer, cut off from radio and television in a rural oasis, I recall how we used to stare at Italian newspaper headlines and devoured the English ones that William had brought with him. Telegraph poles and aerials and printed columns would brief us back into the wide world with the jargon of the moment: inflation spiralling and Gran worrying about the cost of groceries; Britain plummeting into a balance of payments crisis – the macro economy looming over micro lives. We returned to it all from the Casa dell'Avventura in early September.

Whenever we entered our family home in Guildford, my first impulse was to look for Gran, while if Grandpa wasn't in the living room, Paul would quickly enquire, 'How's George?'

'He's more tranquil,' he hoped Mother or Gran would say, 'fewer of those moments,' as Gran called them. 'Considering what he went through in that terrible war, it's all we can hope for.' She had to be crisp and bustle around to avoid remembering Frank and dissolving into tears. Dan needed his tea or washing had to be hung out, and she'd hurry off hoping mother and I wouldn't notice that she could still be upset, after nearly sixty years.

In the autumn of 1975 I remember Grandpa and Paul happily poring over a book of Rembrandt's etchings. Thinking back, it makes sense. Paul had been talking about possibly restoring a Rembrandt portrait, though at the time it appeared they were mostly studying landscapes and cottages. Paul had even persuaded Grandpa to visit the local print shop where they bought frames and in the attic workshop, next to Tim's bedroom, they remounted Grandpa's much-loved pictures. These had always hung in a corner of the living room, though I'd never looked at them properly until they came downstairs in new frames. Here was the landscape of Grandpa's youth, and Frank's and Gran's, before the war that failed to end all wars: country scenes of fields and copses, of villages with thatched cottages, gardens, clipped hedges, streams swirling round pebbles and men watering horses by bridges.

About the end of January 1976, Gianni's weekly letters became agitated. Some trees had been felled on the land we were buying from the Church. Paul was anxious to return and save the poplars he had sketched and painted a 'shiver dappled green'.

'Their ancestors might have provided wood for altar panels. Most artists used it,' Paul had remarked in the summer when we were contemplating with Gianni the poplars and the dribble of water between them.

'It was cheap because poplar hardly gives out any heat,' Gianni added, 'logs for the wretched.'

Gran and Mother agreed to look after Dan over Easter so Paul and I could spend time together. We thought we'd try to recapture the years we'd never had on our own, just us without a child. Gianni wrote again, reminding us that we still owed the balance for the terraces down to the stream. I wanted to gather more material for my book, now with William's encouragement. He was intrigued by what he thought might be a new literary genre.

'Tweak your readers' curiosity, engage their fantasy and take their minds away from everyday life,' he advised. 'Make it seem as if they're there with you. It's their reality as well as yours.' William was addressing me as if I were on his creative writing course.

'Can one teach creative writing?' He laughed.

'Not really. I just give guidelines and offer practice. And encourage reading, of course.' He said I would be creating a dream for people, a different sort of armchair experience. So I returned even more eagerly to the Casa dell'Avventura that Easter.

The Fabric of Survival – Easter, April 1976

'Disastro. Succede soltanto ogni quindici anni!' Gianni was desolate, repeating 'every fifteen years' as he drove us along the edge of the plain. An unusually heavy late frost had frozen the sap, splitting the branches and killing the trees. It seemed as if a fire had swept the lower terraces of the hillsides, spitefully selecting only olive trees and turning them into charred skeletons. Higher up the slopes and along the track that flanked the hill, the terraces were

not quite so stark. Black branches gesticulated every now and then, yet most olives on the hillsides had survived.

Guido showed us the two poplars felled by the stream, one partially stripped to be cut into logs.

'Tomorrow the land will be yours. I'll come early to stop them cutting any more down,' adding after a slight pause, 'I know who it is. Claudio Panichini's brother-in-law, the carabiniere. He thinks the trees are on their land. It'll be sorted out tomorrow'.

There was a strange, almost muffled atmosphere the next morning. I threw back the shutters on my way to the bathroom: Giulio's fields were hardly visible through falling snow. The ground was already dusted white. Well, it was April and there could be a freak snowfall, even in Tuscany.

'Not as chilly as frost,' I reminded Paul, who was cold and dismayed. He had forgotten to stack logs and kindling wood in the late summer warmth.

Don Basilio's Gazetta was still perched on the mantelpiece, the home for everything interesting – to be dealt with in an undefined future. Quickly we read it. His article was an inflamed attack on, of all people, our lawyer, Cecilia Ferrarini. As cultural councillor for the Communist Comune of Montesasso, she had refuted Don Basilio's earlier claim that the most precious object in the Etruscan Museum, the rather overtly erotic Etruscan vase, was a nineteenth-century forgery! It had been found seventy-five years ago by a peasant toiling in the fields just below San Giuliano, on land belonging to the Prudomini family.

Although Don Basilio appeared rather frayed when we entered his dim office, the moment we mentioned the article his expression became adamant. Obviously the fight was still on. The official version was that the real Etruscan cemetery had not yet been accurately located.

'What rubbish! The Etruscans always sited the tombs so they could look over their ancestors into the sunset. In fact,' Don Basilio was evidently no mean scholar, 'I'm convinced San Giuliano was a prosperous village on the fringes of Montesasso's Etruscan city of the dead, producing simple votive objects for pilgrims. The men were farmers as well as craftsmen while the *women tended the kitchen garden and domestic livestock.'* How little has changed, I thought, over more than twenty centuries.

'Pilgrims flocked to shrines where the roads met on the plain during the winter and summer solstices, offering figurines as pleas or tokens of thanks. You must have seen all those tiny votive bronzes on show in our local Museum? The vase is the only one of its kind found in our area, a sophisticated work suspiciously different from all other artefacts excavated anywhere near Montesasso.' So there we were in the ex-seminary to buy land from the church, embroiled in a heated controversy.

Dottor Riccioni interrupted us, bearing an armful of legal documents through a doorway half-hidden by a wooden filing cabinet. We sat in a circle while he droned out the details of the purchase. Nothing much grew on the terraces above the stream, and there were only four olives on the strip of land at the top of our drive, also owned by the church, and not enough mature trees to make it valuable for timber. I recalled what Gianni had said about the tree cutting, glanced at him, but he evaded my look. The lawyer was at pains to stress that the amount we were about to pay was an honest sum, but a lower one was declared; the Christian Democrat solicitor was up to the same tax avoidance tricks for the Church. We signed.

Others outside were waiting to see Don Basilio. He would meet us that evening at San Giuliano for the patronal festival and answer our questions about Montesasso's saint, as well as prove his point in the forgery argument.

'Ciao! A stasera! I'll see you at the feast of San Giuliano!'

* * * * *

By afternoon only small patches of snow remained on north-facing banks. Gianni arrived, enveloped in an overcoat a size too large, when I was listing everything needed for the kitchen and Paul was sorting out the shelving. Gianni had other ideas.

He was restless and wanted me to go up the valley to find wild asparagus and early shoots that made a special spring salad with dandelions, nettles and other plants I had never heard of before. Dandelions I associated with rabbit food, nettles with *soup. Gianni explained that nettles were eaten in an omelette on the first Friday in March to ward off pneumonia and considered I had much to learn. Obediently I lowered my head as I walked, not so much in humble ignorance but to pick out the shy asparagus. Gianni was tipping leaves back with a stick to uncover plants and even snails. I was not interested in them, but he still persisted. I normally look all around at the countryside, to take everything in while he, like his Etruscan forebears, picks out food from underfoot. They probably toiled away in the little community Don Basilio described near San Giuliano, surviving through cultivation, selling wares to pilgrims and, above all, fruitfully co-existing with nature. Each feature – leaf, bud, flower, toadstool, fruit or nut, berry or bird – was a vivid stitch in the fabric of survival.*

I wonder whether he reacts to spring as I do, stimulated by the gradual reawakening of the earth in infinite gradations of green, fresher and sharper against the wet sheen of newly-turned furrows? Bright green points were freckling the umbrella pine Gianni had planted in front of our house as a guardian spirit.

The sun was now quite hot and the valley hazy with the melting snow. I rested my mind and forgot tensions in the gentleness of the contours and the changing shapes and hues as the mists moved and thinned into snippets of cloud unravelling across the plain. Gianni had found only a fistful of asparagus shoots. Too early in the year, but he was satisfied that, on the evidence, he was the first to gather them.

He disappeared soon after this expedition. To our relief, his disdain for priests ensured he would miss Don Luigi's celebration of San Giuliano's feast day.

* * * * *

It was dusk by the time Paul and I reached the small football pitch behind the church. We were late, unaware of the local poetry contest. The winner, lamentably not from San Giuliano, had just been named. A plump brown envelope, balanced on Don Luigi's anthology of poems in dialect with the landscape cover, was handed to him by Montesasso's mayor. Runners up, all men, stood around dejectedly clasping their copies. Don Luigi's tenant farmer was burning pruned olive branches on the edge of the football pitch and the excited parishioners moved towards the bonfire in fervent anticipation. Don Luigi's timeworn mother, dressed like her son in clerical black, and his plump, cheerfully dimpled housekeeper (any woman younger than forty the church considered a potential Eve) were stirring two immense bowls of batter. Belatedly I realised that all Don Luigi's parishioners had come with plate and fork. Don Basilio reassured us. Ours would be supplied, as would his, by Don Luigi's household. We were special guests. The others were probably churchgoers, but many were not and had arrived only for the feast. One never knows. Their hearts might yet be touched.

As he spoke, the largest frying pan in existence, a metre in diameter, was carried on high from the priest's house and balanced on one end of a trestle table until the flames had died down and the ashes could be raked ready for their heavy burden. It was shifted to the embers some minutes later and five donated litres of luscious local oil poured in, the aroma suspending a glistening gold savour over the assembled company. An expectant hush, filled by prayers intoned by Don Basilio, was partially drowned by the searing sound of batter poured into the frying pan. Quiet again, all mesmerised by the yellow liquid rippling outwards to the edge. The batter puffed into heavy bubbles rising and falling until speckled and ready to eat. Spurred on by tasty memories of previous years, the crowd surged forward, joking and shoving their plates, each closer than their neighbours'. Don 'Ciaccia', as our cherub-faced priest was known locally to honour his San Giuliano pancake, imperiously shooed them off. No squabbling. Children and mothers first. Don Basilio murmured tactfully in Don Luigi's ear. No, guests then mothers and children. Don 'Ciaccia' rolled up the sleeves of his cassock, raised the knife as over the lamb to be sacrificed, and leaned forward to draw a perfect diameter, intersecting it with another, then more and more spokes drawn out with precision from years of practice. I lost count of the final portions, as we were quickly served and followed Don Basilio to a bench in the church square.

It was dark and relatively quiet. The ciaccia was delicious, and the bread wiping up the oil filled any remaining cranny.

The lamp over the church door flattered Don Basilio's thin, refined features set off by his smooth brown hair hardly touched with grey. He remained silent, concentrating on some subtle thought until he had consumed his portion and wiped his plate clean. Replenished, he stood up, aware that his slender frame was shown to better advantage in a modest dark suit rather than a priest's habit, which his administrative duties excuse him from wearing.

'You've found yourselves a house in a locality criss-crossed by strange patterns of history.' Hands behind his back, head lowered, he paced to and fro in front of us with the medieval church as a backdrop.

'You asked me about our saint Jamila.' He was glad to tell us. 'She's called the Saracena, and is always depicted as dark, even black. She is said to have heard Saint Francis preaching to the Sultan in 1219 – or was it 1220? – when he went to convert the Saracens. Unable then to leave the Sultan's harem, she took her chance nearly ten years later in the confusion caused by the Holy Roman Emperor's crusade to the Holy Land. She never forgot Saint Francis, and followed Emperor Frederick II's tough Saracen mercenaries to Italy, unaware the saint had died.' He paused, to check our expressions.

'When Frederick and his army passed below Assisi near San Damiano and his Saracen troops leapt over the walls of the Convent, Jamila saw Saint Clare at a window holding a cross towards the Moors running amok in the walled orchard. She knocked desperately at the convent door and found refuge in the church. It was precisely where the miraculous cross had spoken to the future saint saying, "Francis, restore my Church!" The cross was still hanging from the chancel arch.

'Before she died in 1253, Saint Clare gathered her closest followers around her and, all according to the same source, exhorted them to establish more communities of Poor Clares. Jamila founded our hospital in Montesasso where it still occupies the original building, with additions and some modernisation,'

our friend hastened to reassure us. 'Many followed Jamila – that may not be her real name; it's Arabic for jasmine.'

We enjoyed listening to Don Basilio who looked as if he had stepped out of a dusty portrait, the handsome younger son of an impoverished noble family, destined to take holy orders. Intelligent, and always slightly irreverent, his accounts were refreshingly different from the predictable pronouncements of most clerics. Maybe that was why he had been relegated sideways into church administration, rather than moved upwards to a bishopric.

By now all had eaten. An accordion wheezed in the evening air and couples drifted to dance by the bonfire that sporadically leaped into flame, refuelled from the diminishing woodpile. A northerly wind was chilling the festivity. Mothers and children had already dispersed. Don Basilio shepherded us into Don Luigi's kitchen where his housekeeper offered appropriate vin santo and slices of dry sponge called pane degli angeli, or angels' bread, to dip into it.

As Don Basilio had been so generous with his time and explanations, I hesitated before reminding him about the Etruscan vase and the controversy raging in the pages of the Gazetta. He's not a person one can easily find for a chat, more because his duties take him all over the diocese rather than any stand-offish attitude. He does seem to like talking to us, probably because we come from outside the valley and are assumed to be impartial.

'La questione etrusca...' It intrigued me to find a Catholic priest so steeped in the culture of the Etruscans who flourished many centuries before Christ. 'Here, we're right on the site,' he resumed, 'so it's easier to explain the controversy. As you know, the Etruscans founded Montesasso in the seventh-century BC. These mysterious people were probably the first to suffer character assassination by the hand of Roman historians.' Don Basilio was warming to his theme, his eloquent speech easier to understand than the local Italian flavoured with dialect.

'Over many centuries figurines were ploughed up on Prudomini property near San Giuliano. Count Massimo Prudomini founded the museum in Montesasso and donated his

palazzo and all his ancestors' finds; other gifts followed to form the present engaging but incoherent collection – you must have visited it? The Etruscan part is by far the best. Pride of place, however, is given to the supposedly unique Etruscan vase.'

The priest accepted more vin santo, and glanced at us, wondering whether to continue. We murmured encouragement.

'Controversy flared up over a year ago. The Communist majority in the Comune of Montesasso decided to support local shops and hotels by promoting tourism. The museum was to be given a facelift to improve its elderly appearance. Scholars were dismayed. So many famous visitors had seen it thus, so why should it change?

'Clashes and counter clashes occurred in the Council Chamber, migrating to the local piazze in fine weather and into the bars in winter. To no avail. The proposed design for the new display includes an ambitious centrepiece for the vase with a mirror beneath to enable increasing numbers to admire uninhibited the superb figures ornamenting the underside. Protestations loud and long soon followed from the surviving descendants of the donor. They felt their ancestor's reputation could be debased by mass admiration – for the wrong reasons – of the finest depiction from Antiquity of fauns and nymphs joyfully copulating.' Don Basilio tried to look disapproving, unsuccessfully.

However, he was more concerned with another issue: authenticity. Though this reputedly unique survival from the Etruscan world had been found in 1901, less than a hundred metres from where we were talking, still on the Prudomini estate but bordering church property, Don Basilio was convinced it was a fake. No one had bothered much about any of the numerous figurines, rudimentary bronze animals and pottery shards that had been found near San Giuliano since the early 1700s. They were fascinating, but hardly unique and of scant commercial value.

'Following Count Massimo Prudomini's article on the important new discovery in the Montesasso Gazetta of May 1902, the vase was shown to trusted scholars. They hailed it as a *discovery comparable to that of the celebrated bronze chimera found centuries earlier in nearby Arezzo. The Pergamon Museum in Berlin offered a high price for it, as did the Metropolitan Museum, New York. Here was proof of a sophisticated workshop in the area.'* Don Basilio looked at us tellingly, and proclaimed:

'Total nonsense! Nothing new in all this. What about young Michelangelo burying his faun and breaking its tooth to trick his patron into thinking it was an antique sculpture? He'd have preferred his own work, of course, to be recognised and be properly remunerated! In our case the ruse was to enhance the Prudomini family's contribution to Etruscan studies, and through it, their Academy and their Museum, so Montesasso would bask in the reflected glory and be duly thankful!' A break, to allow us to take this all in.

'You can elaborate it all,' he invited playfully, *'since you don't have to deal with the descendants of the family as I do. Sad, but historical truth, such as we can discern it – which isn't much I suppose – is that the Prudomini estates lie on the site of an Etruscan community lacking the skills or technology to produce such a sophisticated object as this vase. Sad but true. It could of course have been brought in from a workshop in Arezzo producing vases as well as bronzes. But why here, to minor shrines associated with the routes crossing the plain and scattered tombs? Besides, visual evidence convinces me that it was made some time in the late 1800s. The abrading is minimal; the iconography virtually unknown in Etruscan art...'*

Paul was watching him closely. He always disclaims any specialist knowledge of pottery, but he spent more time looking at the vase than the paintings in Montesasso Museum. (I thought he was only interested in the subject matter!)

Less like a cherub as the evening wore on, Don Luigi was betraying signs of impatience at the way his dwelling had been taken over by a discussion he had heard so many times before. From a seat in the shadows, he murmured somewhat grumpily that it was late and there were matters to settle with Don Basilio before he left. Outside it had begun to drizzle, but we hardly *noticed as we walked up the hill homebound, treading Etruscan earth, deep in tangled thoughts.*

On the morning of the feast of San Giuliano I managed to slip away to the church square, leaving Paul staining the kitchen shelves. I hadn't yet told my mother about this San Giuliano, in order not to disturb her secret hopes. She could continue her search in her own way, her own time.

There were two Giovannis on the war memorial: Giovanni Migliorini, missing in the African campaign, 1941, and Giovanni Rupi, 1944, killed as a partisan. No Giovanni Paese. He had still to be alive. Somewhere.

I pushed the medieval lion and bull to enter and sit soothed in soft alabaster light in the church for as long as I dared. I should have been helping Paul fit out the kitchen in a myriad humdrum ways. Instead I was dreaming of a baby baptised in that font, of a slender, alert, brown-eyed child – a Marco, a Gio – and grief slid like a shroud over me as clouds dulled the sunbeams through the narrow windows. I should never imagine Tim where he hadn't been; never allow myself any fantasy of him in my plot in Italy, chattering, playing, jumping around in his jack-in-the-box way. I stood a moment looking at the rose window, blurred rainbows swirling round its hub, before turning to leave.

CHAPTER 17

From that spring onwards I came to expect a seasonal pattern of visits, planned around school holidays, to the Casa dell'Avventura. We didn't exactly exclude Mother, but she never chose to come.

Two unbroken weeks together in Montesasso at Easter, just Paul and me, were both thrilling and frustrating because I wasn't used to his careless, casual ways. I tried to get into the bathroom before he could leave his customary soapy rim round the basin, splattering toothpaste and drips all over Gianni's moss green tiles. He'd leave doors open as if he'd been born in a barn, (as Gran dryly noted) and then complain annoyingly that he felt cold. Strange the way someone immersed in the visual world was unable to put plates, cutlery or even towels back where he found them.

Most of the time he spent restlessly scrutinising trees and streams and inhabited or abandoned farmhouses before drawing them. Going through his sketchbooks with me, he explained he was thinking of rearranging them into a *capriccio*. This would not be the sort of composition painted for eighteenth-century Grand Tourists to Rome, fantasy compilations of the famous buildings and masterpieces they had visited. His would be a new invention combining trees, running water and buildings into a personal landscape of associations – visual, emotional and intellectual. All this was at an early stage, but he was sketching scenes and working out how to bring them into his composition.

In a drought when the sun has dried grass and shrunk the earth, you can scan familiar terrain from a height and discover earlier foundations, usually grazed and ploughed over and hidden. Not long before I went ahead to Italy in the summer of 1980, for no particular reason I looked at Paul eating lunch and noticed that his pattern of reactions and emotional structure had changed since Dan was born.

It had begun with quiet but insistent complaints about how child clutter was spreading all over our bedroom next to the box room where Dan still slept. More protests followed when Paul trod on Dan's toys (the ones he had made), left scattered over the floor of the living room where we ate and Grandpa sat in the corner. When Paul was in the house, if Grandpa seemed restless, he offered to keep him company and look at his pictures with him or to find him when he wandered off. Occasionally Paul complained about being taken for granted and feeling that he was expected to be 'on Grandpa duty' the moment he arrived in the house. Sometimes he asked me why I didn't 'look after myself'. Quite often, I forgot to have my hair trimmed, unconcerned because he used to like it bushy, so he could ruffle it and run his fingers through its waves. He wanted me to stay intensely present, just as he had painted me after we met: undulating flaxen hair; wistful eyes as blue as the sky in the background; nose a bit snub, almost twitching at some joke of his; dimples in a half-smile showing the tips of my teeth and a slight cleft at the point of my chin.

'Cute,' he'd say, teasing me and kissing it. He had a proper cleft in his.

He hinted that my wardrobe lacked flair. Sarah and I were finding it harder to snatch time to shop for ourselves, and I needed her to decide whether the garment looked right on me. William was always too busy and Paul disliked spending time on such activities, never offering to come or even to buy clothes for himself. I was equally irritated by holes in his sleeves or socks, and by fraying collars and cuffs.

'You're losing your "infinite variety", Olivia, and becoming over-anxious like my mother! She always went on at me, buying shirts the wrong colour and the right size or shoes the right make but wrong shape.' I silently sympathised with his mother.

'Routine is ruining your life,' he'd reiterate. I tried not to chant about children needing it, and most jobs requiring it. He could restore paintings when it suited him, as long as he completed them on time. He could go away at will, ostensibly on some errand to do with the works under restoration; I fitted round family and school on weekdays, and him at weekends, when he wasn't on one of his art-related tasks.

'I suppose it's part of your many-faceted character, Olivia, to produce not just one, but two unplanned children!' He was only half-joking, but it sent pangs deep inside me. I didn't then realise how complex and painful it was for him to find his emotional life decided without his consent. To be fair, he only once mentioned how my pregnancies had started about the time we were to spend some weeks apart, but I let it pass, recalling how supportive he had been when Tim was growing up. I always seemed too busy to interpret his underlying feelings. The grass had grown back and covered all traces of the foundations that had existed before.

I couldn't bring myself to tell him about that terrifying time in Greece. It happened so long ago, just after we met. He might have left me, seen me as tainted, despoiled. There was disquiet then but little understanding or practical help for women in my predicament. I felt somehow that it was never the right moment.

Mike had opened a gallery not far from Paul's studio in Camberwell and often appeared at Downs Way, or the Casa dell'Avventura in the summer. When Paul was asked to restore the first Rembrandt, the portrait of his son Titus, he announced to us in Guildford that, without 'outside help' (meaning Mike), he had been given the best commission ever. It was so important that he often stayed in London to work at weekends. I was glad of Mike's occasional company, and of Joe's; he often came along too. Joe was looking for work outside the capital for health reasons, and when a firm of Guildford solicitors offered him a part-time position, he settled in the sitting room we barely used. It was duly transformed, at Mother's suggestion, into his study-bedroom. She knew and liked Joe from our university days together; his rent contributed towards house repairs and he helped fill the gap left by Grandpa's increasing forgetfulness. An adult male was a welcome presence in a house full of women. Joe was a quiet type, 'keeping himself to himself,' Gran noted approvingly.

Grandpa died in his sleep late in 1979, though he had been fading away in his corner of the living room for many years. His presence remained, but Gran missed fussing over him; mother and I felt we should have found more time to talk to him as Paul had done. At the funeral, Paul gave the eulogy: he paid tribute to a hero awarded the Military Cross for having saved soldiers' lives in the terrible Battle of the Somme, where great-uncle Frank was killed. I was surprised when Paul spoke so warmly about grandfather's subtle appreciation of art and, above all, of his gift for friendship. He said their difference in age was nothing compared with their shared interests and companionship. I was proud of Paul, but grieved when I realised how little I had known my quiet grandfather.

In the spring of 1980, Paul was asked to restore a Sassetta crucifixion urgently needed for an exhibition in New York. I would take Dan, now nearly six, to Italy with me, Paul joining us later.

Cross Currents – August 1980

Quinto was still spending most days sitting on the balcony of the pale yellow farmhouse above us, his black-garbed, bowed mother having died. His wife, a handsome, wiry woman with a deeply-lined face who speaks dialect at a gallop, now tends the domestic animals: a pig with only one of the litter left; tiers of rabbit hutches and a goat and kid. Countless chickens and guinea fowl wander happily over the fields and orchards around us, being firmly fenced out of her own flourishing kitchen garden under her watchful and suspicious eyes. Gianni refers to her as the destroyer of his vegetable plot. It was certainly in a pitiful state, with chickens happily scavenging away.

Gianni was especially upset because he had flu when the moon was waning and couldn't sow his lettuce, herbs and tomatoes. He planted costly seedlings instead, only to find them pecked, with all too obvious relish. I insisted on refunding him, though it was too late in the season to replace them. Ignorant of chicken lore, I decided to mention the poultry problem during one of my occasional conversations with the solitary Quinto. Unsurprisingly Gianni didn't seem to be on speaking terms with the family.

Perched precariously on a plain wooden chair, Quinto's shoulders and thighs were unsupported as they rounded into balcony space. Not an easy person to converse with, he was given to monologues spiced here and there with dialect and peppery opinions. He told me I should pay Gianni properly for all the time he spent building and tending my property. None of your business, I thought, knowing that Gianni came when he felt like it, not when asked. So, in reply, I mentioned chickens. His wife dealt with them, but he'd convey my concern. To change the subject, I asked what he thought of the current rash of kidnapping, ransoms and the Bologna bomb.

'*Forestieri!*' All done by foreigners! I hesitated (not a very tactful reply to a foreigner sitting right next to him) before asking him which foreigners might be guilty.

'*Meridionali.*' Southern Italians – so he sees them as '*foreigners*'? He went on a bit about the Brigata Rossa ruining Italy; another Mussolini was needed for law and order...

Quinto ignored Dan staring, as children can without being rude, at the big funny man almost falling off his seat. Before leaving with my now fidgety son, I asked about his arthritis.

'*Bad,*' but he had hope at last. Some admirer had presented a '*santa*' with valueless land in the mountains behind Montesasso; in no time she attracted a devoted band of followers.

'Why is this faith healer so popular?'

'She had a vision and now coach-loads come to be healed in the name of the Virgin. I planned to go there for my arthritis. But then her followers began fervent chants which could be heard amplified for kilometres across the valleys, until some foreigners from a nearby farmhouse shot the loudspeakers to pieces!' He looked concerned, but with a flicker of a smile. 'I thought it better to try elsewhere. A male healer based in Rimini has had wonderful results. My son has met a cripple he cured.' So Quinto is saving to go to Rimini, with Mauro's help.

'You earn more on a building site than on the land, even if you own it,' Quinto reckoned, referring to his son, 'but it's more drudgery than farmwork'.

'More regular pay and hours,' I suggested, 'and no animals to feed'. He reminded me that his wife fed the livestock.

Gianni was prickly when I told him they'd agreed to keep their hens out of his vegetable patch. He resents any time I spend with others in the valley, but refuses to go with me to see Quinto. He has his pride, he informs me. He has been '*offeso*' by Quinto; that's the word so often used around Montesasso, probably to do with a code of honour. Whatever you do, avoid making anyone feel *offeso*, or you'll be in trouble!

In Paul's absence, Gianni was taking command of his adoptive family. We were to have lunch with him. It's amazing the speed his tiny car can achieve when Gianni is hungry. Outside his house he shouted and rang the doorbell simultaneously.

Ada was slightly surprised to see us, and had a skittish air about her. In the background a familiar figure was lounging in the only armchair in the kitchen: Gianni's boss, now the supervisor of all road maintenance staff in the Town Council of Montesasso. Gianni was visibly proud of the visit; Ada even more so as the boss had brought a large radio cassette player for her birthday. We sat down to the meal, Alberto joining us a few minutes later. Amid the fuss over a young child and a teenager, the boss was talking about his son, when he was Dan's age, and I was looking at everyone round the table. Gianni is lightly built, even wiry, a shape he's anxious to maintain; his smoking helps cut his appetite, already minuscule. His boss is thickset, eats well, but doesn't smoke. Ada is smallish and not heavy-boned. Alberto is stocky, always hungry and has a wide face and strong jaw. Gianni has hinted that local government jobs such as theirs are often passed from father to son. His boss might strengthen the tradition.

After the meal Gianni took Dan and me up to the attic. In his letters he had described how Ada obliged him to transfer the living room fireplace two floors up to this rooftop den. She objected to the smoke and ashes and even to the rough stone fireplace – it took up too much space. A pile of my letters lay on a small table next to a brown paper parcel, which Gianni handed to me. I smiled at him, eyebrows raised, wondering whether to open it. He nodded. Inside were two medium-sized frames backed with brown paper. I turned one over and gazed in horror at the photo I kept in my bag for bus or train passes, grossly enlarged. In the other identical frame was Gianni from the wedding photo next to Ada's. I willed it to be still hanging in their living room under the crucifix with the dusty olive twig. Closing my eyes to control any expression of horror and fearing that Ada might have noticed its absence for this copy to be made, I groped for some neutral expression not to offend or nurture his fantasy. Dan was busy murmuring to himself over some Italian comics.

As I faltered, head hung over the photos and my letters, Gianni edged up to ask if I liked the gift and attempt a swift, sideways kiss. He quickly re-wrapped the photos, carrying them out for me into his car and later depositing them inside the Casa dell'Avventura. Where did he think I could put them? Over our bed? In my study at home? Or was I to hide them away, for furtive contemplation?

* * * * *

Sarah, William and their children arrived in early August. They had phoned Paul to find out his plans, but he still had to finish the Sassetta triptych; the final varnishes were taking a long time to dry. He would have called me if we had a telephone. When I spoke to him from Orazio's bar, Paul said he intended to join us as soon as he could, but was clearly worried about the meeting the deadline.

With the heat and the hair washing, not to mention the volume of clothes just to be 'rinsed through', the twenty-metre well might run dry. The pump could expire in a spiteful gush of oil, polluting the water. Gianni had insisted on a padlock, reminding me that one way to avenge wrongs was to poison the enemy's well. He feared Quinto felt offeso and anticipated his family's revenge. So did I. They appeared distinctly hostile.

We peered into the well. No glint of water. William made a plumb line with a spoon on the end of a large ball of string. Down and down and down... out of the corner of my eye I saw Gianni advancing on us with a hosepipe spurting a jet of water in the air. He must have turned on the pump he'd installed in the stream (at our expense) to revive his vegetable plot, the geraniums, our guardian pine, and cypresses along the drive. Was he going to replenish the well with stream water of unknown impurities imbibed during its journey from above Oreste's house? I dashed towards him, arms raised, yelling for William to turn off the electricity in the garage. Dropping the hose to gush, then splutter *silent, Gianni too raised his arms, before swooping to hug and pull me into a series of kisses – neck, ear, cheek, lips, anywhere he could get to in seconds. Retreating, I tripped over Dan in the sandpit, who burst into tears. The clash of intentions was solved by William's return from the garage. Gianni hurriedly bent to pick up the abandoned hose as if nothing had happened.*

Our lunch was an oasis of calm. Gianni had left punctually for his. The drama subsided, dispelled by a perfect day of unremitting sunshine and cicadas and the still silence of the spaghetti hour.

Discussion was cut short by a car skidding to a standstill on the gravel in front of us. The portly carabiniere and his brother-in-law, Gianni's cousin Claudio, got out with no more than a grunt to us on the veranda, marched over to the top of the ruined mill and looked down. Were they calculating the number of stones Gianni had removed to build our kitchen? They returned to the car to fetch a roll of wire, a hammer, and a couple of posts.

We couldn't believe it! There, right under our eyes, they were wiring up the only way to reach our three terraces down to the stream. No one can bar access to land owned by someone else. They must have known this, but their abrupt parting remark was to the effect that the wire barrier would remind us they owned the mill as well as a narrow strip joining it to their olive grove opposite the veranda.

The sun seemed to darken, the sky to turn a deeper, more threatening blue, and the cicadas sounded dissonant for the first time. I felt distinctly out of tune with my surroundings. It might be better to have a siesta and leave the plates soaking, to be washed up later. The children drifted off, not chirpily. Sarah, William and I remained alone. Glumly we reviewed the consequences of the wiring. It could be the tip of the iceberg. We were intruders, after all, even if we had restored a derelict house that no one else wanted. There'd been general amusement at the crazy foreigners who wanted such a hopeless place. Now the age-old rites of property had been enacted before our eyes.

Gianni arrived during the siesta as usual. He was angry about the wire, quick to note it was mainly directed at him for expropriating the stones. He sulked around his kitchen garden kicking stones, pulling a dead leaf or flower, and smoking. William chaperoned me to Gianni's patch. I needed guidance on how we could reach our terraces and the steam. William's presence solved one problem, but the wires provided another. Had Gianni any suggestions? He snorted and moved off. Not long afterwards we heard him revving noisily over the gravel, offeso.

After Gianni left, Sarah disappeared behind the house to sort out the marrow situation. So many were left yellowing on the stems that the plants were giving up production to lie down and die, in spite of all our watering. He said he needed them for seeds. Kate and Dan were enthusiastically removing the yellowing ones for 50 lire each to pile them in front of the wire barrier as a reproach. Andrew and Penny were too superior to join in, though they enjoyed playing games with the discarded marrows. Cameras were pulled out and adults took part with more risqué gestures.

I went to Carlo and Pina for advice. Impossible just to ask them what to do – ignore the wire or pull it down? – and return, so I accepted a drink. Carlo wanted to know if I thought Gianni should be told. What about? Alberto. I tried to look puzzled. Pina broke in with her kind, hesitant voice.

'Non è suo.' Alberto is not his son. Should he be told? After all, he behaves as if he is. I told them Gianni had been quite frank with me about his surprise when Alberto was born. Their employers allowed Ada to work with one child, but not two.

'It cost him the job he really enjoyed, working with her at the villa. Alberto's almost seventeen now. Gianni's fond of him. Why tear a family to pieces? I really don't think blood, in this situation, is thicker than water.' They agreed.

I recalled Gianni describing how Ada had witnessed him seduce a girl in the long grass. It was when they both had leave from their employment at the villa to help at harvest time in the valley. I didn't tell Carlo and Pina. They were working in Switzerland at the time, and might not have heard anything. Better not to complicate matters.

As for the wire fence, Carlo advised us to tread on it every time we legally stepped over to reach our land by the stream. Eventually, remove it!

We felt slightly less threatened by the valley culture as we sipped cool drinks and watched the sun setting from the mill table under our guardian pine. Water was being heated for the evening pasta and the first bats, like silent swallows, were swooping overhead. The moon was rising to spread a furry, yellow-grey light over the mill table, across the ruin and on to the crickets in the fields below, lingering late into the night.

Two days later Paul arrived unannounced in a taxi protesting he had written, but post took so long and anyway, there was no phone. It happened that I had decided to stay behind with Dan and let the others take Mammalucca to Florence, so he was lucky to find someone at the Casa dell'Avventura. On our own it was easier for him to explain the trouble he'd had restoring the landscape behind the Sassetta crucifixion. There was a lot of paint loss and much technical and art historical disagreement among the museum advisors over the amount of reversible touching up allowed. Great care and much time was needed, but the exhibition organisers in the U.S., who were funding the restoration, had turned unpleasant. It unnerved him, as he knew only too well that the triptych was needed by autumn at the latest. He wanted to shrug it out of his mind. He had come out to Italy as soon as he could.

'I'll help with Dan,' he added, 'to give you a proper break'. At last he had come! So we got on with meal preparations. Sarah and William had insisted we were not to wait for them as they might have a pizza in Florence and return late.

Dan was missing Kate, talking to himself in the sandpit. Paul brought a chilled bottle of Orvieto wine to the mill table as the sun began to sink and Monte Amiata appeared brushed sunset pink from behind veil after veil of heat haze. The bats reminded him of the ones that frightened him as a child in the ruin he called his 'House Beautiful'. Sounds of a vehicle crunching the gravel. A blue car braked in front of us and Gianni stepped out, ruffling Dan's hair with one hand, the other hesitating before holding out *printed forms and a box of chocolates as a peace offering. He didn't expect to see Paul.*

'I'm having my telephone installed. You must fill in these if you want one too. A domani.' So he would return as normal the following day.

He started backing into Claudio Panichini's olive grove before turning up the drive. Wheels were racing deep in gravel, dust and grit spraying us buff. Paul slipped planks under the rear wheels and the Fiat lurched forward, only to fall back and hit the post holding up the carabiniere's wire fence. Reversing a second time into the olive grove, it narrowly missed a tree. The fence – well, that hardly mattered – but an olive tree... no! Again a whirr as the wheels flayed the gravel. Gianni turned off the engine and poked his head out in surprise. Paul went to see what he could do and returned grinning; the wheels had been mashing up the marrows, now in a churned yellow mess all over the back of Gianni's car as if it had bowel trouble! By that time we were in hysterics and even Gianni was half-smiling. Paul hosed down the back of the vehicle and, again with the help of planks, Bluebottle belatedly buzzed off, much to our relief. Best of all, one post holding up the wire barrier had been pushed down; Paul pulled out the other.

* * * * *

Paul, Dan and I spent the rest of the summer with our friends in pleasurable rural pursuits, like gathering firewood, trimming the vines and watering the geraniums. Gianni had decided he would build us a barbecue, and pushed a wheelbarrow over our terraces by the stream looking for suitable stones. He was careful not to approach the mill ruin. As I watched him, I remembered what he had told me of his childhood, of thrift in the countryside and the unbroken toil to subsist, going right back to the Etruscans. My thoughts wandered into his tapestry of the four seasons, each strand of rural husbandry woven into the fabric of survival under the phases of the moon. Not the grand visual drama of the plain and mountains, but the intimate everyday consciousness of a valley. Gianni's.

Paul had arrived so much later than expected. With no phone, I'd been edgy, expecting him every day, any time. I felt so strongly then that he should have been protecting me from those Gianni 'incidents'. When I showed him the Gianni-Olivia diptych, he laughed and wondered what on earth I would do with these embarrassing photos. He was the one to wrap them up and put them in a 'safe place' where they were sure to be lost.

CHAPTER 18

Holidays are when loners want company. Paul relaxed in the hammock he took so much trouble to bring from London, watching the poplar leaves trembling shine and shade patterns against changing depths of blue. He sketched and painted scenes to patch into his landscape *capriccio* and played with Dan when he felt like it, drawing him almost as often as he had Tim.

Dan was still fair like me. Like me too, he didn't take to crayons or paint. Tim had started with bun and raisin faces on scarecrow figures, later bursting into aircraft battles and blazing tanks. Older, he added houses, trees, hills and I remember him, his hair darker, painting with his father, side by side in a hum of concentration on our last holiday together.

'Who's that boy?' I had taken such care to conceal Tim's pictures and Paul's sketches of him in the loft, but still feared Dan would see the photo of Paul, Tim and me that I hadn't the heart, or the right to hide: Gran's copy in her photographic shrine, and Paul's. Dan was pointing to the mantelpiece in his London studio. I could pretend – your cousin who's gone to Australia.

'Who is he, Mummy?' Dan had started school and his friends had brothers and sisters, like Kate. Paul moved uncomfortably back to his easel and left Dan to me.

I could have sat him down there with the photo and told him straight; or taken him out to a nearby park to fly his new kite, part-telling him while distracted of the brother he never could know, of the spirit whose room he was inhabiting, of the absence.

'You see, I have Tim here.' Instead it was Gran who, cuddling Dan, pointed to her photo. 'Your father, mother and Tim, your brother, looking out at us.'

'Where is he?' I heard but couldn't answer.

'In a café at the seaside.' Gran hugged him closer.

'I mean now?' Dan was right to repeat it, but there isn't an answer. In heaven. Where is heaven? He is dead. Where has he gone? There are no convenient stork images for the end of life.

'How old is he?' Old the second we are born, our one-way journey. Gran picked up Frank's photo, placing it next to ours. Here in this room where I am writing, she recounted his death and Tim's and the futility of loss that nothing she or Dan's grandmother or his mother or father could prevent. Dan's eyes were large pools of blue darkening into incomprehension. That day he started his journey out of childhood.

Paul never exactly cast me, like Sarah, as an 'earth mother'. However, in the family tradition, I was supporting myself and responsible for Dan. We paid the same amount each month into a joint account to cover Tim's, and then Dan's expenses, maintenance for the Casa dell'Avventura (the capital outlay we had shared) and our travel to Italy. It was assumed that I kept the accounts, and therefore it was easier for me to book and pay for tickets and house bills. He was carefree about such mundane matters, taking it for granted I could find money for the ingenious things he planned to do with me from our infinitely elastic joint account. I had a regular income; his fluctuated.

So I almost stopped writing the new sort of book that no one was likely to read. I still jotted down what was going on around me in the summer when the others were reading after lunch and Paul was half-asleep, sketching pad on chest, in his hammock. Scribbling anywhere, usually down by the stream. Not every day. At odd moments furtively going over it, adding, polishing, deleting.

After restoring Rembrandt's son Titus, Paul was overwhelmed with work, accepting most of it for fear of not having enough. Then came another Rembrandt commission – a self-portrait. He was, of course, pleased to be asked but couldn't – or wouldn't – tell me why he was strangely disturbed. He had always been painfully honest. I was more reserved, never wanting to tell him, or my family, what I feared might upset them. For years I had wanted to tell him about my misfortune, especially now that it couldn't harm anyone else. But I never seemed able to find the right moment. Only at the Casa dell'Avventura, from then onwards, did we really have any time together.

I was promoted to deputy head with an increased workload and helped my mother, now chief librarian, with Gran. When Grandpa died she stopped making us all healthy sandwiches. One night, disturbed by my own nightmare of lying alone in a small boat buffeted by a tempest, I woke to hear Gran call for him, still half asleep. She retreated into herself, silently pining. Soon afterwards Mother decided that all four of us, including Dan, should go to France during the spring half term break and see the monument commemorating the Battle of the Somme. It is where her brother Frank, in name only, remains forever.

Sarah was concerned about Paul; he was overworked and should take a break. She would have Dan to stay over the coming Easter. It was really to let us be alone together.

Rich textures – Easter 1981

Down in the hamlet of San Giuliano the early Christians had left their mark, and Don Luigi clearly wanted to leave his. On Good Friday the valley echoed to celestial choirs amplified by loudspeakers on the church roof. Other recorded sounds included chiming bells, a female solo wavering through Gounoud's Ave Maria followed by what seemed like holy pop ending in an earburst of Saint Peter's bells. Was this Don Luigi's way of bringing good tidings to the valley unfaithful, or to make them feel guilty? Paul and I were busy together, putting the food in the kitchen and crouching close to light the fire with slightly damp wood, using bellows to coax the flames.

'There must be a procession,' he said, brown eyes wide, years sliding away. 'Let's go and see what's happening.' So the fire was stoked, the pasta turned off to go soggy, and we pulled on heavy shoes and jackets. Up the drive, left past Quinto's and Maria Pia's, down the slope, where daffodils gleamed in the dusk by Marco's shrine, past the washing area by the ford, up again to meet others rallying to the sounds. At the crossing of tracks we joined a group of thirty or so contadini, each carrying a candle, clustered round Don Luigi who was poking a match at an oil lamp. It was the shrine at the crossroads where age-old grievances had been settled. A hesitant flame lit up a small statue of Saint Jamila set in the corner of a retaining wall and the

attentive faces around the priest. He moved his flock along the track that wound up the valley to our builder Massimo's house, chanting in an unvaried combination of five easy-to-follow notes. I reckoned it would take all of an hour to reach it, if that was his intention. A small figure turned towards me; Maria Pia always seemed to be watching you, smiling with intense concentration, ever friendly and helpful – a comforting presence. They had fifteen shrines, she whispered, to bless and light lamps in, all in the lower part of the valley; twelve had already been lit. We chanted our way onwards, up tracks and along ridges I never knew existed, to find long neglected Madonnas in dire need of Don Luigi's loving attention.

Gianni worked right up to Easter and only came to see us on warm afternoons. His daughter was coming with her new boyfriend, so he stayed in Montessasso to see them.

We passed San Giuliano on Easter Monday on our way down to see if Sibilla would open up the store; we had run out of milk and coffee. Don Luigi was showing two visitors a new mosaic, set above the medieval door, of San Giuliano blessing the square in front of him. He called us over to introduce the current Count Prudomini and his wife, adding that they had given the mosaic to the church.

'What do you think of it, signor Paolo?' The priest listened to Paul's tactful comments before inviting us into his house. Over vin santo and sponge fingers, Rinaldo Prudomini said he had heard from Don Basilio that we were interested in his family's art collection and invited us to his villa the following morning.

Villa Prudomini lies on the other side of Montesasso, beyond Porta San Domenico where Saint Jamila entered the city. We walked along the cypress-lined road to arrive promptly at eleven, stopping at a door with a bell pull. Not a soul visible. The dusty white villa with its chapel and outbuildings had the flat geometric look of a Cubist painting, the same air of suspension, unexpectedly snapped by a terse, 'Volete?' A woman stuck her head out of a window in the building next to the chapel.

'Il conte is expecting us.' The head disappeared. Another long wait. Then, with noise of bolts slowly drawn back, the door

opened and an elderly man in overalls led us over a courtyard to the front door.

Early in the fifteenth-century, the Count later told us, the Prudomini family had followed the Medici example and shrewdly invested in land round a fortified farmhouse near Montesasso. By the end of the fifteenth-century the castle-like building with its watchtower was outmoded. The family prospered under the first Prudomini cardinal,. who extended the property into a handsome country dwelling. The Prudomini line was honoured by further cardinals in later centuries though, regretfully, no pope.

By the 1520s both the entrance hall and the salone were frescoed. Paul looked closely, but discreetly, at the hunting scene prancing through the entrance hall with horses led and ridden by resplendent youths in motley hose and doublets striped russet, ultramarine or mossy green alternating with cream or yellow. They were all progressing through a landscape of rounded hills that dissolved into the airy blues and greys of the distant Apennines. Clumps and receding rows of sparsely leafed poplars on the brink of autumn gold shimmered in silhouette against the mountains and misty sky. Intensely green cypresses punctuated the frescoed Prudomini avenue, their long trunks with branches bunching out to taper elegantly, swaying in the gentle breezes of pastoral delight.

The adjacent salone proclaimed the joys of music and song in fragrant rose bowers, reaching a crescendo in the dining room with scenes of bacchanalian delight. Tables arrayed with food and flowers were spread before the count's ancestors, served by fauns and satyrs. Even the cardinal was present, Rinaldo Prudomini pointed out with a punctiliousness that amused Paul.

'Scholars are fascinated by my frescoes, but they're in dire need of conservation, which is costly,' the Count remarked to Paul, who remained silent. He didn't restore frescoes.

'Have you seen the ones at the Medici villa, Poggio a Caiano? Our family cardinal didn't want to be upstaged by his friend, the Medici pope Leo X, and was more prudent.' He checked to see if we looked interested. Listening faces reveal more than they realise. 'Cardinal Prudomini frescoed more rooms than

Leo X by employing a less famous local master to depict pleasant, unprovocative scenes, at least in the politics of the times,' the Count hastened to add. He lamented the cost of maintaining artistic treasures, but resisted opening his house to the public for fear of attracting burglars (or income tax inspectors, as Cecilia Ferrarini subsequently enlightened us).

We sampled the Prudomini's own white wine standing beneath the heraldic crest, a stumpy figure trampling a tortoise, carved into a fifteenth-century stone fireplace. The Count sighed over all the properties the family had and could no longer afford to keep. It was all he and the Countess could do to manage this huge place. They had a daughter, married with small children, but the name would die out unless their grandson adopted it, as he hoped. At that point his wife appeared. Would we care to stay to lunch? How kind. Yes, we would.

The Count invited Paul into his library to talk about fresco restoration, leaving me to wander through adjacent rooms and admire the furniture and fittings. The paintings were mainly indifferent family portraits, unlabelled as it was assumed everyone knew who they were. The carved wooden chairs and tasselled cushions could be sixteenth-century originals or nineteenth-century imitations, difficult to distinguish, all equally worm-eaten and worn. The crimson velvet curtains were striped by sunbeams slipping through the shutters to spotlight dust in heavy folds. The marble inlay on the drawers of a cabinet set me day-dreaming of grey mountains, pearly depths of lakes and the blasted shapes of trees. Equally compelling, huge parchment estate maps hanging in the archive room traced the gradual collapse of the Etruscan and Roman drainage systems, returning the ancient agricultural pattern of the plain to swamps. I recalled Leonardo's map in the tourist office of those straggling blue waters and the shivering spectre of malaria they evoked.

'E pronto!' We were summoned into the vaulted dining room where four places were laid at one end of a vast table beneath the frescoed Cardinal and entourage. The Count's ponderous, kindly aspect – average height, well-built without being stocky though tending to the fleshiness of advancing years – matches the dark,

weighty furniture. In contrast the Countess is spare in build, sprightly in character, fairish and competent. She had prepared the meal herself, doubling the amounts to four: hot broth with the abstract trails of an egg; veal lightly fried in breadcrumbs with spring cabbage and Tuscan bread, followed by cheese with apples and pears, slightly wrinkled from their winter storage. She apologised. No asparagus. It was late because of the cold snap. Did we mind? Of course not, enjoying as we did the wholesome, uncomplicated nature of the meal.

The Count doesn't seem to be offended by Don Basilio's assertion that the important Etruscan vase is a forgery. Nor does he appear to be in the solicitor Ferrarini's camp, probably because she's part of the Communist majority in Montesasso. Politically, with almost a pope and lots of cardinals in his blood, the Count could only be a Christian Democrat, along with Don Basilio. That's how the serried ranks of the Church are instructed to vote; in their turn from the pulpit they instruct the faithful to do likewise.

It was only after asking the Count if he could take some pictures of the frescoes, that Paul realised he had forgotten his camera.

On the way back we dropped in at Sibilla's general store to pick up a few oddments and found it crowded as ever. The bar and shop are the focal point of the San Giuliano parish. Need refreshment? They have a wide variety of drinks in the bar. Need butane gas replacement, the cheapest way to cook or heat? Orazio will deliver it free of charge. Need pasta, fruit, vegetables, cheese, ham...? Sibilla will dispense them even out of hours from her throne-like platform behind the counter – she never descends. Whatever is required from the space occupied by her expectant customers, she wheedles them to get for themselves. Thus she preserves her choice commercial aura. But that afternoon the suitor-clients – with more men in a general store than I have ever seen anywhere else in Italy – seemed tense. At the counter Roberta, Giulio's wife, was muttering something.

Sibilla, pirouetting behind the illuminated cheeses, ham and salamis, shook her shoulders and asked, 'Come va questo mio *vestito nuovo?'* What did her admirers think of Sibilla's new dress? Murmurs of appreciation from the male audience – find a man who can resist colourful flounces and furbelows, rippling in rainbow hues against a crisp white background! Sibilla smiled and tossed her dark, shoulder-length curls. Orazio was hardly a typical Italian husband. Either oblivious or dominated, he was safely out of the way tending to his bar customers.

'Sembri una zingara!' You look just like a gipsy, Roberta hurled provocatively, facing the client-admirers. An unfeminine growl forced itself through Sibilla's gritted teeth. Disbelief momentarily paralysed the onlookers as, quicker than anyone could see or think, Sibilla descended to the shop floor, put her knee into Roberta's back to pull her down by her hair and kick her on to the floor. Orazio was glimpsed peeping through the connecting door, and disappearing as quickly. In the uproar the two were separated and Roberta, restored to her feet, heaved and snorted in anger. She was accompanied outside and propelled in the direction of Giulio's farm without whatever she set out to buy. A subdued atmosphere returned as the diminutive Sibilla resumed her height of authority behind the counter to ask, *'A chi tocca?'* Who next?

Somewhat shaken, we returned up the valley with our loaf and salami for a quiet evening together by the log fire. At the bend where I had first glimpsed the ruin, Giulio's son, Antonio, stood holding something with a strap hanging down. He dropped it, scowled and picked up stones to throw after Mammalucca. We accelerated past uneasily. Paul unlocked the main door and disappeared, abandoning me to carry in the stores. He reappeared worried. He couldn't find the camera.

So easy to do. Paul must have left it on the table in the veranda while fetching something from the garage. Seeing us drive away, Antonio returned to prowl around his childhood haunt. I was reluctant to ask him about the camera, but Paul was too angry and insisted a woman could explain things more tactfully.

Antonio was sitting outside the barn, whittling away at a stick with the camera case on the ground beside him. He was startled when we loomed out of the dusk and jumped up defensively, kicking the leather object behind him. Paul slipped round to grab the empty case.

'Where's the camera?'

'Non so niente.' I don't know anything about it. He held his fist out, trying to push it defiantly under my chin before I stepped backwards and retreated round the corner of the dilapidated farmhouse. Paul was already pounding back along the track barely controlling his fury and frustration. Darkness and silence only exacerbated him more. We ate pasta with ready-made pesto sauce in silence. Blood red Sicilian oranges finished the brooding meal.

On his way down to the stream the next day, Gianni noticed a black object, then another, smaller, and sensed the worst. He returned to call Paul. His camera was strewn across the grass with the film exposed in ringlets to the morning sun.

'Report Antonio to the police,' Gianni advised without any hesitation. 'He's filched things before.' The rest of the day we discussed what to do. Paul and I didn't want to tell Carlo and Pina or anyone else, as they all lived in the same valley. It would be better, Paul thought, to confront Antonio's family with the broken camera and spooled-out film after Gianni had left. We did.

Giulio, his parents, Roberta and their son were sitting round the table having supper. Roberta and Antonio shouted unintelligible words at us, and stalked out of the room. Giulio looked up, worried.

'Antonio has ruined Paul's camera. It needs replacing, for his work.' They appeared unconvinced. Giulio's father asked how much it cost. It was expensive; what could I say? Paul held out the remains of the camera and pointed to the model and number, but they didn't even glance at it.

Why hadn't we understood earlier? All, with the possible exception of the culprit who had deserted the scene, were illiterate. I began writing down the details in my notebook and tore the page out for them, rapidly trying to back-pedal. The grandfather said he would try the local camera shop. The acrid *chill of the deeply offesi pervaded us as we returned in the dark, dejected and depressed.*

First we had offended Quinto and family trying to keep their scavenging chickens away, and probably Maria Pia and Renzo next door out of solidarity. Now we had offended our other near neighbours, Giulio and family. We felt wronged; as a result we would be ostracised. At least Carlo and Pina, we hoped, were still our friends.

Most evenings I wrote notes for my book by the dying fire when Paul was in the bathroom or had gone to bed, wary of doing it while he was around. He was too good at comments that, he thought, would prevent me being hurt or disappointed. For instance, I needed to relax and not worry about my writing. I was becoming much more prosaic, he thought. No longer like the diamond necklace he had given me long ago. Dulled, the few facets that remained. He was at time nervous, irritable, unresponsive and didn't follow up Rinaldo Prudomini's request for advice about restoring his frescoes. He could have been an intermediary, providing details of Ridolfi's studio in Florence. Paul might not restore fresco, but there were sufficient paintings and statues and carvings in the Prudomini palazzo to keep him in work for a decade, circumstances and money permitting. Something was worrying him. Things weren't coming together; he had to leave; he had to return to work. He just couldn't cope with our neighbours.

CHAPTER 19

Joe was ill when Paul and I returned from Montesasso after Easter 1981. His sister was staying to give moral support and drive him more or less daily to be monitored at the acute cardiac unit.

'Joe's trouble is a genetic defect,' she explained, 'they call it a hole in the heart. It's been a problem since he was a child, but please, we want you to carry on as normal.' I don't remember much about the months that followed whilst Joe was on the waiting list for surgery, except that Paul was outwardly the same, overworking and worried about Joe like the rest of us. Mike would often visit Joe, his best friend from school.

Oddly enough, Mike never invited us to his flat, though he had been visiting me at Guildford ever since we all met at university. I would see him at his gallery, more rarely at Paul's studio or flat, but most often at Downs Way. He was both mischievous and mysterious, eyes crinkling as he smiled while showing us the endless bits and pieces he'd cannily picked up, confident that they would increase in value. He revealed little about his own life, apart from casual remarks about people he'd encountered – for example, Angélique, his collaborator, was 'luscious'. How did he describe me to other people?

It helps, everyone is told, to share our anxiety and distress. Not with Mike. With Joe, perhaps? I should have confided in Sarah, but when I returned from Greece she was too busy setting up house and joyfully expecting Andrew. I felt so crumpled and disgusted that I kept it all to myself.

I desperately wonder still whether I should have told Paul what happened in Greece the first summer after we fell in love, but I was afraid of his reactions – half submerged, uncontrollable, even unacknowledged. And I was expecting Tim. Our time together was always so special before he was born that we embraced the moments and shared everything – almost everything.

It's so easy to be wise with hindsight. Of course I chose the wrong moment and should have realised how worried he was about restoring the works by Rembrandt, but I thought that, as seven years had passed since Tim's death, Paul ought to know what had happened so long ago. We were alone in the house, undisturbed. Dan was playing with friends in the garden; Joe's sister had taken him out for a drive while Mother and Gran were visiting a family friend. I had to tell Paul – why not now? I described everything as if from a former existence.

Long ago when I went to Greece just after we met (it is etched so painfully into my memory that it is impossible to forget, though I had tried to unremittingly for so long), I found myself in a temple leaning against a column, mind soaring ecstatic into the azure sky, then floating down to the lapis lazuli Mediterranean, breathing inspiration for my first novel. A flock of sheep scavenged in bushes along the rim of the sand and the shepherd looked up at the temple, then directly at me. Was the flash a knife or the sun glinting on a cross round his neck? The rest I still can't bear to recall or relive. Nothing can change the circumstance: I was raped. Now, at long last, I was telling Paul. Unburdened, all I wanted was for him to wrap a cloak of tenderness and reassurance around me.

'You've taken a long time to tell me.' He turned his head away, though I was still looking at him. 'It was better you didn't try to resist,' he continued slowly, clenching his fingers. 'At least that man didn't harm you.' Another pause. 'It's best forgotten now, after what's happened. That... that horrible act, and Tim – they're past, gone. Better not to remember.'

Later in bed, I hoped he was trying to forget what we'd been through so we could go back to when we first met, and fell in love. He was gentle and passionate, trying to kiss away all memory of it. Our bliss was ours alone, I believed, our lovemaking uniquely tender.

To this day I have told no one else about what happened in Greece.

A Tangled Web – Summer 1981

After Easter Gianni served as go-between with Giulio's family. He wrote that the camera had been replaced and he was keeping it safe for us; that Giulio and his parents were offesi, and so was Quinto. His wife was still letting the hens stray over our land and ruin Gianni's vegetable patch. Though I repeated my offer to send money for a wire-netting fence, Gianni was as stubborn as Quinto, for precisely the opposite reasons! He had soured our relations with Quinto, but the way we handled the camera incident had a similar result with Giulio and his family. If this were not enough, Gianni threatened to stop his self-styled guardianship of our place.

His complaints about the state of the track and the damage it did to his car were mounting. Every year, without proper ditches, the rain drained off the hillside and washed away the top gravel. I was rather tired of Gianni's threats to leave us if we did nothing about it.

At Easter, Cecilia Ferrarini had explained over dinner that it was a strada vicinale. This meant that if we all signed a petition, the Town Council of Montesasso would send a couple of lorry loads of gravel every spring when the ground was soft enough for it to sink in and, in theory, form a hard core. All those using the track were supposed to spread the gravel. Gianni had been able to get two lorry loads just by requesting them verbally, though he didn't even live along the route. With some justification, he was now digging in his heels, having done most of the shovelling himself. We were never there when the Town Council decided to dump the gravel and only two of all the others, Giulio and Mauro, helped out. At least six more loads were needed. Something would have to be done.

Gianni brought Paul's replacement camera to Montesasso Scalo when he met Dan and me at the end of July. It was the same make, but not remotely as good as the one stolen. I assured him I'd thank Giulio and any other member of his family who would look in my direction.

'Doors were always left open and nothing was ever stolen in the valley,' Gianni said when we discussed the latest news sitting at the millstone table and trying out the white wine he had brought with him. A new police and fire station was planned in the village of San Giuliano just off the Cassia. There had already been three forest fires scarring large areas of the hillside above us. Massimo, half way up the valley, had lost an olive grove. Gossip, as Gianni always reminds me, is contrary to his principles, but he went on to admit that Massimo was rarely at home. He left his wife to mind their daughters while he frequented the local bars with his latest female companion. The less work he did, the more money he seemed to spend.

The following day I telephoned Paul's studio from Orazio's bar to tell him that, as agreed, I'd invited the Count and his wife to dinner. No answer. I tried his flat. Still no answer. He had promised to follow us early in August so we could renew contact with the Prudomini before they left, like most Italians, to spend mid-August around Ferragosto at the seaside.

Mike arrived unexpectedly to keep Dan and me company. Paul had been infuriatingly vague about when he would finish the Rembrandt self-portrait, so Mike decided not to wait for him, flew to Pisa and took a train to Montesasso Scalo, then a taxi to the Casa dell'Avventura, explaining loyally, 'He has a lot on his mind.' Then, 'Angélique may be coming as well.' I wasn't too keen to see her.

Count Prudomini arrived for dinner thirty minutes after the arranged time, punctual for an Italian, but alone. He thought his wife was already with us.

'She does know how to find your house,' he said, worried, 'and in any case, she can always ask Don Luigi down at San Giuliano.' Gianni offered to look out for her on his way home. Silence. Then Mike asked the Count how he, a landowner, dealt with the local population. It was hardly a tactful question with Gianni still sitting beside me. The Count intimated he was somewhat distanced from such problems. His agent dealt with them. At this point Gianni got up to leave, fortunately without the ritual kissing.

'*E il signor Paolo?*' The Count was impressed to hear that Paul was detained in England restoring a Rembrandt self-portrait.

'I would like to know what he thinks of the Town Council's intentions to remodel the museum in Palazzo Prudomini. Cecilia Ferrarini is behind it all, helped,' he coughed, discreetly embarrassed, 'by her friend who is designing it. She dislikes the old-fashioned but scholarly layout. It's "user unfriendly" people now say. Worse, "unhygienic" they tell me!'

As we talked the Count kept glancing up the drive and turning to the track every time a car passed along the ridge to Quinto's or Maria Pia's above us. The sun set, and I decided to serve the meal. It was consumed in near silence. Immediately after coffee, Rinaldo Prudomini rose with uneasy excuses.

'You must get that phone,' Mike insisted. 'Italians don't write letters, except for Gianni! But they do use the phone!'

Still no news from Paul. I telephoned again from Orazio's bar, without success. Nor had Gran and Mother heard from him. On my way out I bumped into one of Gianni's cousins and he invited me to help with the threshing the following day. He and two neighbouring farmers had booked the machine from an agricultural co-operative. They could only afford one day's hire, so needed all the help they could find, male or female. Dan, now nearly seven, could go with me. I was keen, and so were Mike and Dan.

However, Gianni arrived early the next morning with his road scheme. I was to get all the owners along the track to sign the document he would dictate. So Mike drove off without us. I sat down reluctantly, pen ready. Curious, I thought, to find my young son was my chaperone. I was annoyed, too, as I could easily have looked after Dan and helped with the harvest. But Gianni insisted that the rutted track was more important.

He dictated a list of everyone who used the road to reach houses and fields. All would have to sign and pay for half a load of gravel, promising to spread out their share.

The trek started. Quinto predictably refused to sign, saying that he could not walk, let alone use a shovel, and his son Mauro was out working all day and might not be around when the gravel came. Reluctantly, he did agree to pay his share. Gianni was not pleased. Maria Pia and Renzo said they would ask the owner to pay, but their son, Gino the Silent – we had never heard him utter a single word – would do the spreading. This sort of mixed response was the norm, but the field owners refused outright. The excuses were roughly the same: they paid their taxes, the Town Council should asphalt the road.

Dan took his time as we walked along, always wanting to stop and look at something, to wee, to eat from the walking larder I had become and generally distract us. The last on the list, Marino and his wife, were the first Italians to restore a farmhouse in the valley instead of building a new home on the Cassia. They would pay their share, but warned us that others using the track would not take kindly to our initiative. Some might pay and spread, but there would be a lot of bad feeling. Gianni stared at Marino uncomprehendingly. Why wouldn't people be relieved we were taking the initiative? Are they happy to bump their cars over the ruts? Don't they think we're honest? Gianni was offeso, but it was too late for him to change tactics.

Mike returned from the threshing after Gianni had finally left. Tired but content, he had worked all day from the top of the stacks forking wheat into the steam-powered thresher. Over supper he described how a sulky horse and two dumb-eyed oxen had trundled brightly-painted carts to and fro all day.

'You're irritated at first by the sweat tickling off your body, especially in the small of your back where it's difficult to scratch. Then you get in with the swing of everything and ignore it.'

Mike, who speaks fluent inaccurate Italian, found he understood the local dialect more as the day wore on. The children helped. The ones old enough for school became ambassadors between the foreigner, who spoke funny-sounding Italian, and their parents, who spoke dialect. Zig-zagging round the hens and geese to reach the heated activity by the thresher, the children tried to help. Shouted at to stand clear more often than not, they retreated to the kitchen for titbits.

'It's obvious, isn't it, Mike. The extended family depends on women staying at home? There isn't even a division of labour based on physical strength.' His account set me thinking. 'A kitchen garden involves digging and hoeing. That's hardly light work! Cows, a horse, goats and rabbits all need a lot of attention. The division lies in what's near the farm buildings, the women's task, and the fields for the men.'

'True,' Mike said, taking my arm we continued talking on a nocturnal stroll after Dan's bedtime. The lonely dog in the shack above the track heard us and began barking, followed by Quinto's mongrel, then by another guarding chickens cooped up in an abandoned Fiat 500 on the other side of our stream. We often heard the hens desperately pecking at the rusty doors, waiting to be fed. Meanwhile prolonged howls echoed from homesteads further up the valley. Lights went on in what we presumed was Quinto's bedroom, and a female voice shouted unintelligible words. We froze, thankful it was not a moonlit night. The chorus developed many movements and variations when, just as the yelps were dying into the background chirping of the crickets, a lone dog restarted the chain reaction, all obliged to outdo their canine neighbours. We listened for variations from soprano to bass, but they all bayed and yapped in singularly mongrel tones, to peter out exhausted by their own vociferousness.

* * * * *

Neither Mike nor I recognised the vehicle that crunched down the drive the following afternoon, though the elegant figure that stepped out was familiar. The Countess advanced with utmost composure and joined us on the veranda, complimenting us on the view. Just at that point two hens from Quinto's farm strolled across the gravel in front to peck at the geraniums. Dan picked up a stone and hurled it at them, unexpectedly hitting one. It lay prostrate emitting what sounded like a death rattle; the other in squawking falsetto, raced back to the safety of its own yard. We on the veranda were struck dumb. I thought of justice and a stringy chicken roast. Dan, shocked by his unexpected bull's eye, rushed past the dying hen and up the steps muttering something about it being my fault that he had aimed so well. Caught in the *rapid crossfire of colloquial English, the Countess looked dazed, even horrified, and moved as if to go. Good manners dictate that you should avoid any family row in the making, but also that you should gracefully apologise for a missed engagement. At that moment of human indecision, the bird weakly staggered to its feet and shakily, slowly, unevenly swayed up the drive to join its mates in safety. Dan followed at a distance, curious to learn its fate and wondering whether the incident would teach all feathered trespassers never to dare back on to our property.*

The veranda party relaxed. I rapidly made some coffee for our aristocratic visitor, who was so very sorry she had not been able to join us for dinner. Her car had broken down and she couldn't contact us, as we had no telephone. I was surprised she hadn't thought of calling Don Luigi who would have found a way to send a message a few hundred yards up the valley, especially for his church's benefactors.

'She finds it strange that you don't have a phone,' Mike repeated after the Countess had departed. 'You simply must get one for Paul, your mother and for your local contacts.'

After filling in the forms Gianni had handed us the summer before, Paul had remarked, with him out of earshot, that the telephone could be used to discourage Gianni from coming so often. At Easter, Gianni had complained that our application was still stuck in the bureaucratic machinery. He'd done all he could to speed it up, short of outright bribery. However, after we left in April, he'd nobly prevented a huge electricity booster from being planted in Giulio's fields, directly blocking our view of Monte Amiata. Instead, it was erected in front of Renzo and Maria Pia's farmhouse. Nobody minded. They, Giulio and Quinto can now install bigger water heaters and even washing machines. The consumer age has arrived in the valley.

CHAPTER 20

Sarah and William brought with them a twenty-seven word note. Paul had sent it after telephoning them to say he didn't trust the Italian post and to ask when they were leaving for Italy.

'Your mother's well, but very busy.' Sarah's voice came as if from a distance. 'Joe's sister's helping her and keeping Gran company. They're still not sure when Joe will have his operation.' I read Paul's note and knew I shouldn't have come to Italy.

DEAR OLIVIA, I HAVE FINISHED THE REMBRANDT SELF-PORTRAIT, BUT AM BUSY ON A SLOT FOR A TV ARTS PROGRAMME ABOUT REMBRANDT AND HAVE MORE WORKS TO RESTORE FOR IMPORTANT CLIENTS. WILL COME IF CAN, PAUL.

Roof and walls, cypresses and umbrella pine, vines and olives up to hillside scrub, all shrank into sharpened contours, like scanning the future through the wrong end of binoculars.

That summer I remember observing Andrew, who was growing tall like William and had the same ginger hair. He was probably on his last family holiday. Tim, his best friend, would have been here with him; seventeen years old and thinking of university. What would he have studied? Which hobbies and interests? Might he have spoken Italian? He would have been changing from a slender adolescent into, who knows, a taller, gentle-voiced young man, leaner than Paul.

Late summer Festivity – 1981

On the eve of Ferragosto Mike left as unexpectedly as he had come. He had called Angélique from the bar and arranged to meet her in Rome. Sarah and William arrived by car two days later with a note from Paul. Work and a television programme were delaying him.

The way to catch up on events in Montesasso is to read posters on the walls of buildings. They proclaim the next film at the open-air cinema in the municipal park, announce a Goldoni comedy or a Verdi opera in the main square, regret the recently deceased in large black print or publicise the coming Sagra. These are feasts held on Saturdays, featuring a particular species of local mushrooms, pigeons, asparagus or wild boar; this time it was beef from the cattle in the valley.

The Sagra in the municipal gardens for the mid-August Feast of the Assumption gave Montesasso housewives a respite from cooking. Numerous trestle tables with folding chairs had been laid out under the plane trees, most already occupied by extended families busy eating. Mouths crammed, they pointed at a queue, a most un-Italian phenomenon. Plastic knives, forks and paper napkins were handed out, followed by a grilled steak with potatoes, both seasoned with rosemary and served straight from the vast charcoal barbecue on to paper plates. A dollop of tomato salad, a peach and bottles of wine and mineral water, each capped with plastic glasses, were the rations we struggled to carry in two hands, just managing to reach a table with everything intact. The plastic knives didn't cut the meat so we merrily used our fingers instead. A tasty, but messy meal. All over the gardens grandparents were sitting beside grandchildren, while the middle-aged paid for tickets and ferried the food to and fro.

Just when we thought we might wander into town for the promised ice creams, a band struck up. The sound lured spectators to the edge of a paved area, which was already overrun by little girls tossing their curls and skipping to show off flounces on ankle-length frocks. A few equally smart boys joined them, though the girls pirouetted and ignored their frolics. All around, delighted mothers were pelting their darlings with compliments. Never had I heard such concerted bella-calling! For a while this was amusing, but when adult males infiltrated the female audience, one, then another couple was launched on to the dance floor. A mini-model stomped off, disgusted at the intrusion on 'her' area; others carried on, bemused, then worried when wave after wave of adult couples tacked around them dancing a quickstep. Two mothers on the far side shouted that the children were in danger and would the adults clear off. They were blithely ignored. An accident imminent, mothers barged between adults to save their stranded daughters. The little boys were no longer there, having abandoned the dance floor when the first adult couple sailed past.

Penny and Kate ignored Italian youths judged too callow for their attention. Andrew noticed groups of local girls talking animatedly while glancing sideways, under mascaraed eyelashes, at the men prowling in twos or threes in their vicinity. Some looked in his direction, but he lacked the courage to ask one of them to dance. His Italian wasn't good enough, he decided. Sarah and William had a turn and would have stayed longer had it not been for Kate and Dan's insistent requests. One bottle of mineral water was empty; the other was still on our table, unopened. I picked it up with some paper cups and looked around for a bottle opener, unsuccessfully.

A travelling puppet show had enticed Andrew away from the dancers and we joined him on the fringe of the group around the booth. I found myself translating Pulcinello's patter as he was furiously berating a policeman for not having found the culprit. For what? A man in front of me explained that the twenty-year-old son of a well-known Italian political figure had been kidnapped not far from Montesasso – those brigands from Sardinia again! Punch disappeared, to make way for a young man who was carried off by a dissolute-looking fellow with a paunch like our builder, Massimo. Punch returned to a battery of catcalls and squeaked, unperturbed, that the victim had written a letter to his parents to say that he had joined the kidnappers' terrorist group. All this stirred speculation among the onlookers. Had the son been forced to join? Newspapers were filled with pleas from the distraught family; letters said to be from their son have been found in post-boxes all over Italy. Still clasping the mineral water and plastic glasses, I stood enthralled by the true Commedia dell'Arte threading current calamity into comedy.

Sarah and William were shifting uneasily, especially as my interpretation was frequently delayed by additional snippets from the locals around me keen to fill in the picture.

'We're all dying of thirst. Please, get us some water. Now. Pleeease...' Penny, Kate and Dan were clamouring while I vainly looked around for a bottle opener. They were getting on my nerves. I was the only Italian speaker now, at everyone else's behest, and I wanted, just for a moment, to watch Punch and company without interruption. I put the plastic glasses down, took the glass bottle in both hands and smashed it against a plane tree in a desperate attempt to remove the cap. The bottleneck broke and blood spurted. I yelled, clasped hands to throat and staggered towards the park entrance. Kate was shouting for her mother and I glimpsed Penny picking up my bag and following me. Swinging lights hitched between trees illuminated faces surging towards me or shrinking back in horror to let me pass out of their sight.

'E straniera! Si è tagliata la gola!'' They were whispering, 'She's a foreigner. She's cut her throat.' Suddenly Gianni stepped out of the crowd, grasped my shoulder and propelled me towards his car. How he had come to know I was there (we hadn't told him we were going to the Sagra) speaks volumes for Montesasso's grapevine. He might have gone anyway, just watching and smoking. He drove straight across the pedestrianised Piazza della Repubblica and swooped up the hill towards San Francesco to brake in front of the Saint's hospital where he handed me into the care of two male orderlies framing the entrance to the Pronto Soccorso. Trembling, scared that I'd lost the tip of a finger, I was laid on a stretcher and wheeled into a room where someone looking like a doctor and a nun with a squint leant over to prise my hands apart. No, no, no! I didn't want to know what had happened. I looked desperately away as they all bent over my left hand. Blood that had trickled down the front of my dress was drying, nauseating and itchy. The lights began to fade; I was fainting... no, no, no! I moaned again. Stitches, I heard. Then reassuring phrases; people always say it's all right when it evidently isn't! The nun came closer to speak to me, but I shrank, terrified by her squint. A silent scream began in the pit of my stomach, travelling up to my brain and exploding into a firework of pain in my finger. It throbbed frantically. Remarks half-heard about sewing it on again. I moaned for Paul. They said they would get him.

'*Impossibile!*' I moaned, adding that I should never be able to play the piano again.

'*He'll love you without the tip of your finger. Anyway, some piano pieces can be played without a middle finger, or with one hand!*' It was getting worse; from the tip of a middle finger to the loss of a whole hand! By now the doctor reassuring me was holding my right arm and leaning over with a cigarette in his free hand. Ash would inevitably fall into the wound! He and the nun, whose stare I profoundly and unjustifiably mistrusted, were laying my hand, palm upwards, on a board, firmly stopping my fingers from curling inwards as if to grasp and control the throbbing, while pouring a liquid over them again and again. Then the distant sensation of impact, tugs, murmured concentration, and the lights going green and blurred. Why did I want to play the piano? I hadn't had time to touch the instrument for over ten years. Strange fragments of the past invade a panic-stricken mind.

Then it was all over. I was being wheeled out to Gianni. He'd slipped home to tell Ada. She was expecting me and poured hot broth into a bowl. Gianni handed me a bottle of painkillers he had been given at the hospital. I swallowed two, sipped the broth, and then began to fret about the others. Gianni reassured me. William had driven them back to my house, and he would be taking me there himself.

When eventually we arrived, the children begged to help me and Dan wouldn't let go of my sound hand. Sarah insisted I should get a good night's rest. We deciphered the instructions on the painkillers and found I could take another two with a sleeping pill. In the darkness gold rippled over blue; sounds of children in the bathroom and the valley's canine chorus in full throttle floated on waves ebbing and flowing over me before drowning into a moonless night.

* * * * *

'*You must keep your hand horizontal and rest in the shade all day.*' Sarah peeped in to find me awake. '*I'm going to the bar to phone Paul, your mother, whoever's there. I'll tell them what's happened, but not to worry.'* As I lay in fuzzy enforced rest I felt grateful to Gianni, but wished he would not come to see me then, the next day, or the day after to avoid the strain of entertaining him and interpreting between him and the others. It all turned out differently.

Under another unblemished sky, I lay propped up on pillows and cushions beneath the umbrella pine, the guardian spirit of the house, facing up the valley towards the tranquil amphitheatre of the mountains. William and Andrew had taken the children to a swimming pool near a remote church in the Appenines. There water gushes crystalline from a spring into the pool on a lower level, and out to fill an irrigation trough below. It's arctic cold but chemical free, the surroundings a haven of tranquillity. William hoped to spot eagles, Dan to meet a wild boar, Kate a porcupine and Penny and Andrew to play games in the pool. Sarah stayed to look after me. We were enjoying the childless quiet, engrossed in our books.

From time to time I looked up the valley to the olive groves, tinder-dry broom bushes and a few abandoned cottages. Above the olive line the chestnut trees were already shrivelled brown. I could see the roof of Massimo's new house, and the scrubland above it. Just out of sight, I imagined the new posts and a rather fancy cast iron gate recently installed by the owners of the two renovated houses. Massimo was officially the gatekeeper; in reality his wife held the key, still wedded to the house and plot around it, while he wandered off – for work and pleasure. There was an unusual flurry of vehicles along the road up to the restored farmhouses. Five minutes later dark specks were scattering over the hillside.

'Sarah, can you get the binoculars?' She found them in the dresser. 'I can't hold them steady. Please tell me what's happening.'

'Ten or fifteen men are clambering over the rocks below the higher farmhouse, the one just under the crest of the hill. Strange.' Sarah continued peering through the binoculars.

'Could it be a police raid?'

'In this valley? Hardly.' Sarah was too trusting. There could be a police clampdown after what we had heard from Punch before my accident.

We watched, silently riveted to the activities of the human ants now fanning out near the top of the ridge but keeping their distance from the farmhouse. Then they must have crouched for cover out of Sarah's binocular-aided sight. Nothing happened. After some minutes of total quiet we returned to our books. When I looked up about ten minutes later sunlight was reflected from something high on the hillside – a windscreen?

'Sarah, something's happening.' She picked up the binoculars.

'A limousine is moving up the gated road.' She followed it past Massimo's house and then out of sight at a curve in the road.

'I wonder what that's all about?' I asked Sarah, who was more concerned to see I drank enough, that my injured finger was kept horizontal, and that we both enjoyed the untrammelled peace of a perfect day on our own.

Gianni arrived, amazingly late. It was six, time for an aperitif. Following such a generous siesta, I was ready to thank him for all he had done to help me. He apologised for not coming earlier to see how I was. He was clearly upset. Massimo had been arrested.

He had recommended Massimo as our builder, so this calamity was our concern too. Gianni sipped his wine, lit up and told us how, soon after finishing our renovation (all later additions had been carried out by Gianni himself), Massimo hadn't found much work. He became fully occupied with amorous escapades, leaving time only for his own house and minor repairs to others. His labourers migrated down the valley to better pay and more prospects. As one person can only hold one end of a beam, so to speak, this curtailed his entrepreneurial activities even more. Spare time masons, Gianni stressed, could operate independently and were consequently in demand. It seems Massimo was tempted by money to help with a risky kidnapping plan involving a local politician and his son.

'A letter was sent to the politician. He was told to leave a package of bank notes, today, under the oak below the more remote farmhouse. If he did so, without alerting the police, he would be sent details of his son's whereabouts.'

When the limousine had driven slowly through the unlocked gate and up the cypress-edged track, we knew policemen – the *ones we had seen earlier – were waiting. Gianni had found out that one of them, posing as the politician, had walked slowly towards the oak tree. The car then drove out of sight and Massimo the gatekeeper stepped out of the farmhouse.*

'Was he alone? Was he armed?' Gianni didn't know. Only that the policemen scattered over the hillside closed in, and that was the end of a simple attempt to obtain a ransom. A sledgehammer hitting a tiny nail, but the fear of kidnapping was reaching panic levels, Gianni said, even in the hush of our valley.

He was non-committal about his cousin – beh! If Massimo had succeeded he would have been able to pay his debts, continue his love affairs and strut to general acclaim. Failure was unforgivable.

The swimming party returned. Our afternoon had been more dramatic than theirs, which had passed without sight of a wild boar or porcupine, but with games, and eagles soaring. William laughed when Sarah admitted she was worried their children might be kidnapped.

'We're not wealthy or important enough,' and he hugged her. 'Children are priceless, even if they're not worth kidnapping!' However, I had found a good excuse never to let Dan out of my sight.

Our telephone did not arrive before we left the Casa dell'Avventura, but we were inching up the waiting list. Only three months to wait, Gianni reported. He had also heard rumours that neighbours along the road thought we might disappear with the money for the gravel. So that was what lay behind the leaden looks I tried not to notice as we drove away.

It was a strange summer. Without a telephone, sundrenched, in superb countryside and surrounded by friends, it should have been a taste of paradise in a harassed life. It would have been infinitely better if Paul had been there, if Mike hadn't left so suddenly and mysteriously, if I hadn't nearly severed a finger, if I'd had a phone and Paul had answered. I was saddened at the loss of our summer together, frustrated and fearful.

CHAPTER 21

The dialling tone drilled an echo into my head.

What do you do when someone isn't where you expect him to be? It wasn't the first time Paul had been silenced by work. Deadlines, concentration, need to be alone – the usual. Don't hassle a man, Mother had always stressed. Hold back. Wait. Woe to the female predator! She didn't think Angélique was one. She was an enabler, flitting in and out of lives, never settling, finding a nest for each season of friendship.

Not a single one of us – Gran, Mother, Mike or Joe – had heard from Paul since early August when, having completed Rembrandt's self-portrait, he was working on the television programme. Canvases were still awaiting restoration in his studio. Mike was concerned that Paul had been refusing to take on extra commissions after he started the Rembrandt; he could lose out professionally.

Years slip through seasons clipped into days and months, worn unnoticed until a veil is drawn to reveal gathers on forehead and crinkles round eyes and mouth. I suppose we had been physically together for about eight of the eighteen years since we met. My mental image was of a broad-brush face commanding a strong-boned, reassuring presence. I had traced a fold under his chin and a vertical frown line, but had never before the spring of 1981 noticed a slight stoop from nearly twenty years spent cleaning, strengthening, restoring the past as if bowing before it. He wore his hair shorter, the curls cut back. Not yet a thread of white. I carried the changed image into my search.

So Dan and I returned to Downs Way in September 1981 to no message from Paul. Mother assumed he had gone to find me after my mid-August accident. Mike hadn't seen him since July. Early in August, not long after Joe's operation, Paul had visited him in hospital, but that was the last time anyone saw him. The fabric of my life and Dan's was being ripped apart by Paul's absence. Painstakingly, wearily, I tried stitching it together. I began emotional accounting.

Item 1 Paul's disappearance. Beyond my control. Useless to vent my anger on – who? What? Go and look for him. Man is a hunter, Mother told me as a child. To chase cheapens a woman, so Gran said. But he is Dan's father.

Item 2 Dealing with Dan. Within my control, but very distressing. He's almost seven and is expecting his father because I am; because for the first time his birthday approaches without his father and I'm doing nothing about it, except buying him a coat for the winter. Anniversaries intensify the pang of loss. I'm tired of pretence but shouldn't burden him with Paul's absence. When he asks, I'll tell him his father has work far away, or something similar.

In compensation, Joe enjoyed organising Dan's birthday party without exerting himself too much. He set up Great-uncle Frank's model Hornby train and taught Dan's friends to run and maintain it. It was becoming a replay of my early years, without the war, and with Dan as the child waiting for his father, not me. Gran used to say to a small eager Olivia, 'Look at the sky! If there's enough blue to make a pair of sailor's trousers' – I was wriggling in anticipation – 'then we'll give you a special treat!' I'd be up at dawn pulling back the curtains to scan the clouds. Then, and later with Tim, and now with Dan, they'd billow, drift and ebb leaving uncertain patches of blue.

'Yes,' Gran would say, 'I've stitched them together. They'll just make trousers for a slim sailor!'

Item 3 How does Joe fit in? Though it was my mother who asked him to stay with us, it was fate that determined his inherited heart problem, and his need for shelter with just enough, but not too much, legal work. He has always looked fragile, smaller than his actual size, a childlike frame in clothes just slightly too large. His light brown hair was cut so short in hospital that the waves were reduced to ripples like the carved head of a Roman senator, with the same deep-set eyes and high cheekbones. The tip of his nose twitches when he teases Dan. Kind people call him 'a quiet person'; others find he lacks personality. He keeps us calm company.

Item 4 Coping with work. A teacher reported ill just before term started and another didn't turn up. These are familiar crises and part of the job. Ones I can deal with though I can't stop them occurring. I must keep myself busy. The more outside concerns to envelop my thoughts, the better. Hours at school can be sewn into neat areas of responsibility, but in the evening emotion unravels everything.

<u>Item 5</u> Set up a routine, but avoid upsetting Gran or Mother who have been coping with absence most of their lives. Have breakfast, drop Dan off at school, work, fetch him or arrange for Sarah to help, cook another meal: all require careful planning and interminable lists.

In the autumn of 1981 shopping became a bit of a hit and miss affair. Before, Paul or Joe used to help me load and unload the Saturday stores for the menu planned a week ahead. At first Mother helped me while Dan stayed at home with Joe; when he was strong enough, Joe came to shop with me. Mother often went out in the evening; I didn't, hoping for the phone call and spent evenings watching television with Joe, who was still convalescing. I was in Italy when Charles married Diana; they and the Prime Minister were rarely off the screen. Margaret Thatcher was promising us all serious prosperity with British oil flowing from the North Sea into our homes. It affected me not one whit.

Snippets of good fortune came my way after Paul disappeared – an inverse ratio, which left me even more disconsolate. I found substitutes for the two teachers who hadn't turned up at the start of term and both were proving better than the ones they replaced. There was even an increase in all teachers' salaries.

'Go and find out about Paul,' Joe urged. It was nearly the end of September. 'Go next Saturday. I'll look after Dan.'

I knew Paul wasn't where he used to be. The drill of the unanswered dialling tone at his flat and studio over the summer had been replaced by aching silence.

'Yes,' the operator confirmed, 'both those numbers have been disconnected since early September.' That was all they knew. Or were allowed to say. Should I go to the police? To the place where they register missing persons? I could imagine it:

'We have no record of a Paul Wyatt, Mrs Wyatt. Could I take your details? Name?'

'Olivia Taylor.' Throat clearing.

'Ahem! As we have no record of him; he must be somewhere.'
No body mouldering?

'At least he must be alive, Mrs – er, Olivia Taylor.' A dead body turns up. Usually.

'Play games with yourself,' Joe suggested. 'Since you don't know where he is, pretend you're a detective finding out. That'll make it more bearable.' So Joe and Dan played snakes and ladders, spillikins and noughts and crosses, while I was to play the detective.

Under a deep blue autumn sky on the last Saturday in September I caught an early train to London. The crowds were bustling, chattering, intrusive. I dreaded the chill of forsaken haunts, yearned for a chance meeting or just a reassuring glimpse, if not face to face. Even if he was with someone else.

'No, I must find him alone,' I muttered. 'Work out ways and means. Search. Learn to survive.'

The moment I turned into the street of buff brick houses, I saw a red notice by his entrance: TO LET. The estate agents wouldn't know I had a key. It opened the door for a visit I should never have made into the narrow hall of the basement flat. Sunlight projected twenty-four dusty rectangles on to the boards in the front room where my Moroccan carpet had lain. It had disappeared, bearing the memory of our caresses, strands of conversations, jokes and quarrels; of Tim and Paul crouched over the model cars and planes they assembled together and of Dan crawling towards his father – whereabouts unknown. Gone the gallery of Paul's sketches of us, of friends, and places we'd discovered together. I'd had them framed for him one Christmas, in the plain wood he preferred. Before I arrived on a Friday he'd rearrange them to see if I'd notice, gleefully happy if I did. Lined paper with words in capitals lay torn into shreds, shards of an illegible past abandoned in the dark corner of an empty room. The bare bathroom; the frugal kitchen; the stripped bedroom at the back contemplating the tiny garden. Tangled weeds had invaded it, ivy grasping one leg of our bench. If I had been wearing the necklace he'd given me, I would have scratched with a diamond *'Nessun maggior dolore'* on to the window with the vehemence of our bliss recollected in lone wretchedness. But someone had etched it already on a pane above my head. More torn fragments of paper with ripped words that might once have been mine. I knelt to jigsaw them together – Dar- if I have – aft–. My writing, message indecipherable. I jumped up at a tap on the window. A branch in the garden, or a neighbour? Someone might be watching out for intruders. Bottles had already been tossed through the railings. I knew the widow next door and an elderly couple further down, but didn't want them to tell me when he and the furniture left, if they departed together. I needed to gather the threads myself and weave them into some pattern. I could imagine their patter:

'End of August it could have been, dearie.'

'No, more like early September, Maisie. It was the same day Tom brought the spade down on 'is toe in our allotment. Not a very large van. Budget 'ire it was.'

'Was it? Such a nice young man…' Not so young, nor so nice; but thus platitudes are spun. I shivered, picked up a picture in a broken frame flung into a corner, locked the door softly, and stubbed my toes as I fled up the steps and down the street before anyone could call out in pity to the 'poor abandoned woman'.

'Find out,' Joe had said, 'it's demeaning; but less painful than waiting, or not knowing – even if you end up learning the worst'.

By the time I had turned the corner I was panicking less but was immeasurably more miserable. I needed to find Mike, but a true detective would head for the estate agents.

'Which property?' asked the girl filing her nails.

'26 Carstairs Road.' She nodded when I placed my honest key by her phone. I asked if the previous tenant had left an address. She looked up at me.

'**I** don't know,' stressing the "I". 'Mr Harrison should be here on Monday.'

I walked out bolt upright, turning my emotions inside out, looking crisply the opposite of how I felt – confident.

The heels of my shoes hit a sharp note of despair. I had inhabited that bitter underworld since Tim's death, expecting to hit the bottom and push back up. Paul's studio was a brisk fifteen minutes' walk along suburban streets of front gardens cramped behind cast iron railings. Better to know, Joe said, than to do battle with speculation, panic, dread. I had never been trusted with a key to the studio. It was easy to picture the chaotic still life – easels, paints, solvents, coffee mugs, clothes thrown over the frayed sofa – of our time spent on the first floor. A window opened and a woman leaned out, looking over me to the end of the cul-de-sac. My heart thudded. Before I could call up to her, she had gone.

Better a confrontation than more emptiness. Better to fill in the vacant space – with indignation or sufferance? He would be there, relaxed, leaning back on two legs of his chair. Perhaps, in the throes of a middle age crisis, the abstemious Paul had returned to smoking pot, though he had never really started. Better to know, or to leave the imagination unfettered? I vacillated, tossed by a tempest of scenarios, all of them inconsolable, as I paced up and down the cobbles outside. People would notice me: a female loitering – or a shady individual casing the joint?

There were stabs of sound and colour: sparrows hopping along the eaves, scavenging in the gutters; a cat purring on a bench, paws up to the sun; pots of red geraniums shedding petals from a balcony and pale pink Japanese anemones peeping through iron railings. Grim fact or feverish fantasies? I knocked. She was older than she had seemed when leaning out of the window. No, she hadn't seen the previous tenant, a picture restorer. She'd just rented it with another artist on a short lease. Six months. After that? He could be returning for all she knew.

Away over the rough cobbles. (Where had he taken the paintings he'd kept to restore when less busy? The ones he cleaned for Mike to sell to rich clients? The others for thrifty collectors, who had less money but little haste?) I turned right into Camberwell Church Street. (Had he stored or sold our bed, our settee, our – my – carpet, the table?) I ran to catch a bus to Oxford Circus. (The sketches were mine. I'd paid for the frames.)

'How could you take everything away without telling me?' I shouted silently.

Crowds were bunched round sandwich kiosks, shuffling in and out of shops and department stores, their voices gibbering at a muffled distance although I could have touched them.

Mike has always been nifty on his financial feet. He had his eye on the Queen's Silver Jubilee in 1977 when he moved his gallery into new premises off Oxford Street. Visitors to London could be enticed into the wide, low space flowing tastefully round the sparsely displayed artworks, mostly paintings and pottery. Less expensive photographs, posters and the new trend of ephemera were in the basement. There was a trace of expensive perfume and a figure stirred behind the reception desk at the back.

'Allo!' A distinct French accent I had heard before. Angélique, Mike's on-and-off companion. They had once come to a scratch dinner at the now empty flat. It was not an enjoyable evening because of her shrill voice and attention-seeking restlessness. Her new incarnation as his gallery receptionist must mean that something had happened to this haughty, provocative woman. Previously she had hosted expensive dinner parties to introduce Mike to her wealthy friends, who might buy slightly damaged works by known artists. He would then present his restorer, Paul. She could be seen gliding from a Rolls Royce in a stunning pearl grey suit slit to the hip and a vast black feathery hat partly shading her doe-like eyes, lips just parted to reveal, or not, the tip of her tongue. She skilfully fashioned this considerable allure from the sum of just above average parts. It was known she enjoyed innumerable contacts in powerful places.

'Oleevia, I am so sorree!' What did she know about Paul? She advanced through the spacious gallery. Hats in 1981 were for weddings and Ascot, baptisms and funerals. Angélique flaunted a wide-brimmed pink one with a black ribbon holding a real or fake white rose, blushing at the edges. Even in my state of agitation, I thought it inappropriate, as was the matching pink suit with black buttons, collar and cuffs, slightly on the tight side to accentuate her hourglass curves. She must have dressed for a dinner date. She was the last person I wanted to see.

'Sorry?'

'Mike iz not 'eere. Bizzee.' She sighed and sat down again, 'Zo much bizziness. I 'elp at veekends.' She probably had nothing else to do except wait for him to take her out to dinner. I would have to catch a train before then. She held out a shiny paper shopping bag for the broken picture I was holding.

'Vor Mike?'

'No.' I could have laughed. It was the saint in the rococo frame which Mike himself had given me many years before and that I had presented to Paul! Turning away to look at the nearest work, I found a disgruntled gentleman in a blue jacket and cravat looking coldly at me, quill in hand. By a follower of David, perhaps?

'Ow iz your babee?' – a rising tone, like a bored socialite filling the void with polite chatter.

'Fine.' This time I would fill the gap. 'Actually, he isn't a baby. He's just seven.' I wouldn't let her ask after Paul; so, 'Why are there so few works on display if business is good?' Perhaps this had something to do with Paul's disappearance. He may have relied on Mike too much. It has been said that a move up-market presages disaster.

'Ow do you say, a glut, then prices descend.' So it's all a market ploy.

'How can I contact Mike?' She looked at me suspiciously, having always met me in Paul's company.

''Ee come in 'ere, peraps, dis evening.' Her accent became more exaggerated the longer she stayed in Britain. With a Gallic shrug of the shoulders, she held her hands out, palms up, her eyes raised as if in prayer, lids gently fluttering. In other circumstances, for other people, an irresistible performance. I would ask Mike, not her, about Paul. Question him like a detective.

To her credit, Angélique did subsequently tell Mike that I was distressed. To his, he came to Guildford the next day, a Sunday, when Paul should have been with Dan and me. He was silent when told of the empty flat and re-let studio, the silence of another wounded soul. He thought he was Paul's best friend, the one who had helped him most (while furthering his own dealing activities).

Mike had last seen him some time in July, when Paul said he would join Dan and me in Italy. That's why Mike didn't contact him, certain he was out of the country. Unlike Joe, he counselled the hardest course. Wait.

'He was restoring for the best museums. He might have been offered a studio, rent-free.'

'Then why doesn't he phone us?' He didn't know, nobody did. I was learning only too well how inaction saps hope, leaving acres open to vagrant despair.

'Reconstruct your life, Olivia,' was all he could say. 'Don't go to the police, yet. Don't let Dan know how you feel.' Don't, just don't.

Week followed week and this new pattern became a routine. I rarely went to London, but Mike would turn up at Downs Way when he had work in the area or wanted to escape from the city. He brought no news of Paul. If his parents or his brothers had heard from him, they didn't tell me; Paul could have asked them not to tell Olivia where he was, not to... His family hardly knew me or Dan, an unofficial grandchild when they had plenty of accredited ones. I convinced myself it was kinder not to telephone and distress them. So my thoughts would stumble on.

Sometimes I discussed Paul with Joe when Dan was asleep, Gran in bed and my Mother out on one of her evening engagements. I still hesitated about going to the police, see-sawing between anger and resignation, hope and despair, the unending anguish of waiting and not knowing when or what to expect.

Nessun maggior dolore. Memories crept through pauses into my itemised day. Once there was no greater grief than to recall Tim's past without present or future; now it was too harrowing to remember the sixties when Paul and I thought everything was possible. We danced to the same tune of abandon, shared the same spliff and communed with the world. I knew plenty of men before Paul, and they seemed more fluid, more available. Paul instead was selective and secretive; he found the sixties emotionally confusing. I picked over everything I could recall. Was he naturally monogamous? He was always different while seeming to go along with the rest of us. He was hopeless at small talk. Everything about him was tense: his body, and his manner in company. He was one of the nicest people I'd ever met, but he didn't have a clue what others were really like. He thought that if he ignored awkward questions, they would evaporate. I soon gave up asking how he felt, because he never answered the question. I thought I was emotionally open when I talked to people; he had a shy, nervous social smile and gave nothing away. He could be impulsively generous, then distant. He was often overcast, then came unexpected gashes of brightness, bursting out passionately, unrestrained like the midday sun in an azure sky. He was like no one else ever could be, standing there at the door of Downs Way with the street lamp illuminating him softly from behind. I tried writing him out of my mind, using my notes and Gianni's letters for my story, but nothing worked. He was indissolubly part of my dream.

At the end of October I phoned Paul's bank in London to find out why it had stopped payments into our joint account.

'We are not allowed to give confidential information but -' a long pause, 'generally speaking, we monitor overdrawn accounts.' This only revealed that Paul was paying nothing into his account; he could be alive or dead. It was then that I went to the police. As I feared, it was the Mrs Wyatt, er Taylor, treatment; no, we haven't heard anything. We don't think it's a crime or anything of the sort. Then kindly, hand on the shoulder of an abandoned woman, I was advised to try the missing persons' route.

CHAPTER 22

I started looking at my mother differently when she explained how she managed her emotional 'loss adjustment'.

'Distance him. Put him into a frame,' she advised as the days, then weeks stretched painfully into months. She pointed to my father, fading into distance, the only photograph taken when films were even scarcer than their time together. I glimpsed the beauty that he saw in her, as she told me how she hid his photo in a pouch made from a shirt left secretly for her to repair; he never came back to collect it. For years afterwards his image hung inside her blouse. When I was three, she framed it and set it beside the latest photo of me on her bedside table; the War was ending and my father would return. I found no comforting reason for Paul to be restored to me, so I festered in ignorance, in powerless anxiety – above all, in futile anger. Was his behaviour caused by me, my negligence, my insensitivity? It had none of the tragic finality of Frank's fate in the trenches or Tim's outside his school gate; only the intimate wound of not knowing.

'Accept him as framed by the past. Don't let him sour your future. Fill up your time so there's not even a chink for him to creep in and haunt you.' Mother knew it all. She had reacted by dividing her free time into neat portions for friends and films and bird watching and whatever research she was doing with her companion in the reference library. It paid off in promotion at work, but I wasn't so sure about the rest. In November, when the last leaves were blowing off the chestnut tree at the end of the garden, I placed every photo I had of Paul in a plastic bag and pitched it into the farthest corner of the loft. Except for one. I couldn't pluck Paul out of Gran's favourite picture with Tim and me in the happy days I was excising from memory.

Christmas 1981 was not as dreadful as I had feared, and Dan was fretting less about his father with all the attention he was getting. Joe had adopted Dan's wayward habit of total deafness when called to meals, heads down together over a model boat, aeroplane or whatever, blissfully ignoring all appeals or just simple questions. As Joe got stronger his restored heart rejuvenated him, almost like a new lease of childhood.

Tim and Marco had been killed by mindless fate. For all I knew, like Giulio, the van driver had continued a 'normal' life after he skidded and knocked Tim down. My father, then Paul, had walked out of our lives to play another part elsewhere, unknown. If we were not to be loved, at least Mother and I needed to know. Or were they both dead?

I shouldn't have gone back to the Camberwell area in London but when Mike invited me to the theatre, I found that without thinking I'd taken the underground to go to Paul's studio, getting out at the Oval instead of Oxford Circus. I turned back, jittering inside. Mike had waited for me before closing his gallery. It was Saturday and he was without his assistant who always reached him with messages, but never revealed where he was. No sign of Angélique.

'Angélique's gone to Scotland,' he said in his typical offhand way. It struck me he had changed; rounder contours, more congenial though still assertively marketing his unusual looks. Full of fun and boyish absorption, like Joe, he enjoyed playing with Dan at weekends.

Not long after Christmas Mother decided she would like to see for herself what was happening in Montesasso at Easter. She arranged it all. Sarah and William invited Dan to stay and Joe would keep Gran company. She began packing with almost girlish excitement.

'Olivia, how cold will it be?' She was asking: 'Olivia, how...?' along with, 'Olivia, when...?' and, 'Olivia, where...?' until I started laughing at her, thinking of all the times she had taken herself off to Italy when I was a child.

'D'you know they don't call anyone Olivia in Italy? Oliviero for a man, but Oliviera doesn't exist.' Concerned, she said, 'I had to choose a name, and I thought your father would like Olivia. It would remind him of his Tuscan hills, the silver olive leaves all year round, and the golden green of the oil.'

'Didn't you act Olivia in *Twelfth Night* at school?' She nodded, smiling this time, and I thought of all the lovers who chased Olivia, from the besotted Count Orsino to the ludicrous Sir Andrew Aguecheek and Malvolio, but it was only Viola/Sebastian she loved. Not too bad a prophecy for me at university, when one man stood out from the rest. However, Shakespeare ended his play where the consequences of requited love begin.

I had never seen my mother look so skittish. How pretty she still was, with her fine cheekbones, slightly pointed chin like me and dark Taylor hair, touched up for the trip. She had joined a tennis club and lost weight, though I never thought she needed to.

The spirit of the valley – Easter 1982

After I left Italy at the beginning of September in 1981 Gianni sent me letters at least twice a week. The telephone was connected and gravel tipped in piles along the track but, as usual, only he and Giulio were there to spread it, with some help after work from Mauro and the silent Gino. No mention of Marino the hairdresser. Gino's sister, Caterina, who had hastily married Mauro next door, miscarried, Gianni tartly adding that they needn't have married after all. At least her father, Renzo, gave her away before he died some weeks later of a heart attack. We had new German neighbours.

I had been the first foreigner to buy a ruin in the valley, and remained so for many years. Nearby, but well out of sight, is a tiny house where Ada's grandmother had once lived. It has been sold, Gianni duly reported, to an elderly German professor and his wife. All these changes intrigued my mother, increasingly curious about the Casa dell'Avventura and Gianni.

Gianni was delighted to welcome two women on their own. He was clean-shaven and sprightly. The gaps in his teeth had disappeared and his smile was full and unstained. There was also a whiff of after-shave. I squeezed into the back of Bluebottle, leaving Mother to retune her rusty Italian to his update of local news.

'I'll introduce you to my brother-in-law. Pina, his wife, is cleaning for the firemen and Carlo finds he pays less for a drink in their bar. It's also a hotbed of gossip.'

Carlo was loading a lorry when Gianni drove into his yard. Pina gave us coffee and asked how Paul was. I explained he had urgent work to complete for a television programme. She was impressed.

As we left, Carlo took my arm and propelled me into his workshop, leaving Pina talking to Mother and Gianni.

'*Stasera?*' Was he mad? This evening? Here I was alone with my mother, so in Carlo's mind, perhaps in the collective valley mentality too, I was up for grabs. I feared a Carlo version of Gianni's sulks and the local tendency to be *offeso* if rejected. I whispered something about showing my mother the house, and he breathed out, '*Un'altra volta...*' with a quick pouting kiss and a knowing squeeze of my arm.

Something had changed at the Casa dell'Avventura. I left Mother on the veranda with Gianni, who was overjoyed she could speak some Italian, and walked a few steps up the drive. The only remaining view uncluttered with poles and wires had vanished. From Quinto's house, ugly cables forked across the stream and down the drive towards me.

'*Telephone wire,*' Gianni called after me, pleased. '*You're in the telephone directory!*'

Quinto's wretched hens were scavenging on our land. As I walked up the drive, I tried shooing them in front of me towards his wife. Penned inside her kitchen garden, she was talking to Maria Pia. I went over to tell Maria Pia how sad I was to hear that Renzo had died. She was both tearful and excited at the prospect of a grandchild. Caterina was expecting again and had only three months to go. Quinto was in great pain from his worsening arthritis and could hardly move. His first visit to the 'saint' at Rimini on a chartered coach had been helpful to a point, but he couldn't afford another journey, and in any case it hurt him too much to jolt over mountain passes in a bus.

'*I'm sending my singlet this time!*' he shouted down from the balcony. '*The saint will bless it for a much smaller fee.*'

'*Good luck.*' *There was a pause while we all nodded in hope.*

'*Venga a trovarmi, come and see me,*' *Maria Pia said as I was leaving,* '*and bring your mother. I'd like to meet her.*'

'*She's a bit lonely,*' *Caterina whispered, walking with me to the top of the drive,* '*do go and keep my mother company.*'

I returned to find Gianni showing Mother everything he had done in the house and garden. They enjoyed it, she practising her Italian and Gianni showing her what he had built. In the afternoon he took her on a walk we had done years earlier. I'm happy to see her so amused by Gianni. After all, they're the same age and enjoy reminiscing. As he did with me at first, he's inserting odd English phrases.

'*Where d'you think he learnt them?*' *I asked her.*

'*Beh!*' *she replied, as Gianni does,* '*Could be like a musician I knew. He was in the Allied army advancing north from Naples and partisans were offering help on all sides. He managed amazingly well with* "*andante ma non troppo!*" *or* "*piano, pianissimo!*" *tucked between the usual colourful swear words picked up in male company. Gio – I mean Gianni – is typical. He can't manage verbs very well, so I don't think he's ever studied English. After all, he comes from a deprived background.*' *Yes and no. Gianni had not been deprived of a loving family, from what he told me. Perhaps he had given her a different tale of his childhood?*

I wanted to introduce my mother to Caterina while Gianni was on his stretch of road in the morning. She liked company when working at an old pedal sewing machine in the ground floor storeroom. We sat and watched her hands deftly placing two pieces of cloth together and seaming them into a sweater. When the two piles had been sown into one taller heap of finished work, she relaxed and said she would take us to see her mother next door.

Maria Pia's wooden kitchen table had been replaced by a Formica one and the small black and white television by a larger colour set. Otherwise the kitchen had hardly changed since she invited me in after washing clothes together in the stream. That was when Renzo gave us the old bread cupboard and the writing desk I'm still using. The walls are whitewashed every other year, time intervening with warm, shadowy traces of wood smoke from the family hearth. There's no attempt to create the prim 'country kitchen' or 'designer rustic' styles that have invaded restored farmhouses in Italy. The bread cupboard is still in the corner, used now to store flour and sugar for cake-making, not as in the old days to keep dough while it rose before the weekly baking session in the outside oven. At midday a van brings fresh bread to the farmhouses. A pot still hangs over the hearth to provide constant hot water, and herbs dry, hung from rafters in bunches accompanying cured hams and strings of onions, garlic, sun-dried tomatoes, corncobs for animal fodder, red peppers and figs, some stuffed with almonds, all suspended on string looped and twirled round nails. It has a calming effect on me. Gino the Silent has now graduated to the armchair where his father used to sit and converse in dialect with whoever had time to listen. This too adds to the atmosphere of what I fondly imagine is life enduring since Etruscan times.

However, that morning we found Maria Pia sitting in the armchair, her left foot resting on a stool.

'I've strained it. Nothing much. I've used egg white for a plaster cast.' Caterina butted in.

'She wouldn't go to a doctor!' Maria Pia's wide smile shone in the threadbare room.

'It isn't swelling. I don't need to go. We didn't have doctors where I come from.'

'Where is that, signora?' Mother likes nothing better than hearing how other people live. When she travelled to Italy she used to stay in small hotels and saw the public side of Italian life in museums, churches, bars and restaurants. This was what she really wanted to sample: everyday life.

'Over the mountain...' then Maria Pia paused. We nudged her on, encouraging her in turn, so she began her story.

'There were three cottages, three families in a clearing for charcoal burning.' The fire flickered across the browned walls meeting streaks of sunshine through the open door. 'I looked after the goats first, sometimes the sheep or pigs. The kids skipped

more than the lambs.' I thought of Mauro's mother, the nonna taken on walks by her nanny goat, stopping here and there to tug at the banks above the track or crop our clover and dandelions. The goat would appear under our olives, blinking, nose up at us as if we were trespassing, while the old lady would be gathering brushwood some way behind.

'We were five living children. Two – or was it three?' she looked up at Caterina who shrugged her shoulders, 'died as babies. I did go down through the woods to school when I was six or seven. It was opposite San Giuliano where the cobbler and blacksmith were, more than three kilometres away, I think, very far anyway, and I was cold and hungry. I cried so much that Mamma said I could stay behind. I was the eldest, and my brothers and sisters copied me. We were all busy anyway. The woods were alive then, animals moving around with children or old folk looking after them.

'I helped Mamma carry baskets to the market in Montesasso, one on each arm, and one on my head. We got up in the cold, before dawn. She let me fill them with bundles of charcoal, kindling wood, eggs and goat or sheep cheese, chestnuts – it depended on the time of year – also mushrooms. We didn't keep eggs for ourselves because they sold first, and we needed the money. Then the cheese usually went. What we didn't sell we tried to exchange for flour, yeast, soap – things we couldn't make. If we were very lucky, we sometimes bought a pair of shoes for Papà. The only money we had was from selling produce at the market, so we were always short of what we couldn't make or find in the woods. Most was done by barter. I was cold and hungry but Mamma was pleased if the baskets were heavier going home. We were exhausted; it was slow going uphill. If they were light, we'd be carrying back what we hadn't sold or bartered, but if heavy it meant plenty of flour for bread and pasta, soap, paraffin and candles, potatoes and onions and some other vegetables if in season. Mamma and I got so tired in Montesasso, sitting all day on the ground. If we were lucky and arrived early enough we'd find a place under the eaves to shelter from the sun or rain, but where people passed by. Especially rich people. Sometimes they gave me an apple or a sweet, or occasionally shoes, a bit of clothing, even money which Mamma quickly took when nobody was looking.

'No, we didn't have a kitchen garden like here. Papà said the padrone Gadini would come and take whatever we cultivated, and he couldn't read or do numbers. That's why he was suspicious, and so was Renzo. If you don't understand what's being written down, you think you're being cheated.

'We were too high up for olive trees. We had snow, a lot of snow in winter. Oh, the cold. I can never forget the cold! The chilblains. I couldn't sleep for rubbing them, and still they went on tickling and aching. And going to bed hungry. Mamma made bread, occasionally pasta with the flour we carried up from the market, but there was never enough of it and we always seemed to be hungry.

'On feast days the priest before Don Luigi sometimes came up to bless the Madonnina in our shrine, bringing old clothes and such like. Mamma would be anxious and got up especially early to make egg pasta if she had managed to find enough flour, as he expected a meal. She had to use the eggs she was saving up for market and some of the ham from the one pig a year the padrone allowed us to keep for ourselves. We occasionally had chicken. I learnt how to kill and pluck the old ones that didn't lay any more. One chicken didn't last long. The priest seemed to eat too much! We didn't eat red meat as the animals belonged to the padrone. He came, or sent his farm manager to count them after lambing. At Christmas, if she remembered, his wife would give us a few bottles of olive oil, which had to last a whole year. Otherwise Mamma used lard.'

She was smiling and wriggling the toes on her injured leg as she recounted these hardships that were becoming history as she spoke.

'Granny died when I was quite young, but I remember her spinning wool, and Mamma did too. The spinster was an important person, always a woman, as without her the others couldn't weave cloth. We helped make rag rugs and patchwork covers from old clothes and tufts of wool or we knitted by the fire in winter – socks and leggings and pullovers and blankets. There were never enough covers so we slept with all our clothes on. And still it was cold. Mamma cut down men's shirts and trousers for my brothers, so they flapped around like scarecrows when they chased straying animals, or were fooling around on the woodpiles. We didn't have enough clothes or shoes. Papà made wooden clogs for us but our knitted socks got so cold and wet in the rain and snow, and heavy with sticky mud. Everything took days to dry. The only thing we had in plenty was firewood. We could take all the dead wood we could find.

'There was a lot of quarrelling over garments. The first to get up took the best clothing and shoes even if they were too big, and the last had to use clogs or go barefoot. We had to walk everywhere. I remember once,' she laughed, 'when I had to wear Mamma's old skirt and blouse held up by string and hurriedly tacked down the sides, because the others had taken all the clothes! In summer it was better. We wore less and went barefoot. It wasn't cold and it was easier to find food in the woods.

'In the war my sister got polio and nearly died. Everyone – Germans, English, partisans – passed by us. All three families in our clearing helped an escaped English prisoner of war. They took turns to leave bread for him in a little hut high in the mountain, where he'd collect it when the coast was clear. We children weren't told why they were carrying food into the woods, in case someone asked us.

'Sometimes we'd just meet and tell stories or sing together. We'd gather outside for dances in the woodland clearing, round a bonfire in winter with leaves and twigs to absorb the mud. Polka, waltz, mazurka, quadrille with the best accordionist we could find. I'd meet other woodlanders and one, an old woman, used to ask me to run errands, even giving me some money for it!' Maria Pia lowered her voice to a whisper so Caterina wouldn't hear. 'I was careful not to tell my parents, because I had to scurry off and leave the sheep while I took the little parcel to someone. For some sort of cure. Later I learnt they were potions or spells to have, or not have children, or little cloth dolls to stick pins in to – magic, that sort of thing. I suppose she was a kind of witch.

'Spirits? I remember a man used to shout out about spirits and told us not to go to some parts of the mountains. Older people said it was because he knew there were truffles there and was trying to frighten people off. Others said that the wolves were all those who had died a violent death – the unquiet spirits. They would howl in winter and padded outside the house whilst we were shivering inside. If you opened the door you could see ten or twelve red specks, eyes of devils. Sometimes we made a huge bonfire in the clearing to keep them off the sheep pens and chicken sheds as the hens wouldn't lay out of fear, and away from us, especially babies.' Caterina, busy round the stove, reminded us.

'Wolves used to prowl down here in the winter, right down the valley.'

'True,' said her mother, continuing. *'An ox panicked and killed a child by the ford where we first met. It was frightened by sprites, the souls of children who die young, like my brother and sister and my two little girls. Not bad spirits, just mischievous. Was Marco killed after you came? He was Oreste's grandson. Or great grandson. A nice little boy, but always straying down the valley. Not that there was anything wrong in that. These things happen.*

'Try washing clothes without soap! I can still see Mamma counting the egg money in the market and thinking what she could buy with it. Soap always came first, then flour, then paraffin for the lamps, and candles if there were any coins left. I helped her wash in a mountain spring, freezing cold in winter. It wasn't far, but wet clothes were so heavy and the ground rough. I would hold one end of the trousers or shirt while Mamma would twist and twist until it ran dry. Then she would shake it out and put it in a wicker basket. We pegged the washing outside or on a rope across the room where we lived and ate and slept. Sometimes the sprites would play with the garments and pull them off the pegs, so they fell and got smudged on the earth floor and Mamma had to rinse them again. The wrung clothes still dripped. I tried to get away from them, close to the fire, but the men blocked it from the rest of us. They played "beggar my neighbour" or "scopone"' by

firelight when the paraffin lamps and candles ran out, with Mamma as near as she could get to the hearth, mending and cutting down clothes, patching or knitting. Always busy.

'When it was hot we had fun washing ourselves in the waterfall on the far side of the clearing. More often than not we heard the sprites, my little brother and sister, giggling and tumbling around in the brambles and rocks above us, often making us spill the water we had to carry to a large metal tub. In cold weather it stood by the fire warming all day. Then hot water was added from the pot always hanging near the grate before Papà took the first bath. Then my brothers, then me and my sister. Mamma was always last, because she had been rationing out the bits of towels or old clothes we'd dry with, making sure nobody used too much soap. Except Papà. She herself usually bathed when we were all in bed across the room. Other days we'd wash in cold water using a bowl on the stone ledge where we rinsed the plates after the dogs had licked them clean, and poured the water out through a spout in the wall. I was always afraid a snake might wriggle in, but it never happened! There was a lot of water carrying all week, but Monday for clothes washing and Friday for a bath were the worst days.' She looked at us, heard our unspoken question, and laughed.

'Where? I knew you'd ask me that. We went in the woods, usually. Otherwise in the hole Papà dug leaving two planks on each side, a pile of earth, a wooden spoon, and a heap of big leaves if he remembered – dock, or chestnut. If we found a newspaper we'd save it to light the fire or tear into squares for the leaf function. He made a sort of tall shed out of poles with twigs woven between them, and moved it when the hole was full, after he'd dug another one. Each of the cottages had its own, and they'd move it around their nearest edge of the wood.

'In winter the pigs were in the sty and fed scraps from our meals, but in spring, summer and autumn I had to take them into the woods until sunset. Nobody had a watch. We returned at dusk, got up at dawn, or earlier in winter if it was market day. The wind blew all the time in winter, except when it was very, very frosty and the air bruised noses and cheeks. I chewed grass, twigs,

anything I could find, and was always hungry. I liked the late spring and summer best, and autumn before it got too dark and bleak, with the chestnuts roasting on the fire, though it wasn't so nice when they were all we had to eat. Those months weren't so lonely, as there were more people in the woods, more to gather and eat, much more to do while looking after the animals. Berries, wild lettuce, mushrooms. I was bending down early one June looking for tiny sweet strawberries, when I noticed a pair of old shoes on young feet standing just where I knew the plants grew best. I sat back and looked up to see Renzo who had a wide smile on his face,' and she cupped her hands round both cheeks as tears gathered above them.

'That smile never left him,' Caterina said, *'even when losing at cards!'*

'We got talking. He was a woodcutter, but did a bit of everything. Most days he came back with his mule – nobody around us could afford one – laden with sticks or logs, sometimes charcoal. He always gave me something: flowers, berries or nuts, or bits of wood with funny shapes – anything to make me happy! I had to move around with the animals, but he always found me. That was the best summer of my life. I had no shoes, only clogs and two frocks to my name, but I was happy as a skylark. I was warm, I wasn't hungry because we found a lot to eat together in the woods.' She was whispering again. *'I had hidden the witch's money in a tree trunk and told nobody except him.'* She continued in a normal voice. *'In September he asked me to marry him. Then he went to Papà who said he would give me a she-goat for a dowry. We had to wait for two years to find a landowner willing to have us farm his land. Families like ours who owned nothing and didn't work for wages were still expected to find dowries for daughters. Signora Gadini sometimes gave us sheets she didn't want, or cloth she had left over. I was given some white material, so I spent the next winter making my wedding dress, and there was enough left for underwear such as I had never had. The stitching was wobbly, as I couldn't see properly by firelight. Even so, I felt quite a lady, especially when the signora returned with shoes for me and two shirts for Renzo.*

'After the war, the other shepherds began to move down to the hillside farms. When Renzo and I married, we were the only

mountain family left. We walked more than three kilometres to San Giuliano to get married, but our return was much slower because everyone called us in for refreshments. We and our friends sang on the way up to my family for our wedding lunch. It took so long that our guests had already arrived and stood looking out for us at the edge of the wood! That evening we went to Renzo's house where we ate supper and danced the night away to the best accordion player from all around here.'

There was radiance in her voice as Maria Pia gathered us into her wedding story.

'Soon afterwards the farm next to Quinto fell vacant, and here we have stayed. Gino was born a year later. I lost a girl. Then Caterina here. I lost another baby girl before – or after – Arturo. I think he was the last.' Caterina was frowning, mumbling something about not wanting me to take her mother's photo because she was wearing her mother-in-laws cast-off dress. Maria Pia just smiled and wriggled her sprained ankle in its egg white cast.

'Am I better off now? I'd never go back. To the snow and the rain. And hunger. Everyone has left the mountains, even the charcoal burners. A few return by car. Nobody wants to live up there, not even strangers like you. All the shepherds' cottages are in ruin. My children work on building sites or in factories and all their children will go to school. Gino keeps this farm going in his spare time and I tend the kitchen garden, hens, rabbits, the usual. I don't want to go back to see the ruins, not even to get the mushrooms or strawberries in the places I know they grow best.'

Mother's subsequent silence continued almost unbroken over lunch. Maria Pia had told us of a way of life that went back to when the first woodlanders cleared the undergrowth and settled with their flocks in mountain glades, high above the hillsides where Gianni's ancestors later began cultivating his valley.

'Did I hear Maria Pia say she was married at a church called San Giuliano?' Mother asked me over lunch. I hadn't mentioned the name of the church. Now I could see her listening to what my father had told her all those years ago.

CHAPTER 23

'It was my idea to take Gianni,' Mother told me, 'to visit San Giuliano. How could I have missed it?' She was thinking of her post-war pilgrimages to all the San Giulianos in Tuscany.

'It must have been too small to put on the map,' I suggested. When I arrived in 1974, all the tracks from the hillside farms converged on the church square at the heart of their community before heading north or south along the Via Cassia. Only the priest's house and his farmer's stood by the church, with the school and the smithy on the other side of the stream.

'I've checked it's on the most recent map of this area,' she said. With all the new buildings like Pina's, Sibilla's by the fire station and more spreading along the Cassia, San Giuliano had earned its mark on the map.

'I asked Gianni to show me the names on the War Monument,' she continued. 'He dropped my arm and said instead that he wanted to show me the church and the priest's unusual collection of bones! Then I called him back to see if he knew anything about the two Giovannis on the inscription.

"That Giovanni," he pointed to the one at the end, "was at school with me. He was shot by the Germans". He was shying away again.

"Why?"

"I can't remember exactly. A partisan."

"And this one?" I was keener than he wanted me to be.

"Oh, he was a prisoner of war."

"Where?" I was too persistent.

"I don't know." I could see him hesitating, as if he knew more than he was going to tell me.

"He was parachuted back, for some reason. To do with radio contact, I think. Anyway the Germans found him."

"Shot?"

"No, a land mine. He was trying to escape. Why are you so interested?" He wanted to set himself adrift from his history. I didn't. Inside the church, Gianni ran his hand round the font where he'd been baptised and told me what he'd learnt at school about the two Saint Julians. We couldn't find Don Luigi in the church or his house, so we didn't see the mammoth bones in his museum. I did manage to find him later and ask what he knew about the two Giovannis on the inscription. It was clear he thought it an odd question. He couldn't tell me much more than I already knew. They were innocent men tangled up in the tragic events of the war. They lost their lives in one way or another and were all remembered in prayers at his church. He hadn't heard of a Giovanni Paese of their generation or any other. He remarked it was an unusual surname.'

Gianni was spending his free time with mother, abandoning me to my book though I didn't have fresh ideas or even the will to write. I went on solitary walks to direct my thoughts. On my return, I tried to draw them into sentences, shaping paragraphs to blot out the anguish of not knowing mingled with a desire to hold Paul close. It echoed the ache of Tim's absence.

Cecilia fights back – Easter 1982

Gianni wanted to show my mother his childhood haunts.

'You've already seen them, Olivia,' he said, and that suited me. She asked him to take her to the church of San Giuliano. Mother and I were developing our separate agendas for the afternoons when Gianni came to the house.

I drove up to Montesasso hoping to find my lawyer friend, Cecilia Ferrarini. She was busy rearranging the Montesasso museum. An architect, born in the valley next to ours, had won the competition for the design and she was keen for me to meet him. On Good Friday Mother and I went for a morning walk down to the Via Cassia where new houses were being built. San Giuliano was just a hamlet with a church serving a large and scattered parish when I first crossed the square eight years ago and glimpsed Don Luigi. It has now become a village, and is spreading further along the Roman road.

'Olivia!' Sibilla was watering her front garden when we passed on our way to the bar. Mother was badgering me to

venture inside a new house on the Cassia and Sibilla was just the person to ask.

'Grazie a Dio I don't live over the shop any more! My doctor told me to sell up after a bad attack of hepatitis last Christmas.' She narrated the symptoms, returning with the frequency of a verbal tic to her 'pi-pi color bronzo'. Or perhaps her fixation was with the colour of bronze, starting from the brazen pots on the veranda stretching the length of the house. The now familiar deep brown furniture shone in brassy tones to accompany bronze ornaments and matching pots and pans in the kitchen.

The tone lightened in the sitting room where Sibilla seemed to have thrown streaks of peppermint into thick cream, stirring a couple of times before leaving it to flow into an imitation marble table top. It looked too smooth and tacky to invite touch. Mother's eyes were on stalks. All was squeaky clean. The sofa cushions rose like a soufflé around us as we sank into them, concerned whether we could rise to our feet in the politeness of time. Sibilla mounted the platform behind a bar counter across one corner, reminiscent of her former raised position in the shop. Grandly, against the backdrop of row upon row of liqueurs with a mirror behind them, she offered us a drink. We both chose safety in Camparis, preferring the known to a voyage into uncharted colours, tastes and high alcohol content. Orazio hovered in waiting behind the sofa, making approving noises. Two little women, kept carefully in the background, watched us from the door: her aunt and his mother.

'We bought this plot not long after starting the bar and shop in the house where Orazio was born. We continued building, on and off, over fifteen years.' Their new house stands where the valley sinks into the plain below the Cassia, cold and clammy in winter, hot and humid in summer, but at the hub of anything worth happening.

Extracting ourselves from the sofa, we were ushered upstairs past a cabinet of Orazio's guns, noticeably larger than Carlo's, the hunting rifles pointing upwards in a tight rank, all highly polished. Only the wild boar trophies that adorn Carlo's dining room were missing. We were not shown the old ladies' quarters, but their son's was on our circuit. He was married without any children, Sibilla noted regretfully, but had a good post in an Arezzo bank.

She was keen to reveal the master bedroom with its own vast bathroom; the others shared a smaller one covered in sunflower-dominated tiles. Hers instead was clad in bronze coloured tiles with a poppy motif, perhaps to induce sleepiness. The bed contradicted this assumption. The vast Italian-style matrimonial couch was designed with a console to hold television, radio and tape recorder. Over it a huge glass chandelier dangled dangerously, only slightly smaller than the monumental one in the sitting room. Pictures of animals with ribbons and cute expressions hung around the walls to cheer up their cuddly counterparts, dejectedly nestling among cushions heaped over the pillows. I imagined Sibilla, exhausted, throwing herself onto them to watch her favourite TV programme, though if she hit a tiger's paw, a teddy's foot, or a pretty doll's leg, it could be an uncomfortable landing! Before retiring to bed, can you imagine the task of undressing it to find space for themselves? Sibilla relished the way we surveyed it in detail, murmuring appreciatively.

'You have taken a lot of trouble over your garden, signora,' Mother said, standing on the porch. Each shrub or tree had been planted in isolation from the others, many in discordant bloom. A magnolia with wax-like flowers, a mimosa in full yellow cascade, an ornamental cherry sprouting pink buds and numerous standard roses, all smartly upright in circular beds surrounded by neat gravel. In their old house Sibilla had green fingers. Her cherished pots of plants used to squat haphazardly up the steps out of pecking reach, tended singly and lovingly; the wax-white arum lily found on church altars and the rarer strains of geraniums stood beside culinary basil, parsley and fennel. Her villa garden had been created, Mother thought, just by gathering together plants that caught her eye.

Pina spied us with Sibilla and ran over the yard as we passed to invite us to a family supper. They had begun their houses at about the same time, Pina told us, but Sibilla's was far more ambitious.

'People with connections find the best jobs, like the banking one for Sibilla's son.' *Carlo was egging Pina on, smiling at me and wiggling his eyebrows.* 'First Sibilla managed to get her son an invalidity pension when he injured his hand helping in their shop.' *It didn't stop there, according to Pina. Taking full advantage of his misfortune, he had slipped into the banking job on its invalidity quota. Carlo interrupted,* 'So now he has a double benefit from an accident: an invalidity pension for life and a much-coveted job at the bank – short hours, good pension and retirement after thirty-five years! That can mean in one's fifties if one gets in early. No mean prospect!' *We all nodded agreement.*

* * * * *

Cecilia arrived late on Easter Friday. I tried inviting her to come at seven, hoped to see her by eight, but it was nearer nine when she drove down the drive. She explained she has to dance to the tune of her clients, and they all sleep during the siesta, emerging after four in the afternoon expecting shops and her services to be available until eight, their supper time. With her was a younger, quietly spoken man. She introduced him:

'Francesco designs airport interiors, but he's here to put the last touches to his museum display for the Prudomini bequest.' *Then, looking round,* 'Hasn't Paul come?' *Mention of his television activities caused silent respect, his absence regretted.*

Our conversation wandered pleasantly to arrive at the strange ways of the electric current.

'I have the maximum domestic allowance, referred to as "three kilowatts", but the lights are always fusing.' *Cecilia and Francesco were already smiling at my foreign ignorance. They remained silent, so I rambled on.* 'I've only two water heaters – a smaller one in the kitchen, and a fridge. No washing machine. My neighbours have sprinklers, saws and many more electrically powered appliances than we have, but none of our problems!' *By then Cecilia was laughing.*

'They only have a bath once a week,' she said by way of explanation. Mother and I looked at her in disbelief. The inhabitants of the valley were involved in far more physical labour than we were, surely they had to wash more often than us, not less?

'Only one bath a week,' Francesco agreed with Cecilia. 'Electricity has just come to the valleys around here. I know because the farmers on my parents' land in the next valley are very frugal. Electricity still seems a luxury to them,' he explained. 'They worry about not having the money to pay the electricity bills every two months. When the candle burnt out or the oil for the lamp was exhausted, they could only replace them when they had the money to pay. Now they fear losing immediate control of their expenses.'

'Understandably,' Mother nodded.

'Pay for three more kilowatts of power,' was their advice.

When I stopped serving the food to sit down for the first course, I thought it a good moment to ask Cecilia about Don Basilio.

'Why do you want to know?' She looked a bit startled. I reassured her that I had only met him when buying land from the Church and he gave us a copy of the local Gazetta with his article on the famous Prudomini vase. It was clear he disagreed with her about it and the recent finds.

'They aren't forgeries! He's completely mistaken.' Cecilia was warming up.

'Volete saper tutto?' Mother and I were eager to hear the whole story.

It seems it all started when the Prudomini decided to donate their famous Etruscan collection and other valuable works to the Montesasso Museum.

'I'm the elected representative of the Town Council of Montesasso with particular responsibility for culture and tourism.' It was easy to see that Francesco admired her guts. The young architect gazed fascinated at Cecilia, eyes flashing. She had vivacity, a mischievous allure, and not a grey hair twisting among her dark curls.

'I'm determined to modernise the museum and attract more people to Montesasso. This would give a much-needed boost to local traders, hotels, bars, restaurants and also the traditional crafts, as well as stop families moving down the mountainside to Montesasso Scalo.'

I noticed Mother was also aware of the body language between Francesco and Cecilia, as she was saying little and watching intently.

'It's sad that just when I was coming to an understanding with Don Basilio – the Prudomini never reply – there were elections and, as prominent Christian Democrats, the Prudomini returned to their villa to whip up votes for the party. All communication between Don Basilio and me ceased.' Cecilia paused. I could well imagine the Count and Don Basilio's consternation when the local communists (Cecilia was one of the more popular) increased their support. As her family comes from Rome, it's easier for her to make contact with the leading Etruscan museum there, though she's loath to get it involved in this controversy.

'It's a risk.' Cecilia paused as Mother cleared the plates to move on to fruit and cheese. 'If the Roman Etruscanologists prove me right and the vase is a genuine Etruscan artefact, Montesasso might never see it again. You have to allow for all the political rivalry, as well as the competing claims of the larger archaeological museums in Rome, Florence and Arezzo.'

Mother and I discussed what we'd learnt long after midnight. I want to believe that the Museum's most famous treasure, the erotic vase discovered and authenticated by our Count Prudomini's scholarly grandfather, is not a forgery. Cecilia is my friend, but she is no Etruscanologist and could well be mistaken.

Towards the end of our stay, Joan and Gianni would potter in the garden while I went over my writing. Spring had given sheen to the air and a touch of shrill green to the unfurling leaves; I should have been inspired. Instead I didn't manage to settle down to anything and I couldn't help hearing them communicating in a mishmash of English and Italian. She would call him 'Gio' short for Giovanni, instead of the normal 'Gianni'. I should have been more grateful. No unwelcome squeezes and kisses; a relief, I told myself. Gianni looks so much better, quite handsome, though I'd hardly noticed it before. Still lean but not so bent and drawn. Even his limp has gone, and he's been buying new clothes, the old rascal. He's smiling and talking more. Springtime, new sap, renewed vitality.

* * * * *

After our Easter visit, Gianni has been addressing his weekly letters to Joan, now signing himself Gio. She relates most of the news from his letters, but doesn't give them to me to read. Quinto saw his first grandchild, Susanna, before he died of pneumonia in hospital. His vest arrived back from its blessing by the saint in Rimini two weeks after the funeral.

'Gio,' Mother announced, 'says Wolfgang is using your field at the top of the drive as a building yard. He's extending his house and seems to think that piece is his. Mauro says it's yours.' Was Gianni moonlighting for Wolfgang at double the going rate while I was away, I wondered? He had hinted as much at Easter.

Cecilia phoned late in June to ask about people to invite to the preview of the new installation and recent finds at Montesasso's museum. Everyone she knew would be invited, of course, but she wanted to make a splash. Near San Giuliano on Prudomini land another significant tumulus had been discovered. She was very excited.

'I'll tell you more in the summer.' As an afterthought, 'Could you try and persuade Count Prudomini and his wife to come to the opening on 7 August? The new installation for the latest Prudomini bequest will be ready and it's important for the museum to keep the family connection. Get Paul to do it. They admire him, a restorer and working in television. They still don't acknowledge any of my letters.'

Political rifts can divide people with similar cultural interests. However the Prudomini seem to be shunning me too. I wrote to the Count and his wife without expecting or receiving an answer.

Mother and I were both now thinking ahead, with different expectations, to summer at the Casa dell'Avventura.

Paul had been missing for eight months. I hoped he might have contacted us over Easter. Joe or Gran would have told him our new number in Italy. Gianni put it in my name and I hoped that Paul might consult the International Directory. While Margaret Thatcher was triumphantly leading the nation to victory in the Falklands War and loved sons and brothers were being sacrificed for a glorious cause, the case of a missing man shrivelled into insignificance. Gran had a telephone call from Paul's mother. She was distraught, saying his solicitor brother had already been in touch with every existing organisation for tracking missing persons and had run out of options. Her husband had made a television appeal for information whilst we were in Italy. She hadn't telephoned because they didn't want to upset us even more; precisely the reason I hadn't been in touch with them. No payments or withdrawals had been made on our joint account since he had visited Joe in hospital. I felt deprived and emotionally destitute. My makeshift responses to reassure Dan were wearing threadbare.

CHAPTER 24

The phone had rung many times in Downs Way while I was with Mother in Tuscany. No male voice, just Paul's mother tentatively asking Gran if she had heard from him.

'He used to not contact us for months on end,' she admitted plaintively, 'and he didn't want us to disturb him in his studio.' A pause to blow her nose. 'His brothers have done all they can… but it's many months since we've heard from him and I'm so worried.'

Gran sighed and told her that I, too, had been in touch with every existing organisation for tracking missing people and had run out of options. Everyone was distraught. When I rang Paul's mother on my return I found her almost incoherent.

'My husband… won't mention his youngest son… makes matters far worse.' I didn't tell her Paul's payments for Dan had stopped.

'I'm relieved you've phoned.' Sarah's voice was higher than usual, a tone of slight disapproval. 'Dan's been asking and asking when you and his granny were coming back.' She sounded upset.

'I'll tell you when you come. Be quick!' I took the car, though I could have walked.

Dan always enjoyed playing with Kate in the attic, where a bed was kept snug for him in a small room under the eaves. She had a larger room next door. Penny spent interminable hours in her own poster-lined bedroom on the floor below where, ostensibly, she was doing her homework but usually, Dan reported (probably because Kate told him), preening herself in the mirror. Andrew was out most evenings working unsocial hours at a pub. Dan would follow him around when Kate was otherwise busy and didn't want to play with him. Sarah was fascinated by Dan who imagined growing up by modelling himself on the young man about the house. Irrationally, it upset me. Tim should have been his role model, and now Andrew was taking Tim's place.

Usually Sarah wove a web of calm around her home; untidy and lived-in, there was always a glow. She offered an unruffled harbour to soothe the shifting winds and squalls of teenage temperament. Sarah had William, and was infuriatingly content. She didn't ask for more in life, even if, she said, it made her boring. And she laughed at herself. All life is a trade off. Some of us grossly miscalculate.

But I had never seen Sarah so disturbed.

'After you left, Dan settled in as usual,' she started. 'He knows he has his own room and his teddy.' She had thought of everything. 'But after he'd been with us for about four days, when Andrew went off fell walking over Easter, Dan began asking when you were coming back. Then he wanted to know where granny was, and I said she was with you in Italy. He seemed puzzled and asked if Daddy was in Italy too.' Paul was in everyone's mind. How could he be so heartless? Or had something horrific happened to him?

Guilt smears my memory of that Easter. Shame too, and helplessness.

Sarah seemed on the verge of saying, 'Take Dan, he needs you.' She could well have added, 'and Paul too!' But as I cuddled Dan, a small bundle of sobs, the loss of Paul and Tim reverberated in the emotional void inside me.

It was Mother, with more experience of absence than most, who steered Dan and me through the emotional turbulence in the wake of Paul's departure.

'No fantasies. Expect the worst. Dead or disappeared; in practical terms, it's the same. Physical survival comes first – food, shelter, it's as basic as that.' Did she hug me in wartime, when the flying bombs were dropping on us? For her, hope shone in through a half-open door, rang with an unexpected knock, lay in the scent of wild roses and the tart sweetness of blackberries from that summer long-ago when she and father passionately loved me into life. As years wandered away, it was gathered into the companionship of her colleague at the library, and now the Joan and 'Gio' letters written in hybrid English-Italian.

A leaden weight bore me down as soon as I awoke and as I bustled around Dan at breakfast, getting him ready for school, dreading more questions and repeating the only answers I could think of: Daddy's away working, busy abroad. With Paul gone I seemed to be losing Tim a second time. Their absence wore into me, until I arrived at school, slammed the door on them both and got on with the business of survival. Mother had managed pretty well without my own father, and I must exist without Tim, and now Paul. But I clutched Dan close to stop him following them.

I forged a new persona: Olivia, successful professional woman, sophisticated, trim, organised forty-year-old single mother and attentive daughter with precious little time between school and home. My colleagues were all emotionally preoccupied elsewhere; they provided few social opportunities for chance encounters. It can't have been long after Easter 1982 that I was made Head of School with a significantly raised salary. My professional fulfilment was progressing in inverse ratio to its emotional equivalent. A mother with a sliver of ice in her heart and a seven-and-a-half year-old hanging on to her supermarket trolley.

At weekends I took Dan up to the Downs, sometimes with his friends, more often alone. We'd look at trees, birds and flowers and I'd remember, with a stab of pain, how Tim used to sketch the same scenes: horses galloping, kites flying, people out in wide spaces. Together we'd jump over low branches in the rhododendron tunnels as I'd done in childhood, imagining myself a steeplechaser, and he'd ask, 'Did you come here with Tim?' A heartbeat missed. Or deep in sunken lanes we ran our fingers over moss and round knotted roots. 'Like Gran's hands,' Dan said. Or touched ferns curling out of winter leaf-mould smelling brown and green, rot and growth, and avoiding red spotty toadstools – 'Poisonous!' he cried out. Colours that remind me of Paul, I thought, wishing they didn't: green, brown and red. The stones were striped with the strata of time and mottled with landscapes of the imagination – that's what Paul had told Tim about Leonardo, here, by this wall, this gate, this field.

'Did you do this with Tim?' When he asked it, he looked smaller than a seven-and-a-half year-old and was sucking his thumb.

We took a train to fishing villages on the south coast, scouring the beaches in all weathers, collecting shells: surf-sounding pearly ones veined pale green, flat grey tortoiseshell husks or a tiny white cushion with fluted openings, rough to touch, where life had escaped leaving a void. Together we pictured scenes below the water surface, with seaweed and coral plants waving their tentacles as shoals flickered through them, and the sea bugs, as Dan called them, slithering inside his creamy white shells with brown spikes like hedgehogs.

'Don't break them!' That was unfair for me to say; I was far clumsier.

'I won't,' Dan said. 'Did you go to the seaside with him?'

'No I didn't,' not strictly true. We did take Tim to Ostia, near Rome. A waiter at a beach café took that last photo of the three of us.

Gran was Dan's home anchor while Mother and I were working late. She told him all the stories of the photos on her bedside table unchanged since my childhood, especially about her parents who bought this house, the first to be built on Downs Way. He asked to hold the Great Exhibition medal still in the same place on the mantelpiece. Gran had taken it down for me to handle when I was Dan's age, saying proudly.

'My grandfather was awarded it in 1851, for helping in London's first great international exhibition.'

Once he sat on her lap, sobbing. Words tumbled out, 'Gran, why do you have the photo of your brother in uniform who was lost in the war, and of my granny and mother and father and Tim, but not me? Why?'

'I took his face in my hands,' Gran told me, saying, 'I don't need to. You're a living image, and my hands are framing you in the shape of my heart. He hugged me, and then, do you know what he said?' He was playing with her fingers, his light and smooth, the childish dimples hardening into knuckles, the tips widening.

'Your hands are like Kate's tortoise!' he was grinning with tears on his cheeks, 'and you have brown spots on them.'

'They were left by the fairies of time dancing their muddy feet over me.' Gran was smiling and Dan was too.

I found myself escaping more often into my story mapping changes in a Tuscan valley. Mother was dreaming too, even contemplating early retirement.

'Perhaps in Italy,' she hinted.

Ties and tensions – Summer 1982

When Mother and I arrived with Dan and Joe in late July, the stream between us and the church square was almost dry and the pump in the twenty-metre well had burst, spattering the returning water with oil. Gianni and Joan took plastic containers to fill in Montesasso, leaving Joe and me round the mill table to ponder our misfortune and Dan to construct a Lego lorry.

The old well slowly filled up again, but the water could only be used for washing bodies, assuming no objection to an aftershower aroma of engine oil! Over time, Gianni assured us, the new pump would clear the contaminated water. The faster we used it, the better.

So much had been happening that I hadn't even shown Joe our land. Dan went wild, shooting imaginary beasts down the terraces and floating rudimentary log boats on the trickle of a stream. The flowerbeds had faded, except for the sturdy geraniums in pots on each side of the veranda steps, randomly watered by anyone who remembered. The cut grass on the terraces down to the stream was still lying on the ground like an abandoned hay crop, clogging the surface; Joan insisted Gio was right, it did inhibit new growth. In other words, he was disinclined to rake it up. I didn't bother to shoo off the hens pecking the flowers whilst Joe and I walked up the drive to see what had changed on my land next to the new German neighbour. He had cleared away the building material, knocking branches off the plum trees and mulberry in the process, and was now using it as an off-road parking place. Joe thought I was right not to protest. I wasn't using the land and Wolfgang and his wife didn't peer over it at us.

After Gianni had left and just as we were watching bats darting over the crimson sunset below a sky shading pale blue into green, splutters of unconnected notes and the ominous clearing of a throat rose from the foot of the hill, disturbing the twilight. A few coherent sounds followed, hugely amplified, swooping into the latest romantic song followed by a foxtrot. All this drifted towards us from beneath a canopy of floodlights on our side of the fire station.

'It's the Festa dell'Unità,' I said, somewhat perturbed.

'If you can't beat 'em, join 'em!' Joan commented, half-joking. So I turned the pasta water off and we walked down, curious to see what was happening and find something to eat there.

Carlo and Pina were not at home, nor were Sibilla and Orazio. They had all gone to the Festa in aid of the Communist Party newspaper, L'Unità. It was held on the football field originally laid out for the firemen and carabinieri, but soon taken over by the youngsters in the vicinity. The current Italian hits, coy or brash, boomed out of loudspeakers while all activity was concentrated under awnings where people were eating.

A curious company of youthful grandmother, frayed mother with male friend, and a small boy sat at a table and looked around for familiar faces. It was too crowded to think in the animated chatter that competed with the music, each rising in decibels as the evening wore on. I thought we might return home after the meal, a futile idea, since the music and disc jockey's commentary would disturb us until the early hours. Joan took Dan off to watch the skittles and side shows while Joe suggested a turn on the dance floor to a quickstep, followed by a samba, and then a calmer romantic waltz. A smiling face swayed by and I recognised Carlo with a small curly-haired woman on his arm – Marisa, who had given Gianni and me cake, lemonade and good company. A few minutes later, when the makeshift plank floor was reverberating to rhythmic feet, shouts and screams seared the night air. Couples slowed down, looked round, and then recoiled in horror. Pina had grasped her rival's curls and was jabbing a plastic knife into her plump arm. Women gasped in surprise. The music blared on while two men struggled to part them. Carlo meanwhile had vanished. Pina rushed sobbing from the dance floor and the spotlights, fleeing from the renewed indifference of the couples, now rhythmically involved in the frenzied samba next on the tape – the dance must go on.

'I'll see if Pina's all right,' I shouted over the noise to Joe. 'Find Mother and Dan and take them back to the house. I'll just look in to make sure she's not alone.'

No lights through the slats of the shutters; not even a yelp from the yard shrouded in silence. I hesitated before mounting the outside staircase. The door was open. In the tiny kitchen lit only by a light through the scullery door, Pina's son and Lisa, his girlfriend, were leaning over her. Vincenzo looked up and nodded me inside. Pina was moaning that she couldn't stand it any more; Carlo only came back to eat and went out again, returning to sleep in the early hours. Lisa, less voluble than usual, was busy in the background making coffee. Compressed into that small clammy room one marriage was unravelling and another was still being deferred – to Lisa's fury.

That summer of 1982 Dan shadowed me, trying to hold my hand in case I wandered off. Together we dug and hoed a patch at one end of Gianni's kitchen garden, without consulting him about the phases of the moon and what we might sow. We vied to see whose seeds sprouted first and what we could produce to eat.

'When's Dad coming?' His eyes held me to answer.

'When he can.'

'Can takes a long time, and I want him to come swimming with me.' Dan had noticed the new municipal swimming pool at Montesasso. Instead I taught him to swim.

'We've got a phone now, so why doesn't he call us?' Why give him imaginary excuses?

'What if he comes and we're not here?' He hovered anxiously around me and the phone, blue eyes imploring, clinging to his two points of reference.

'He'll wait for us.' As we are waiting.

'Does he know we're here?'

'He can find out.'

We both think with the same fear and pain but don't say aloud, 'Why doesn't he?' Not to wound each other, we sheathe the question. Then, 'When is Andrew coming?' He wanted male company. 'Or Penny and Kate?'

'Soon.' More waiting. So we created our adventures.

Dan found stones sticking out of the retaining wall to serve as footholds up to the field Wolfgang had invaded at the top of the drive. We'd lie there and pick leaves and flowers from as many different plants as we could find. There were faces in cloverleaves, luck in ladybirds that ran over the back of his hand, honey bees in the clover flowers and nasty wasps crawling over the fallen plums. Butterflies, from handsome red admirals to run-of-the-mill cabbage whites, were there for us to chase around the olives, plum trees and mulberry, while moths fell into your glass of water at night or dropped dead on the table, immolated on electric bulbs.

We sat in Maria Pia's kitchen and she told us how hard-earned cash had come from silkworms living on the leaves from our mulberry tree.

'Cocoons sold well until nylon was invented after the war. In less time than it takes to think about it, no one would buy them. The silk industry was finished. One less way for us to find ready cash since landowners, for some reason, didn't demand half of the cocoons as they did for everything else in the *mezzadria* system.'

I asked her to identify the flowers for us. She pronounced, I wrote the names down but couldn't find them in my Italian botanical dictionary.

'Is Maria Pia making them up, Mummy?'

'No. They're probably dialect words.'

'What's dialect? Do I speak it?' He did, picking up words heard about him in the valley.

Dan and Olivia entertaining each other: two figures fading into a distant landscape. I became peripheral, my story of the ruin rebuilt inconsequential, all part of an unvaried pattern of change from chrysalis to bug to moth to death to eggs and rebirth. Everything waiting for the next act, outlines prescribed, details indistinct. Something would happen and there was nothing that mother and child, bent over wild flowers and insects, could do to change it.

CHAPTER 25

When the phone rang, Dan always picked it up, said 'hello' and listened, usually to put it down in tears. A woman's voice.

The plot thickens – Summer 1982

Joe was talking to Joan on the veranda and Dan was piecing together a jigsaw puzzle on the table while I prepared supper, when the telephone rang. It startled me, unused to the sound at the Casa dell'Avventura. Dan ran inside to answer it. I followed him to find it was Cecilia.

'Quick. As many of us as possible,' I said urgently, 'I've forgotten about the Etruscan exhibition. Cecilia counts on our support at the preview.' I was embarrassed because she had changed the date to suit me. Joe offered to stay behind with Dan, who had disappeared round the back of the house in case he was roped in to do something useful.

Italians usually arrive at least half an hour late for social events. It was a relief to mingle with others trickling into Palazzo Prudomini across the courtyard, up the outside steps and along the corridor into the vast assembly hall.

From outside it seemed a steady stream of people would give creditable support to the exhibition preview, but this immense chamber with coffered ceiling and tall windows absorbed them and still looked half-empty. A strained atmosphere emanated from knots of people balancing glasses and canapés. Cecilia rushed over and asked, 'isn't Paul with you?' while propelling us towards two figures isolated under the central chandelier: Count Prudomini and his wife. We exchanged pleasantries and I asked politely what they thought of the new display. They were non-committal, enquiring instead what Paul was restoring, impressed that he was away working on another television programme. They were already looking over my shoulder for the next guest, lost for conversation. The more I felt them withdrawing, the more perversely imprudent my conversation seemed to become.

'I've heard more artefacts have been found on your land near San Giuliano.' I paused; they remained silent. 'Don't experts from Rome now say Montesasso was an important Etruscan city because key trade routes met on the plain below?' My stilted conversation petered out. All this was amply expounded in the fat and costly catalogue conspicuously for sale at the entrance. Cecilia's architect friend was hovering by it; I longed to break away and ask Francesco for a tour round his new display. Instead I asked how Don Basilio was, expecting to see him there, but the Count replied brusquely that he had not seen him for many weeks; everyone had been so busy.

'Don Basilio is convinced that the Montesasso vase, authenticated by my scholarly grandfather, is a forgery, and the new finds as well. He could hardly come to a preview of an exhibition displaying works from the celebrated Prudomini bequest which he happens to consider are fakes, could he?'

I had always thought the Prudomini agreed with Don Basilio. However, their presence at the preview implied support for Cecilia's authenticity argument, assumed by the stylish display. The Count seemed to read my thoughts.

'We're here because this Museum was founded and, until the post-war era, funded by my family.' His tone of voice made it clear he regretted that his family had relinquished control.

Cecilia came over to introduce the Prudomini to the Mayor elected in the spring – on a Communist ticket! They shook hands, limply exchanged a few conventional comments and drifted apart. By then the Count obviously considered that he and the Countess had made their presence felt just enough to show they were not ostracising the whole affair, yet did not fully approve. As they processed diagonally towards the main doorway, silence fell and people shrank back against the walls.

'Portano iella!'' I heard someone whisper to her neighbour behind me. So the Prudomini were bearers of misfortune, of the 'evil eye'. That was a new twist for me. All gazed in silence at the couple disappearing out of sight and, as their attitude suggested,

out of my acquaintance. Their steps had hardly begun to echo along the wide, arched corridor of the Count's former ancestral home, when the chandelier crashed down into iridescent splinters of glass, just where they had been standing.

Nobody breathed for an eternity, ended by an apprehensive hum of relief; groups were reformed, glasses refilled, canapés consumed with increasing relish as the fragments were swept away. The Mayor roared with laughter, circled by hangers-on. Cecilia hastened back to thank us for dealing with the Prudomini. Francesco took us round his new layout while the guests were chatting and refreshing themselves. The main gallery had been redecorated, but most of the pictures displayed were where they had hung for decades, if not centuries. Only the glass cases showing Etruscan artefacts had been changed. They were new slim-line versions surrounding the central installation, spot-lit from inside. There, in pride of place, the trophy exhibit seemed to float just below eye level under a shower of light, the revelries – to everyone's barely concealed delight – sensuously revealed to all by a specially positioned mirror. The Mayor chortled at them unashamedly with his deputy. Joan hummed a popular number she had picked up from her Gio as she looked round the displays. Other less sensational vases and miniature stone deities, formerly in the central showcase, had been relegated to peripheral ones. In a room apart, pulsating with chatter and incipient intoxication, the latest Prudomini bequest of recent discoveries from their San Giuliano property, was elegantly displayed and ignored.

The sun was setting over the Etruscan tombs as we returned from Montesasso to our valley. When we passed Carlo's yard, I asked Joan to drive herself back. Pina and the whole incident with Carlo's mistress had been on my mind.

Not a light was on. A neighbour shouted she was with Lisa's parents three houses past Sibilla's former shop. I found a subdued Pina sitting with Lisa, both lamenting Carlo's amorous adventures and Massimo's ongoing misdeeds. Released after the kidnapping incident through a government amnesty, he was in trouble again. He had been accused of robbing Etruscan tombs behind San Giuliano, a stone's throw from where we were sitting, and illegally selling the artefacts to a criminal ring of dealers in touch with foreign museums. Don Basilio had hinted that Count Prudomini's grandfather might have dabbled in shady dealings around the early 1900s, when foreign museums would pay anything for the best antiquities on the market. Something similar could be happening now.

'Do the new finds belong to il conte?' I asked Pina and Lisa, to turn the conversation away from Pina's plight.

'Yes, the tombs are on Prudomini land.' Lisa assumed Massimo was in touch with such illegal activities through his involvement in the kidnapping affair. I was sad. Our builder had been ruined once through his own folly and ignorance, but he was not a hardened criminal, nor essentially unkind. To add to the emotional confusion, Lisa was saying she had broken her engagement to Vincenzo because he wouldn't marry her.

Pina began sobbing after Lisa went into the kitchen to help her mother prepare supper.

'Lisa is expecting Vincenzo's child,' she whispered, 'and wants to marry before it's born. I wish he would.'

At last Vincenzo came in, pulled a chair over to sit by his mother and put his arms round her. She relaxed, weeping even more. Promising, I thought. Five minutes later Vincenzo had declared to the assembled company that he would marry Lisa and I was invited there and then to their wedding! We began to laugh and tease him. When would it be? What would he like for presents? He blushed, and seeing that, Pina smiled. Everyone drank to Vincenzo and Lisa, tactfully not mentioning their future offspring.

There were more intrigues going on locally, Vincenzo said, something to do with the Vatican and banking. Limousines, police escorts, bigwigs and secret meetings at the villa in the next valley. I had noticed it from the Cassia, a substantial white stuccoed building with green shutters at the end of a cypress-lined avenue. A hush. All faces turned to Vincenzo, who settled comfortably into his account. After tales of financial rackets masterminded by politicians or financiers – all equally corrupt in his eyes – of bank notes used as stuffing for cushions; of motorways costing billions *leading to nowhere, no one was surprised to hear rumours that local Christian Democrats were involved in something sinister. But what exactly? One in particular, onorevole Bintoni, had retired behind the high walls round that same villa. He was involved in some sort of masonic lodge and, it was rumoured, in money laundering. One scandal followed another with a regularity that made them appear almost normal to the practically-minded folk of San Giuliano. Once so farfetched, the dubious activities of distant people in power caused little more than a raised eyebrow and wise look. Now they were too close for comfort. One of the main culprits was living in this villa, though his status was so financially elevated that Vincenzo called Don Bintoni a stregone, or wizard!*

Vincenzo accompanied me to the Casa dell'Avventura before going to deal with his father, no light task for a young man who had just been eased – not really trapped – into marriage! Joe, Joan and Dan were playing 'snap' at the mill table when I returned. They were not in a hurry to hear my news, just asking if Pina was all right. Everything Vincenzo had told me concerned the outside world; it was curious but irrelevant to our piece of life at the Casa dell'Avventura.

The following day Joan and 'Gio' went with Dan on a walk, leaving Joe on a deckchair in the garden, lost in a book. I intended to spend a quiet afternoon writing, but kept on thinking about the green-shuttered villa. I had also picked up, probably from Carlo, the half-envious joke making the rounds of Montesasso bars about the blind and lame running all the way to the bank to withdraw invalidity payments. He hinted at Claudio Panichini's war pension and his subsequent fighting fit existence in his hardware store, and Sibilla's son working in the local bank on their invalidity quota. Another nagging issue was well pollution caused, Gianni said, by the increasing use of fertilisers and insecticides. Twice he took Joan with him to have the water analysed, each time paying a steep fee to the government laboratory in Montesasso, for both samples to be declared impure. After the first analysis he was advised to pour chlorine into the well and leave it undisturbed for a while, but the advice was not to drink the well water. I reckoned there was a brisk trade in expensive analyses, redone in perpetuam, or discontinued on the assumption that the whole process was a 'fix' designed to increase the laboratory's income. Up to now we have drunk ours and no one has fallen ill. Or was there a movable standard, forever unobtainable? Joe suggested some officials might have shares in the thriving Italian industry of bottled mineral water!

Thriving indeed. I went to stock up in Montesasso. When pausing by the Prudomini palazzo, now the museum, to contemplate the Saracena's statue and the surrounding buildings, I was interrupted by an indecently large car, the type that provokes a stare. The passenger side passed a hair's breadth away and a once-beautiful, still striking face looked open-eyed at me. I could have sworn it was the Countess, flattening me against her husband's palazzo.

'Was it the contessa?' I asked the statue, puzzled. Santa Jamila looked at me unflinchingly, as saints tend to do. The gaze either comforts or disarms. That day it did both. In the busy general food store nearby, caustic comments could be heard about 'pezzi grossi' stirring things up for ordinary people, who only wanted to live honestly and pay their taxes like every other decent person. Such sentiments reduced all to silence.

'Cosa succede?' I was the last in and so asked what had happened. Hadn't I seen the huge American car scraping the walls and sweeping the inhabitants aside? That was the onorevole Bintoni, a local lad who had made it with a vengeance.

'Eravamo ragazzi insieme,' said the man serving behind the counter. They had grown up together, both sons of contadini suffering under the mezzadria system. Luciano Bintoni soon got in with the local priest, a certain Don Basilio, who was mighty ambitious. This was many years ago. Bintoni was sent to the Catholic University in Rome. Oh yes, he was bright, but a bootlicker too. He'd steered dangerously close to taking religious orders while never avoiding a chance to bed pretty women, especially starlets. He was a young man to note in the 1960s when the Italian film industry was booming.

'Once he'd been selected for the Christian Democrats' list of parliamentary candidates, he soon rose near to the top,' the storekeeper explained to enthralled shoppers, 'meaning that he could really start his political and business career once the priests and nuns had elected him for being such a good Catholic!' Resigned murmurs from the women; disparaging comments from the men.

'He hardly deigns to recognise his former schoolmates,' the storekeeper continued, 'and feels he can break laws with impunity. Not just financial ones, which are the easiest for politicians to get round, but,' fired by his own indignation, 'here in his home town he can drive dangerously through a pedestrian area and get away with it!' All protested in agreement. He hadn't even married a local girl, but, predictably, a banker's daughter from Rome instead. Rarely in Montesasso, it seemed that morning, exceptionally, he had an appointment with his mentor. Don Basilio had done well too, starting in a poor country parish and rising to be in charge of the Church's finances for the area. Hand in glove they were from early on. The company assembled nodded in unison, and slowly turned to shopping. I left with four bottles of mineral water, too preoccupied to carry any more. The sun was setting and the others were waiting.

Evening is the most soothing time of day at the Casa dell'Avventura. You can't let your mind dwell on the niggling taxes local politicians appear to be manipulating, or the roughly cut grass Gianni has left strewn over the terraces, or the polluted well water. August is the best month for shooting stars, and many fell, to Dan's delight, that evening.

CHAPTER 26

'This must be Paul's secret place,' I said.

'How do you know?' Joan was curious, but Sarah (the Thompsons had arrived later than expected) glanced at me and said, 'Shall we go somewhere else?'

I hesitated. The clump of holm oaks by Sant'Anselmo fitted Paul's passing reference to it years earlier. It hurt being there, with the three of us sitting in his shade. The sky was clouding over and the humidity beneath the branches weighed even more heavily on me. I changed the subject.

'Why isn't Gianni here this afternoon?'

'He's at some family affair,' Joan said as we stood up hastily, the hail suddenly pelting down. 'It's odd how I enjoy his smell of tobacco,' she continued, 'and I haven't smoked for forty years!' I studied her as she stared into the storm. I'd never heard her talking about her personal life to anyone. Perhaps it was because she looked happier than I can remember, away from her work and duty and reassured daily that friends were taking care of Gran. Or was it because the hail didn't stop and we had time to spare, standing still, just waiting?

'I'm not tempted to start smoking again – don't get me wrong! It's just that I'm reminded of wartime when everyone smoked. Offering someone a cigarette was a way of opening a conversation, saying you liked someone. Even sharing one,' and she smiled almost skittishly, 'though I'd judge it unhygienic now!' (I'd seen her take a puff at Gianni's when she thought I wasn't looking.) 'It was the smell of friendship, the match that lit up a glimmer of hope, eyes glistening, a mouth smiling.' All three of us silently thought back. Youth, that wishful land of elusive hopes.

'I do understand,' Sarah almost shouted to be heard above the hail, 'but I'm glad no one smokes in my house. Nor any of my friends,' she paused, 'at least, in front of me.' I wondered if she was anxious about Andrew and, if not his present friends, his future ones. She admitted she had sniffed his clothes, fearful of any trace of cigarettes, or worse, drugs, not that she or I knew exactly what smell to expect.

The last of summer – 1982

Sarah and William arrived after Andrew had finished his vacation job. He was starting university in the autumn and, though she didn't admit it, I knew Sarah feared this might be their last family holiday. I caught her watching Andrew more than usual, the first to fly from the nest. Dan had missed them and was much happier now he had Kate to play with. She's small, like her mother, and not much taller than Dan. The rest of the time he shadowed Andrew, who had grown like William, rust-haired, tall and lanky. Andrew reminded me of his father when Sarah and I first met him. He wasn't my type then, but I had come to admire William's assured manner and even found his ginger hair quite attractive. He had always been a good listener and encouraged my writing, but this summer I appreciated his company and help more than ever.

On a late August afternoon Sarah, Joan and I had wandered off to pick blackberries, leaving Joe and William reading and the children lolling around at the house. Sarah led, Joan and I following her. I hadn't noticed Sarah from behind before and saw how dumpy she had become, with wisps of grey weaving through her light brown hair in need of a tidying trim. She turned round, smiling.

'I think we'll find berries nearer the spring by Sant'Anselmo.'

She was right. We gathered all the ripe berries and, mission accomplished, sat round a pool on weathered stones overshadowed by evergreen oaks.

'Could they be Etruscan?' we wondered together.

The storm had caught us just as we were starting back, hail bouncing off and stinging bare skin. We retreated to wait under the trees and silently breathed in the wet air as hail melted into rain and water gushed into the Etruscan pool. Standing in a row under the trees, and smiling as drops bobbed down our faces, we chatted and waited. No let up in the rain. Summer clothes dragged on our shoulders, clung to midriff and legs. When the downpour slackened, we dashed to the priest's house behind Sant'Anselmo and knocked.

'He's there,' I shouted through rain battering the roof of an outhouse, 'I can see a light'. No response. We looked a fine trio, bedraggled, teeth chattering and skin like plucked hens.

'Chi è?' A balding head peeped out from the upper floor. Once he'd seen us, the priest came down and unlocked the door. We might have been itinerant labourers from Sardinia or gypsies, he explained.

'They'll pick over the church if they can. Then see if there's anything left in here.' Hardly. We sat on plywood nailed over the original frayed rush seats, sodden garments pressing dark shapes onto them. No desk in the upstairs room, but a table, its surface invisible under piles of pastoral paperwork. A threadbare bed lay in evening shadow on the far side. His hands, folded plump, unfussed on his worn black habit, matched his resigned face.

'Yes, I know Don Luigi. Yes, please use the phone,' voiced in competition with the clatter down the passage from the forty year-old female preparing supper.

Andrew came to fetch us in his father's car. I sat behind him, saddened that this might be his last holiday with us. Bring your university friends, Andrew, I thought.

He stopped the car at the top of the drive to the Casa dell'Avventura.

'Olivia, the sun's out!' Sarah exclaimed. 'Look at the earth steaming under the olives like -' Andrew interrupted his mother.

'It's like Noah's ark finding land after the rain.' When the dove came with the olive branch.

The mosquitoes have been particularly bad this year, breeding in pools of smelly water in the channel between Giulio's land and mine. It dribbles out of a pipe from Wolfgang's extension into a larger one from Caterina and Mauro's house. Cautious after the chicken saga and the slow reconciliation, I was unwilling to say anything to them, even though we were all busily scratching bites.

In cooler weather after the late August storm we went on longer walks. One idea was to explore around Oreste's house and the source of our stream, but Joe and I were keen to follow a track over the ridge into the next valley. Joan and Gianni joined Sarah's family group up the new asphalt road past Massimo's house to Oreste's. Our trail into the next valley led through terrace after terrace of olive groves, many abandoned, unpruned, unloved. Dan ran wild, slashing at the high grass with the 'snake stick' he always carried. Below us, almost in the middle of the valley, was a cypress avenue leading first to a group of farm buildings, then continuing up to the green-shuttered villa, the largest for miles around. We climbed down to the avenue and prowled around the villa's high walls. A mastiff sniffed and snarled at us from behind the wrought iron gate. The shutters were ajar, the front door slightly open, cars scattered around the drive. Not a sound. We were about to turn back when the small but assertive figure of onorevole Bintoni, the 'stregone' himself, appeared framed in the doorway, then vanished inside to return with a woman. She looked familiar. It was the Countess who was speaking to someone inside. A tall man in a sober suit followed her towards one of the smaller cars – Don Basilio. She was about to leave and would see us peering round the gateposts. We retreated rapidly along the avenue shushing Dan, who was intrigued by our proximity to the wizard's lair, to find cover behind a clump of oaks. Don Basilio closed the gates behind her neat sports car and the Countess drove past us down the cypress avenue. We were safe.

Sarah, Joan and I were planning for the holiday to end in a double treat: jousting at Arezzo for Dan and Kate, and probably Penny too, on condition that we could listen to the choirs' festival created around Guido Monaco. He was a tenth-century monk born in Paris, but appropriated by Arezzo after he settled there.

We straggled up the main street leaving the statue of Guido musing in the middle of the station square where we had left Andrew; he had been lured to Florence by friends before returning home with them. I called Dan and Kate over to join Joan and me at a window display of illuminated tomes, each showing the new-fangled staves that Guido invented to teach his choirboys sight-reading.

'Before the 900s the choir boys had to learn the music by heart...' Penny was entranced by the window displays of early autumn styles. William passed us humming up the street on his own followed by Joe gazing at the architecture and Sarah with her nose in a guidebook.

A small audience was scattered around the nave of the Pieve where the first choir was singing in front of the high altar above the crypt. More chairs than usual had been set out in the nave, but people preferred to stand at the back. We sat, found the Romanian choir better than expected, and waited for the next one from Paris to start. There was some banging of doors at the entrance; the conductor waited, arms raised, baton poised. Then the first few notes; a solo boy soprano soared, climbing to a pinnacle of sound, when yet another latecomer opened the door to let in a dissonant thump of drums and trumpet blasts. Even the odd neigh. Some standing at the back left, to admit endless seconds of crashing and banging from the town band. Yet others hurried out, the brass volume doubling as they opened the doors, only muffled when they swung back after a sequence of rapid exits. Furious, the conductor stopped his choir in full throat to lean over the balustrade and glare down at the small audience still there. We at least had stayed, though Dan and Kate were fidgeting to see the procession outside. Probably Penny too. William tiptoed them out.

When we had at last joined the others, after hearing more excellent choirs and applauding the winners from Paris, the historian in me explained that jousting had been a popular sport in the Middle Ages. It kept the young Aretines fighting fit, just in case they'd have to drive out the Saracens – code name for any sort of non-Christian enemy from Guido d'Arezzo's time onwards. A teenage girl standing next to us described how, after prayers round the horse and rider in the parish church of each district, they would be blessed by the Bishop on the cathedral steps at the top of the town. The band then set off past the Pieve followed by the flagthrowers, horses and knights in procession to the Main Square bustling with supporters.

Squeezing our way through the crowd, we settled on a vantage point under a portico. The dummy Saracen waited for the four contestants, parading in turn to the sound of drums. Each district's throwers spiked the air with furled flags, hurled higher and higher, then caught with a leap sideways, a curl of the back and outward thrust of the hips, all contoured by the multicoloured stripes we'd seen on the hose and doublets in the Prudomini frescoes.

'So supple!' Penny enthused, imagining herself there, with her father's long legs and her success in athletics. No other square in Italy can have more wooden balconies and truncated tower houses, once rising to rival heights. In the Middle Ages, citizens felt distinctly superior looking down upon neighbours. Maintenance costs and other grubbier and less eye-catching ways of showing superiority have levelled the towers into low-pitched roofs behind parapets. These were now covered in spectators. Ordered down by the police with loudspeakers, they melted away, to reassert themselves a few minutes later. The whole scene was a repeated comic interlude.

The sky turned a deeper blue, tinged with pink in the west; bats swooped in loops and arabesques as the last of the flag throwers left the arena, to frenetic applause from their supporters. It struck seven; a cannon exploded and the first knight entered the lists. An intake of breath, followed by silence. Then from a standstill to a gallop, lance tilted towards the Saracen, the rider made what seemed like a direct hit on the top right section of the shield, ducked as the grisly balls attached to the Saracen's arm swung round, and raced out of the square. When the judges had talked, the maiden in Renaissance clothes had waved to the crowd, the Mayor had bowed and the hubbub had calmed down, the verdict was boomed out on the loud speaker. The next horse charged mouth open, tongue lolling, towards the target, its knight thrusting his lance under the Saracen's raised arm. The infidel's fistful of balls hit the rider's unprotected neck just below the helmet, felling him with a heavy thud onto the sawdust. A moment later he was accompanied off limping to barely suppressed titters, his supporters furious. The following riders all scored before galloping away into the upper town.

Much argument ensued while the judges conferred over the final result and the town band reappeared to thump tunelessly round the square, vying with the peels of church bells. The dappled grey from the Quarter of the Roman Amphitheatre appeared with its jubilant rider, followed by the district's flag throwers clad in red and yellow.

The slight Aretine girl who had been crowned Queen of the jousting stepped gingerly towards the dappled grey, more accustomed to a short skirt than heavy damask. Amid boos, shouts and applause from rooftops to balconies echoed by the crowds in the square, she presented the golden-tipped lance.

And so our summer ended.

Bring your university friends, Andrew, I thought. No, don't. Tim would have come with you. He would have been as tall, hair curling down to the nape of his neck. He wouldn't have driven so fast while talking as you did, Andrew, turning corners and your head to include me at the back. Tim's voice would have been deeper, like Paul's. I had to crush my emotions and stop filling the void with an imagined embrace, a wave and a smile over a broad shoulder as he turned and vanished into a future that will never be.

* * * * *

My story is about threads from the past woven into the texture of a Tuscan valley, living history in the countryside tilled by generation after generation passing on an uninterrupted pattern of survival. Their history and ours is intertwined in a tale for others to recreate. Those were William's words. But I couldn't expel Paul's from my mind. Not long before he disappeared he said.

'Olivia, why don't you write a novel? That's what you always wanted to do.' When I stared at him, he added.

'Look, your book's neither fish nor fowl.'

'What do you mean?' I didn't really want to hear his reply, but it came.

'Your writing's part travelogue, part memoir, a hybrid that doesn't work. Too many different bits and pieces.' My expression troubled him.

'You did ask for my candid opinion. I can't bear to see you disappointed.'

CHAPTER 27

Saint Mary's struck eight-thirty. Smoke and mist wisped up the road to the Downs. Satchels over shoulders, children chattered past, veering right to wait at the zebra crossing with the lollipop lady, spangles of sun on her luminous 'STOP' board. Dan, nearly eight, crossed over with me into the pushing, bustling gaggle of children heading towards the school gate and another lollipop lady who stood by the railings protecting the spot – just a stretch of asphalt by a school entrance – too late. Perhaps I should have followed advice at the time and left teaching after Tim's accident.

Dan's birthday fell on a Saturday. It was a breezy day with tufts of cloud, like when Tim and Andrew went out to slide down banks, shoot logs over rocky rapids or rampage through the rhododendron tunnels. Joan stayed behind preparing the birthday tea with Gran, while Joe and I took Dan and his friends up to the Downs.

September; a year since Paul left; the first anniversary of another loss. Excising images from my mind satisfied anger, but fed frustration when memories crept back to haunt me. So I gripped tightly to a routine cluttered with crucial and humdrum decisions: syllabus, meal rotas, Dan's sports equipment, staff illnesses, class checks, school lunches – and Dan's. All the donkeywork off-loaded onto a single mother, the head of a medium-sized school.

Joe usually accompanied my evening walks and we both played with Dan. Joan would sometimes come with us to the cinema, diluting our companionable warmth. I got the message: her house, her garden, her space and us in it to manage firmly, kindly and with her no-nonsense formula.

She agreed with Paul's mother and Gran that all I could do was to keep an endless vigil, the one that none of us wanted to mention. It was life with dread deep inside, and hope unexpectedly choking me, breathless. A sighting – there he is at the bus-stop balancing from one leg to the other, tousled hair to be stroked smooth, green jacket, brown corduroy trousers comfortably sagging and a red scarf.

Closer, it wasn't him or his colours. Was it my face I saw in the mirror, a crumpled one, twisted and carved by sorrow?

'Gio – Gianni – sends his greetings.' Joan had opened yet another letter in his squiggly handwriting. 'Just the usual stuff,' she said, as reticent with those scraps of lined paper as she was when I asked her about any missives or gifts she might have had from my father.

'It was difficult to get films in wartime, Olivia.' So just one indistinct photo was, she still said, all she had of him.

I told Joe how uncommunicative she usually was about my father, but he just smiled.

'We need to keep part of ourselves secret. She'll only tell you what she wants you to know.' The darker, soft area around his eyes and the hollows on either side of a slender nose made him look vulnerable, in need of protection. Joe had a sort of warning halo; a light handshake, a touch on the shoulder, but no embrace allowed. This fragility lingered on after his operation, endearingly.

I climbed the narrow stairs to Dan's room under the eaves to find an eight-year-old totally absorbed. A miniature football table, cardboard boxes overflowing with Lego, cast-off books, models with broken or recycled parts, grease-marked text books, exercise books, a scatter of pens, pencils and a rainbow packet of crayons. Unused. He didn't draw or paint like Tim. I tried to forget how the room had been before him. It's now Dan's, strewn with everything he had asked for or needed, without trace of a former presence.

Dan was more practical. He would be an engineer, a problem-solver. He was spending a lot of time at Sarah's, especially when Andrew was home from university. Their house was still a welcoming jumble of cast-off clothes, books, pine furniture and unwashed mugs.

'Sarah's helping with a campaign to let parents stay in hospital with their children,' William told me with an itch in his voice. 'She's out one or even two evenings a week.'

Once a week, on Fridays after school, she orchestrated a thorough turnout when everyone was allocated a task, usually cleaning one's own room and another designated area. Even William had to return from the university in good time to deal with their bedroom and his study. Sarah cleaned the kitchen and the room where they got together and ate. Dan was asked to help her so he would feel part of it all. Clutter started to reappear on Saturday morning before I called in after shopping to fetch him.

One October evening when we were alone together, I asked Sarah if she ever wondered what William might be doing when he returned late.

'Why should I ask?' she was rummaging in a button box to match a shirt button. There was a rumour that William interviewed students singly and thoroughly, some more than others.

'I don't pry,' Sarah continued. 'Why should I? He'd shut himself into his study with "Do not disturb" written in the air in front of it if I did!'

She looked at me. 'Think of what you have here and now, your springboard for tomorrow, and the next day, and so on.' The way she proposed it felt manageable, at least for the small slice of future I could swallow.

'As long as William's back to cut the lawn, clean his part of the house, wash the dishes and do handyman jobs, I'm happy. What point is there in worrying what he's up to?' She found the button and a nametag for Kate. 'We can't be together all the time. I wouldn't want to anyway.' She was hunting through the sewing box for thread to match Penny's jumper. 'More seams gaping under the arms,' she mumbled with a needle in her mouth.

'Dangerous! Gran says you might swallow it!' Sarah took the needle out and laughed.

'That'll be the day!' I expected Sarah to repeat her favourite advice – worry corrodes – but she wanted to tell me something else, choosing her words carefully not to open my wounds.

'Marriage, old-fashioned conventions and so on, happen to suit William and me.'

As November winds blew over the snow falling in the mountains behind Montesasso and the nights turned icier, Gianni's letters became gloomy. Joan told me his circulation was bad. He spent the days in his kitchen looking at television, bent over the butane gas heater. The central heating Sergio had installed for a special price didn't work. I thought of the gutter along the edge of the veranda tilting back from the downpipe and the illogical way Sergio worked. Gianni bemoaned the fact that he couldn't go to see how things were at the Casa dell'Avventura, to make sure the geraniums had not perished in the cold and the pipes had not burst. He was yearning for the countryside, for his valley.

In late November after the olive harvest, the sun shone fitfully. Mother relayed that the pipes had not burst and some of the geraniums on the veranda had survived. He watered them and they thanked him by pushing up etiolated shoots. The moment he began to shiver in his heavy coat, he drove his ageing Bluebottle up the drive and took refuge in Pina and Carlo's kitchen, warming himself through and through before returning home.

Though I'd given up writing to Gianni now that Joan had taken him over, I did, rather stealthily, send him a letter at the beginning of December without telling her. I asked him directly how he had learnt some English and where he had been during the war. It was curious how little he had told us about the time between his youth and his marriage beyond: 'I was with the partisans in the mountains,' which was what all men his age asserted.

A week later Pina phoned. It was six in the evening. Gianni had died that morning. He had keeled over under the laurel tree above the mill. When he did not return for lunch, Alberto, now nineteen with a car of his own but no job, left to search for him.

'A heart attack,' Pina said sadly. I was the first person outside their family to be told. The funeral was the next day, a time-scale still assuming an immobile community. I was more distressed than I realised, and Joan was so upset that we couldn't get to the funeral in time. I sent Pina the money for our wreath and wrote to Ada and her children. Dismayed, I didn't know what else to do.

Five days after Gianni died a letter came addressed to me in his spidery handwriting. I left the unopened envelope quietly alone for over an hour before going into my bedroom to read it. He had written and posted it before his last journey to the house he had inspired. He would be going out there because the sun was shining and he felt much better. He was practising English for when Joan and I returned at Easter. Was this an indirect answer to my questions, or hadn't he received my letter? He was going to light the fire up at the top of his house later on in the evening as he was tired of spending all the time in the kitchen. He went on to tell me he had taken the 'special photographs', as he called them, down from the wall in his den and propped them on the table where he could see them better. Those were the bogus 'wedding' photos that he had contrived. A diptych for us.

Tuscany without Gianni was unimaginable. We were all saddened and shocked. In spring and summer we had seen him at his best. But, with bad circulation, his smoking aggravated matters. We felt bereft.

If Sarah and William hadn't invited us for Christmas 1982, we would have made a mournful household, just Gran, Mother, Dan and me. Joe went to see his sister and ailing father. For days we amused ourselves choosing presents. Kate and Penny, easy, something light hearted and colourful; the men, Andrew and William, more difficult. Something very special for Sarah, which she would never buy for herself. We thought about them, mesmerised by the coals of the living room fire, three generations with the fourth busy in his room at the top of the house.

'Gianni reminded me of your father.' Mother had never admitted this before. I winced. 'About the same height. Brown hair and eyes. Rather wiry.' A normal Italian male. She didn't mention any secret sign of recognition: the tone of voice, the curl of his lower lip, the pattern of hair on his chest, a mole on his left buttock?

'Details slip out of memory; atmospheres remain.' She looked tired, older. 'One remembers what one wants to, how one wants...' her voice trailed away into silence. The logs sizzled and flickered in the hearth. I noticed her hands for the first time, the raised veins and freckles of age. Gran's fairies had started dancing on them with muddy feet.

'Not much of a coincidence, I suppose, but they were both Giovanni,' she continued. With both men she shared a special language, his broken English and her phrase book Italian, each wrapped around the other's ignorance. She had never told me much about the summer of 1941 before, of its intense uncertainty.

'We didn't have much chance to be together. Landgirls worked hard...' and were penned in, though she didn't admit it, almost as much as the 'Itie' prisoners doing the heavier work on the land.

'They weren't seen as the enemy. Not seriously... They weren't trying to invade us,' though people would have censured the Englishwoman with the Italian prisoner, had they noticed. All she was left with was that small framed photo, very worn at the edges; my father yellowing into history. And me.

I put my hand over hers. I don't remember doing it before, except perhaps as a child. She thawed.

'Didn't he give you any presents?'

'He gave me bits of wood with interesting shapes – a sort of natural sculpture – posies of meadow flowers or berries and leaves with the colours and textures he liked. In wartime nobody had any means to speak of, just emotions. They were free and dangerous.' She hesitated. 'Even in wartime there are moments worth remembering. Fugitive happiness. Your Gran,' Mother paused, 'found it hard. Loss. War. Her brother Frank. I don't know if she really loved – ' I was relieved she didn't say it. Mother might have been the child of Gran's make-do marriage. A sort of post-war clearing-up.

'I can't explain it properly. In wartime, it was like being young and old in an instant. Not knowing what might happen, you lived for the moment. It could all end any second – an air raid, a crash, an invasion. Only now – then – counted.'

I had to be the result of a passionate encounter circumscribed by conflict. A passing chance for love.

'He did say he might have to move away. No reason given. Deployment of prisoners, I thought. They were used for their skills, paid and fed like our servicemen. Some civilians resented being more strictly rationed than prisoners. He may have been parachuted back into Italy to liaise with the partisans. The Allies were making plans for an eventual invasion. We only thought ahead to the next meeting, but couldn't count on anything. I told him I might be expecting a child. He was glad and asked me to marry him after the war. He said that he lived in a Tuscan village called San Giuliano. Do you know how many there are?'

I did. That's why I decided not to awaken her hopes when I found another, our San Giuliano.

A day or so later, when we were clearing up in the kitchen, she said, 'More than anything else, I wished you would never experience what I've been through.' She told me how she'd waited for a gesture, the touch of fingertips, the tone of a smiling voice, a whispered syllable, the smell of cigarettes and a warm body, to know that she was wanted not just when close, but that she haunted, inhabited another. It was easier, she supposed, for her. Part and parcel of wartime living. She loved him desperately, believed he'd return and would cherish his child. Other women in a similar dilemma, most of them, gave their children away. She didn't.

'Gio and I talked about having children on an evening that seemed eternal. It was always "when the war is over".'

Precisely. It was over and he didn't return. He didn't even write. He might not have known her family name. So many Joan Taylors. They could never go to Downs Way together, so how might he find her address? Secret relationships leave few traces. In their case, just me.

So she waited, keeping me for him. In dark moments he, like Paul, was dead. At others she imagined him round the bend in the road, near the footpath by the haystacks no longer there, or behind the ruined windmill high on the Downs. At first he appeared to her as a soldier. Then as a successful businessman or farmer, artist or engineer. He remained the age she last saw him slipping agile into the night.

As time passed, self-doubt throbbed profoundly inside me and then began thumping through each day. The betrayed assumptions of trust. The memories of tenderness, soft to touch, the sharp tang of salt on skin – moments of refuge in hope. Desire drifting into dreams of a homecoming. Then the harsh tone of base, incremental anger: how could he desert us, abandon his child and me to a life spent filling the gap left by him, deeper and darker as months lengthened into a year? A twilit future of an imagined knock, light streaming through a half-open door with a cautious hand pushing, a presence desired.

Joe's return after Christmas delighted Dan and set Mother and me back into our old routine. January brought the snowdrops Gran had planted a forgotten time ago, followed by purple and yellow crocuses venturing further over the lawn. Hers too. By March daffodils and primroses were blooming under the chestnut tree at the far end of the garden. Rooks cawed in gutteral monotones from their nests, like the desolate voices that echoed inside me.

Gran hardly left her bedroom all February and was visibly fading in March. She did not die on the day of the accident I wanted to forget, only lasting until the end of the month.

It was strangely comforting, I thought from an emotional distance as we drove in the rain to her funeral, how the different brick, stone and plaster facades in Guildford jostle chromatically. The five storey blocks of rough stone and rubble lining the streets of Montesasso were dreary with damp grey patches in winter and spring. They had once, it was said, been painted in rainbow colours. I liked to imagine them clad in varied shades, just as in Renaissance paintings, perhaps to indicate clan loyalties: the Montecutes and Capulets of Montesasso.

William came to Gran's funeral with Penny and Andrew, while Sarah looked after Dan and Kate. Mike arrived with Angélique in glowing black velvet with a glistening fur collar to cup her face under a wide hat. A theatrical flourish, creating admiring space as she swept through the cool air to embrace Mother and me. No Paul. No way of telling him. As before with Tim's funeral, not told and very absent.

And so, Easter 1983. Mother's little candle of hope was snuffed out. No Gianni, no Italy. It wasn't exactly despair, only her feelings shrinking back into the present.

'There's a lot to do here. To tidy up,' she said, distracted. 'I could look after Dan, but he'll prefer Sarah's family.' I, too, wanted to stay behind.

CHAPTER 28

We are old the moment we are born, a second old. Sometimes we slip imperceptibly into a looser, rumpled skin; more often it is a sudden perception of small white flecks on a hand darkening into a filigree of veins. By the summer of 1983, Mother had placed the solitary image of my father in a never-lit corner of Gran's gallery of memories. In the same corner more photos joined hers to continue their silent fading into dust-rimmed frames. I put Tim, the three of us, at the back and turned all the photos towards the wall. Mother closed the door on Gran's room and locked away the last but one chapter of her life. She settled into age.

Warm weather, birdsong, summer time. I began, hesitantly, to picture the Casa dell'Avventura in a distant, hazy image. At least it was something tangible that could be let or sold, if people were prepared to pay for it. Though emotionally fragile, I knew I had to return. Because Sarah and William needed a summer holiday; because Dan wanted to be there in his territory with Penny and Kate and, he hoped, Andrew; because Joe offered to book the flight for Dan and me to go there with him.

It turned out that May and June had been unusually wet. No Gianni to open the windows, inspect the roof, trim back the vines and clear the channel. Gravel had rolled down the drive with the rain and all around the building it had surrendered to underground pressure from couch grass, chickweed, ivy and bindweed. From the pergola at the front, the vines had wrapped the house and fingered through south-facing windows. At the back, soft blue flowers cascaded from Gianni's favourite plumbago; to the east by the channel and Giulio's fields, the rose, entangled with white-scented jasmine, waved a pink bouquet beyond the roof in unsupported exuberance. Gianni's kitchen garden was in mourning. Shrivelled cabbages leant over dying beans; carrots had given up growing to retire into wrinkled roots in the company of dried-out fennel.

The familiar summer throb of bees and somnolent flies; the cicadas' seesaw notes; the daze of delight and savour of summer. No touch of Gianni in the air; no wry grin at my 'ahs' of satisfaction, cigarette between fingers and a hand on my arm with, 'Is good, Olivia?' in his eyes.

Two gasping red geraniums had toughed it out through the heat. Someone had placed them as sentinels on either side of the last step to the veranda. The tamarisk had spread its feathery leaves over the kitchen shutters, and flame flowers from the trumpet vine embracing Gianni's pillar had blown on to the veranda. Still there behind the heat haze lurked Monte Amiata, an anchoring note in the unruly dissonance around us. The lock took a fraught moment to worry open. Shutters pushed outwards through cobwebs embroidered with moth wings and bluebottles. Mould impregnating cushions and blankets, nurtured by months of rain sliding inside the shutters and under the windows, stung into nostrils. Stillness. Not even the memory of cigarette smoke. A newspaper abandoned in the hearth, half burnt into curls: 9 December 1982, the day Gianni died.

Open wide, the windows let in the zizzazz of Giulio's strimmer, chain rattling and yaps from Quinto's former house and a plough groaning along the hill to the west. An angry bee hit me as I followed Joe out, both laden with cushions and blankets. He intuited what had to be done. He never struck me as handsome, but he had a rare loveliness of being. Of being Joe, himself, ready and here, now.

'I'll air these,' he said, about to sling a couple of blankets over the clothesline.

'Wait, I'll wipe it.' Of nearly a year's grime, I thought. He piled the bedding on dry grass under a stone wall, returning with more blankets to flap fresh in the sun. We smiled like children helping mum.

'Simple pleasures,' he said, 'the ones remembered'. We rested on two stones, dislodged from the retaining wall by the roots of oak trees on the terrace above. I turned to hug him, tearing free from Paul's shadow enshrined in a dark corner of the past. Joe shifted sideways, from his stone to a hillock, and leaned forwards, lifting the corner of a blanket. In its shade we peeped out over the maturing grapes, over dust green veils on knobbly olives, over sunflower fields and drainage canals into haze enveloping the extinct volcano, Monte Amiata.

'What shall we...?' I looked at Joe, still hitching up the blanket and gazing beyond.

'Carpe diem.' Joe was never discursive. Breaths of air from the south bearing sunbeams blew off musty particles, stroked away year-old crumples, teased out worn or flattened pile to redefine texture and colour.

Not the moment to fret about finding someone to strim the grass, to cut back the rampant vines and bushes and revive some semblance of order. Joe didn't move.

The silence of the past enfolded me as we sat, separately contemplating. A soundless film of Etruscan ploughs slicing twists of iron red earth, of oxen chewing, flapping tails, steaming manure and creak of harness and axle, as reassuring as the drone of bees on the lavender at my feet. Bursts of strident cutting and growls of neat tractors bred to weave round olives on narrow terraces sporadically crunched the silence before lunch, and after the siesta hour into evening. Along the Cassia the coaches, dray carts, an assortment of wheels and hoofs clopped, clanged and jolted into timeless echoes. Nothing obtrusive. Part of the medley of sound through time. Then a lone military jet gashed the midday blue, a contrasting colour in the weave of life happening.

Like releasing heavy clothes, slipping off sweaty garments, throwing away yesterday's newspaper, showering off past heat, dust and passions, so I finally let Paul go. Hope became too emotionally painful. Never again could he loom up apologetically from the mists over the quilted pattern on the plain, nor sit silently sketching by the mill table, nor appear framed in the sitting-room doorway, nor round the corner by the channel offering me a rose. Nowhere now could he ambush me with memories to fuel hope. I had suffered unsummoned presences enough. Fully adjusted, framed and finished, his photo with Tim and me was facing the wall in that corner shrine. Done.

I looked at the first brush strokes of sunset across the plain and he didn't reappear; nor when I turned to the deeper colours in the hills, nor to the east where Montesasso just tipped the brow of hills, nor silhouetted against the ball of fire touching the crests to the west, nor in the shadows ranging over sunflower fields, vineyards, cypresses and umbrella pines and back to the rise and fall of the horizon. Vanquished. My past history.

Joe was smiling at Monte Amiata. He felt my eyes and turned his smile to me.

'What about finding someone to cut the grass?'

'Maybe.' He was looking back at the valley. How non-committal he always was. Perversely, he would then come up with the best ideas.

'I could ask Carlo and Pina?'

'Good idea.' He was still dreaming across the plain, untroubled over the future. I wanted to shake and hug him simultaneously.

Dan was whooping down by the stream with the boats he and Joe had penknifed from old branches and twigs. Joe was thwarting my apprehensive attempts to rein my child in and stop him slipping off as he had just done. It was too shallow for him to drown and he could swim. But I should have gone with him.

'He's nearly nine,' said Joe. 'Let go, Olivia. What will happen, will happen in spite of you. The future will come, whatever you plan.' So I bothered about the grass cutting instead.

'Let's go to Carlo and Pina tomorrow?'

'Whenever.'

Joe was more demonstrative with Dan than me; heads down, their hands moved pebbles and small rocks to create a waterfall and dam water into a harbour for their fleet. Joe pointed and they shared the shift of a stone, freed the same log to strengthen the bank below their harbour, stood side by side to observe their liquid sculpture. Still no touch of the arm, no shoulder hugging, no ruffling Dan's hair.

* * * * *

We found Carlo clearing out the storage area on the ground floor so he and Pina could eventually move down there, relinquishing their quarters to Vincenzo, Lisa and baby Dario. The neighbours were objecting to their huge white water heater, incongruously installed by Sergio, our plumber, on the outside wall of their new bathroom. It breached the legal distance from the boundary fence. *'Pettegolezze!'* The usual silly little grievances, but Carlo was much more relaxed with Dario to distract him.

'They still have the weekly bath mentality,' he snorted. 'We've bought more kilowatts, but they're still on the old three kilowatt allowance!' He pouted, raising his eyes to the ceiling to show how foolish they were – and me too once, in the days of our frequent short circuits. Some in the valley now wanted bathing options; others husbanded scarce resources, the economy of survival still resisting the allure of consumerised hygiene.

'I've heard someone is setting up a land maintenance business for absent owners,' Carlo said, looking at Joe; he didn't ask after Paul. 'Beppe Orietti. I'm sure he's in the telephone book.' Joe, alone with me at the Casa dell'Avventura, was regarded with as much interest, though less curiosity, than Mike ten years earlier. Olivia's men came and went, they presumed. Sibilla's son had provided the valley with its first divorce. He was rumoured to be co-habiting.

Almost ten years. 'Time to give up?' I thought out loud. Joe looked up from the documents on Gianni's table. He was sorting out the car question. It was bad enough having no one to meet us at the station. Taxis were erratic; a row of them, or none at all.

'Mammalucca's costing more in repairs, insurance and worry than she's worth.' A lawyer's voice. I pulled my chair closer to look at the insurance forms he had laid out. He smelt gentle and reassuring. 'There's a problem over ownership.' I had forgotten it was bought in Gianni's name. 'Let's hire a car. Cheaper in the long run and less hassle.' The low compelling voice of clarity. 'No insurance, repairs, or ownership problems.' He held his hands out, palms up. I had always warmed to his quiet consideration, spare frame, and direct manner. We walked up the drive and along the track in the twilight cool. Dan was ahead of us, poking around in the hedgerows to see if any fireflies were still there. I wanted to hold Joe's arm, but he blithely kept a clear close distance.

* * * * *

I drove the old mustard-coloured car for the last time to Montesasso, dropping Joe and Dan off to hire a vehicle. Ada seemed pleased to see me, offered an aperitif and began weeping.

She had expected Alberto to take his father's place in the road maintenance unit, but that didn't seem to be working out. I thought of Gianni's boss, the one whom Alberto so resembled, but she would already have pulled that particular string. Had Gianni's family fixed its flag to the wrong political party, the local Communists whose power was declining, while the boss was propelled by the Christian Democrats who reigned on the plain where he lived? His son was in the *carabinieri*, another prized governmental job found through weaving the web of influential connections. Meanwhile Ada and Gianni's daughter Giuliana was well; married, working up north, too far away and still childless. I left Ada an envelope with money for what Gianni had done, told her to keep Mammalucca for Alberto, and asked if I could have Gianni's set of keys to the house. She started weeping again as I went down the stairs.

So much to do. Gianni's spirit was everywhere. He had insisted on paying the electricity and telephone bills. My bank would pay them, but mandates had to be signed after endless waits in dismal offices impregnated with stale cigarette smoke. I waved to Quinto's widow, *la nonna,* sitting in his place on the balcony and imagined his family still chastising me for paying Gianni too little. He was always there on your land, poor man, toiling away for you. They never realised that Gianni came whenever he chose to and cultivated his own kitchen garden, keeping his family in vegetables during the winter, if they used the freezer I'd bought them. Couldn't they understand he was a landless *contadino* who had become a mason, but still yearned for the countryside of his youth? We had lent it back to him. Quinto's family remained unimpressed. What mattered were work and money. They were tied to the land with memories of mud and toil, of the frost-shrouded winters and animals requiring constant attention; they could hardly understand Gianni's claustrophobia in Montesasso.

* * * * *

'I like staying with Dan,' Joe said when I apologised for leaving them to see Cecilia on my own. It was only my unease and thanks, too effusive for the shy person he was, that made him add, 'Children take me as I am. That's how I want it to be'. He said something about not liking to be defined in terms of his work, of wanting companionship, not close proximity. A revulsion, perhaps from the bodies Mother described crammed into bomb shelters, from lying by warm, sticky, spongy flesh and the wafts of sour air as limbs stirred; from the people who sat too close in trains and buses and splattered when they spoke?

'I am as I am,' Joe's movements were saying. 'Don't ask any more. My genes aren't worth passing on anyway.' Before and after that conversation he talked about everything else but himself and the defective genes that had led to the hole in his heart and the operation.

The Saturday morning I went to see Ada I'd bumped into Cecilia outside her favourite bar in Piazza della Repubblica, the haunt of Montesasso's intelligentsia.

'Let's have a meal together, at home,' she whispered, glancing into the café. She looked drained. 'This Thursday?'

Cecilia was waiting for me at the same bar wearing a crisp-cut linen trouser suit and a conspiratorial air. Figures walked rapidly along Via Garibaldi, disappearing into hidden doorways or the shops that had not yet pulled down their blinds. She turned sharply under a dark arch and I followed her through the twilight to a tiny square at the end of the alley. The lights were on when she opened the door, spaces filled with mouth-watering smells. I followed her into a large room with a sofa and matching leather chairs at one end and a table partially laid at the other. Papers were lying on the top of a desk, and books rose in shelves from floor to ceiling.

'*Mi dispiace.* It's untidy. I've only just returned from Rome.' I knew she often went to see her parents. Her father, himself a well-known solicitor, had a huge practice with politicians as clients. I mused idly whether he could have been Bintoni's lawyer, but thought it unlikely since his daughter was so active in the Communist Party.

The meal that followed deserved to be remembered, but was obliterated by what she had to tell me. She was leaving Montesasso. There had been threats, anonymous letters pushed through the door. Insults. She had been to ask her father's advice; he immediately said he needed her in his office. Probably a strategic response.

She was deeply depressed. Fifteen years earlier she had decided to leave Rome and set up her own practice in Montesasso. She was disgusted by the way that foreign aid for Italy was not only being used for private advantage but was also channelled into shadowy right-wing organisations to prevent a communist coup or, others hinted, to relaunch the fascists in disguise.

'Young graduates were full of ideals then,' she remembered, 'and sick of the smug metropolitan complicity, if not outright corruption.'

The food was getting cold. It didn't matter. She was driven by some inner compulsion, resting the serving spoon and fork on the dish, her brow furrowed, her eyes fixed on me.

'*Hai sentito di questi intrighi?* D'you know about the Italian political sub-culture? Not that it's entirely Italian. It all goes back to the fall of Mussolini in 1945, which my father helped to bring about. He was young and idealistic, like so many others who had risked everything to oust that impostor. But Italy was devastated by two armies: the Allies, intent on defeating the Nazis, consequently destroying all that seemed to impede or delay that end; the Germans, enraged by the betrayal of their Italian allies – turncoats who were helping the British and Americans – were out to punish them. The countryside was ravaged; the little industry there was, annihilated.'

She was describing the Italy my father returned to; the Italy Gianni knew as a partisan.

'After the War,' she explained, 'Italy was seen as a bulwark against the threat of Communism from the East. More money was secretly channelled from abroad; a covert anti-Communist network set up and, in the seventies when the Italian Communists were almost voted into government, things came to a head.'

That was when we were restoring the ruin, the bomb exploded at Bologna station and the Red Brigades' activities penetrated our valley through Massimo and the kidnapping.

'You must have heard it all; rumours of secret Swiss bank accounts and dubious underground activities have been circulating for some time,' (Cecilia probably knew odd things were going on in the green shuttered villa) 'followed by revelations of financial and more salacious scandals.' (Does she know the 'wizard' Bintoni?) She told me how her father, a retiring person, had for decades been working fruitlessly, risking his family and career, to clean up endemic corruption. There was a price to pay, even in provincial Montesasso. It came to a head over the Christian Democrat and Communist rivalries in the area, and her growing awareness that all jobs, including hers, were politically determined.

'I hadn't paid anyone anything, or given any advantage to anybody, not even the members of the local Communist Party. Francesco is my friend, but his was by far the best design for the museum display, and I was one, on a panel of six, that chose him. That didn't stop tongues wagging. It may have helped that he comes from Montesasso, but our friendship didn't count at all. I thought Montesasso was an attractive, less corrupted place not too far from my family in Rome, where a single professional woman could be taken on merit alone. I'd discounted my father's reputation, the risks he'd taken in open opposition to Mussolini, the enemies as well as friends he'd made then who are now in high places. However, it seems I was welcomed to Montesasso initially as a key route to the corridors of power in Rome. It was naive of me not to realise this at the time; my rapid rise to a high position in the local party hierarchy was, I assumed, in recognition of my own abilities. What a fool I was! I tried to use it to smooth the way up for other women. I was effortlessly elected town councillor since I was placed near the top of the list of candidates.'

Success spawns jealous enemies, from outside and within. She bewailed her own innocence caused, she thought, by her profound belief in equal rights, especially for husband-and-church-dominated Italian women, and in social justice, both embedded in her from an early age. She assumed all other rational humans would share her values.

'It all began in Montesasso,' she confessed, 'back in the Fifties, long before I came here, when Don Basilio, a parish priest, was sent to the Catholic University in Rome. He returned to administer church property in the diocese of Montesasso, perhaps over a wider area – I can't find out how far his tentacles reach. Then Luciano

Bintoni, an uncritical supporter of Don Basilio, was processed through the same educational channels in Rome and rapidly scaled the Christian Democratic Party's electoral list. So far, nothing unusual. I discussed it with my companions in Communist Party circles, and went about my business.' She broke off to clear away the dishes.

'Things came to a head when the Town Council voted money to modernise the museum display. Count Prudomini distrusted me from the start. I was undermining his control of the family's ancient heritage. However, as councillor in charge of cultural affairs, I had to encourage local crafts and tourism. I was amazed when the Count resented my efforts, seeing that he had no legal rights over the Museum, or the building. Count Prudomini has managed to delay its refurbishment for nearly five years! There was even a rumour that his father bequeathed the family's collection to the museum to avoid the expense of restoring the paintings. When the present excavations started on Prudomini property near San Giuliano, I sent a routine notification to the Ministry of Culture in Rome and to Count Rinaldo himself.'

The pastries for dessert lay forgotten on the pine sideboard.

'Normally the Count took months to reply, if at all. I was mildly surprised when he wrote to say that Don Basilio, an Etruscanologist, had already examined the new finds and that he would be offended if others came to check the priest's "expert and considered" findings. Cecilia thought it tactful not to insist. She was no Etruscan expert after all. That was, it seemed, that. Then the bombshell. Don Basilio published another article to prove the new finds were all late nineteenth-century fakes from the same source as the famous vase in the Museum!'

The whole point of spending so much money on the museum refit was openly challenged, and not only by the Christian Democrats on the town Council; there were also murmurs among Cecilia's Communist colleagues. She argued forcefully that the money had been voted, the designer appointed and the work started before any of them had voiced opposition. The museum was attracting interest worldwide and Montesasso hotels were reporting an upsurge in bookings. She kept the refurbishment going, but only just. However, it took far too long and her reputation was tarnished. From that moment, the smear campaign took off.

There was sniggering behind Cecilia's back. She was having affairs; she was even a seductress! She was aware of hostile eyes prying. Attractive, vivacious and always well dressed in the latest fashions, her tailored trouser suits and mini-skirts became provocative in the judgmental climate of Montesasso gossip. There was also tittle-tattle about Cristina Prudomini and the *onorevole* Bintoni, but that waxed and waned without anyone knowing much about it – after all they didn't live and work in Montesasso – whereas Cecilia was under a constant spotlight, spending people's taxes on displaying fakes so that each action, each word, each glance, each outfit was analysed and interpreted to distraction. She felt and resented it. Her innocent trust trampled. Only after some months, and prompted by her insistent questions, did her friends admit it was so. They had been trying to shield her, but the flood was overwhelming them, too. They assessed their options and retreated to their families and jobs. Cecilia's friendship was less crucial, and her political connections proved ineffectual after the 1978 murder of the former Christian Democrat prime minister, Aldo Moro, by the Red Brigades, but unjustly blamed on the Communists. Members of her party were found guilty of corruption, though to a far lesser degree than the Christian Democrats; even so, some were tempted and succumbed. Her father's influence had been eclipsed, though his reputation as a brilliant lawyer survived.

With Massimo's second arrest for handling stolen artefacts, there came another twist. Cecilia incurred more wrath from her Christian Democrat enemies – the Prudomini Don Basilio and Bintoni axis – by insisting that Etruscan experts from the Villa Giulia Museum in Rome should inspect the 'fake' Etruscan objects and give their far more specialist verdict. The recently found artefacts were unavailable for inspection, she was informed. The experts intervened directly. They were grudgingly shown small votive figurines and animal statuettes, which were duly authenticated and dated. Cecilia was thrilled. It was just what she had hoped, indicating Montesasso must have been a major Etruscan city. Scholarly interest was increasing by the month.

After his release, Massimo from our valley had been giving his vivid version of events to rapt audiences in the Bar dello Sport on the Cassia. Count Prudomini was evasive, but Don Basilio continued to disagree with the scholars from Rome, though not so openly. Don Luigi's parishioners on the way to Sunday mass had noticed foreigners visiting the Etruscan tombs. Massimo was called in again for questioning. He might, or might not have given the police the information they were seeking. A raid on the *onorevole* Bintoni's villa had surprised the Countess and the politician *in flagrante,* but such revelations were the order of the day. More important, some of the Etruscan objects that had 'disappeared' were found, and others were soon to be accounted for by following up some easily decoded telephone numbers in Bintoni's possession.

The 'fake' issue turned out to be a cover for the sale of Etruscan objects to foreign middlemen, probably the ones financing the tomb excavations. Then more intermediaries were involved until the artefacts disappeared into the sales rooms of the world's most prestigious auction houses, their authenticity guaranteed but their provenance never traced to the Prudomini lands in the parish of San Giuliano. That international anti-Communist network had proved its wealth-giving properties yet again.

Cecilia was vindicated, but the whispering persisted. No approval for being right all along. She had lived her life openly, asking to be treated as an equal with men; to have a professional and public service career based on her native ability, and a love life such as men had ever enjoyed, albeit of a rather sober kind, she admitted a touch ruefully. After the rumours started, she noticed she had fewer clients. The political cause she had espoused and her father's heroic wartime exploits had become irrelevant. Personal ability and her palpable achievements counted for nothing in Montesasso. Her relationship with Francesco was knocked sideways. He was now busy in Milan with fresh clients, commissions, and emotional bonds.

The Countess disappeared after we had witnessed her drive away from the villa. Unsurprisingly, so did the *onorevole* Bintoni. The Count was in his Roman *palazzo* and not speaking to anyone. It was rumoured he would stand in future elections as a neo-fascist. Wherever the *onorevole* and the Countess were, apart or together, people were convinced that the same international network was providing them with hideouts and money laundering facilities. They were hardly in financial straits, or even feeling the need to account for their actions. Don Basilio has been glimpsed from time to time protesting his good faith in declaring the Etruscan finds to be fakes.

Where was Cecilia in all this mess? Returning to Rome to help her father in his practice, perhaps to take it over eventually. Not too bad, she admitted. But that was not what she had wanted to do with her life. She would return bereft, her ideals shattered, her efforts to advance the cause of women and of open government belittled, and throughout she had denied herself the conventional option: a husband and children.

'*Prendiamo un caffè?*'

* * * * *

That evening I knew I was losing a friend. Cecilia invited me to stay with her in Rome, but it wouldn't be the same as having someone to count on in Montesasso. The lights were out in the Casa dell'Avventura. Joe had forgotten to leave the outside one lit to welcome me back. The moon was rising over the hill to the east, and I sat on the veranda to watch it silently spread a luminous sheen, mantling the valley in softness, in deep, dark, mysterious folds. It was uncannily quiet. Usually dogs barked and rattled chains, crickets chirruped and owls hooted. Stillness, and the silence poured over me. I stopped thinking and sank into myself – no past, no future; just mindless forgetfulness. Then it came. The crunch of gravel up the drive near the back of the house. Blood chilled into barbs of terror. Heart thumping chest, mouth open, tongue curled to shriek. Another crunch, a step, a mat grey cut-out of a man in the moonscape.

CHAPTER 29

Did I jump into his arms with everything ending happily ever after? I was fearful. If your wish is granted, then there has to be a reckoning in the aftermath of absence. Paul was my Lazarus, and when resurrected, I required an account of his two buried years.

It would have been easier if I had seen his expression, but he stayed like a statue, face in moonshadow.

'Where have you been?' He stood, silent. Would I drive him away if I probed?

'Do you need somewhere to sleep?' A raw question. Had he been stalking me? Did he know Joe was here? That Dan was old enough to have a room to himself on the ground floor? Or think he could wipe his slate clean by slipping into the far side of the bed we had bought together?

'Can I have a shower?' said the dark granite statue. I thought of mother in the air raid, of Joe and physical revulsion, and feared the running water above his bedroom would wake him up. I wasn't ready for any encounter outside my present.

As he moved towards the veranda steps, I made out the rough edge of a beard. His clothes were probably clammy and dishevelled. A destitute return.

'No. It'll disturb the others.' I wouldn't admit Joe was here until I had to. 'You'll wake Dan.'

'Your mother?' I didn't answer. Why should I?

'You can use the sofa.' Under the cushions was the emergency bed. I didn't offer bed linen or pillow or towel, and turned into the house, going straight to the bathroom. He was still outside when I closed the bedroom door, trembling. A dream come uneasily true.

* * * * *

Healing the wound of two wasted years would be harder than I feared. Presences. No mother here, only Joe. Neutral, but Paul might not believe it. All the explaining to do, the silences, the polite conversation smoothing over turbulent undercurrents. I was unprotected by a routine to fill painful time gaps. No flood of forms to complete, humdrum calls to make, preparations for classes or listening to the concentrated needs of the young could ebb and flow in my mind until I floated, exhausted, into a haven. Deep, dying slumber. This Tuscan sanctuary should have convivial spaces for relaxation and pastimes planned together round drinks at the mill table.

Or should I send him away? Now. Before he saw the others, especially Dan. I feared I'd yell at him, furious even because he was sleeping. I could hear soft snores fluttering his nostrils on the other side of the partition wall. How could he fall asleep, like that, after walking back into my life just as he slipped off, without any warning? I crept past him across the sitting room to lock the main door so Dan couldn't come in the morning and find him. On my way back I stood over him wondering. Should I demand to know what he had been doing? Now? Wake him up? If I shouted or became upset he might shy away from me. No. I should wait for him to justify his absence.

Too much had been left unsaid; too much had unravelled between us.

* * * * *

Joe was sitting on the veranda when I unlocked the door in the morning. He looked up, puzzled.

'I thought I heard you in the shower?'

'Not me.' He followed into the kitchen, silently watching me knock the used coffee out of the funnel (nobody ever cleans it out after use) and refill it with deliberation. It could have been my mother. Mike. Even Angélique. No, he guessed who it was.

'Paul slept on the sofa last night.'

'I'll leave if...'

'Please don't go!' I was crying. A dream come true never feels as anticipated. I resented the clutter that had accumulated between Paul and me. The justifications. Other people wondering – Dan, especially.

'When are Sarah and William arriving?' he asked.

'I can't remember.' I set a tray on the kitchen table, too muddled to think. Three mugs. No, four. I couldn't be bothered with a milk jug; a carton would do. Joe carried the tray out to Gianni's table, scrubbed till its grain rose in hackles, and went back to the kitchen for the biscuit tin. Or we could have jam on yesterday's bread, but neither bothered, half talking of nothing important. And still Paul didn't emerge. Dan came up the steps and I didn't bother to ask if he had washed his face and brushed his teeth. Joe was uncharacteristically quiet. Dan looked at us curiously. Or was it just because he wanted Joe's advice on the next stage of the bamboo den they were planning by the old mill? 'Is Andrew coming? When will Penny and Kate be here?' he asked before scampering across the drive to the ruin.

The door to the upper storey remained firmly shut.

Would Dan recognise him, or even want him back? I filled a bowl with his cereal and, leaving my half-empty coffee mug with Joe on the veranda, followed Dan out of sight behind the mill rubble, to slump beside his clear morning chatter.

'Can't Joe come and help me?'

'I'll ask him.' Steamy heat was already rising from the channel between us and Giulio, the mild-mannered killer who was strimming his terraces, facing west and us, edged by the light of the morning sun. Zizzazz, zizzazz, drilled into my dazed mind. Zizzazz, zizzazz. Anything better than seeing Dan's eyes wide, hair tufting up in surprise, recognising, or turning away from his father. Sarah would come sometime – today, tomorrow, the week after – I couldn't recall precisely. I already heard her soothing me.

'Relax. It's your holiday too, Olivia.' That meant time left free for my mind to wander down tracks dried in ruts, over skid marks wounding the earth or along streams veining the land. By the mill ruin Dan was humming, talking to himself, or me, or Joe. Peopling his new den.

'When are they coming?' He'd been asking about the Thompsons every day, on and off. I mentally rehearsed my reactions: elated, apprehensive, too vulnerable in the dream-come-true scenario. It should all end here and now with the coda 'happy ever after'. I peeped round the bay tree where Gianni had his heart attack and across the sun-beaten drive to the veranda. Two men sitting; fraternal, familiar, a murmur of voices over coffee mugs. Nearer. I couldn't face the taller, darker one, but glimpsed he had stood up to stare at me. I wanted to retreat back to Dan and avoid the encounter. Giulio had stopped the strimmer. No birdsong. No bees, bluebottles, cicadas or trespassing chickens. Deep blue silence pulsating overhead.

'Olivia.' The familiar melodious voice, a shade deeper. Hesitant. Hair longer, curlier, lighter, and no last night beard, no torn soiled shirt, frayed jeans, scuffed trainers. A green short-sleeved shirt over fawn chinos. A well-groomed Lazarus.

'Olivia?' He stayed where he was, back to the valley. I stood sun-beaten on the drive. I had missed his entrance, framed on the threshold, restored into my life.

The telephone rang behind the half-open door he'd come through. No one stirred. Three, four, five trills, then Joe moved to answer. Paul was standing, looking as if he'd just returned from an explicable absence to latch on to the family chain of events; spruced, sprayed, deodorised. Olive branch assumed.

'For you, Olivia. It's Sarah.' I walked up the steps to brush past him into the sitting room turned bedroom. Paul didn't respond.

Joe went on chatting inessentials. Not 'What have you been doing since you came to see me in hospital?' because he wouldn't require justifications from another man. Just innocuous, 'We haven't been here long. Not done much, too hot,' and so on. I didn't really bother to listen, thinking instead that the Thompson family would fill the ground floor. No room for Paul except where he was – or I was. He had starting spilling his belongings over the sofa and floor. As usual.

He was standing, back against the column and, as I came out framed in the doorway, I was reflected in his dark glasses. Dan came talking up the veranda steps behind him.

'Joe –' he paused at the top step seeing the back of a stranger. The dark glasses turned.

'Come –' Dan looked from Paul to Joe and back '- and see what I've made.' Another longer than normal look at the tall dark man in a green shirt and fawn trousers, and he turned back down the steps across the burning gravel followed by two men.

'A natural survivor,' I said out loud, not knowing whom I was referring to, 'doing as men always do,' not exactly sure what I meant.

They turned out of sight past the bay tree. I went into the kitchen to find the shopping pad and hit it with the nearest pen, engraving in white lines milk, bread, cheese, fruit, vegs, etc. The pen had run out. I tossed it across the marble top, not wanting to search for another by the telephone and risk reawakening associations with his possessions scattered over the sitting room. I'd have to remember what was needed. When I stepped down by the bay tree to say I was going shopping, Joe and Dan were weaving bamboo rods through upright poles; Paul was sitting apart, hands round knees, watching. Then he reached out towards Dan.

Changing forcefully into second gear, the hired Fiat ground up the drive carrying me away with the after-image of an arm faltering over the child's head, not quite touching. It was as if Paul was trying to paint over the image of his absence and rework his relationship to Dan – a human *pentimento*. At the supermarket, I grabbed a jar of apricot jam off the shelf (still seeing Dan, startled, looking up at his father). Two bags of ground coffee with their brown aroma, (thinking of the fresh, sharp after-shave of men talking inconsequentially, mug in hand, as if nothing untoward had happened). Bread, thick unsalted Tuscan bread (imagining the child and adults sitting, standing, leaning, waiting famished at one end of the veranda). A fat slice of speckled gorgonzola layered with mascarpone (his favourite cheese – was he emaciated? I hadn't noticed); tangy thin-sliced local ham, Milanese salami and matured sheep cheese, best dry, desiccated, dispassionate. I was shedding pounds from my emotional burden. He was alive.

Driving back I pictured Paul, sitting against the mill ruin, one hand on the warmth of the stones, the other twiddling grass in his mouth, hesitating to caress his child, then reaching out to Dan who was weaving a bamboo wall with Joe. Restore the original, or is the afterthought more truthful? *Pentimenti*. Repenting or rethinking?

Sarah and William had arrived, to my relief, and we sat on the veranda as if summer two years ago had been seamed into an unbroken present. William, the *cantastorie*, true storyteller of our imprint in Tuscany, had completed the pageant of the valley he'd been writing for years. His words sounded reassuringly across the tableau framed by the beam from the kitchen wall to Gianni's column at the top of the veranda steps. From the drive I could see Dan looking at his father surveying the plain, both as if they would never have the chance to do so again; Kate next to Dan, wide-eyed at the goddess of love whose legs were projecting from the boot of William's vehicle; Sarah behind her, eyes moving from me to Paul and back; Joe watching from a corner; Penny and Andrew leaning on either side of the kitchen door.

William had ordered the statue a year ago from a garden centre. It was to be a surprise for us. In a flurry of conspicuously secret activity, he had prepared a plinth for his goddess above a flat area to serve as a stage. Venus turned out to be much heavier than eyes could estimate. He called for help to ease her into her place. All gathered round the back of the car, gazing in reverence at the three-quarter-size goddess (a sub-Canova version in pulverised Carrara marble), lying in abandon on scratchy straw. She was slowly carried down to the stage, Andrew her head, Paul and William her feet, with Joe and female followers in train, and then hoisted on to the plinth framed by bay trees.

'We should put Apollo somewhere for company,' Penny suggested. Instead, all eyes were on Venus while Joe was cementing the goddess into her tutelary position above the stage, and William was casting his pageant. There were plenty of would-bes: Penny would be the Virgin painted for a local monastery by Fra Angelico, with Kate as the angel Gabriel. William fancied playing the artist himself, if no one else offered. Paul was cast as Leonardo who had mapped the whole area – a copy of the Queen's original was still hanging in the Montesasso tourist office. Andrew filled in for the engineer who had finally drained the plain and Dan would be the head and trunk of Hannibal's elephant with Joe for the hind legs, as well as lead the 1944 allied liberation army in the last episode. Sarah would prompt and Olivia provide the audience of one.

Rehearsals were to be held at William's command.

* * * * *

No one asked Paul what everyone must have been thinking: why had he left and where had he been all that time? I was relieved. Nobody wanted to cause friction or embarrassment. Neither did I. He had to explain himself to me alone, and to Dan. I kept busily vigilant, tidying myself away into our former bedroom. Sarah had found him bed linen and a blanket, soon strewn with a sketchbook and unmatched socks. His wallet lay with a long, thin gold and blue box on top of the old bread cupboard he'd restored; the familiar trousers and shirts were slung over the back of a chair, two equally scuffed pairs of trainers underneath.

Wolfgang had convened a meeting to be held that evening at Giulio's farmhouse. Something had to be done about the ruts and car springs, but I didn't want to go alone. I had never needed Gianni more than now to accompany me along the road. The Thompsons had already decided to explore Montacuto, with Joe taking the overflow from William's vehicle. Penny was researching a school project on World War II in Italy and needed to find out what had happened in this hilltop town about thirty miles from Montesasso. Dan, thinking we would all go on the outing, chose to sit behind Andrew driving his father's car. There was room for Paul with Joe and Penny but William suggested he should stay behind to sketch and paint undisturbed. Or that was the reason he gave to leave us alone together.

I put some bread and cheese on the veranda table, with only one glass of local red wine to remain clear-headed, and concentrated on jotting down some points for the crucial meeting. Paul stood by me for a while but I didn't want to look at him. Then instead of sitting, he fetched his sketchpad and went down by the stream with a hunk of bread and cheese. I tried to concentrate on what Gianni would have wanted me to do. Our efforts to improve the *strada vicinale* had not just been pointless, but counterproductive, making the neighbours suspicious. Now I was alone and unsure about my role in the meeting ahead.

Paul came with me. We walked apart along the track in question. Some neighbours stared, though nobody seemed surprised to see him back. Spindly wooden chairs were already set out in a semi-circle on the far side of Giulio's farmyard, a few already occupied. Prominent at one end was the self-appointed patriarch, Wolfgang the retired professor with his wife. Giulio, Roberta and Antonio were sitting under the walnut tree at the far end of the straggly semicircle. Wolfgang, ironically the last to come to the valley, was shuffling papers and coughing impatiently with undisputed authority. He summoned everyone to be seated. The chattering groups broke up and drifted to the chairs still unoccupied. Others sat on an abandoned wagon, a dry-stone wall, and the edge of the well.

'*La condizione* of our unpaved road is a disgrace. It's ruining our cars.' Wolfgang started with the pure Italian of a born linguist as Marino slipped into the semi-circle, pulling up a chair next to me at the end nearest the road in question.

'You should be in charge of this meeting,' I whispered to him, 'shouldn't you?' Why didn't he, a well-established inhabitant in our valley, run the meeting? It was clear that the *contadino* families who had emerged from the *mezzadria* system to buy their own houses were used to the rough road and, as I knew to my cost, unwilling to take much part in improving it. Only the incoming element felt the situation had become intolerable. Wolfgang pointed out in his eloquent opening remarks that his car, and his wife's, had been seriously damaged by frequent journeys over those ruts. He added, glancing round the attentive semi-circle, that most of them here returned from work for the full Italian lunch, before going back in the afternoon.

'*Pace,*' was Marino's whispered reply. He had opted out of the rat race, and was only too happy for someone else to take it all upon himself. Wolfgang, who let it slip that the new mayor of Montesasso was a close friend, was now talking about the cost of sixteen million lire, and that was a fine reduction on a quote of twenty-one million. Thanks to his efforts, the Town Council would pay five million. But we had to find the eleven million quickly, otherwise we'd lose that subsidy. I opened my mouth to 'why?' but closed it again.

Wolfgang fell silent and people spoke in little groups. Nothing seemed to be happening. I glanced at Paul but he didn't speak.

'Can't we get other quotations?' My voice trailed away into uncomprehending ether. All eyes on me, puzzled.

'*Perchè?*' Wolfgang asked. 'This quotation is from the firm that does all the roads for the Council. What's wrong with that?' I felt under accusation. Why did I suspect his judgement and, by implication, that of the relevant elected councillors?

A lull. No one appeared willing to consider my suggestion. There seemed to be a consensus that the firm chosen would do the best job for the lowest cost. Wolfgang the Patriarch cleared his throat loudly and repeated that if we delayed and asked for other estimates, we might lose the Council's subsidy. He, in any case, was unwilling to ask around. Someone else would have to take that on. He had more than done his bit for the road, he emphasised, looking pointedly at me. I remained silent to sense the reactions. None.

'*Siamo d'accordo?*' Agreed? It seemed as if he had a gavel poised, before tapping it smartly on the documents laid on his knees. Done! My recommended firm. My price. His wife was already working out how much each had to pay. One or two in the semi-circle muttered that they had not discussed it enough. The Patriarch settled back into his chair, the largest of all, and said he needed agreement from each individual involved. I willed him to ask me last, or at least towards the middle, but ill luck would have it that I was on his left, and the natural place to begin, rather than with Giulio at the far end. He turned towards me.

'*Signora?*' Here it comes! I visualised the yellow plastic pipe poking through the stone wall below Mauro and Caterina's house to join another from Wolfgang's new extension dripping steadily into the channel alongside our property and relentlessly feeding those five mosquito-ridden pools instead of soaking away into Mauro's fields on the far side of the track.

'Go on!' murmured Paul. All eyes were on me. The evening refused to cool off. To the south, a rumble. Not a breath of air stirred.

'*Mi dispiace,* the kitchen overflow from the house above us feeds the pools in the channel running past ours. They're a breeding ground for mosquitoes. The water must be piped underneath the road before it is asphalted. Then, and only then, can I settle my part of the cost.' Householders had to pay four times as much as the others, so if I didn't do my bit, the road couldn't be surfaced. There were immediate protests.

'That's a private matter between you and your neighbours,' several protested, 'nothing to do with the road'.

On the contrary, **all** to do with the road. How could a tube be put under the asphalt? If not done before surfacing the road, then we would be eternally plagued with pools and mosquitoes. Some guests have had to leave, bitten into pincushions.

The semi-circle disintegrated into knots of people talking and gesticulating with unusual vigour for such a sultry evening. A clap of thunder, but still far off. The Patriarch stood up to shout at me. I felt tired and weepy and turned away, wishing Paul would speak out instead of me. No one else wanted to discuss matters; no attempt to monitor an agreement with Mauro who was there, saying nothing, next to an indignant Caterina waving her hands in the air, eyes flaming at us. She was *offesissima* all right. It was their gaping outlet, their dirty water (and also Wolfgang's), but **our** fault for mentioning it, and especially in front of their immediate neighbours. Silly foreigners making such a fuss about pinpricks no worse than nettle stings, their eyes were saying. I remained silent. People stood up, some drifted off. As I moved towards the track I heard Marino talking to Paul. A fist suddenly appeared in front of my face, '*Via, o vi dò un pugno in faccia...*' I fled as Antonio chased me up the incline till his hand grasped my shoulder, the other clenched beneath my chin.

'*Via!* This is private property. *Viaaaaaaa!*' he shouted at me, face hardly six inches from mine, his knuckles now tilting my chin back. A figure appeared, grasped Antonio's fist, pulled it firmly away from me and whispered, 'Go back to your house!' He turned the young man towards his father's farmyard and frog-marched him off.

'Who was that pulling Antonio away?' I whispered, shaking.

'Marino,' Paul replied, just behind me. 'I'm sorry. I didn't realise what was happening.'

'He told me to go home.' So we did.

The night was still young, very oppressive, yet I was shivering and sweating at the same time. Paul took my arm as we returned down the drive.

The others were back waiting for us on the veranda picking at bread, cheese, tomatoes and peaches, since no one felt like cooking.

'People were locked up in the church, everyone from the small town of Montacuto,' Penny was telling us. 'Then the men and male children were taken out and shot. There's still a lot of bad feeling, not just about the Germans, but also the partisans. They had blown up a vehicle and killed German paratroopers knowing full well, from posters and other warnings, that there would be reprisals.'

Paul was standing behind Joe near the front door. I was sitting diagonally across the table, back to the plain. Something was fluttering behind his head. A bat, I thought, unmoved. Dan straddled the top of the steps fiddling with some Lego.

'There was the usual inscription on the town hall. Date, numbers shot,' Andrew explained. 'We happened to sit down outside a bar next to a table where three men were drinking beer. They pushed spare chairs over to us and wanted to know where we were staying in Tuscany. When I mentioned San Giuliano, near Montesasso, they asked if we'd heard of Giovanni Panichini. Small world!'

'Why? Did they know him?' Paul said. Why hadn't he asked about Gianni before then?

'He must have been one of the partisans who ambushed the German soldiers,' Penny continued.

'They didn't know Gianni had died,' Kate said. Andrew added, 'They just nodded when we told them. No surprise, regrets, or questions.' I turned towards Paul.

'You knew, didn't you, Gianni was dead?' I couldn't help asking. 'How?'

'Angélique.'

I might have guessed. The crickets thumped the heavy air. The usual pattern of lights across the plain seemed doom-ridden. Lightning etched the horizon at infrequent intervals. The storm was undecided, the night airless.

'We've done exactly what we've tried so hard **not** to do all these years, alienated the whole valley,' I said.

'An exaggeration,' William tried to console me after I explained what had happened, 'only your near neighbours.'

'Worse,' I went on. 'Nobody seems to care if we're all being ripped off. And what about Wolfgang's role in all this? The last person to arrive, and now he acts like the local patriarch and he's not even Italian! Why on earth do they all put up with it?'

'Because he's the only one who bothers,' Joe said, 'and it's in their interest not to become too involved, or to have to grease the palm of some flunkey to get the road done. Someone else is doing it. So much the better! No time to waste on such matters. That's what you should do.' Joe was right, but we'd have to stop complaining about the mosquitoes. So what then? Pay up, let the road be asphalted, and then try to get Mauro to cut a trench in the tarmac to lay the pipe? Impossible. I felt trapped.

All gazed into the darkness. I wished the crickets would shut up. The previous evening Dan had found Harry, the giant toad and mosquito eater, in the back garden and near him, the last of the glow-worms. Now both had deserted us, just like the rest in Giulio's farmyard.

'Time to sell the house?' I said. No one answered. 'It could become very unpleasant. We might be ostracised again.' The very air around us seemed threatening. The thunder had changed tack and was approaching. Jagged lightning tore at the sky across the plain. No one felt like hazarding the usual evening stroll. It would mean passing under Mauro and Caterina's house (their bedroom light was still on) and along the rough road that had caused all the trouble an hour earlier. Marino had advised us gently but firmly not to venture away from our house that night. We obeyed, subdued, and from the veranda we watched the storm move away to hide behind Monte Amiata.

CHAPTER 30

The following afternoon Sarah insisted that William needed more rehearsals with the others. Dan was to help Andrew work out the lighting for the evening's performance. As the audience, I had nothing to learn.

'Just return by seven for a bowl of pasta. You've got your script, Paul. It's quite simple. You only have one scene as Leonardo.' Sarah was prompting us to move off-stage and on to our own devices.

The clouds had returned grumbling over Monte Amiata while snatches of sun dried the rain from the previous storm. Paul and I stood awkwardly together until Sarah and William led us towards the car, light-heartedly discussing the pageant. I sat in the passenger seat though Paul wasn't named on the hiring agreement, not caring whether I drove or not. Until two years ago, he usually drove my car. He set off tensely to nowhere in particular. Nor did I mind.

Two figures with space between them in a hired car faced the plain with no plan to hand and diverging horizons. Aimlessly they started over the first map page opened, turning south-east by a drainage canal towards Sant'Angelo d'Orcia. Do you remember, remember, remember?

Drifts of sheep grazed the hillside; furrows etched fields, scoring contours chalky white to creamy brown. A solitary farmhouse stood abandoned amid an ocean of crests, vapour curling off them. To the right rose a jumble of rocks at the end of a track.

'There,' I pointed. 'Let's go to those boulders.' I don't know why I said it except to find some aim, some purposeful movement. The track started at the bottom of the hill by a tangle of acacias and continued past poplars bordering a stream.

'They always grow by water,' he said, out of the car before me. Another rumble. 'Most panel paintings were on poplar. Bad for fire wood but good for panels. It doesn't split when you hammer nails into it.' He was wearing one of his short-sleeved, red shirts open at the neck, chest hair curling grey. I glanced at him gazing, eyes narrowing tensely, at the poplars and then the boulders at the top of the slope. Still looking away he continued. 'They say Christ's cross was made of poplar. A humble wood, but the nails couldn't crack it.' Stuff of popular legend, I supposed, like Piero della Francesca's frescoes of the Story of the True Cross that I'd taken the children to see in Arezzo, long ago. Paul, I remember, hadn't come with us. The poplar leaves shivered, ruffled by a rogue breeze as the storm stirred. While we walked a hand's width apart to the boulders, clay furrows greedily imbibed blue-grey strokes of rain. Stranded cypresses were bowing to the tempest. A black speck hustled sheep towards the desolate farmhouse with a dovecote, a toy-like shepherd tramping after them over the ridges.

'Come,' was all he said, striding ahead towards the outcrop, his shirt clinging and touching the hidden birthmark on his shoulder blade. Crouching beneath two rocks, he left space for me to squat beside him in damp warmth and tangy closeness. One arm supported him; the other clasped a knee – no attempt to embrace.

As long ago at the beginning of memory, we sat like specks on earth's skeleton; veined boulders washed bare by streams into rivers and out to the sea.

He continued to lean on his right arm, his left hand traced patterns in the rivulets coursing over the rockface. Hairs bristled over the pulse in his wrist and the thread of a scar I had forgotten. Was it there two years ago? Blown together by the storm, this could be the moment for me to snuggle up, feel his heart beating and end all happily ever after. Instead I tried to let him bridge the space saying, 'Do you remember the fresco in the Prudomini villa? The landscape in the background was like this.'

All the remembering – tentative 'when's', timid 'where's' – to cobble together and mend or strain the fragile patching of absence. When did we – not I? Where did we – not you? Beware of 'Why?' I placed my left hand next to his – not touching, just near – and observed every gesture and glance, flinching at any turn of his head. Paul hadn't yet looked into my eyes without sunglasses. It had stopped raining. I waited, then propelled myself up and out of the shelter.

The rocks were steaming in the sudden heat as the steel blue squall rolled east to the Apennines leaving pockmarked swirls of dust.

'I missed these landscapes so much,' he said, walking back to the car. 'All the faces seemed to suck me into them.'

'Why?' I had no idea what he was talking about.

'Why?' he repeated. He wasn't connecting, as when darning a hole, the needle misses the other edge and swerves back on itself. He was contemplating instead the curtain of rain moving away over the ridges towards the Apennines. So I linked back.

'It's just like the storm clouds behind the young man on the white horse.' He listened motionless, still gazing beyond his horizon. 'Do you remember? The one we saw when we visited the Piccolomini Library the first time we went to Siena together.' I drew my breath before adding, 'with Tim'. There I was filling in gaps, embroidering silences and leaving no space for him. He turned slowly, this time looking straight at me after two never-ending years – brown eyes speckled green and rimmed by dark lashes. They hurt. Tim was in them somewhere.

'Even if I went away,' he said with an effort, face desolate, 'I didn't want anyone else to have you. Or Dan – or even Tim's memory.' I heard him, having nothing to tell him of my two years apart, nothing that he couldn't have pieced together himself.

He stopped by the car and leant on it, looking out towards the greener foothills of the Appenines, away from the still eddies of bare clay cliffs with whiskers of yellow broom and a spare cypress craning over a gully.

Inside the Fiat he looked straight ahead, the engine a drumming counterpoint to his hesitant monotone.

'Do you remember?' (He's assuming my thoughts, my reactions. I'm silent with effort.) 'I was restoring a Rembrandt self-portrait. As I was carefully cleaning away the dirt he began staring at me, a face scored by debt, eyes sad, unfathomable brown pools. He would have looked at Titus like that. I saw myself there, gazing with Rembrandt's eyes at his son whose picture I'd already restored.'

It was hot and humid, nostrils sated with smells of moist soil and damp clothes drying. I didn't caress his bare arm moving predictably with the gear changes or his thigh flexing to brake. His light trousers clung, damp and warm. I lowered my window still further and Paul turned at the blast of cross air.

'At least Angélique understood.'

'What?' Relieved I didn't have to mention her first.

'That nothing can follow everything – as night follows day.' Another pause, then 'Shakespeare?' Better not to probe. I could see Angélique hastening to help, elegant and assured.

'That painful restoration of Rembrandt himself, the publicity, television programme, all crowding in and finishing together. Then no work at all.' I waited.

'I never realised how quickly debts mounted, how difficult it is to find enough money to rent a London studio and flat, however small.' He was driving back towards the foothills and Montesasso. 'I should have found someone to share. But not many people are around in July and August.'

That was, perhaps, why he didn't confide in me. I was away in Italy waiting for him, without a telephone. I imagined him in the flat with the sketches I had framed for him round the walls. Me. Tim. Dan. Then he must have scratched *nessun maggior dolore* on the windowpane. No greater grief indeed, than to remember happy times in present misery. Dante exiled from Florence and his family; Francesca and Paolo languishing in *Inferno* for illicit love but we were now driving together into tentative sunlight after a storm.

'You were always too busy.' Did he mean with Dan and career, mother and grandmother – all but him? Once he would have teased me like a schoolboy, '*Varium et mutabilis semper femina*' – 'woman's a various and changeful thing', which is why, he said, I had enchanted him.

Straight on over another crossroads. Paul always drove sticking his neck forward from his shoulders, as if to deny his height. The end of his nose was rounder; the sag behind his chin gave him the profile of a Roman emperor. Alone with me in the car, nobody else could listen.

'Angélique always had solutions. One of her clients owned a castle and had numerous paintings to restore. I could have a whole floor to live in–' (so that's where our furniture went) '–and the baronial hall as a studio. It seemed an ideal way to sort myself out. Then I would contact you.' (I might have known. Angélique provided every easement: client, castle, paintings, cash flow – what else?)

'She found me mediocre portraits of stiff figures to restore. I was to cheer up maiden aunts in funereal black by painting in fur trimmings and silk furbelows, according to the style of the desired period. She was good at filling any cracks in family history and upping my fee. It would only be for a few weeks, to pay off my debts.'

Did he keep our bed, our carpet, our bits and pieces and his portraits of us? I imagined them in a high-ceilinged bed chamber with mullioned windows; sketches of Tim and Dan, even me overwhelmed by vast stone walls. His studio in an echoing, vaulted great hall stacked with flaking figures. A slender spectre glided through it all, whispering in her beguiling accent. Paul drove towards the next wave of storm clouds glowering over the afternoon sun. Straight on at another crossroads along a gravelled track.

'She found the works, got the money, sorted me out.' Yes, I thought; deftly, charmingly manipulative.

'I couldn't have survived without her.' He repeated her sad story: a child unloved by a philandering father – a French count, no less – abandoned by a society mother to emotional poverty, imprisoned in a château with priceless treasures and not enough to eat. However, her father provided her with invaluable aristocratic connections all over Europe and particularly, it seems, in Britain. Prominent families needed help with ancestors, inherited or acquired, such as plain Edwardian girls on the eve of marriage or spinster Victorian great, great aunts in unrelieved black; or dull founders of fortunes burdened by chains of office; or pining Georgian heiresses and bewigged speakers of the House of Commons – all to be pampered, cleaned and restored to glory. A mean face was to be rounded and rouged into a smile or timeless glance of distinction; a maiden to be garlanded in flowers; a stodgy man of substance enhanced against a background of added acreage. Most of them Angélique was able to sell to her admirers, their ancestry cheerfully altered to fit an aspiring but unadorned wall.

And all this came after restoring two Rembrandts.

'When Angélique's friend was away,' (he was careful not to mention the name) 'I was given free use of the staterooms and spent time examining the portraits in the long gallery. It was a good place to pick up motifs to enliven a dull portrait,' he admitted with disgust. 'A vase of flowers. Different garlands. Another fur or lace trimming or more luxurious robes.' Is this what 'lovingly restored' really means? Paul was 'restoring' what, in Angélique's view, would be saleable.

His profile tensed, Rembrandt brown shadows under his cheekbones, nose more salient, eyelids slightly drooping. Was he trying to vindicate his long absence? Where was Mike in all this dubious moneymaking? Safe, perhaps, in ceramics and small scale sculpture.

Thunder again. Paul drew in on the left verge, blocking my view of the returning storm.

'We've been here before.' For two years my world had reverted to 'I' and 'you'. The deserter was using 'we'. I needed to get out, to stand in the squall and float over the hoar green of my trees, olive branches churning above the puckered earth. More agitated cypresses marked a boundary. Folded into the valley, evergreen oaks underlined hard folds of clay; ploughed ribs tumbled on the left into a scrub-filled gully with yellow daubs of broom. To the right parallel lines curved up to drop into ridges beyond, and above all the brassy glow of thunderclouds, a forked gash of light. Kettledrums grumbled deep in the throat of two angry, wasted years. I shifted a few steps to my left and there, framed by holm oaks, lay the road we had discovered before. Leaving umbrella pines in the valley, it zigzagged across the clay – a scar stitched by cypresses snaking up the shoulder of the hill, curving over it and beyond into endless roads, paths to possibilities.

Before the last growl, before the wind twisted and turned to blow the storm sideways, before the last tear in the backdrop, a sudden blast of sunshine raked the grey skin of the land, ruffling the ridges and throwing long shadows sideways. I swivelled round as the rays veered away, searching across the valley to catch that same road, forever climbing.

He was sitting in the car, face towards the winding road, brow creased, saying nothing.

'I don't know if we can have the play tonight,' I said returning to the passenger seat. 'It might rain. We'd better go back.' He silently reversed, leaving the zig-zag road behind to drive towards our house, away from the bleak lunar landscape.

So he had been lured by Angélique's financial solution. His only comment about money over the past eighteen years had been that he didn't have a regular income and I did. So I paid for whatever our joint account couldn't cover, like fares or the car. It was his assumption that I resented, not the paying. As Gran would have said, when he was in luck, he could always have opened his mouth and offered.

He was still silent, and I was still dejected as the Fiat tipped over the last bare ridge into the plain quilted with drainage canals. We drove through elongating shadows of cypresses and umbrella pines spreading east into the foothills of the Apennines.

'I don't think you like Angélique.' You can say that again! I scrutinised him while he was concentrating on the road. I wouldn't react or provoke. 'She was easy to confide in …' So I wasn't? I was so deeply slashed that I had either to scream or take refuge somewhere, somehow. I shrank into myself and let him speak on, 'I didn't ask for help, but she happened to drop by, saw what a mess I was in – ' His voice trailed off. Another long pause. Quite a ménage in that castle: the laird and Paul with Angélique benignly flitting back and forth, an angel with canvasses tucked under her wings. What web was she weaving? The golden lining of sombre clouds hung ragged over a watery pink sunset as we turned down the drive.

* * * * *

The actors had been hyper-busy in spite of the storm. The play was now ready. The oak tree to one side of the theatre had been strung with spotlights. Props were in piles at strategic points: under the tailrace of the mill, to one side of the bay tree behind Venus and inside the ruin itself. Rehearsals had been taking place all afternoon, resulting in some tantrums and grumpiness. William had both directed and stage-managed, Sarah reported, with calm assurance.

She welcomed us with a glass of cool white wine and stuffed olives. Shopping at the new Co-op was quick and easy and the meal soon prepared. The crickets were already chirping and the moon came on cue, now clipped on the waning side. I sat on the ledge under Venus, restored by theatrical companionship to muse on my role as the Audience. I should be practising ventriloquism to sound like a crowd. Fluttering out from the ruin, up to the oak tree, then squeaking into the clear air, away went the bats... Did I just catch the shadow of the *stregone*, the Wizard Bintoni, before he swooped off westwards to confer with his coven behind those high villa walls?

No more musings... The Play's the Thing to catch the conscience of a wizard – if he had one? We would sup at the end of the performance. The night was yet young and the thespians more impatient than hungry. Paul left his wine and olives reluctantly for a quick rehearsal of his entrance as Leonardo. The play started when my grey blanket arrived on stage with the vacuum cleaner tube as trunk; Hannibal's elephant had crossed the Alps to pasture below our house. Off stage Paul kept on staring at Dan, as if mentally sketching the stoutly diminutive Hannibal, who was shouting and giggling his rhymed couplets to uneven effect, before doubling as trunk and front legs, first prompted and then supported by Joe at the elephant rear. Fra Angelico painted the Virgin Penny, smiling in embarrassment when Kate arrived as the angel Gabriel just before cue. The *beato* William painted on serenely. Paul entered, hiding behind Leonardo's flowing beard. The actors not on stage swelled the audience, whose hands were beginning to ache, as her cheers became hoarser. Andrew, who had spent all afternoon on the lighting, took a well-earned place centre stage as the worthy eighteenth-century nobleman, Fossombrone, whose canal system had restored the swampy land of the plain to agriculture.

The later personalities were not so engaging, however necessary to the history of 'our' valley. Searching for a major note to end his pageant on, William had quickly read up its more recent history. Dan had excitedly kitted himself out with army surplus uniform and toy pistols. Chinese crackers provided gunfire as the Allied troops moved northwards to liberate Florence. So the battle raged, with enough clatter to alert the enemy for miles around.

'Shusssh! We don't want to offend our neighbours!' I called after the disappearing troops. There on the ridge above our highest terrace stood Wolfgang and his wife surveying the activities below.

'*Fuochi d'artificio per una festa*,' party fireworks, I called up to them airily. We always communicated in Italian, though they probably spoke excellent English.

Afterwards we toasted Venus in *spumante*, supped on the stage and mimed works of art in candlelight. Having conjured up the spirits of the past, we now put the valley to rest. An owl hooted. Then a dog howled.

CHAPTER 31

Nine figures relaxed in dramatic exhaustion round the millstone table. Dan was dozing against Andrew, who disturbed him to take Penny for an ice cream in Montesasso. For five minutes there were seven, with the smallest flopped on to the table. Kate offered to put Dan to bed. The moon rose higher to cast creamy cloaks on five dark, intermittently silent shapes. Joe left a gap between Paul and me when he stepped over the back of the seat, saying goodnight. Now we were four. I knew Sarah, hushing William's sporadic *post mortem* on his play, was watching Paul, the gap left by Joe, and me. Paul contributed something banal about everyone being tired after all the preparations, rehearsals, assembling props, and so on. William stood up to stretch at the moon; Sarah followed. Two left, watching to see who would be the first to react. I was, but he, moving almost simultaneously, thought he was.

I was first up the stairs and across the veranda into the open sitting room doorway. First into the bathroom. He could wait. After all, he'd waited two years before returning. He smelt hot, steamy like the road on our return from the lunar landscape.

In other times the two of us would have walked up the drive together, marvelled at the moonlight masking the valley and listened to owls hooting. Instead he slumped in a cane chair by the sofa, waiting his turn. I couldn't see his eyes and whether they followed me as I moved from the bathroom to close myself alone in the bedroom.

Long moments later he went into the bathroom; noise of flushing and brief splashing in the basin, then out to the veranda – hoping I might choose to join him? He exited when he felt like it, entered when it suited him.

I heard a car on gravel and Paul's lilting friendliness to Andrew and his sister, their words and laughter, inspired no doubt by his comments. Tim might have been there; grown tall, still slender, face hidden inside my fantasy. At university, probably with Andrew, he could have…

The crickets resumed their chorus, punctuated by howls to the moon. I wasn't asleep when the outside door clicked slowly shut, followed by a silence. Was he hesitating outside my closed bedroom door? Then the sofa creaked and bumped, just slightly, on the far side of the wall between us.

* * * * *

I must be born gently into the day. Woken by the sound of voices below the bedroom window, I reluctantly pushed the shutters to let in a crack of light. Men's voices from behind the fig tree on the boundary channel. Grumbling to myself after a bad night, I dressed and slipped through the sitting room, to the bathroom and then past ruffled sheets on the sofa towards more voices on the veranda. Something was going on in the boundary channel. I didn't want to face any neighbours, all furious with me after that meeting. The others didn't get into trouble there; better for them to go and see what's happening. I opened the sitting room door.

Neither Joe nor William or Paul would do anything without first having an undisturbed breakfast. Paul didn't look straight at me, but was the first to get up, disappearing with William and Joe towards the voices on Giulio's side of the boundary. Inside again to peer out from behind the bedroom shutters, I could see a number of heads, more precisely Mauro's, Giulio's and, ominously, Antonio's. Paul and William had found spades and were helping them dig a trench down the dry channel to the stream. I slipped back to the veranda for a cup of coffee, sat and waited in trepidation. Sarah and the children were still asleep.

After bursts of discussion, the men came up the steps by the ruined mill. I retreated inside to avoid any adverse reaction. Their voices sounded amicable enough while they all stood below the veranda. Listening behind the sitting room door I could hardly make out what they were saying; Paul seemed to be offering them coffee, (his Italian had survived two years of silence) which was politely refused. I heard the crunch of gravel and opened the door a crack. Not a soul. I whispered, 'Have they all left?' William came out of the kitchen, surprised at my furtive behaviour.

'They've gone up the drive to decide where the drain will go under it. They're measuring how much plastic tubing to buy. I'm making some fresh coffee for Sarah. Like some?' He disappeared, unperturbed. He hadn't been the object of Antonio's fist flexing, nor particularly concerned about the simmering hostility of the valley. What had happened to change it all? Surely Antonio couldn't have been civil?

It turned out that he was neither civil nor uncivil; silent and sullen, unless directly spoken to. The others were more than civil; decidedly pleasant. I could hardly believe my ears. Even so, when Paul returned with Joe, I looked straight at him, saying, 'I'm glad you're here because I need your written consent to sell this house.'

'Why?' he said, surprised. Had he already forgotten our miserable time, prisoners of the valley on our own veranda, fearful of taking a walk on the property and the public way? Paul was staring at me as never before. No, all was fine. I was being too confrontational. Silence. I felt strangely relaxed. Care seemed to float off my body; no need to arrange cleaning, bush-clipping, grass-cutting, vine-pruning, all the Gianni attention that was missing. The coffee percolated: liquid, aromatic manna. William brought two mugs and sat down beside me, saying, 'The people here are used to you running the house. You speak fluent Italian and you even understand the local dialect! Believe you me, they are all perfectly amicable. I think someone must have...'

'It was Marino!' Paul said unexpectedly. He was looking fixedly at me, ignoring my request as he continued, oddly loquacious. 'Marino must have hinted how each could benefit. Wolfgang will put his cesspit pipe into the tube they've gone to buy. It'll join the overflow from Mauro and Caterina's kitchen and be piped down the channel past us into a site underground.'

'On somebody else's land?' William voiced my thoughts.

'Of course,' Joe agreed, with a lawyer's complicity. 'Giulio will be there to make sure it isn't on his, or he'll demand payment. You must watch they don't perforate the pipes from your cesspit; plastic is cheap and easily cracked. Mauro will attach the overflow from his washing machine and... but Wolfgang is the real winner here, as I am sure Marino has already told him. As long as there's no smell and no standing water to affect this property, then all should be happy. That is, until some unsuspecting owner, Claudio Panichini's farmer perhaps, realises that pipes are discharging on to his land. Until that moment – can't smell it, can't see it, so all are content!'

Sarah stopped at the bottom of the steps.

'Nobody's listening to me.' I thought I said it quietly, but Sarah looked startled. 'I can't manage everything here without Gianni.'

'I can.' Paul stood up, about to bang his fist on the table. Two large bees started buzzing against the beams above him. I didn't remember how fiery and youthful he could look, fresh with enthusiasm. 'Of course I'm sad Gianni died, but he never left us in peace.' Paul paused for some response. None. At least he said it openly, coping with the silence, jostled by bees. He shook his head and drew a hand through his hair.

'He was always following Olivia, getting in her way, making her irritable.'

There he was again, thinking for me, making assumptions that suited him, misreading my mind.

Angrily, I said, 'I coped pretty well with Gianni and without you. I just haven't the time or energy to manage this house and the land on my own.' Paul froze by the door into the house, more bees bustling in the corner above him without anyone noticing. Sarah hurriedly came out with a suggestion.

'Why don't we go to *Rigoletto* at Sant'Angelo d'Orcia this evening? We can have an early lunch and leave Andrew at the station on our way. He's meeting friends in Rome. We'll all enjoy it.' She frowned at me and I narrowed my eyes back. Why was she blaming me for the spat? It was their holiday too, she seemed to be saying, and they'd had enough of our tension. Separate us, diffuse it, and just let matters resolve themselves. So we set off, Paul with Sarah and Penny in William's car and Joe taking Dan, Kate and me.

It was one of those almost unbearably lovely days, poignantly memorable when peeping out of an emotional prison. Joe, humming away at the wheel, wasn't my companion any more. He had neatly side-stepped to make space for Paul, and I needed him back, on any terms. I wanted his unemotional, physically remote, reassuring, total friendship. He drove across the parched landscape with evening shadows lengthening over the ploughed land and a spare cypress guarding another abandoned farmhouse topped by its empty dovecote. The clay ridges, hills of unremitting toil and little return. All eighteen years of Paul and me and two children, now one, lost in arid futility. Sarah and William, Joe as well, would be storing such moments of pure delight for a feast of scents and textures to savour in future recollections. Mine would be as barren as the furrows swirling away in parallel distance to an unobtainable horizon, one crest after another to more beyond. I had showered painstakingly, put on a long and pretty dress, tucked up my hair and made some attempt at make-up, but could still smell my despondency.

Rigoletto was due to start in the cool of a summer evening at nine. A wooden stage had been erected in front of the town hall in Sant'Angelo d'Orcia. William bought seats opposite the large *palazzo* with a portico and much agitation on the third storey loggia. Spotlights were being tested, and directions shouted from loggia to stage. It was nearing nine, but the square was only a quarter filled. We sat conspicuously alone, me at one end of a row with Dan and Kate, then Sarah, Penny and the three men. Nine fifteen; a few more stragglers. Nine twenty and the seats all around us were taken. Nine thirty and a rumour that the founder and patron of this music festival, a distinguished foreign composer, had still not arrived. Children played hide and seek under the stage; a dog lifted its leg to mark one of the tubular supports. The orchestra continued tuning up, just to remind us it was not late. At last a flurry of people settled into the best seats just before the Mayor appeared with the great man who was, it transpired, to conduct. Cheers laced with boos as he mounted the podium and a spotlight caressed his balding pate. The first chords and all was forgiven.

Another moonlit night, soft and benign. Sarah was amazed we could hear the voices so clearly. The atmosphere was working. I became totally uncritical and let it soak in. Leaning forward I caught Paul smiling and relaxed between William and Joe. Whole families were out for the evening; it was their festival, their scene. Two dramas co-existed: below stage, children and dogs; above, singers at full throttle. The elegant *palazzo,* the blank façade of the cathedral, the stern battlemented town hall, the whole square and its inhabitants gaped, horrified witnesses of Gilda's abduction off the stage, through the crowd of café bystanders under the portico and into imagined skulduggery deep in the shadowy alleys beyond.

On our way home, floating on melody, thrilled by the drama, no one noticed the starless sky and the irresolute storm wandering back our way. It came on us suddenly, rain slashing the windscreens and pouring down on an endless battalion of toads slithering across the road.

'Stop!' Kate yelled from our car in front, 'we're massacring them!' It was a horrid feeling. Both cars braked; the road seethed as far as the headlights reached.

'I'll turn the lights off. Perhaps they'll go away,' Joe said. 'William will do the same.'

'Are they migrating somewhere in the storm?' Kate again. Phosphorous eyes were moving from right to left, sporadically spotlit by gashes of lightning. The rite of passage ended, we moved on, gingerly, nobody willing to stop.

* * * * *

It was to be a lie-in, lazy day in the valley after the *Rigoletto* evening out. On such a day I would have written about *Rigoletto*, but not now. Paul couldn't tease me because I wasn't writing any more. Instead I started to read a book William had given me about someone renovating a tumbledown house abroad. Everyone was talking about it; others were now writing my sort of book. My despondency increased.

But it came to pass that we were disturbed by four men: Mauro and Gino the Silent, his brother-in-law from next door, Giulio and Wolfgang, who mostly just watched and commented. In no time whatsoever, the pipes were laid, joined to others from all directions, set under the road to be asphalted, hidden down the channel between us and Giulio under silt and vegetation, to the unspecified place of disposal – forgotten until someone protests or there's a stench and the whole process restarts.

The men accepted an espresso, all of us standing on the veranda in relieved tranquillity. Wolfgang's wife would collect my share of the road money before I left. Serenity had returned to the valley. I felt accepted. The sun caressed the garden, Giulio's fields and the *nonna's* hens pecking at my flowerbeds. After the August dog days when heat shredded tempers; after the storm and Antonio's threats, more serene days with deep blue skies heralded autumn. A yearning for the early days at the house rippled inside me, for the times we washed in the stream, when people in the valley were less gripped by money, more open, more Arcadian. Attitudes and expectations were changing fast, leaving me stranded.

I was dozing over the book William had given me and nobody was doing anything in particular, when shrieks from the house splintered the siesta calm. Figures from all directions dived towards the deserted veranda, William pushing the sitting room door into darkness. He tried to open the shutters, but something was slumped against them. A strange sort of whimpering. Buzzing and whirring around the room and up the chimney. Joe pulled me back and locked the door by mistake after thimble-sized bees raged out at us. William rattled it, yelling above Paul's moans.

'Open it! Get a doctor!' Words clipped with urgency.

'Better the hospital.'

'Ask Maria Pia, Caterina, whoever's up there.'

'Joe, can you explain in Italian?'

'Let us out of here!' Silence, except for the moans inside, whispers and shuffling outside. Joe turned the lock and the door burst open pitching two figures on to the veranda in a cloud of dark angry bees. We plunged down to the drive leaving Paul slumped against the low veranda wall, hands over face, while William stood dazed by the door.

'Shut the door,' said Sarah, returning up the steps. 'Keep the children away,' to me as she tried to release Paul's hands from his neck. Dan, Kate and Penny stood in the drive behind me.

'William, have you been stung?'

'I don't think so.' All over the beams there were bees as big and brown as the knobs on the mahogany chest of drawers.

'Get the car, Olivia.' Sarah saw I hadn't been stung. 'Move slowly so they won't swoop on you.'

Thinking of her and Joe coping at the house comforted William and me after we reached the hospital and were sitting on hard tubular chairs in the *Pronto Soccorso*. Paul had been wheeled away by a man in white overalls without a word or glance. The same orderly re-emerged.

'*Moglie.*' A statement, not a question. 'Wife,' he repeated. 'Family?' he queried, eyes pale under a receding hairline.

'*Documenti?*' The word was fired at us by the system's bureaucratic needs. William nudged me. 'Partners' weren't then an accepted stitch in the social fabric. Female companion or mistress were the formulas. And anyway, we weren't partners any more. His decision.

I was allowed in. The nurse uncurled Paul from the foetal position he had frozen into, stooping from veranda to car and hospital wheel chair. He was lying on the surgical couch I recognised, a male nurse holding his hands away from his throat while a doctor chucked one syringe into a waste bin behind him and plunged another just below his shoulder. His face was turned towards me, lids closed, flickering. Tim had the same long, dark lashes. I hadn't noticed the three deep furrows, crossed lower on his brow by a vertical gully flattening into the bridge of his nose. It was long, not too narrow, rounding out into wide nostrils. Like Tim? I tried, but couldn't remember. As he didn't open his eyes, mine travelled over him, half-hearing he could have died and that the bees only missed an artery in the neck by a millimetre. Could have been fatal. Poison right into the system.

'You're his wife?' Again. Papers to fill in: his name, place and date of birth, address, parents. The same round for me. Glancing at him, completing the forms, then glancing back – was it a tear, or just moisture from under the left eye, spilling slowly over the lower lid? Then another. To lean over, touch with a forefinger, kiss shyly, understand silently. I leant forward, moved a hand, but the orderly motioned me back.

Afterwards I learnt that I needn't have fretted over names – his, mine and all that rigmarole. In Italy married women always keep their family name. Nowadays, who bothers?

* * * * *

'*Pericolosissimi!* They must be nesting in the chimney.' Maria Pia's views took precedence over her daughter's. Other suitable 'issimos' were repeated by son-in-law Mauro, stressed by Giulio and Gino the Silent who had accompanied his mother, alerted by Paul's screams and Joe.

'*Il collo! Pericolosissimi!*' Maria Pia restarted the 'issimo' chorus when Paul, his neck bandaged, stepped unsteadily out of the car. Her hand went automatically up to hers. 'The artery! He could have…'

'My uncle died.' Giulio this time.

'*Un'epidemia quest'anno!*' An epidemic of bees?

'*Api?*' Bees? 'No,' Maria Pia insisted. 'No, hornets,' triumphed the chorus. Nests in every chimney in the valley that year, it seemed. No wonder the hospital took one look at Paul, and responded so rapidly. Paul was installed in a deck chair under the guardian pine, dazed, the rest crowding near him by the mill table, all a safe distance from the veranda.

'I won't go back to that room.' Memory looms and obliterates. I hadn't noticed in the hospital that someone had cut handfuls of hair from his head. The hornets had buzzed down from the chimney and swarmed through the door with him, bobbing round his head and tangled into his hair. Somebody – Sarah, maybe William? – had bravely cut them out close to the scalp.

'I've cleared Dan's bed. Come and lie down.' So Sarah led Paul into the ground floor room Kate shared with Dan, away from the chorus of concern.

'Get the firemen,' trebled Maria Pia and her daughter.

'Now,' the bass of Gino (no longer silent) together with Mauro.

'*Urgentissimo,*' came Giulio's tenor.

Joe and I left for the fire station, taking Sarah's shopping list with us. The older of the two firemen on duty looked as if he had been born tired; he heard us while tipping his chair back and consulting his watch.

'*Difficile.*' I glanced at Joe. There was one empty chair and I didn't want to leave him standing. It was clear we'd need the politics of emotion.

'We're understaffed.' Predictable excuse. 'Vacations.' Strange for firemen in the midst of a blazing summer, but vacations were for

August, whatever the job. Ferragosto stretched farther back and forward every year. He yawned.

'Hornets, did you say?' It was a new word for me, so I stressed it – *calabroni*.

The younger man moved closer to us. No uniform, but presumably he was a fireman too. The older one stirred uneasily then, turning away to the papers on his desk said, 'I'll send people round this evening, after dark, when they're nesting. In the chimney, did you say?'

* * * * *

With the veranda out of bounds, the kitchen was too. Supper was a makeshift buffet on the mill table with the provisions Joe and I had bought in Sibilla's former store. There was no cool water from the out-of-bounds fridge, but the mineral water in the garage had to be fresh enough. I took a bottle to Paul, with a bread roll, ham and cheese and a sliced peach. He was asleep. I would have stretched out on Kate's bed if all her and Dan's possessions hadn't been piled on it.

Everyone was restless, afraid of going anywhere inside the house until the firemen came. Joe improvised a trip to Montesasso for ice creams, leaving me behind with Paul to wait for the firemen.

I sat alone at the mill table, uneasy with the image of Dan staring from the rear window reminding me of – I couldn't picture Tim's face anymore. Soon I might only see Dan's if I dared think of Tim. The sun was an orange yellow suspended over merging greens and the shadow lengthened away from the guardian of the house, the umbrella pine Gianni had planted and where he used to stand and watch me. Crickets started sawing slivers of air in an identical jarring groove, like the endless parallel etching of the plough in Giulio's fields. The uneven patchwork of the plain spread pink then grey, before a bead of light was sewn here, another there, then strings of them. I wished I was having an ice cream with the others in Montesasso, not waiting at the house for firemen while a man who might have died from a sting was sleeping inside and a dead weight in my stomach anchored me to the stone seat. I turned my back to the sunset to look up the darkening valley, and saw Dan – or was it Tim? – taking his first lone steps. I pushed my elbows forward on the round table, head in hands, eyes closed into palms where the swirls of blue and yellow stilled into three silhouettes around a table.

When I looked up one of them was sitting opposite, head forward, shoulders humped. I could only see Paul's shape, but felt him looking. He flicked a match to light a candle I had found in the garage, dripping the first melted wax on to the millstone for it to stick upright. As he bent over the flame I could see the patches of bare scalp where the hornets had been cut out surrounded by tufts of unruly curls. Tensions quivered and burnt pinpricks, jabbing at me – ask him, now! No angelic mediator for him to escape to here.

'Why didn't you come to me for help?' He winced, looked down and sideways, pulling his hands off the mill table, ready to bolt away from my reproaches. The chirping space whirled into a tussle of wills. To explain, admit, resolve, pardon in some sort of jumbled sequence.

'You women were all over me at Downs Way. Either asking probing questions or offering treats. A cup of tea and specially made cake with, "how many works do you have to restore?" A sort of accounting.' Looking down, the candle accentuated his brows, heavier than I remembered. Light, trembling, ran up a deep frown channel. I waited.

'Your grandmother fussed around asking questions, expecting so much of me. A man should be the breadwinner, the usual.' Another gap. No, I wouldn't bridge it, as Gran would have done. Mother too. He was looking at me now as if trapped. My hand wanted to reach out to caress curls back over the raw patches of scalp. He leant back, shifting his feet on the gravel.

'Why didn't you tell me what was happening?' I paused, waiting for him to speak. 'You didn't tell anyone. Not your parents, your brothers, Mother or Gran – or Dan and me.'

I hadn't noticed the tic in his cheek before, or the way he mouthed dumbly. Then a gust of words.

'You all ignored your grandfather. But I noticed the way he was lovingly packaged into irrelevance. He and I shrank into sort of male ornaments, hanging socially on to the household. That annihilating assurance of all you women!'

His hands were back on the table, clasping, untangling, and then gripping again. His cheeks had begun to hollow into a fold by the line of his jaw. He said something about our 'open relationship' shrinking into conventional expectations of him, as Gran put it, 'supporting the family'.

'That's all they could think of.' He spread his hands palms up on the gritstone. 'There was no space just to be.' He hesitated. 'Mike held me between pincers too. He found me the studio and works to restore. I owe a lot to him. But he ignored me when I repeated a painting had to be X-rayed so I could restore it truthfully. He insisted the owner or dealer would not pay for one, or it would make the work too expensive. He went on about his gallery rent being so high. So was the rent of my studio. I tried assistants. They all did what Mike or the owners wanted and refused to listen to me. "Buyers like 'em bright. Status baubles on their walls," or so Mike said.' Bright is beautiful: subtlety, dull. That's what Paul used to lament when we talked in his studio.

'So I tried to work for museums who **did** X-ray the paintings. A few works came, famous but not well paid. Not for the time it took. The Fra Angelico, you remember? The Sassetta, and a Perugino, all with landscapes I loved. Then came Titus. He was the first of the Rembrandts.' His hands reached for his throat, probing the bandage; mine stretched out to guide them away. They were moist, clinging, vulnerable. He withdrew them to lean on the table and look into the approaching headlights of William's car.

Dan ran unthinkingly up the steps to the kitchen and a squadron of hornets dive-bombed him. No direct hit, but he retreated terrified. The hornets had stung Paul, chased us and violated our space. It was almost dark and they should be going back to nest in the chimney. Paul felt dizzy and returned to lie down. Dan stood on the mill table to fix a baleful look on the track above Giulio's terraces and chant his spell. 'Abracadabra, bring the firemen here **now**!' The phone was in the sitting room not far from the chimney. Dan was fretting. His spell hadn't worked, so I decided to take him and find out whether the firemen had forgotten our hornets' nest. We met excitedly, car engine to fire engine on the narrow track. I gave way and watched the cumbersome vehicle bruising our olives and narrowly missing geranium pots to halt as the rest of the household lined up to welcome it.

'*Calabroni?*' shouted the driver from the cab, cocking an eyelid above almond-shaped Etruscan eyes in a fleshy face. '*Pericolosissimi!*' Three firemen tumbled out in hot helmets and gloves, eyes hovering over the company to alight briefly on Sarah, pause on me and discard us both to home in on Penny; tall, slender and nearly eighteen. A small, plump one with full lips and an aquiline nose jostled in front to scan her in the headlights.

'Mustn't be aroused,' he said, staring too long at her. She didn't feel the length of stare but just smiled back.

'Keep well away,' said the tall, conventionally handsome Italian behind the plump one.

Another, older and swarthier, asked, 'Where are they?' while joining the others to gawp at Penny and her long auburn hair. I pointed to the chimney. Dan, as close as he dared, was gaping like the rest of us. All four pattered up the veranda steps and into the sitting room, the driver leading. Lights flipped on, and as soon off again. Back down in reverse order to the fire engine and spectators. Busy muscles levered off ladders, uncoiled hoses and unloaded canisters of sinister intent.

'Keep away,' said the full lips.

'Fumes,' continued the swarthy one, 'very dangerous!' The other two were worrying ladders over the roof tiles. Shouts up, demands down, incessant coming and going into the house. Etruscan eyes and his bouncy, aquiline companion were hauling hoses and canisters into the sitting room. I started to follow them, but a huge leather glove pressed heavily on my shoulder.

'*Signora, è pericoloso!*'

'The doors. Please close the doors to the bathroom and bedroom,' in my most pitiful voice.

Mutterings, a whoosh from the chimney and a burst of chemical particles hung like an atomic mushroom over the house, slowly permeating the hush below. Four helmets, blue shirts with epaulettes, dark blue trousers above shiny black boots stood in a contemplative row with spectators straggled around them, floodlit in the headlights.

Then, galvanised into duty, hoses rewound, canisters retrieved, ladders hung back alongside, the fire monster backed ponderously up the drive scraping Florentine lily bulbs off the bank and olives off overhanging boughs. Relief, silence and darkness surged back and slowly dispelled the chemical stench hanging over us as the headlights tracked away along the ridge.

I hadn't noticed until then that the moon was rising or that Paul was standing in the dark behind me or that Dan had his arm round Paul's thigh and a firm hand was stroking his hair.

* * * * *

Released back to the veranda, we relished cool water and melon from the fridge, and choc-ices from the freezer. Gradually the fumes cleared leaving a sniff of chemicals and dead hornets like embers in the sitting-room fireplace. The bedroom door was shut. So was the bathroom.

Paul said, after the others had gone and we were alone on the veranda looking at the moonclad valley, 'I can't sleep in that room.' My stomach gulped. Excitement twittered inside. This, the real moment of return? No hand held out to walk me into the moonlit valley listening to the crickets. No gazing together at the plough hanging over Maria Pia's and Mauro's farmhouses to navigate by the North Star. Still less to catch a shooting star. Silently we sat at each end of Gianni's scrubbed beech table. If not in pain, he must have been in shock.

He followed me through the diminishing particles to the bathroom, where I quickly shut him outside. He was still standing there when I came out. I heard the bathroom door open, close and later, much later I heard him say 'May I?' outside the closed bedroom door. May I travel two years back? I was sitting on the bed in my night-dress. Gently opening it, he stood there, as the moon slid into the window frame, cool and with a scent of soap. As I got up, arms open, something cold and hard crushed under my foot.

'Help! I've trodden on a scorpion!' and hopped past him to the bathroom.

When I returned he was lying on his back on the far side of the bed with the sheet pulled up to his chin. I settled beside him. Two silent effigies in the oblong light of a winking moon. As I was about to reach out under the sheet, Paul groaned and turned away. The moon closed its eye and sailed out of the frame.

CHAPTER 32

Paul and I were sleeping together as strangers when Mike returned to the Casa dell'Avventura. He rolled up in a clapped-out Deux Chevaux he had borrowed.

'Hornets,' he said, cheerfully treading on a corpse outside the kitchen door. 'Angélique told me you were here.' I smiled, clenched teeth barring any outburst. Even now she was pulling our strings wherever she was. Couldn't she be kept out? Here at least. The urbane businessman, unruffled, stood with the sun behind him, hair shining. Paul was sitting in his usual place, a corner of the veranda where he could turn away and let his mind soar over the plain to Monte Amiata, though still physically with everyone else.

'Paul, there's work waiting for you. Interesting stuff, paying well.' (Paying Paul well or Mike well? Both, perhaps, in the best of all worlds.) Paul turned slowly towards Mike.

'I'll have to see the canvases first. It depends on what condition they're in.' He was wary. 'Are they portraits?'

'Yes. There's also a still life.' Paul looked back across the plain to his horizon, uncommitted.

'And by the way, Angélique's contacts are paying up at last,' Mike continued encouragingly. A red-hot jab in my stomach. A lizard peeped above the parapet. Leonardo had drawn envy as a lizard on a face, Paul once told me. This one was a dry, cold, green-pocked, yellow lizard; uneasy, not repugnant.

'Look at the lizard!' Mike glanced at Joe to help him out and received an unfocused smile back.

'Angélique,' Mike was trying to combine a face-the-facts attitude with compassion, 'has had a tough life. You've no idea what she's been through.' (I could hear her using her accent to charm him.) 'Her father…' and so I had to revisit her tragic childhood. 'Her mother died when she was two…' (I thought she'd jettisoned the daughter for a lover?) 'And she was abandoned in the huge château, a little child…' Mike echoing Angélique made Sarah's eyes widen in disbelief. William's glazed over as he sat jotting down improvements

313

to his pageant for some future performance. Joe, attentive and sympathetic, remained silent. Paul was concentrating on the lizard.

'She has a lot of influential contacts from all the travelling she's done as her father's agent.' That explains her speculation on elderly men and potentially profitable introductions.

While conversation meandered around Angélique's sad childhood, I shifted my thoughts – as William was doing. Paul wasn't meeting me, even halfway. No glances, no gestures, at least that I had noticed. Why should I always be the one to reach out, throbbing inside, and offering the moonlight caress that wasn't returned? His sleeping snuffles and sighs that I had yearned for now unnerved and irritated me. I resented his newfound chemical cleanliness. Angélique must have enveloped him in an exciting range of fragrances. He had lost the warm familiarity of pigments, the uncommercialised zest of white spirit and his own tang that sat in my nostrils tingling excitement, expectation. That pulse within.

Joe surprisingly, almost nonchalantly, brought the subject up again.

'Olivia, why do you talk about selling this house?' He, of all people, should have understood. Paul turned to me, eyes like eddies in muddy water.

'Yes, why?' He didn't wait for my answer and returned to the landscape.

I swallowed an indignant reply, sniffing the silence instead. All eyes on me. Flatly, I said, 'Paul owns this house too.'

'Yes, so why sell?' He was looking at me again, uncomfortably. Sarah got up to do something in the kitchen.

'I've already explained I can't run this place without…'

'I'll do it!' All swivelled to look at Paul, except for Kate and Dan who were playing down by the stream and Penny reading under an olive tree.

'Oh! Thank you.' I was outraged. 'After two years' absence, I'm sure you remember the ropes!' I raised my fist to bang it dramatically on Gianni's table but William restrained me. Sarah came out of the kitchen with a tray of glasses filled with cold lemon tea for us to try. It was to break the tension, but didn't. We needed more hornets, another unexpected arrival, a fire engine, the postman on his Vespa, even Angélique herself! The drink was cool though too sweet and the returning heat pounded, punctuated by an intoxicated bumblebee and the unrelenting late-summer leg-rasping cicadas. I wasn't looking into the sun, but all I could see were camouflage colours, ugly splodges, sun yellow, grass green and mud brown. Like the lizard. Like Paul's eyes.

I couldn't stop the outburst, though I didn't want the others to hear me, just Paul.

'I miss writing my story that you laughed at. Why describe a place nobody wants to read about, how we'd found it, the history of the valley, all that stuff? How naïve foreigners bought a ruin and did it up with the help of the local Giannis. I really wanted to write it and get it published and live inside all those silly dreams. You chucked it back at me, so I gave up, like that–' I tossed my glass over the veranda. The dregs of lemon tea splashed glints onto the gravel. Space swirled with scratching cicadas and sizzling flies. Sarah looked angrily at me before running down the steps to brush the splinters aside. No swallowing back my words now.

'It was a world to escape into. A fantasy that didn't hurt anyone. To stop Tim possessing me.' I was weeping and no one moved, till Paul said,

'You're not the only one to have dreams shattered. We all do, and have to get on, for better or worse. Usually worse,' and he retreated into the house, shutting the door behind him.

The sun shone on, the cicadas sawed away into the afternoon and the haze rolled down from Monte Amiata across the brown ribs of the plain and the drainage arteries to cling to the olives, an evening veil pierced by cypresses and umbrella pines. Paul had chopped away at my refuge, clearing the undergrowth for despair to prey on me as it pleased. The next day he and Mike left for London. Not long afterwards William drove Joe, Dan and me to catch a train to Pisa airport before they started their long drive back to England.

* * * * *

From my desk in Gran's room I was too often pleasantly distracted by the garden. The school year that September had blasted off in a gust of urgency. I was catching up on a dull Saturday morning, papers scattered in organised piles all over the floor. Joe had finished mowing the back lawn with juridical precision and tidying the scene framed by my window. Sarah and Kate began setting up trestle tables while Joe looped balloons in and out of the trees. My task was lunch. I tapped the typed pages into a neat pile, sheathed my pen and was about to get up, when I heard the rapping. Mother opened the front door.

'It's too unsettling. You can't turn up unannounced just when you feel like it.' Interrupted making biscuits for tea, she had a rolling pin in one hand and the other on the doorknob. Mother and I had hardened into 'they're the practical type', without Sarah's consideration or gentleness.

'It's not fair on Dan,' she continued. 'He's thoroughly bewildered, doesn't know what to expect when.'

After returning with Mike, Paul must have been marking time in the Scottish castle, possibly back to creating ancestors for Angélique's clients. He probably had still not worked out what he needed most: us, money or some satisfaction from his work. After two blank years, two considerable sums had been paid into our joint account days before Dan's ninth birthday. They added up to a quarter of the twenty-four monthly payments he owed, though that wasn't the debt I needed repaying.

'Yes, Paul, it does happen to be Dan's birthday,' I said, glancing at his new shirt and tie. He lingered awkwardly at the door, childlike, waiting for Mother to chivvy things along. She looked him up and down, as if about to comment, before returning to her biscuits.

'I want to take you and Dan – and everyone here – out to a birthday dinner. Or a film. Later, perhaps?'

Oh Paul! No warning. He always avoided letters but could have phoned before materialising, framed by the doorway, neither in nor out.

'I do want to take you.' He was looking at me, diffident, eyes retreating under lids and brows into a frown.

'I'll see what the others say,' moving him inside to shut the door on neighbouring eyes. He had never appeared before with such a big case and so many bags.

'Where's Angélique?' I couldn't, wouldn't stop the green and yellow lizards crawling all over me. Paul was never much good at dissembling.

'I've no idea,' he said, non-committedly. Mixing in circles where she hooks clients for him, I added silently. He stood clumsily marooned in luggage; he'd have to clear himself away somewhere. There was a pleading in the way he stood, his suit, his luggage. I should have been getting lunch and making sandwiches for Dan's party.

'I'll take out Dan's present.' Stooping, he avoided my eyes. Was he assuming he could dump his clobber in the cupboard under the stairs, crammed full and with Mother's invisible label 'to be sorted' hovering in the air in front of it? Or in my bedroom?

'Is this all you have?' Curiosity won, reluctantly. He looked up with what I took to be a nod. Despite the slight hollows below the cheekbones, the white daubs in front of his ears and a softness padding his jaw, he was still almost youthful.

'Dump it all in my study.' He hesitated. 'Gran's room.'

That afternoon Dan's class burst into the garden. He ran all over the place with the other boys, gripping shoulders, grappling, tumbling on the grass and weaving in and out of girls sauntering arm in arm, hopping in a circle or skipping in a surge across the lawn; yelps, babbling, chirruping. Joe marshalled them into three-legged and egg-and-spoon races, then apple-bobbing fun.

Fetching something I'd forgotten in my study I found Paul looking at them through the window, stranded with his flotsam around him and as diffident and vulnerable as when I met him. From the door I hugged him in my thoughts, fleeing inside myself when he said, 'I, I've something for you as well as Dan.' He opened a tattered brown bag, the old bulging type that snaps at the top, and took out a slim golden box to balance on his left palm towards me. It was the one I'd noticed in August lying on the bread cupboard he'd restored.

'Take it,' gravely. He was still looking at me, eyes in shadow, but I could hear the plea in them. I bit back a shrill 'Why now?' or 'Too late!' Glimmers of remembered sunlight touched the deep blue necklace when I'd sneaked a look at it in the Casa dell'Avventura.

'Lapis lazuli,' he said. I knew it was the pigment of the Virgin's cloak, for the patrons who could afford it. More valuable even than gold. It is also the first pigment to wear off.

'It's the colour of your eyes.' Real lapis lazuli! Resonant blue with gold specks. I asked him to fasten it, but he didn't kiss the nape of my neck as he used to. I left him silhouetted against the window watching the children play, a tubular container crooked under his arm.

More than giving, it's being here, now, that matters. Being present.

September can be a fickle month. We were lucky that the afternoon was benign, comfortingly mild. Kate, acting as Dan's elder sister, had helped Sarah spread Gran's damask tablecloth over the trestle tables for tea. Paul knelt on the grass, opened the container and unrolled two huge sheets of meticulously painted snakes and ladders; fewer snakes than fabulous monsters with prehensile tails, scaly skins and dragonfire mouths; a splayed phoenix at the start and a dodo, wings in tatters, beak open at the winning square. It attracted a flurry of keen contenders, divided by Joe into judiciously mixed boy and girl teams. Game over (I think Dan's lot fortunately won), Paul carefully rolled the sheets back into the container. Dan, an arm flung over his friend of the day and talking to two others, ignored the familiar female gang – mother and grandmother, Sarah and Kate to-ing and fro-ing with dishes, plates, mugs and glasses – to play with side-glances at the two men, Paul in particular. Abandoning the debris of sandwiches, buns, cakes and games after the last of his friends chattered out into the street, Dan crouched on the living room floor with his presents around him, oblivious.

'Happy birthday.' The child froze, hand half-opening over a plane kit. Paul leaned down to add a red and gold package.

'Open it.' His right hand hovered over Dan's head, defining an arch, a caress in the air. Dan turned sideways to look at his father, now squatting beside him. Heads together over the crisp wrapping paper, Dan stripping it, Paul's arm stretched out again. Another *pentimento*. The shoebox was covered in marbled paper, found only in Florence, of frenzied storm clouds above fantastic towers and spires and arches over red and white caverns like a coal fire, flickering dark and light underneath. Dan looked up and smiled at Paul for the first time since this return. Paul touched his shoulder, lingering there.

'Lift the lid.' Settled in dusty ruched paper, the top layer mottled green, the one underneath rippled like the inside cover of a bound book, the third a harlequin pattern, lay pebbles and shells and fossils of every shape and size, with delicate networks like veins, capillaries and arteries. As before with Tim, Paul was telling Dan of whorls and eddies, of the earth's molten convulsions over centuries petrifying life into fossils in inconceivable ages past. Of whirlpools, pinnacled cathedrals, fortified castles of infinite imagination – Leonardo's, his, Tim's once and now Dan's: their shared fantasy. I listened disconcerted. Should the present after nine years be a present again?

'Did Tim like these?' Dan held out a fossil and looked hard at his father.

'Yes,' a pause. 'Yes, Dan, he did. A lot.' Paul tightened his shoulders, and then added softly, 'Or would have done.'

In my study he had strewn his packages over Gran's former bed and turned her photographs to look out at us: great-uncle Frank and his school friend George, my grandfather, at some birthday event; George marrying Gran; the one photo of my father; Mother as a child and me as a baby, but the photo of him with me and Tim round the café table was missing. So was his suitcase. He had moved them to the floor above, into Grandpa's odd-jobs area next to Dan's bedroom. Mother had disposed of her father's workbench and tools, abandoning in their place a utility 1940s wardrobe she had probably bought for another home, and a spare bed for Dan's friend or hers to stay overnight. By no one's leave, Paul just stayed.

'What about your studio? The Scottish castle?' It ballooned into my vision, brooding fantastic, with Angélique fussing over him and the prosperous laird. He shrugged.

'Too far and too cold.'

'What about your work?'

'I'll manage.' He did. Significant payments showed up irregularly in our joint account as canvases mounted the stairs, usually after he'd been away on some trip. They were stored in the room with a water tank next to Grandpa's area. He began restoring and smelling of turps and white spirit and pigments.

If he turned up and settled as it suited him, who might follow? Knock, knock – here's Mike, here's Angélique, here's 'I'm Paul's friend'! Joe came for a temporary nest and is still roosting. Now Paul. He had always refused to stay more than a few days in Downs Way before, so what had changed?

That's what I disliked, the assumption that I would accept anything: his self-amputation from the family tree; now his return to branch out over the top storey next to Dan, who didn't object, even liked it. Stopping the agreed contributions to the family account, then starting them up again at his pleasure. It irked me that Mother and Joe accepted Paul's undefined presence without bothering. She had said her bit, and left it at that while Paul neatly inserted himself into underused space, turned up for meals, helped with the dishes or charmingly excused himself if he had to be away for some days. Gran had brought Mother up with an unquestioned attitude that Men Were Special. She automatically found him a house key, though I suspected he had kept his original one. Mike had been given one like Joe, so why not Paul? Don't create discord, Olivia. You'll need all the friends you can get.

I stayed late at school, adding papers on my return to ever-growing piles in Gran's room. Joe was usually at home on the days Sarah brought Dan back from school; he bumped his schoolbag up the stairs hoping to find Paul and play around in their eyrie. He had his father back, which is more than I ever did, and I should have been glad. In the living room where we congregated before meals, or the front room where we watched television, people were always coming or going or gathering. To be alone, we retreated to bedrooms or, in my case, to the study. We rarely met in twos or threes. I was nervous tucking Dan into bed and sorting his clothes if I could sense Paul next door. He didn't come in. It was my time with Dan.

I paid the bills, though Downs Way was actually Mother's house. This suited everyone else; fewer decisions, less bother. There were slight undercurrents, reconciled by the convenience of our living arrangements, and out of deference to the oldest and youngest.

'Cherish what you have,' mother would say, wise through lost hope.

How could I have let the man who walked out on Dan and me slink back on his own terms? I slipped into the casual mode where our relationship had begun and concentrated on survival at work, waking alone to the sound of early birds and a town stirring and cars braking at the foot of the hill outside. I was down first to prepare Dan's breakfast with mine. Paul had his later and cleared up after us. Weekdays were sated with routine bustle and spiced with off-menu actions and resolutions. When the elderly clock above my office door chimed four in the afternoon, I phoned to check who would be at home for Dan's tea, and found excuses to stay away longer. Weekends threatened confrontation. The one after Dan's birthday, had it been fine, could have been saved by our old habit of walks along sunken lanes to the Downs looking for hazelnuts, lingering, making up jokes, stories and games. Instead it rained. We locked ourselves into our solitary spaces, coming together in safe numbers at meals and discussing whether to take Dan to the cinema or Sarah's or a friend's. The dance of spatial deference disguised tensions.

Paul explained he had to go to London to meet colleagues. He helped, if he wasn't away, on my weekly trek to the local supermarket. He was contributing regularly to the food kitty and sporadically to our joint account. Opt out, I spat at him when I was alone in my bedroom, when it suits you. Don't mind us! I probably meant me.

* * * * *

The clock struck four and opened two more hours of a possible Friday retreat into school paperwork, my mind constantly tweaked by doubts, uncertainties, fantasies – on minimal visual or spoken evidence. A helter-skelter of castles and rich lairds. Angélique lookalikes rushing at Paul with armfuls of portraits to touch up, heels in the air, leaping into his embrace, his bed, the laird's, or both. Separately or together? Visions of Angélique vaulting over the end of a Jacobean four poster, tossing shoes, price labels on each instep, over carved figures merrymaking at the foot of the bed. Harvest frolics. Fertility dollies. Squeaks and grunts fluttering out into the ruddy Scottish sunset on a scatter of baronial bats.

'You can't go on like this,' Sarah told me. 'Uncertainty feeds anxiety and rots your guts. Why don't you confront him?'

Paul might open up if we went on a walk with Dan, but then again he might not because of the child. Most evenings I heard him talking to Dan. I stopped going up as I used to at his bedtime, letting Paul tuck into a family role. Should I suggest a weekend away with him? I wished Angélique would turn up unannounced and provoke an outburst. We could go into the garden for the confrontation. Tough on the neighbours, but at least it would spare Mother and Joe. And Dan, if he was in the house. I could turn on Angélique, accuse her – though I wasn't sure of what.

In the event, when I returned after six o'clock on that Friday evening, Mother said he had waited to see me and then left to collect some canvases, returning on Sunday evening, or Monday. That was, for the moment, that.

And so another week with October winds and the first leaves swishing down the street. About that time I overheard Paul asking Mother whether he could pay for the water tank to be transferred into the attic to free up more space for the canvases.

'His money, his idea,' she told me after it was agreed between them, 'and an extra room in the house, which is always useful.' More space to perch.

I tried not to look from my office towards the school gate. Although the accident didn't happen there, over the years school gates had merged into one particular gate, pavement and memorial plaque. So much advice then and over the years, from clergymen and friends to the current mode of psychotherapist or counsellor. Some were still repeating that I should have left teaching altogether, just when my salary and career prospects were rising. Others that I was right to stay on and defy fate. I convinced myself that I had the best job I could get close to a home with help for Dan and without mortgage.

Anxiety about the weekend started earlier now. Confrontation had to be the only way, I kept muttering to myself from Thursday morning. But sometimes I wanted to see Dan on my own. So, before supper that Thursday, I crept up the stairs, back earlier than usual. Engrossed, Dan and Paul stood, heads bent, over a workbench. Pictures were stacked against the lower edge of the dormer window overlooking the back garden to the chestnut tree, slate roofs and the spire of St. Mary's. A genteel, placid, boring residential district, just what Paul and I had vowed to escape. Paul looked up first, then down again after attempting a smile, saying nothing. Dan turned excitedly, 'Dad's letting me use his new bench! I'm learning how to make a box for my fossils.' He'd found a new friend, like Joe. Maybe Dan didn't want a father figure. Friends are chosen, fathers are bestowed or withdrawn. Dan seemed at ease with him. No questions asked; just life latching on to the present offer.

The weight of the day wore me down. Before dinner I normally buried myself in my study, but my eyes were burning tired. I lay on my bed as afternoon sank into evening with sounds of Dan on the floor above in Tim's room. An accident happens; railings were put up too late. The street lamp was splattering light through the branches on to my bedroom ceiling. Count up to ten. Breathe deeply. Relax. A tap. Some branch on the window. Another tap. How many sheep did I count last night before waking up with a more feverishly active mind than ever? Over 200. A tap.

'Olivia.'

I sat bolt upright. The door opened as I switched on the bedside lamp.

'Can I come in?' he said, standing just inside the open door. One chair had clothes on it, the other a pile of books, manuals and reports I should have found time to read. Books on the floor were waiting for shelf space somewhere in the over-furnished house. He hesitated, arms dangling, then sat on the edge of the bed, the only free space.

'I'm sorry. I do things unexpectedly.' I didn't move. 'I've nearly paid back the months I owed.' Oh yes, stopping and starting, the same old tune. 'I have money now, if you need it.' Needs there always are. Count on Olivia. She's competent, reliable, efficient, while you can be inventive, erratic and inept. I observed the piles of books and clothes, the worn curtains and coffee stains that wouldn't release their grasp on the green carpet, anything but his eyes, sometimes deep brown like a spaniel, at others flecked lizard-green.

'Liv, I've told you why it all happened. After the success with Titus and the Rembrandt self-portrait – have you forgotten already?' That was the old reproach: you only remember what you choose to, then worry away at it like a terrier, never letting go. However, I hadn't heard him call me Liv for, well, for too long.

'I spent so much time I should have been working chasing payment for restored paintings. People are quick to collect them, slow to pay.' Was Mike one of them? 'Then Angélique came to help out. Without her…' Dan ran noisily across the landing and down the stairs calling out, 'Dinner's ready!' Paul got off the bed quickly enough and I followed.

That night Angélique invaded our former bedroom. She had beguiled him, Paul said, with paintings to restore and clients she herself would pursue for payment, leaving him in peace and quiet just to work and gradually pay off his debts. It was her pleasure to do it – I bet! Angélique, the immaculate, slender, sweet-tongued French import; irresistible, and she knew it. Paul would present himself as the victim – of circumstances, of course.

The next day was Friday, and that evening I went straight to the top floor, the spell broken, ready to tackle Paul about Angélique. Dan was there alone, humming in concentration over the new workbench in Grandpa's odd-jobs room that had become Paul's. Alongside the workbench stood a table and easel with familiar stains of white spirit, trails of sawdust and shavings.

'Dad's gone to London,' Dan said without looking up. 'He had to go.' No mention of when, or if, he'd be back.

So October winds buffeted Joe and me that Saturday when we took Dan and a pack of friends to the Downs. Joe kept insisting they were old enough to go on their own, but Dan had entered his tenth year and I was fearful. I didn't let them wander out of sight. I stood back and watched Joe gazing at the billows of vapour hanging over the sunset, infused with the moment. The end of the day was creeping up on the afternoon. Though he never came close, I could still feel Joe's intense, untrammelled joy. Live for the moment. Just be.

Paul might, or might not, return. I crept up to the top floor before Dan went back to his room after supper. I shouldn't have looked to see whether Paul's clothes were still in the old tank room under the eaves. He had transformed it into a cramped bedroom with garments hitched on nails along the bottom of the skylight and dropped next to sketchpads on makeshift shelves. Nor should I have checked the letters and sketches scattered over his bed, or pried into the stacked canvasses in the workshop and studio next door. A still life stood half restored on the easel. I was only concerned about his present safety, after all.

I felt free to tuck Dan in, chatting and sorting out his clothes.

'Why don't you come every night?' And when I didn't answer, he just said, 'I miss you'. Then, 'you've never left me alone before.' I thought he stressed 'you'.

I have always kept an engagement diary, but was now jotting down comments as well. The entry for that Sunday in October was filled with frustration, even with Dan, who didn't seem to question his father's behaviour. It was all he had ever known: a piebald father, around in irregular patches of presence and absence.

That night the irregular father crept back up the stairs like a burglar. The new boards where the water tank had been creaked as he slid into bed. The next day, when we were all sitting politely at dinner (which he never offered to cook), he asked if I could find the lapis lazuli necklace to show to my mother.

'Where did you find it, Paul?' She was impressed.

'In Florence, a shop on the Ponte Vecchio.'

'It doesn't look antique.' She was turning the beads over carefully, before, 'it's beautifully strung. A friend of mine returned from India with a lapis lazuli pendant, but this is lovelier.' Paul put down the plate he was washing, took the necklace and, opening my right palm, poured beads like drops of sky on to it.

'Wear it next Saturday. I'm taking you out. Just you.'

Who'll look after Dan? Mother? Joe? Sarah or Dan's friends? He had started staying overnight with them. I reined myself back; why should I always do the organising? Why indeed, but I fretted all week. He wasn't one to say, 'let's leave at eight or ten or eleven on Saturday morning, and Dan will stay with so-and-so.' No forethought. 'Excitement, Liv,' he used to insist, 'comes with unpredictability and surprise!' I'd long lost any appetite I might have had for the unexpected.

I worried myself off food that week, but no one noticed. I recall flavourless salads and sour apples. Talk at the table touched on it being a good year for fruit, though growers never admit it. Not too much rain. Just enough sun to ripen the crop, and so on with pleasantries smoothing the undercurrents we tried to shut out of our individual rooms. It was easier now summer had ended and doors were closed to keep out draughts.

I asked no questions and made no arrangements for that Saturday, annoyed that Paul had kept his keys to my car for those two years, and then assumed he would drive saying, 'I think you need to relax,' while backing out of the garage at eight-thirty. He had announced an early start the previous evening, forgetting that on Saturday mornings I stocked up for the week ahead – that was before Sunday shopping. I opened my mouth, then closed it without asking who was taking care of Dan and buying the stores. Something would have been worked out.

Paul drove me through countryside and suburbs, bypassing London to head north to Bedfordshire and stop on the road he had cycled along as a child, ten years old and out on his own for the first time. It was just as he had described. Black and white cows grazed the slope below Bunyan's 'House Beautiful'. The brook was still running over the dam he was sure he had built. He gathered pebbles, gleefully offering me a handful to play ducks and drakes across the widest pool. Speckled stones worn into aeon-old strata, toffee colour and slate grey. We wandered with the stream across water meadows. Higher, in the fold of the hill, a copse undercut by shadow lay like a green epaulette on the earth's shoulder. He whittled sprigs off a branch, slashing at bracken and brambles with it, clearing his childhood trail up the slope to the footpath along the crest. Where was Dan now? He was asleep when we left.

'Did you collect rabbit food?' Did I not! We looked at the verges together, tipping dock leaves back with the toes of our shoes to uncover mottled cloverleaves and the tenderest dandelion shoots. He bent to pick a dandelion head grey with seeds, then stood in front of me, nosing it tentatively to blow 'love me, love me not...' until we bumped foreheads, he throwing it down at 'love me' with some seeds still left on the stalk.

'Cheating!' I laughed at him. About then he might have kissed me – or just a hug. A bramble tore at my arm. Would the shops still be open by the time we returned?

The wind stirred the bronzed tips of oak leaves, a few ash trees fluttering yellow between them.

'The dandelions were bigger then.' He was looking at the verge again. 'More succulent.' He crouched down closer to a ten-year-old height.

'It felt so good,' he said as I looked down over the navy windcheater to his hair, now grown and trimmed over the pink patches, 'to bring home basketfuls of rabbit food.'

'Or hips from the hedgerows.'

'That was later in the year.' Or was it?

'When did we follow the plough picking up potatoes?' Our post-war contribution; our sense of purpose.

'Did we miss school to do it?'

'I can't remember.'

'I think we did.'

'Acorns for the pigs.' Our memories jumbled up year, school and seasons.

'Did you like rose hip syrup?'

'Ugh, too sweet with vitamins!'

'Mother chased me round the kitchen table, spilling spoonfuls, begging, "Paul, be a good boy".'

'Gran did the same with cod liver oil!'

'Lucky they never invented acorn bread or cake! You bet they'd say they were full of vital vitamins!'

'Pig vitamins!' and we walked along giggling, shoulder to shoulder. Soon afterwards, I was sitting on the sill of a vacant window and watching Paul relive his 'House Beautiful'.

'I used to imagine this ruin as the house John Bunyan saw centuries ago.' He leant against the lintel of the front door, mentally restoring the carved oak panels that had first opened in 1615, fingertips in hollows where hand-wrought hinges once swung.

'Bunyan would have looked up at the sun scattered over a myriad diamond-shaped panes.' We imagined the casement windows inside these mullions clear of moss, mirrored in the wide eyes of youth. John Bunyan would have been ten, about the same age as Paul then, as Tim, as Dan. Ten, before secondary school takes them over and when you should stop mothering them. (Let the child grow up, for heaven's sake!) Then a random white van, the innocent assassin.

'I used to come sketching here with my great-uncle.' He'd moved inside and was smiling at me through an empty window to make sure I was listening.

'You told me about him. Wasn't he your gruff childhood hero from the trenches?'

He came to sit by me, scintillating past excitement.

'Great-uncle Bob was working on a project for local schools. They had to recreate John Bunyan's "House Beautiful". He helped children imagine the building as it was. They made drawings, plasticine models and bigger cardboard ones.' He paused. 'It was the first time I won a school competition,' he said shyly, 'and the last'.

No bombed-in roof, no jagged, fire-snagged trees that Paul's great-uncle Bob, a war artist in World War I, had painfully recorded in France. This mansion, built for Mary Sidney, Countess of Pembroke, was destroyed by the slow dust of neglect; by roots and overgrown trees; by innumerable generations of worms and ants mining the foundations, of insects gnawing the beams and doors; by centuries of wind and rain fingering the mullions and bees battering the precious glass. A tiny hole, a hive inside and bees buzzing in and out abrading the panes. Sooner or later the lead would have been pillaged.

Paul recalled his great-uncle sketching, recreating the world of Mary Sidney, who gilded more than three and a half centuries ago through the doorway into the garden with musicians, poets and perhaps even Shakespeare. He was seeing himself as a ten-year-old looking up from the valley, just like John Bunyan, at the 'House Beautiful', imagining it restored and resplendent again. At last I had found the link. The ruined house revived by his great-uncle led to

Paul, the restorer of paintings, of the old bread cupboard, and the Italian ruin.

When I turned round he wasn't there any more.

'Paul!' No answer. I found him in the main hall where his great uncle had described the tapestries that once hung there, weaving tales of love, hope and despair. Keep what you have as best you can. Leaning on a wind-stroked unglazed window he was still, head in his hands, shoulders more rounded than usual.

'Paul?' I put my arms round him for the first time in two years and two months. He didn't respond.

Then I felt him sobbing.

CHAPTER 33

We sat leaning against the 'House Beautiful' looking over Paul's childhood valley. Running down it was a boy tugging at a kite, a ten year-old Paul soaring with the eagle at the end of the string, wild and free in the land of infinite promise – before tests, commitments and confusing choices. That fabled age of innocence.

'Try harder, Paul. Your spelling's all over the place'. The teachers went on and on at me. 'Don't you **like** reading?' Mother was bewildered. I jumbled things up, not like my clear-minded elder brothers. So she prodded me with books for birthday presents, giving me a comic for a Christmas treat.'

When we were back in the car he remembered belatedly to tell me that Dan was staying overnight with a friend and Joe was helping my mother with the shopping. I hadn't asked; he had taken responsibility. Driving home, he continued, 'I was Dan's age, about nine, when they started letting me go off in daytime. 'I must know where you'll be', was all Mother said, 'and when you plan to be back'. I roamed, saw great-uncle Bob a lot, and had adventures with friends. Then the torture. Curtains drawn to stop me gazing out, though I went on sketching in my mind's eye or on the back pages of my exercise book, covering them up when the private tutor was looking. All those written exams had to be passed.' He was silent for a while.

'Haven't you realised I'm dyslexic?' I hadn't, just that he disliked writing letters. I thought he used capitals because his handwriting was illegible, and he wanted to tease me with VARIUM ET MUTABILIS SEMPER FEMINA. I laughed it off as a typical public schoolboy joke about women always changing their minds, though Paul hadn't been to public school like his elder brothers. He scraped into the local grammar school with a head that knew about dyslexia, rare at the time, and had heard that Paul Wyatt was 'good to outstanding in all aspects of art'. He was the only one who asked to see Paul's portfolio. That evening Paul gradually fitted the jigsaw together over dinner in a pub with a log fire and low beams, warmth and friendliness. His father was only mildly interested in his wife's watercolours; 'her hobby' he would say to fill a sag in the conversation, art being an extra adornment when there were the means to support such leisure activities.

'There's no money in art,' my father kept repeating. 'How could you support a family?' Mother tried, rather feebly, to encourage me but I sensed I was disappointing them both.'

He was gathering the strands and beginning tentatively to mend the tear he had made in our relationship. When I'd first seen him restoring, it had set me thinking of the threads of varying hue and texture that people take and weave into a personal pattern. His brown and green with highlights of crimson are more sonorous than my green changing to silver in a different light, shot with varying hues of blue.

* * * * *

'Should you let Dan breathe in all those solvents?' Sarah had noticed Paul restoring in the room next to Dan's when she brought him back from school. She was more outspoken than usual. 'Woodwork's fine. Dust, maybe, but not white spirit, paint and all the fumes, Paul.'

I ought to have realised that myself. If Dan shouldn't sleep next to the chemical smells from Paul's studio, then he shouldn't either.

The following day Paul transferred his pictures and solvents to the garage, with proposals to move his studio into it and my car on to the road. The garage had electricity, a window and a door into the garden. I rather enjoyed designing rooms after my experience with the Italian ruin, but Paul showed me his plans, found the builder and worked with him, using the skills he had learnt with Gianni to save money. He paid for the new wall and large window where the garage doors had been, leaving a parking space in front.

As Dan would be ten on his next birthday, I illogically dreaded a repeat tragedy. Ten is the age Tim remains. The clock on the wall ticked, the hands turning irrevocably. Railings outside school entrances give little reassurance when imagining a vulnerable child hopping alone along streets and running past the lollipop lady at the pedestrian crossing, or lured into shops to overspend, to be pushed drugs, grabbed and abused in an upstairs room.

The evening after moving his studio into the garage, Paul told me what I would never otherwise have known. I was lying on the bed resting my eyes. Soft light from the street lamp dangled on the last plane leaves outside and twigs were brushing the windowpanes. His words stung from shadows so dark that I couldn't read his face.

'Two policemen accosted me by the school fence the winter after Tim was killed, with "Sir, will you come with us?"' I could see his shape, hunched on the end of the bed. 'They only questioned me. A man had been reported prowling around school gates.' I moved closer along the bed. 'It was horrible. Only wrongly suspected, but I felt tainted.' He didn't stir until my forefinger touched the thin-lipped scar on his left wrist, hoping he'd tell me about it, and drew a soft line up from his pulse to the tip of each finger, starting at the smallest. He drew his breath in sharply.

'Tim came unexpectedly. I thought that the new contraceptive pill was safe. We had no life together before he was born and immediately craved attention and devoured time. Mostly yours.' Another pause. 'How old was he – about two? – when I went to Florence in 1966. People said he looked like me. His hair was turning brown, and had always been curly.' He hesitated, wondering whether he had already told me. I waited. He still had to justify himself.

'Everything was confused. Florence was in turmoil after the flood, works of art drying out all over the place. I saw a Rembrandt self-portrait on a wall somewhere. He was looking at me, curls twisted over a wide forehead, a dip, a slight furrow between the brows above gentle eyes and his straight nose widening into nostrils like mine, too large. His half-lit face was turning to look at me. Rembrandt painted it at the same age I was then, about the time he married Saskia and was more successful than he would ever be afterwards.' Paul clenched his hand under mine.

'Years later, when I was invited back to work in Florence, I couldn't cope with Tim's death. I can't explain it. Not just images jabbing at my concentration, but annihilating waves of despair. Restoring Titus came at the right time professionally, the wrong time personally. It was about two years after the accident and I was taking as much work as possible to force it out of my mind. I needed to pay all my debts and accept a lot of pictures so that I'd have no space or time to grieve. And I was unnerved about Dan arriving neatly, again unexpectedly, to fill the gap – except that a baby is never the same as a ten year old. Tim was my companion, my friend. Born tragic, like Titus.

'I took one look at Rembrandt's son and almost refused the offer. Mike warned me that such a refusal would set people thinking I couldn't cope with more work. Vital commissions would go elsewhere.

'You know how we have to write a report: the painting's history, its condition, paint loss, discoloured varnish, frame and so on. What needs to be restored and how. It was the historical bit that hit me. Titus's mother died when he was only a year old. When in 1657 Rembrandt painted that portrait of Titus, aged sixteen, he was bankrupt. All the pictures and etchings still in his studio were sold.' Paul's words wavered in the faltering lamplight. Better just to hear, not to see him.

'Titus was taught to draw and paint by his father. So was Tim. I've kept his sketches and paintings but still can't bear to look at them. When I restored Titus, Tim looked out through his eyes. The same slight frown, Rembrandt's or my wide nostrils, brown eyes and hair curling over the collar. Ten years after this portrait Titus married, to die before his daughter Titia was born, and before his own father. It didn't end there. Like Titus, Titia lost her mother when she was a year old. I spent hours, days and weeks bending over Titus, reliving Rembrandt's paint strokes that created the image of his one child, out of four, who lived to be an adult. A studio once buzzing with assistants, collectors, the great and the good of seventeenth-century Amsterdam was now silent: he and Titus the only sitters. I had tried to wipe Tim's image from my memory, but with Titus his face returned. Touching Titus, the father Titia had never seen, felt or heard, I imagined that all she knew of him was this portrait. Now I was restoring it for the world to contemplate.' He stopped. 'All this probably sounds silly and sentimental, but one spends long hours alone with whatever one's restoring.'

Restoration, conservation, and so on are scientific activities, so Paul tells me. All the restoration he does must be reversible. He has to find out about the artist to decipher his technique, discover his *pentimenti,* interpret his changes of mind, suggest what to do about pigment deterioration, later additions or enhancements, and so on. It sounds like detective work.

'I kept referring back to the museum experts, of course. They knew Titus's portrait had been trimmed on the right and bottom, keeping R and losing "embrandt". I speculated it was because Titia tried to fit it, say, between her four poster bed and the clothes press, so as not to lose sight of her unknown father. That loss I could never restore.'

He had to continue.

'From 1977 Titus haunted me, bringing Tim with him. Following Titus I had so many commissions that I could choose: landscapes, still life, animals – anything but portraits. I dreaded something would happen to Dan.' That was probably all he wanted to tell me, but I remained silent, just in case.

'All these hours of painstaking analysis – of paints; of the artist's technique, the use of brushes, tools and glazes; the need to make agonising decisions about what to restore, or just to stabilise what remains – bring a thrill of recognition, moments of shared creation, of being there and here together. A strange sort of out-of-time feeling. I can't really explain it; an epiphany is what they say, isn't it?

'Mike began to irritate me. He was always dropping into the studio when I had a deadline, just because he was at a loose end. He'd still bring in pictures, assuming I would always do his first. Then when you arrived in London so we could be together, he was always hanging around. It was better when Angélique came along and we could slip away to be on our own. He always seemed to be around you too in Guildford.'

Leonardo's lizards of envy. That must have been when Paul started drawing them.

'Then not long after Titus and probably because of him, I was asked to clean one of Rembrandt's self-portraits. I should have refused, as I had with other portraits. It would get around – too bad. But to refuse a great work? So I agreed and started the research to find that the bankrupt fifty-one-year-old artist was portraying himself just as he looked when painting his only surviving child. I was contemplating his steady, sad eyes as they looked at Titus. I knew as I touched Rembrandt, that he had only eleven years left to live, a year more than his son. Day after day we scrutinised each other more clearly. Call after call from a television company persuaded me to appear on a programme restoring, explaining and looking out like him at an unseen public. For weeks there was too much to do and I refused everything else. Then, nothing. The television money didn't arrive in time to pay my rent arrears. Like Rembrandt, I was deep in debt. I simply couldn't face going to Italy.'

* * * * *

On a late October morning I picked up the papers on my desk in Gran's room and slipped them into a file. Paul needed the car and dropped me at the school gate. Placing the file on the larger desk in my office, I watched the children bustling in through the school gate and the parents standing outside. He had only been questioned, and that was now far in the past. Paul was starting to enjoy the children chattering along the road outside his garage studio, collecting conkers on their way.

'Sometime you'll have to let go.' I wrote in my diary. 'Dan is nearly their age, Tim's age. His next birthday is his tenth.'

'They throw conkers at the window of my studio,' he said.

'Just playing.' Blaming them is blaming us thirty years ago. I knew sometimes he'd go out and say, 'Mind the car!' if he were up early. But if I'd already driven away he'd join in the fun, inviting the schoolboys into the garden to find bigger and better conkers under our chestnut tree, helping them string the plumpest and swing them into competition. Returning to park the car by its former garage, I'd unlock the garden gate and shuffle my feet through the autumn medley of leaves to pause by the side door into the garage, maybe knock.

'How's the old lady?' I'd ask of the portrait on his easel.

'She's better,' he'd say. 'Early stages yet.' She still looked vaguely forbidding without her frame, but I didn't enquire whether he had to spruce her up for commercial or family consumption. I was curious but didn't ask, and he didn't say.

In early November after the counting of days to Christmas had started, I was invited to give a paper at an education conference in Rome.

'If we're going to sell,' I told Paul, 'we could add a few days after the conference and set things rolling. We both own it, so you have to be there to sign.' We had avoided talking about Montesasso since we left in September.

'But we're not going to sell,' he said. So we went to Rome together. As usual, I bought the tickets.

* * * * *

Since Gianni's death there had been no regular source of information from our valley. Montesasso slumbered in my mind until Paul and I returned to Tuscany after the conference to pick up some strands, untangle others. My friends couldn't believe that after nearly ten years owning olive trees in Tuscany, I had never helped with a harvest. I longed to pluck the ripe fruit from my shimmering silver-leafed trees.

Paul hired a car in Rome and three hours later we were at the Casa dell'Avventura surveying the sodden grass, now nearly a foot high, the bare vines and the mists up the valley plumed by smoke trails from fewer inhabited farmhouses. The afternoon was drawing in beneath a watery-blue sky, leaving just enough light for logs to be carried from the summer pile and kindling wood from the edge of the stream. Just as when we bought the ruin, I felt in harmony with the valley. There is a deep sense of reassurance on seeing, in the hot summer months, logs neatly piled and brushwood stored under the projecting eaves of outhouses. Paul reported that our woodpile seemed strangely depleted. Sitting by the fireside, we calculated how many logs would be needed for a family to cook and keep warm all winter and whether it could be done from the two acres we owned.

The telephone rang. It was Pina who wanted us to have supper with them and discuss the olive harvest. I had called her from Rome, asking for advice. We pulled on our coats, having tried to stoke up the fire and damp it down simultaneously to keep the rooms warm until morning.

Pina was seated by the hearth evidently in pain. She whispered that I wasn't to tell anyone, but she had cut her leg when getting into the car with Carlo. He had driven off impetuously without checking whether the door was closed. However, he'd been kinder to her since their daughter-in-law Lisa had come to live with them.

Tongues were wagging in Montesasso bars about a local mother who was having an affair with a much younger man. Vincenzo recounted the gossip over the meal.

'Why shouldn't she?' Lisa said sharply. 'Men have done it for centuries,' glancing at her father-in-law.

'Not the same,' Carlo retaliated. 'A mother knows whose child it is. That's why she must be faithful to her husband so he is sure the child is his.' A long pause, then Vincenzo stated.

'Dario looks like me.' It was not a question, though glances from baby to father revealed it wasn't obvious to everyone else. Vincenzo peered anxiously at Dario, innocently asleep in his carrycot.

'He takes after me, doesn't he?' Actually, he looked more like Lisa, but everyone murmured consent. Liqueurs were poured and plans made. Carlo would come at eight the next morning with nets for the olive harvest and show us how to go about it. Then we could get on with it ourselves.

'The story of that older woman eloping with a young man is spreading like wildfire round the valley,' I remarked to Paul on the walk back.

'Yes,' he said, stopping to stare at me in the lamplight outside the fire station. 'Makes you wonder why Alberto looks like Gianni's boss, and Ada's sister has an albino son and a swarthy husband.' I continued for a step or two, though he wasn't following. I couldn't go on, leaving him staring into my back.

'What about Mike?'

'What about him?' I turned my head. Who was his companion when we were apart? His brows overshadowed the expression in his eyes.

'Dan is very fair,' he paused, 'though not albino.' His tone cautious, tinged with fear. 'Tim was dark at Dan's age.' Tim, his perfect companion at the age of remembered innocence, of infinite hope. His genes, his stake in the future, his continuity – why did it have to matter so much, anyway? He knew about Greece. There were no DNA tests then. It all happened when rape was somehow seen as one's own fault; a humiliation. One didn't tell anyone about it before feminism became an issue. My mother had managed with me. I loved, I wanted Tim; I wanted both my children. He came up close behind.

'I couldn't ever say anything to you about it. About being afraid Tim – and even Dan – weren't my sons.'

'I told you that if I'd struggled, the shepherd might have killed me. I thought he had a knife. When I knew I was pregnant, I passionately wanted him to be your son. Like Dan.' After a pause, Paul said, 'So did I.' And we walked together into the night. The fire had gone out but we did not feel the cold.

* * * * *

No sign of Carlo the next morning. We were up at seven, an ungodly hour for us, but the skies had opened. We had remembered to pile logs and brushwood under the eaves and on the veranda. I stood there watching the downpour gloomily while the coffee percolated and Paul laid the fire. A slip of a figure rising like a wraith from behind the mill ruin moved, bent double, past the steps.

'*Signora! Venga!*' It was Quinto's widow, the *nonna,* bowed under her load of brushwood and logs. She looked up, rain running down a handsome, furrowed face.

Paul ran down to help her put the load on the gravel and climb the steps. She sat willingly by the fire, water trickling off hair, face, hands and legs, and squiggling out of sodden shoes with half-torn soles. Damp had penetrated three jumpers with snags and holes and a long patched skirt. Paul gave her hot coffee, politely enquiring where she had found the wood. She replied, in her homespun blend of dialect and Italian, that she'd taken it from 'the Germans' land'. He didn't ask her why she preferred the longer route home past our woodpile and house. As she got up to leave, she mumbled something about not knowing that we came at this time of year. I explained we were here to pick the olives and she nodded, saying they were about to harvest theirs too. She had probably run out of fuel and gone foraging on our land. Paul helped hitch our logs and bundle of brushwood on to her back, and we both watched her slow determined trudge over seventy years towards home, heat and survival. She truly belonged to the valley.

Carlo came the following morning punctually at seven-thirty. It was not raining, so he assumed we would realise he was coming. The fire was out, the house profoundly cold. We hurriedly brewed coffee in the kitchen while chatting with Carlo. The weather looked promising. Monte Amiata stood robed in dark purple on the horizon, wispy clouds circling the peak. Above us pale blue was just peeping through a lattice still tinged pink from the dawn.

'*Non pioverà,*' Carlo reassured me over his *espresso*. He looked contentedly at the skies and said that they had rained themselves out. It would be dry and frosty. Emptied in one draft, the cup set on the table far from its saucer, he was down on the drive sorting out a pile of fine netting. He pointed to the outside edges and told us to carry them round the large olive tree behind him in opposite directions until we met and the bright orange apron circled the tree fanning outwards. Carlo busied himself pulling it closer to the trunk and flattening it so it billowed out, rising towards the edges. He then shook the tree gently. A few black olives plopped down, not many.

'*Bene! Sono in un ottimo stato.*' We had arrived at the best time to pick them. He climbed the tree and motioned Paul to follow. Each perched on opposite sides, Paul copying Carlo who gently half plucked the olives so they fell into the net. When Carlo descended, he told me to gather the other two corners and help him ease all the olives into the deepest hollow. He then deftly tipped them into a tin container. Each tree would be the same, he said, after initiating us into the ritual cull of the olives. My plants, my colour, our peaceful and productive pursuit.

'*Eh! Mi sono dimenticato. Orietti verrà domani per parlare del prato.*' Carlo had found us a man known as 'Orietti the father of five', who ran a land maintenance business, and would cut the grass for us. Perfect. The job would be done, paid for, with no strings attached.

Carlo left as the sun shone more steadily though there was still a bite in the air. We tackled the maturest trees first as they gave more fruit and greater visual and tactile satisfaction. We had just started to follow Carlo's instructions when the *nonna* reappeared in a differently patched skirt and equally worn layers of woollens. Talking without a break she headed towards Paul, already roosting happily in an ancient olive tree, and climbed to a self-appointed perch opposite him. Her gnarled arthritic hands fluttered over the ripe fruit at three times our speed, shedding a relentless olive rain on me harvesting from the ground. Some, bouncing off my shoulders, came to rest outside the net. Following them came a shower of dialect, which I roughly interpreted as directing me to pick them up. I obediently hopped out of the magic orange circle into the grass and pecked around for the errant olives. Once they were back on the net, the *nonna* seemed less anxious and turned her patter towards Paul. From time to time he glanced desperately at me.

'I can't get the hang of what she's saying!'

'Nor can I, most of the time. Just pretend, and nod, giving a *sì*, or *va bene*, or *è vero*, but **never** *no!* It was the word that, I had found to my cost, caught you out! Her onslaught of words would stop abruptly with a '*come?*' when one hadn't a clue what she was disagreeing with! The shower of olives continued unabated on the *nonna*'s side of the tree. More dialect and she transferred herself on to a branch neighbouring Paul's; his hands trembled under her critical gaze. Hers were like a humming bird hovering over the boughs, tapping the olives deftly into the net.

'She's been doing it for at least sixty years!' I reminded him.

By mid-morning the mists had fled into the deepest crevices of the valley. The *nonna's* daughter-in-law joined me on the ground under the fourth tree, leaving baby Susanna well wrapped in what Gran would have called a Moses basket. Caterina admitted that she preferred to climb the trees with a companion and recount her grandparents' stories of what happened in the valley many years ago. But since she was pregnant again she stood with me, picking olives until she left to prepare lunch. By the time Mauro came home for the main meal of the day we were on the tenth tree and his mother had retired to her kitchen garden, probably to gather vegetables for

Caterina, who seemed to do all the cooking. Mauro climbed up number eleven and chatted to Paul in standard Italian because he had spoken it at school, on and off, until about fourteen. His mother was illiterate. Words and numbers had long retreated into the deepest recesses of her mind through chronic disuse. Mauro mentioned in parting that a few days earlier, below the house he was stuccoing in Montesasso, he had heard shouting and seen Don Basilio in furious argument with Cecilia Ferrarini, back from Rome to close up her office. As far as he could gather it was all about the recent Etruscan finds and their disappearance.

'Who,' I asked Mauro, 'took the Etruscan objects from those recent excavations on Count Prudomini's land?' He shrugged his shoulders.

'Nobody knows. They've disappeared. So has the *onorevole* Bintoni. Everything's gone very quiet.' Mauro didn't have any precise details, but something strange was happening.

'Paul, we must see Cecilia before she leaves for Rome.'

'We must finish the olives first. It's frosty but dry. We've only done eleven out of twenty-five trees.' Paul was adamant. We'd come to do a job and it had to be finished. Anyway, Cecilia was trouble prone, and that was not where Paul wanted to be.

We had a quick lunch, and on with numbers twelve, thirteen and fourteen while the light and sun lasted. The *nonna* returned with Caterina and Susanna in her Moses basket to help us for another two hours in the afternoon. The yellow sunset glowed warmly as we gathered the net, tipping olives into the centre. They only filled two thirds of Carlo's metal container. It didn't seem much for a day's work, or the equivalent of four *contadini*, two of them slow and clumsy.

As the sun slipped out of sight, the frost bit. Paul went inside to relight the fire in the sitting room. I tried to contact Cecilia in both her office and home, but she had already left for Rome.

A plate of pasta on our knees, the flames mesmerised us. Scents of the rosemary and olive twigs used to rekindle the fire before piling on poplar logs, all found on our land, mingled in our nostrils and permeated our thoughts of slanting olive leaves, plump fruit and perched conversations – the essence of rural life. Never, I recalled, had I slept so peacefully.

The following day Paul was out soon after sunrise to arrange the net around the next tree. I could smell the coffee percolating. This time I climbed to a bird's-eye view feeling light and rather uneasy. I feared I might squawk and try to ruffle my clothes, though Paul seemed unaffected by such unseemly reactions. The valley was a symphony of greens, rising from the silvery dew-washed grass to the darker pearl green olives and the cypress sentinels, marks of sombre green along the drive below us. The gaunt poplars lining the path of the full-flowing stream branched yellow grey, and up the terraced hillside russet willow shoots stood out against evergreen oaks. On the ridge, pine trees marked the edge of the mushroom wood. My soul was floating out and up in celebration. All was peace...

A muddy car bumped down our drive and a small, spare man got out to stand expectantly.

'*Buon giorno!*' The newcomer stepped forward smiling.

'*Sono* Orietti.' Of the five children, I added automatically to myself; one child per Italian family was now becoming the norm.

Orietti was a good listener, observant, a true countryman. In less than thirty minutes he informed us he would have to widen our paths to get the grass cutter down to the lower terraces, showed us how he would prune the vines and fruit trees, warned us the grass should be cut at least twice a year, depending on the rainfall, and gave us a price.

His business-like attitude impressed Paul. Orietti found, of course, other things that needed doing: an immense branch was dragging down our beautiful oak below Venus. That would need cutting in the spring. Paul had snipped the ivy strangling the poplars, but it needed killing or it would just grow up again and suffocate his trees. March would be the right month. And had we noticed the *processionaria*? He pointed out the remains of nests like balls of cotton wool hanging from pine trees at the top of our drive.

'Oh no!' Paul cried, 'they won't eat our guardian pine, will they?' I pointed Orietti round towards the mill table and our precious focal point in the garden.

'*Forse. Vanno bruciate in marzo.*' Those caterpillars hatched out in warmer weather, and after they had devoured one tree, each clinging on to the other, they 'processed' to the next. Unwittingly we had provided a good processional route for them, all pines and cypresses down to our treasured guardian one. Orietti was reassuring. He would cut down the larvae nests in March and burn them.

'*Addio!*' He airily waved us farewell.

'Have we budgeted for these extras?' Paul enquired thoughtfully. Needless to say, we hadn't.

Another meal enjoyed by the fire, just the two of us, in rural contentment. We had finished the last olive tree before sunset. The following morning Carlo took us to the oil mill. The one on the Cassia where the fire station is now, had closed ten years earlier. Since then another two in the vicinity had stopped business. The only oil mill remaining stood in the next valley and was owned by the absent *onorevole* Bintoni. I had noted the cluster of buildings lower down the cypress-lined avenue to his villa.

Arriving with Carlo, born in the area, we were immediately greeted and introduced to the manager. Our offering was weighed to determine the amount of oil and our share of the payment, then taken up a rickety ladder and through a trap door to the top floor. We followed to see our olives tossed into a six-foot diameter drum that was churning a crunchy mass of olives. The circular movement and thudding entranced us, until a shout came and a lever was pulled back to let the sludge down to the next drum. This unappealing mass was more forcibly churned and the first pressing (unadulterated and so to the Italian mind, not just virginal, but extra so) flowed into a smaller container beneath. I gave Carlo a mischievous look and asked him, if it was virginal, why did 'extra' have to be added? He answered seriously that the purest olive oil, the first pressing, was by far the best, and very expensive. The second pressing, plain virgin, produced good oil and then came the stuff that was squeezed from the olive stones, just cheap cooking oil. It was also useful, he added, for recalcitrant locks. Carlo asked us to bring five two-litre bottles for just over nine litres of the best olive oil imaginable: thick golden green with particles of genuine quality clearly floating in it.

The manager insisted on showing us old wooden barrels and terracotta containers moulded with olive boughs and cornucopia to ensure a fertile and profitable season.

'They haven't changed,' he told us, 'since the earliest days of oil making and were only discarded here a generation ago. I remember the back-breaking work on the hand-operated presses'. He grimaced at the memory and I thought of how *onorevole* Bintoni's modern electric machines had put neighbouring oil mills out of business. They only had equipment fit for a museum.

The frost snapped at us under clear skies, the cold segment moon now shrunk into a sickle. Montesasso sparkled sharply in the distance. So with our extra-virgin oil safely back home and the terracotta roof tiles on the Casa dell'Aventura 'coupling' (as the locals put it) over us in the ancient Roman manner, we were part of a fertility rite reaching back beyond the Romans to Etruscan times.

Paul covered Venus to protect her from the cobweb cracks wrought by winter frosts, and I polished the furniture, leaving it shrouded in dustsheets until spring when, without saying it, we knew we would return.

CHAPTER 34

When was it – ten or more years ago perhaps? – Paul was up and out before the sun began to dapple the olive groves and ripple light and shade over ears of wild wheat on Giulio's abandoned terraces. The thump of metal on stone. I looked up at Paul's arched back and his pick rebounded, loosening shale down the slope.

'Coffee?' I held out the mug that was Gianni's, cracked and stained with memories. Paul straightened up, sleeves rolled back, arms bronzed with wisps of white over a fretwork of lines. Seasoned. Stones lay haphazardly around him.

'Thanks. I hope you like the path?'

I raised an eyebrow, then blew him a kiss.

'You'll decide when it's finished.' I nodded, waiting for the empty mug.

There he was the next morning and the following ones before the sun crept over silver leaves touched by a dawn breeze. I noticed he winced when his left hand bore the weight of a stone, so I asked him at last about the scar; it came from the missing years.

'I broke my wrist, tripping on an uneven paving stone when running to catch the post.' That was all. The letters – or razor? – would have been in his right hand.

'Not enough stones,' he announced three days later when I brought him coffee. He was scraping the shale away from *pietra serena*, the silvery grey stone of Florence, to start cutting steps into the hillside.

There should be no work in our Garden of Eden. Nothing to do with either restoring or teaching. Pottering in the garden, walks, reading, sketching or scribbling at whim – learning to relax. Together.

A year later, Dan dug holes where the earth was deep enough to plant the cypresses that Paul and I had been unable to find in the local nurseries. He had just started university and returned to La Casa dell'Avventura inspired to create a sustainable environment. His compost heap didn't attract a neighbourhood of scavenging cats like Gianni's, but it did sprout peach seedlings. Dan meticulously planted them along the edge of the terraces.

Not one of our local garden centres had the cypresses we wanted with the long trunks and branches curving out to end in a point like an exclamation mark. The only ones they had were bushy from the roots up. Plant experts were called over to help us.

'We're looking for the cypresses found in paintings,' Paul explained.

'These are all we have,' they replied, puzzled.

'No, they're not the ones with clean trunks.' He paused and they waited. 'You see them in paintings and all along roads here in Tuscany.'

'These are the same ones!' The experts were smiling, almost laughing. 'All you have to do is to cut the lower branches off as they grow. It's quite easy.' And has been done for centuries, perhaps to stop highwaymen hiding behind them?

When Paul's steps reached the top of the slope, my cypresses following them were over five feet tall but I had cheated a bit, buying them at my height and paying a little more. I enjoyed shaping my mark on our landscape, trimming the lower branches back to the trunk. Where I could cup enough earth around cypress roots I tucked white and blue lavender, planting behind them a dark edging of rosemary with spikes of deeper blue flowers. They aren't thirsty plants and are prospering on the dry slope.

Silhouetted against the sky, Paul was staking out a path to zig-zag across a higher terrace when I stepped up two short flights, coffee in hand, just as the sun glowed round the edge of his head. He enjoyed leaning on his wide Piero della Francesca spade, stripped to the waist for early morning action. Paul, a bulldog, unlike the whippet Gianni, who years ago bent over the stones, eyed, sorted, divined the rocks and built the pillar while we were driving over the clay ridges south of Siena. It was then we first chanced on the sinuous road with cypresses – a human imprint upon the bare hillside.

That spring we planted an umbrella pine at the first zig and three more cypresses back along the zag that Paul had curved up the hillside. On August evenings we crouched together breaking up bulbs of sky-blue, sun-speckled Florentine lilies. Now they nestle to multiply amid the lavender and rosemary on both sides of our path.

Last Easter some lilies flowered in time for our San Giuliano patronal festival. The cypresses are now taller than Paul and, after curling the path round to the top of the Z on the upper terrace, we planted some more.

Over the years the path has become our Easter and summer ritual. Paul is always there soon after sunrise. The regular chop, chop, chop, of a pick breaking rocks or dry earth when I take him black coffee with two spoonfuls of sugar. Habits of place we create and pass on. I tend and talk seasonally to the rosemary, lilies and lavender, annoyed that I've been sold more blue than white lavender plants, syncopating my anticipated melody of colour. He looks across the plain, appraising the weather for the hours to come. I picture the next stage of the path. We don't discuss it, each feeling the other already knows. A zig-zag road with cypresses is all over postcards, drawing the eye over a typical Tuscan landscape. But it is not like ours.

Even now, after he has started to work with a group of London restorers, Paul tells me he dreams of our landscape, of cutting the steps, edging the stones into the earth and shoring them up to create a way over a slope and a terrace. It soothes his mind and spirit during the slow and painstaking removal of accretions, reviving delight in an artist's fantasy of trees, mountains, lakes and hilltop dwellings behind an Annunciation or Crucifixion, skies of imagination opening above. I asked him whether he had seen such a distinctive road in a painting. He knew he had, but couldn't recall where, though it was lodged in his mind. Perhaps in the Uffizi galleries when he was helping back in 1966 after the flood? We returned there, just to look at the landscapes behind the figures in the Sassettas, Peruginos, Ghirlandaios, Botticellis and Raphaels. No winding road with cypresses. Then the earlier ones: Giotto and all his Gaddi and Daddi followers creating smooth grey rocks with a cheeky animal or a plant peering out of a crevice. No luck. We went to see the Fra Angelicos in the former monastery of San Marco. There were plenty of white-robed Dominicans praying by cypresses against a backdrop of grazed pastures and grey boulders, but no cypress-lined sinuous path. We returned to the Ambrogio Lorenzetti landscape, which we discovered together so long ago in Siena's Town Hall. Not one winding route with cypresses.

Mother returns occasionally. She has an arthritic knee, but that doesn't stop her gardening or taking, more slowly, the hillside tracks where she and Gianni found wild asparagus, mushrooms, the best blackberries or wild orchids and the deepest purple thistles imaginable. He showed her all sorts of cacti that grow in dry crevices and erupt into flower when least expected. She prises them gently into the bucket I hold, to thumb them, as Gianni taught her, into Paul's low dry-stone wall that edges our path.

After Carlo finally handed his business over to Vincenzo and had time on his hands, Mother took us both up the valley to the best places Gianni had found for broom and juniper seedlings which she wanted to try planting near the path.

'Gianni must have discovered these places during the war,' Carlo said. 'Nobody comes here now.' Dark, secret spots, where oak trees shelter the next generation of mountain plants. 'No one knows when Gianni returned here in wartime. He was reported missing.'

'When and where did he go missing?' Mother stopped to stare at Carlo.

'Don't know. I was a child. I think they said he enlisted for Africa in 1942. No, earlier. 1941 perhaps. Poor families sent their sons. One less mouth to feed, and the sisters took over their farm work. He was missing for a long time, and then turned up here with the partisans.'

'When?'

'I'm not sure.' Carlo paused to think. 'It must have been after the Armistice, I suppose. In September 1943. There was no way of finding out where he was. His family was very worried. I don't think he contacted them.'

'Shall I try Ada?' Mother asked me. 'She's older and might remember more.' Someone sometime had whispered about Gianni being a prisoner of war. It might have been Ada. If a man disappeared in wartime, Mother told me, it was because he was captured, on a secret mission or dead. We did ask Ada, but she knew no more than we did. Something had bound Gianni to an anonymous existence for two years of his life. It is sad how fear silences people. Some now blame partisans for provoking German troops to kill innocent civilians in reprisal, as happened at Montacuto. That might explain why, by the time we knew him, Gianni was keeping part of his life to himself.

Carlo continues to wink at me behind Paul's back, and squeezes my arm as if in strange complicity. Invitations to dine and dance are still made whenever I appear on my own. I fear the impact of the male ego *offesissimo,* and would do anything to avoid a confrontation, just as I had funked it before with Gianni – or Gio, or whoever he was. The valley is too contained, its grapevine sprouting far too many tendrils. It is not worth the risk. Recently Carlo asked me casually, *'Cos'è successo al giovane biondo?'* What has become of Mike! Carlo hasn't forgotten how I moved in that first summer with Mike's help. His presence was speedily misinterpreted in the valley.

So I'm fair game. Like the thrushes, partridges, hares and wild boar, here for the trying. If lucky, for the taking. I ruefully suppose I must have caused some entertaining gossip over the years, much speculation, even rivalry and some wagers. At last I understood why Gianni sulked, refused invitations and tried to be so possessive about me. He was staking his claim; Mike, Paul and Joe had together revealed I was, as far as the locals could see, literally up for grabs! I suspect that Gianni let rumours of our relationship kindle, burst into flame and then rampage round the valley so he could bask in the glory of his supposed triumph. Carlo, and probably others I hadn't even noticed, tried to challenge his apparent supremacy. He fought back. Gianni's death and Paul's absence released me to a potential valley free-for-all. Later the grapevine began to give contrary signals; the situation might not have been all Gianni had made it out to be, but suspicions still lurked.

'Cos'è successo a quel giovanotto?'

'He's not so young now,' I laughed in reply. 'Mike's just a friend and he sells paintings.' Perhaps, at long last, Carlo could see I wasn't a perfidious 'daughter of Albion' playing fast and loose with men in the valley! Whose fantasy was that, anyway?

Mike now looks a bit older than Joe even though they were in the same year at school. He seems slim from behind, relaxing in worn blue jeans and open shirt, blue to match his eyes, but the waistband curves lower than expected. Casual wear reveals more than his light grey or dark blue suits with ties to display his latest diversification: Art Deco or Nouveau or Rococo, whichever is the current theme in his gallery. Timing his display to coincide with a spectacular Art Deco exhibition in London, he made a tidy profit, appeared on radio and television and was moderately pleased with himself and his latest partner.

'What's happened to Angélique?' Mike was on his own when I asked.

'She ended up marrying the laird in that Scottish castle. It was a lavish society wedding, only just in time; she was starting to fade.' He half laughed, ending in a nasal giggle. 'She became Lady something or other. Odd, she always seemed so proud of her noble name – what was it, de la Tourelle? Angélique de la Tourelle.'

So the castle and the laird really do exist. I had suspected they might be Paul's way of avoiding awkward explanations.

Loud events often have equally loud repercussions. Marriage in a Scottish castle progressed to a tabloid divorce, with Angélique featured on prime time television. Mike came to Guildford so that he, Paul and Joe to could watch the programme together. They were astounded to learn her real name was Pauline Curtis, born in Lewisham, South London. Her negligent parents and indifferent teachers left her to strike out on her own path to wealth and notoriety. There she sat, recounting how she fled from a drunken father who abused her, face demurely bowed, newly blond tresses sleekly rounding her head, eyelashes over cheeks, cherry lips, nails manicured red to match, slender fingers over sleek knees and her legs neatly inclined. So sad and poised, the victim's stance from tip to toe. Viewers were initially deprived of the details they desired. Not for long. That evening at Downs Way two men in particular were watching Pauline from Lewisham apprehensively, tight-lipped. Her mother thought she should earn money as quickly as possible in an office or hospital, anywhere that paid. They gaped when poor Pauline from Lewisham explained how she turned into Angélique de la Tourelle after weeks immersed in fashion magazines and language tapes, and launched herself to become a celebrity among the wealthy.

'I love art,' said Pauline, alias Angélique, gazing at the viewers as her accent changed from South London to exotic French, 'zo I learn about it wiz my men friends'. Paul leaned forward between Joe and me, shifting to the edge of the sofa as if about to leave, while Mike stiffened visibly in his armchair. Mother sat in the other armchair, smiling.

They needn't have worried. She wasn't going to poison any relationship or name any names except her unfortunate ex-husband and her parents, too elderly now to bother.

Mike cleared his throat loudly and said he had to leave. There was a lot to do the next day – new clients, the usual. He would never admit he had been fooled. Paul did, after Mike left, even finding a few excuses for her behaviour. I listened and haven't to this day asked about him and Angélique during those two years. Prying, I thought, destroys trust. I almost did when Dan told me he happened to find her website offering costly advice on how to ensnare a rich husband. Paul could hardly have fallen into that category.

* * * * *

'You'll have to repair the retaining wall, just along the terrace by the third curve in the cypress path.' Dan, upbeat about his first job as an archaeologist with the North York Moors National Park, had become, like his father, an expert on dry stone walls. 'If a couple of stones are out of true, the rest soon follow.' Paul stood up, arched his back and looked affectionately at his son, at least half an inch taller and with the same hew of shoulders and thick curly hair. Fair like mine.

'I've done stonewalling since before you were born,' Paul reminded Dan with amusement.

Not long afterwards Paul called me to come and see what Dan was up to. Without a word to us he was planting oleanders at each curve in our path. Dan was quick to get in first.

'They don't need water. And they have white or pink flowers as,' and he glanced anxiously at me, 'I know you don't want strong colours.' He came down to us at the bottom of the first flight of steps. 'I wanted it to be a surprise. I've been thinking about it for some time.'

'Shouldn't we all be designing the landscape together?' Paul asked.

'I know you'll say Tim never actually came' – Paul and I stared at Dan – 'but I miss him not having something here. Just something to keep him present. That's all'. He paused for a moment but, as we didn't say anything or move, he climbed back to his planting.

Some refrains echo more, the deeper they lie in the memory. My mother, no longer hoping my father might return, talks more openly of how passionately she loved him, and how he remembered, as he held her, where he lived in Tuscany. A clutch of houses round a barn of a church, San Giuliano – enthralling stories of a faraway place. She still smiles at the way they mixed his attempts at English and her rudimentary Italian. She describes him seated on a wall swinging his legs, while his eyes, voice, hands and arms portrayed more feeling than faltering words could express. I overheard her telling Dan how he taught her gestures; one to bring good luck, index and small fingers in the upside-down sign of the cuckold, and you had to say at the same time, *'in bocca al lupo!'* Strange indeed, imprecating into the wolf's mouth, and intriguing. Or finger in cheek, a tribute to some tasty dish. Later Mother found out these were rough gestures, but Gio was intelligent all right. She enjoys recalling the San Giuliano tale of a bright child who did better than his parents could ever dream of. Then came the War. He went ill-trained, badly-equipped to Africa and was captured in that underfunded campaign.

'What did he really look like?' Dan asked.

'You've seen the photo, of course. Dark and handsome. Wide, expressive eyes. Very loving. Curly hair like yours, but not fair.' I joined them.

'Tell me something I don't know already.' I was thinking of some birthmark, like Paul's on his shoulder. 'A birthmark, scar... I don't know, like...' but I couldn't think of anything unless she could. She sat silent for a while. I'm learning to be patient and wait for her.

'It always seemed to be dark when we were alone, with the fear that something was about to happen – like being disturbed, or having to go to a place at a certain hour, or an air raid. Perhaps I didn't really look at him to notice things. It was his presence that was special. Just being together, as one.'

Being, surviving. Gianni's ancestors – Gio's, too, perhaps – tilled our valley over the centuries. From sunrise a light wind strokes the grasses and oak seedlings sprouting between the stones of the banks shoring up the slopes, and the vines running wild on Giulio's unploughed strips beyond the channel to our east. To the south, it breathes over terraces ploughed twice a year and olives irregularly pruned. On the far side of the stream towards sunset, bulrushes wave rust-coloured batons at the brambles tangled with fig leaves, the last to stir in the breeze. Light-leafed poplars, embraced by ivy, flicker by our stream to the west and in spring cast seeds soaring feathery over us. A whisper suffices, and the sycamores to the north shiver over the olives, denizens of the hillside. The woodland advances on layers of time older than farmers and their terraces or even the hunter-gatherers.

* * * * *

We have a different bedroom now that our furniture from Paul's London flat is in our room next to Dan's. I was a bit concerned about Mother's 1940's pieces, but she said she didn't care for them any more and was willing to give them to charity. We love it up there, having coffee when we wake up and drawing back the curtains to see how the seasons are behaving in our garden.

'Television seems to be prying into our secrets,' Paul thought out loud.

'How do you know? You don't watch many programmes.'

'True. But I've sampled them. I'm sad, something is lost...' he was saying what I hadn't found the words to tell him. 'Remember how we once thought our love, our tenderness, every caress and crevice of our being together were unique? Now everybody knows everything.' He snuggled up. 'It's difficult to explain, but it's as if people are machines and their physical satisfaction is a question of measurement. Frequency, intensity and so on.'

'Isn't it like looking into rooms with one side open to anyone who wants to tune in?' I said. 'People don't seem to want privacy. They either perform or peer. It's a public display of emotions; there's nothing intimate or personal or passionate that's just between two people.' I was emphatic. 'Our love can't be put on display.'

Shush!' he said, 'Dan's home this weekend. He might hear!' We laughed and said together, 'He's grown up now!'

* * * * *

Dan says our attic is a treasure trove.

'Do you remember?' He was holding up what I had tried to forget, now kept safe in his room – a fur bonnet, a squirrel hand puppet and much else to make me sob inside. Those were the special things I couldn't give away when Tim's bedroom was cleared. Dan has no respect for brown paper, stripping it to uncover the contents.

'I like having my brother's things around me.' He had found his father's sketches of the three of us that I'd had framed to hang in Paul's Camberwell flat. Dan immediately took the ones of Tim to his bedroom, arranging the others in our living room and obliging his parents to eat in the company of their younger selves. Paul worried about 'the cacophony of frames'. The plain wood round our portraits did not match the black frames Grandpa had chosen for his etchings. Mother looked on amused, happy with anything as long as her father's pictures with his countryside scenes remained where they had always been, in his corner.

Deep inside I am glad Tim has returned to his room to keep Dan company, but it is still painful to see him there. It is their territory now. I'm relieved that, while he was scavenging around in our loft, Dan didn't unwrap the diptych of Gianni and me, or if he did, no mention was made of it. It was Gianni's fantasy. A present best forgotten.

'It's not fair, Dad. Let's hang Tim's paintings and sketches here where you eat.'

'No room,' Paul stated in a tone that was final. 'They're in our bedroom.' He had always kept Tim's artwork to himself, until he asked me if I'd like his paintings and drawings in our bedroom and how I'd like him to arrange them.

'I can always give them a home,' Dan repeats from time to time.

Paul came across the saint Mike gave me (which I passed on to him) at the back of our wardrobe, still in the carrier bag Angélique had found for me. He has never told me whether he broke it and deliberately left it behind when he moved out of the London flat. After repairing the frame, he has hung my rococo saint on the landing outside our bedroom.

CHAPTER 35

Paul has been working on his *capriccio* in the garage studio for some time now, in between commissions. He consoles himself with the thought that, if he doesn't get enough landscapes to restore, at least he can go on creating his own fantasy one.

Over the years Giulio's farmhouse has become the cardinal point in our approach to the much-restored 'ruin'. It stands where the road turns sharp left revealing a view across the valley, with our Casa dell'Avventura right in the middle on a spur jutting out towards the plain. Over more than a decade, his farmhouse had stayed reassuringly unchanged with its porridge-grey plaster peeling off the rubble walls of stones cleared from terraces. It descends the slope, articulated in two parts, one inhabited, the other for the rabbits, poultry and general storage. Across the public track on the other side of the yard where the dramatic road meeting was held, there used to be pole haystacks, sculpted differently every time we passed. Here we first glimpse our valley on arrival and lose sight of it on departure.

'Why don't you paint Giulio perched on a ladder under the eaves?' I was looking over Paul's shoulder at the work in progress. He has located Giulio's farmhouse off centre, doors and windows open, with hayricks, poultry and other animals but no people.

'Perhaps,' Paul said. 'Right now I'm editing out his ungainly butane gas cylinder'. It intrudes into the field at the back of the house, but who would begrudge Giulio and his family their central heating? On a summer evening, they now eat in a paved front garden separated from the farmyard by raised beds of roses, bay trees, oleander and mimosa as well as the traditional geranium pots surveyed by an arum lily or two.

Social mobility comes complete with a new sign, bang in the middle of the track that local inhabitants have used for centuries: *proprietà privata*! We assumed it was a hallowed right of way, but now keep off it for fear of provocation. Giulio still tends the olives on his terraces, but Antonio's heart lies in self-assertion and driving a small red Fiat as if it's a Lamborghini, never giving way when any unfortunate vehicle meets him along our narrow lane. The asphalting has speeded up his latent tendencies.

Paul has at last painted in a human being! A younger Don Luigi stands in front of San Giuliano, not as I suggested in the middle section of the canvas but placed low down by the Roman road which, for the moment, he's only indicating with a straight sweep of brown across the bottom.

'I'll elaborate the Cassia later. I'm working on the church and the priest. I like the black of his cassock against the grey stones and the green cypresses.' I did too.

'Why are you scattering the mammoth bones and other bits and pieces from his museum round the church square?'

'Liv, I'm painting a new type of picture, a sort of landscape *capriccio*. It's a fantasy. I'm juxtaposing the landscape and buildings I care about. The canvas is my space and I'm free to put what I want where I like! Don Luigi's important and so are his fossils. They come from the substructure or skeleton of the valley.'

Elderly Don Luigi hasn't engaged with the forces of modernisation. I was relieved Paul omitted the football pitch next to his church. It is covered in straggly grass with one goal post askew, the other collapsed on the ground, superseded by the full-sized one floodlighting the games of a new generation. Paul has ignored the new ground and the fire station, though they should have been down near the Roman road, as well as the *Festa dell'Unità,* still limping on in spite of the collapse of communism. Peeping down on it, he might represent an intriguing bird's-eye view of a boisterous rustic feast and include the two women fighting. There's no way of painting Don Luigi's change in records broadcast over the valley at Sunday mass. Out with Gounod's *Ave Maria* and in with some 'holy pop' from the Vatican radio station where Don Basilio has contacts.

Paul relishes the thick oil strokes on the rutted track leaving San Giuliano to wander up the valley beside the stream and the poplars; I can see the wind rustling their branches and hear birdsong as he works. He has ignored the asphalt and caught the mud and the drystone walls sprouting wild mint, thyme, tender asparagus shoots in spring and mottled brown succulents in summer, spiked here and there by couch grass. On one occasion Dan and I were watching as Paul pushed the track up with the tip of his brush between terraces to become the spine of the valley, paths branching out like ribs. We both hoped it would end at the top with the source of our stream by Oreste's house. Instead it forked, 'like a wish-bone,' Dan said. One branch went through an unlocked gate to a house we might have bought.

'What about Massimo and the politician's son?' Paul turned to look at me, puzzled. I'd forgotten he hadn't been with us in the summer of the kidnapping and quickly switched to, 'please add Massimo selecting beams with Gianni on a stifling summer day. We drank white wine and fizzy lemonade – d'you remember? I was talking to Oreste while you did a lot of sketches of Massimo's builder's yard, and the little old millhouse down by the stream...'

'Maybe,' he said, but he hasn't included Massimo. Not yet.

'Will Oreste's house be at the top of the right fork?' It was his creation, his *capriccio*, but I couldn't help asking. He likes Dan and me peering over his shoulder to see how he's getting on, with an 'um' and 'Oh, good!'

'Yes. I've already thought about the oldest man in the valley. I'll put his farm at the top.' He started painting the fork right through the olive groves I dream about, to reach Oreste's dwelling.

We could hardly have expected to find things the same when we returned last summer. Initially they were. The same opening high up near the crest of the valley, just below the ridge that shelters Oreste's farmhouse from the north winds and the worst of the winter snow. Some evidence of life, though nothing moved, not even the old man asleep under the walnut tree. But something had changed. Further up the glade, to take advantage of a clear view across the plain for miles and miles to the range of mountains beyond Monte Amiata, stood a new construction, roofed but unfinished. It is built of rough stones, but mechanically arranged, not as Gianni did it after eyeing their shapes for some minutes, puffing away and figuring in his mind's eye how to fit the masonry puzzle together as if preordained. The man turned to look at us and broke our trance. It wasn't Oreste.

'I'll paint it as we first saw it. He's there in spirit. Can't you feel him there, just by looking at what I'm painting?' He used his earliest watercolour for Oreste's old farmhouse, not the way it is now, spruced up into self-catering apartments for holidaymakers wanting a pool, a view and tranquillity.

We knew that over the years Angelo, our electrician, had been building a home near the Cassia. It would have proper plumbing, up-to-date gadgets, and no cobwebs! We originally found him living near Sant'Anselmo in the outbuildings of an ancient farmhouse boasting its own tower and pigeoncote. The *padrone*, a Ferini, hadn't spent a lira on it for over ten years, neglect lending it a friendly down-at-heel, rather apologetic look. Paul once painted quite an elaborate watercolour of these buildings, but it doesn't seem to have found its place in his *capriccio*. The fortified farmhouse, low-lying and stifling in summer, is now being restored into holiday apartments. But if you look up to the skies risking a crick in your neck, you can just make out Montesasso.

The Ferini are also up-marketing the only genuine *villa suburbana* in the valley, built higher up the hillside by their ancestors to oversee their land. Carlo used to visit Marisa in her house outside the villa walls. Paul's secret place where Mother, Sarah and I sheltered from a storm is nearby, his deep green pool trickling through an arch of hewn stones into a lower, bluer one, which he fondly imagines is an Etruscan sanctuary, a perennial watering place, the abode of nymphs. Now their quietude and his are rudely disturbed. Villa Fontanina has been restored into luxury self-catering suites with the shared use of a spacious swimming pool, all let at a *prezzo profumato*, according to Angelo. The adjacent farmyard has been gravelled over for a car park and wrought-iron gates inappropriately enclose a trim forecourt with potted azaleas and oleanders. Neat and nice and, according to the publicity, an 'authentic Tuscan villa'! An up-market restaurant, the sort that does not deign to put prices on the menu, spreads over the garden. An arcade has a niche in the centre where a statue of Bacchus grins inebriated at the diners through bunches of grapes. Above them the twinkling lights of Montesasso and swooping bats remain; beyond over the plain, more hills and bright specks beneath a night sky pricked by stars. Villa Fontanina is just now emerging as Paul first saw it from his secret place to the right of the canvas.

'What about more buildings?' Dan has been photographing them with the complicated new camera Paul gave him for his last birthday.

'I'm including the ones I want,' Paul said. 'Only a few and not if they have changed too much.'

'What about Carlo and Pina?' I said. Every time we pass Carlo's yard, seemingly unchanged, Paul laments that there's nothing there he wants to paint, only lorries and a house made of breeze blocks.

'I've photographed them with Vincenzo and his family.' Dan found the snaps to show his father, who said he'd think about it. They all did appear later on in what he pointed out was, 'For you, Olivia, your olive grove,' just above the middle of the canvas. Pina joined Caterina under a tree with the *nonna* perched above them (you can see her chattering away!) and Carlo helping Paul and Mauro spread the orange net round another olive with Susanna and Dario, older than they were at the time, wriggling under it, creating havoc and fun.

'Deliberately inaccurate,' Paul said, 'but true to the spirit of our valley'. No sign yet of our house.

He dislikes the antiseptic atmosphere of the new Co-op on the Cassia as I do, but it's convenient to shop there. It resembles a vast supermarket anywhere in the world, selling, impersonally, everything from food to household goods, clothes, garden tools, barbecues and pool equipment.

'You don't really expect me to include it?' He wants to animate the Cassia but it remains just a straight brush sweep at the foot of the canvas. I was expecting him to spread buildings splayed out on either side of the valley's link with the world beyond, but he doesn't like the way it's changing with factories jostling houses and shops along our nearest stretch.

Montesasso has been spruced up in the new mode. Peeling plaster is stripped to reveal bits of brick thrown in with soft grey *pietra serena*. Paul wants to show the buildings built from stone gouged out of the land they stand on. Human toil has shaped the mountainside into dwellings, touched up, adapted, half pulled down and rebuilt since the Etruscans, more than two thousand five hundred years ago. Many who moved down to new houses in

Montesasso Scalo in search of every conceivable modern convenience, are now restoring the old town and returning to the air, views and character of their former homes.

The corner store, just to the right of the niche with Garibaldi's statue where I used to go for bread, fresh pasta and a chat, has closed. Instead there's a fashionable hairdressing establishment. A beautician has taken over a former fruit and vegetable shop. Down Via Garibaldi there are expensive boutiques selling tourists' goods, from designer clothes to the local pottery. Wines are marketed together with impenetrably wrapped hams, truffles and cheeses, all found at half the price in the back alleys, or for one third at the Co-op. Montesasso is changing tone. Young voices are speaking standard Italian, relegating the local dialect to their grandparents.

'I want to include Montesasso,' Paul was thinking out loud, 'but I don't like all the new tourist shops'. He was trying to work into the top right-hand corner an outline of church towers, roofs and chimneys inside town walls, with an ox and cart about to enter the Porta Etrusca, sweeping the road in firm brush strokes under the hoofs and wheels down to the plain.

At weekends he has started bringing his *capriccio* inside the house to hang over the living-room fireplace so we can enjoy it at mealtimes. Mother and I were following our particular ways into it one evening when Dan interrupted.

'What about this photo?' and stuck it on to Montesasso's town wall with Blutack. Paul was horrified.

'Why are you doing that?' He tried not to shout. 'Do you expect me to paint it? Use it for ideas?'

'Yes.' We all sat still, silent, waiting. In Dan's photo Italian school children, foreign tourists and students on study-abroad courses were gathering outside the shop selling sandwiches in Montesasso's main square. Both sexes sported interchangeable T-shirts in trendy acid colours over the international uniform of jeans. Some smartly dressed adults in the background were parading up and down to view themselves, and others, in any reflecting surface or eyes. In this digital age, if you are not worth scrutiny, with a click you're edited off screen and out of mind! For the young, even for Dan, it's a major preoccupation to get oneself included with more than just a passing glance, not to be condemned to formless oblivion. Dan's photo catapulting people onto Paul's fantasy landscape was a good idea, but I didn't say so out loud.

'Thanks, Dan, I'll think about it,' Paul said with difficulty, 'but remember, it's a *capriccio*, not a collage'. Predictably, that didn't please his grown-up son.

'It could be one.' Dan was unabashed. 'Why not?'

'The scale in your photo is wrong.'

'Your landscape fantasy has no coherent scale,' Dan insisted. 'Look at the individual scenes. Some are painted as if you're looking up into them, others splay out to show many viewpoints, and still more are just bird's-eye views, as if you're floating over them.' Dan was right. Together they made a patchwork quilt of country scenes with just one town, a tiny Montesasso shrinking top right inside its walls which Paul threatened to paint over – a *pentimento* – and redo. He had decided to feature the street where I first met Gianni.

That was because further out by the Porta Etrusca customs change more slowly. The passers-by still nod the time of day. People are still reassuringly familiar, though time has passed through here as well. The one-legged rag-and-bone man who sold me the bedsteads has died; his area has been sluiced down and set with white plastic tables and chairs, an overspill from the transformed Taverna Etrusca. Its owner of generous proportions has retired, leaving the familiar tobacco-stained interior with worn and scrubbed trestle tables to be transformed by her jovial, equally tubby son. He has expelled the old wooden tables and rush-seated chairs, imported washable plastic gear, and set up a tiny *spaghetteria*, which the locals now patronise for the best *spaghetti alla carbonara* in town. The Pompeian-style shop has its shutters open over the venerable stone counters to provide the frozen-yoghurt-in-ten-flavours dessert for clients of the *spaghetteria etrusca* opposite. I was beginning to feel a bit lost. Paul wasn't. He painted the street as it was when he first saw it.

The stream and the track marking the spine of the valley support the whole composition. They are the valley's lifelines, but the stream is threatened with extinction. Still more ominous black tubes snake up the enfeebled waterfalls above the ford. Another owner higher up is constantly pumping stream water into a reservoir on his land to irrigate his vast lawn and flowerbeds. *L'acqua è un bene in comune!* Water belongs to all. Paul has brushed in the source above Oreste's house and, looking at it, one can imagine his spirit outraged by the thirsty gluttons plundering the water from the spring on his land, in his time shared by all in the valley.

Even though some older members of the Panichini tribe filter back to their valley, they no longer cleave to the peasant lore of their youth. The *cultura contadina* they grew up in is firmly rejected with its mud and slog, perennial tiredness, dirt ingrained under nails and into every pore, bitter cold in winter, sweat and toil in summer, animals to feed day in day out and the only time off on Sundays after church – all for little material reward.

Nowadays on warm and sunny Sundays, three generations of the Panichini who fled the countryside when people like us bought the buildings they willingly relinquished, return to the valley. In spring squeaks of joy greet the wild violets and primroses. The grandchildren pick posies, guided by their grandparents, while the sons and daughters search for wild asparagus and lettuce.

'*Roba genuina!*' they squeal in delight. Some also pluck snails into buckets, the edible kind we are told. It makes my stomach churn, but then I wouldn't know one snail from another. Paul has depicted them with the plants. In June there are small, stingingly sweet wild strawberries where Maria Pia grew up and the partisans and Allied soldiers hid on the mountainside above Oreste. After summer rainfalls they come in search of mushrooms, too late Gianni would say to find more than discarded ones. He cut away the brambles round our ruin 'because of snakes and fires', but in August the hedgerows and hillsides are speckled with blackberries – *frutti di bosco!* Wild berries nowadays adorn menus in fashionable restaurants, a health-conscious, exotic and pricey dessert! They could have come right from beneath our noses, our valley's crop. The way Paul is painting the trees and plants in their valley is, I've come to think, how Gianni and his Panichini ancestors would have seen them: a rich tapestry of survival.

Now the former *contadini* have earned the time to enjoy the sensuous delights of nature: songbirds in spring, the summer scent of lavender and pine needles, the kaleidoscope of greens and the shimmer of silvery olives before the more sonorous autumn tones of ripe pomegranates, rose hips and purple grapes.

'Is there snow in your paradise?'

'Why not?' Paul smiled. 'D'you remember the April snowstorm?'

'Please paint it in, somewhere.'

'I'll try,' he said thoughtfully.

Paul found it hard to depict the passing of the *mezzadria* system. Few initially bewailed it. Look at the way Giulio has bought his crumbling farmhouse and gradually modernised it for himself, his parents before they died, and now his intransigent son, Antonio. Our valley is sliding into modern times. Outwardly I rejoice at these gains; inwardly I fear it is the end of the terraced hillsides, the backdrop to Paul's anthology of human survival in this valley. The broad beans Gianni looked forward to every year are not now cultivated under the olives. Many of the groves are abandoned and the terraces, clogged with weeds and dead branches, not even ploughed once a year. A generation ago brushwood, gathered by children and the elderly, promised warmth from the damp winter chill, a pot of hot broth bubbling over the hearth and crusty bread baked in the outside oven. Giulio, Mauro and Carlo are the last of countless generations to take a personal pride in vineyards, gnarled fruit trees and olive groves. So every year more terraces are abandoned; the couch grass, brambles, broom, oaks and chestnuts seed and take root and multiply unmolested. Elderly couples, both landowners and *contadini,* provide one another with eggs, vegetables and company. Their children, like Francesco who designed the Montesasso museum display, work elsewhere. He often invites us into the next valley where he grew up. His parents own part of the hillside above the *onorevole* Bintoni's villa and the oil mill.

'What about hillside farming?' Dan asked him.

No crops are sown under the flickering silvery light. With nobody to shore up and trim the crumbling terraces, shoots are pushing out of the slits and dislodging stones in the retaining walls. No machine can repair such a wall.

'The wooded crest of the valley is creeping down on us,' Francesco replied. 'The hillsides are returning to their pre-Etruscan state.' I can hear him now.

'Italy imports most of its timber, so we need trees. With no flooding on the plain for over fifty years and no more malaria, there's no need for the terraces. After all, they've only been here since the Etruscans, and what's that? A mere two thousand years of history.'

'What about the olives?' I asked anxiously. 'They don't do well on the plain with the humidity and the frosts. Keep the terraces for the olives at least.'

'The multi-nationals are taking over.' Francesco echoed Dan who had already taken us further south to see new Italian olive plantations. The trees are tall and thin, looped together by black irrigation tubes and planted to allow space for machines to plough, spread manure and harvest the crop.

'I've been studying areas like these valleys,' Dan said, looking intently at Francesco. 'They are patterned with settlements, tracks, graves, burial grounds, a mass of evidence that has created a three-dimensional map of four thousand years of history. Wars only began when hunters settled, started farming and forming communities. Possession meant survival.' We sat silently facing the plain where, in 1944, Francesco's parents had watched Allied troops passing our side of Monte Amiata.

'It must be easier to manage historic landscape in Britain,' Francesco said after a while, a half statement, half question to Dan who should know. 'Where there are low-lying ploughed fields, moorland for pasture and hillsides for forests, there's no need to terrace the slopes.'

'Perhaps.' Dan nodded, pausing to think it through. 'Difficult to say. People see land differently. For its beauty, for its past, for what it says about humans since history began. For its heart, the way the earth sort of beats, with or against us.' He spoke cautiously. 'Looking at landscape touches a pulse inside me. It sounds silly, but I have to think about it in my work. How and why should we preserve the human imprint on nature, even when the farming that creates its pattern on the land is no longer economically viable?

Keep it for recreation and spiritual sustenance? It's a question of whether to intervene, when and where. Should we let the mark of countless generations gradually unravel, as is happening here on these hillsides, or restore it to how it has been for centuries?' He was speaking unusually slowly. 'Everything is in flux, both disintegrating and being restored. The woodland is reclaiming these terraces.'

'So,' Francesco said, resignedly, 'there's no stopping the flow of history on the hillsides. And that means the olive groves will retreat to the low land and then, who knows, to Africa, and vines to the large uniform estates on the plain below us. We humans have tampered for more than two thousand years, from the Etruscans onwards, I suppose, then nature takes it all back to start over again'. We listened, silent. 'I hope we don't have to be hunter-gatherers once more. Not for the moment anyway!'

The mountain is the host and the trees are the guests. Already the brambles are extending their territory over the terraced hillsides and I fear for my olives.

I yearn for Paul to show more of the wide sweep of the hills looking up the valley. Instead he is painting much more detail close to the eye at a variety of angles and vanishing points. He says he wants more sound, so he has included a nightingale and a lark at the edge to sing into the picture.

Paul has finally accepted that his *capriccio* might be even more unusual if it became a *collage* as well, but he and Dan disagree (sometimes too vociferously) about where to paste the photos, or even how large they should be. I think the canvas has space enough for both father and son.

'Isn't the Prudomini villa part of the landscape?' I'd enjoy looking at a Renaissance building and wondering at the changes in one privileged family. If not quite managing a saint or a pope, over the centuries the Prudomini had practised a form of wealth redistribution by contributing to religious foundations for the sick and destitute in Montesasso. Their town house became a museum, giving Montesasso status in Italy's competitive cultural climate. As Cecilia hoped, the town is now a centre for Etruscan studies and Montesasso's carving and maiolica traditions are thriving after centuries of neglect. Paul tells me he isn't sure where to put the villa in his scheme of things. He paints the exterior of people and houses, while I try to recreate what goes on inside them.

'*E Don Basilio? Il conte?*' Over the years Don Luigi has updated us on what has happened in our valley. The Prudominis haven't been to their land below the church for some years. The excavations were abandoned after *lo scandalo*, and all is managed by a rather grim *fattore*. The land agent, the dreaded 'middle man' is everywhere, and Don Basilio, nowhere. I didn't dare ask him about the *onorevole* Bintoni and the Countess, since truth and imagination might be disconcertingly similar.

Years ago, when I was still shopping at the old Co-op tucked away in a Montesasso Scalo back street near the station, I found my secret place, a refuge from Gianni. One afternoon, tired, hot and bothered by all the shopping I had to do for a perpetually hungry family, I wandered under an arch into a wide courtyard edged by two-storey buildings. It stands between the Roman Cassia and the oldest building in Montesasso Scalo, a large villa owned by a younger branch of the ubiquitous Prudomini family. Once a posting house, over the centuries it was frequented by merchants, pilgrims and travellers to Rome. When the railways came in the late nineteenth-century, soon followed by motorised versions of horse carriages, the buildings fell into disuse, maintaining a stubborn air of timeworn neglect. Paul could place them on the Cassia at the bottom of his *capriccio*, but this is my secret place and he hasn't found it yet.

In the far corner is the sign of an *osteria*, an olive branch. An open wood fire fumigates the interior all winter. In the spring, I drop in for a glass of local wine with ham sliced on Tuscan bread, or just a cup of coffee. In summer the wooden chairs and tables settle comfortably under a vine pergola. The regulars still play *scopone* hunched over their cards, wine glasses and cigarettes to hand. The tavern keeper, who lives with his family above the empty stables, has shuffled a bit with the times. A fridge has arrived to cater for ice cream in hot weather, but the tables remain scrubbed and venerable. Narrow stairs leading to haylofts and lodgings for stage coach passengers in this former hub of highway activity, survive untrodden, still and silent. My refuge remains an unrestored secret.

Paul has at last included Marco's shrine in his landscape. The roughly cut, red-etched inscription *Che Dio ti benedica* now has tiles balanced above it on breeze blocks to protect the flowers. Paul hates the Florentine lilies there now, a permanent dusty plastic blue and yellow remembrance from people who are too busy to replenish living flowers. We walk past the shrine to the trickle over the ford; no crabs, no toads. This rutted track crosses the new asphalt road up the valley past Massimo to Oreste's chestnut woods. The crossroads shrine that has just lost Saint Jamila for Padre Pio, has a stiff bunch of artificial marigolds needing a dusting of rain. Paul sees them as tributes of neglect.

'Why don't you paint us in?' Dan asked, a bit irritated. 'You don't want the photos I've taken of Andrew, Sarah and the family, Joe, or any of us. We're all left out.' As an afterthought, 'and you are, too!'

'What about Gianni?' I asked.

'Look at the Casa dell'Avventura and the way we've planted the path with cypresses to wind over the terraces above it. I'm painting it at the centre of the canvas now, at the heart of my *capriccio*, so I imagine us all in it, and you should too. I'm not going to insert people hither and thither. You're all involved just by looking at the picture and imagining what you will. The *capriccio*'s for you to explore however you like. You're all there in spirit. So is Gianni. He restored our ruin.'

Paul has received his first commission for a landscape *capriccio* and is trying to curb his excitement.

'It can wait until after Christmas,' he said, outwardly calm. I helped him carry his original *capriccio* back across the lawn to the studio. We were standing together thinking about the unpainted areas of his invention and I was missing the interiors, the hidden stories, the quick of it all, when he remarked without looking at me, 'Liv, I haven't seen you writing much.' I didn't know what to say. 'How's your story of the valley?' He must have forgotten that he had laughed at my idea.

'Paul, you didn't think anyone would want to read about our experiences. Others have long since been writing that sort of book and created a veritable industry. I don't want to be part of it.'

'Olivia,' he was looking at me now, eyes like pools. 'I know now I was utterly wrong. I'm really sorry, so very sorry.'

'In any case,' I said, 'I've missed my chance.'

Or have I?

This is a book about landscapes and homes and hearths – the life of the valley and of us all.

Our elixir.

It is Tim's book. Without him it would never have been written.

* * * * *

Tim

'D'you remember Tim smiling for the first time and clutching your necklace?'

'Yes, the diamonds you gave me.' (Or the many-faceted glass beads he said were like me!)

'His soft, helpless, milky smell?'

'His tiny curling fingers with dimples for knuckles?'

'Chuckles puckering his cheeks?'

'I loved him peeping out of the fur bonnet in winter. He was wearing it when he began walking determinedly away from us – '

'How he yelled when he tugged at your Gran's damask tablecloth, sliding it off to break her best plates – '

'D'you remember banishing all the photos, vases, lamps, all Gran's clutter to higher shelves as he pulled himself up, reaching out–?'

'Wobbling uncertainly from the bathroom weighed down by nappies and dragging a trail of toilet roll behind him?'

'Odd how a small child understands so much but can't control his bowels –'

'But can toddle around and laugh with his whole body – '

'Quivering from toe to topknot, finger to eyebrow, all over, gurgling – '

'Or like a rod, rigid, mouth a trumpet of fury.'

'Then go hopping and skipping – '

'Blissfully – '

'Just like piglet in *Winnie the Pooh* – '

'With nappies sagging – '

'D'you remember he wanted a piglet more than a teddy? Both were demoted when the red squirrel hand puppet appeared.' (I had secretly acquired it for myself.)

'Then, after we bought his first two-wheel bicycle and he went–'

'On his own to the rhododendron tunnels and the Downs, frustrated when his bicycle ran into the sand –'

'But sped spectacularly and dangerously home on it down our road.'

'Don't remind me.' I shuddered.

'Also the sledge – which year was that snowy winter when he nicked all the tin trays he could find and skidded with his friends dangerously past the door, only just stopping at the road junction?'

'They were nearly ten years old. I think it was Andrew's idea to make one out of wood – '

'With a holder for a whiskey bottle in case they felt cold!'

'The snow melted before they could try out their invention! It's still hanging from a rafter in the garage – your studio.'

'My fault. I shouldn't have read him the *Just William* books! Self indulgence, it was, because I found them so funny. So did your mother and Gran, always sneaking in to listen. A licence to outwit, tease and frustrate adults!'

'Gran was upset because he would only wash his face – it positively shone above his neck which always looked grubby! I don't like to remember how many bribes there were to get him into a bath. It was the locked door and "I'll do it myself" stage, floating boats in clear bath water.'

'About then, I remember, he went in for models: ships, planes, cars; anything that could be bought in a kit. I'm guilty here. I loved doing them with him.'

'I enjoyed finding you both, heads down, in total childlike concentration, blissfully oblivious. I couldn't get into his room without dislodging a ship with my sleeve, or hitting an aircraft hanging, dust-laden, from the beams. Dusting was **not** allowed. I used to check, when tucking him into bed, where the dust had slid off through its own weight. Just like snow.'

I used to envy their double-minded concentration, cutting me out as observer, and winced thinking back, a shadow looming.

'No regrets,' said Paul dispelling it, arm round my shoulders and leaning over my desk. He reached out to the photo now back in Gran's shrine, so lovely that it hurt. As he brought it closer, the three of us – Olivia, Paul and Tim – surged into the warmth of the moment, the scent of a summer breeze and embraced the quick of the past.

'That's how we'll remember Tim.' Paul tightened his arm round my shoulder, 'facing him, retracing, reliving our time with him forever.'

'You take it,' I said, 'for your studio. It's the only copy left and the negative has disappeared.' I had to turn away from Tim's photo and his face that Paul had pencilled and shaded in just to keep the pulse of him inside me, his unmediated presence – his brightness of being.

('How do I figure in all this?' I can hear Dan saying. Here and now; living and loved; making your own landscape.)

Paul was the one to confront our secret fear, the one with the courage to dismiss it tersely:

'As far as I'm concerned, Tim is, and always will be, my son. Uncontested.' When he added, after a moment's thought, 'Dan too,' I cursed again the way I still weep so easily even when there's no cause for it. And for my father too who could have turned up then, now – if thoughts created more than fantasy, he would have returned long ago.

They lie in the fellowship of memory.

Tim
Marco
Gianni
Gran
Grandpa
Frank
Gio?

Lie in peace.

PRINCIPAL CHARACTERS

British

Olivia Taylor   school teacher

Paul Wyatt   picture restorer
Tim   their first son
Dan   their second son
Joan Taylor   Olivia's mother
Gran (Alice Palmer)   Olivia's grandmother
Grandpa (George Taylor)   Olivia's grandfather

William Thompson   lecturer in English
Sarah   his wife, school teacher
Andrew   their son
Penny   their daughter
Kate   their daughter

Mike Smithson   art dealer
Joe Hallam   solicitor
Angélique   public relations agent

Bob Hepworth   van driver

Italians

Gianni Panichini   stonemason
Ada   his wife
Giuliana   their daughter
Alberto   their son

Carlo Tondini	Ada's brother
Pina	his wife
Vincenzo	his son
Lisa	his daughter-in-law
Dario	his grandson
Marisa	Carlo's girlfriend
Quinto	neighbouring farmer
La nonna (grandmother)	his wife
Caterina	his daughter-in-law
Mauro	his son
Susanna	their daughter
Renzo	neighbouring farmer
Maria Pia	his wife
Gino the Silent	his son
Arturo	his son
Caterina	his daughter
Oreste	neighbouring farmer
Marco	his great grandson (deceased)
Giulio	neighbouring farmer
Roberta	his wife
Antonio	his son
Pasquale Panichini	former owner of la Casa dell'Aventura wife
Claudio	his son
Franco	his son
Daughter and *carabinere* husband	
Massimo	builder
Bianca	his wife
Rosella	his daughter
Sergio Palombini	plumber

Son and daughter

Angelo	electrician
Beppe Orietti	gardener
Orazio	local store & bar owner
Sibilla	his wife
Andrea	bar man
Silvano	land agent
Marino	retired hairdresser
Conte Rinaldo Prudomini	local landowner
Contessa Cristina Prudomini	his wife
Onorevole Luciano Bintoni	politician
Don Basilio	church official
Don Luigi	parish priest
Dottor Riccioni	lawyer
Cecilia Ferrarini	lawyer
Francesco Spaventi	architect
Gadini	landowner
Ferini	landowner

Germans

Wolfgang and his wife